KATHRYN JOHNSON

THE DEATH of a MAVEN

I0769348

CHAPTER 1

VERITY CADE HELD the match between trembling fingers. For the third time, a pale blue flame flickered weakly on the wick of the slender white candle. F-f-fizzle! A thin trail of sulfurous smoke rose toward her kitchen ceiling.

Tears of frustration pricked the corners of her eyes. She pinched the bridge of her nose to make them stop.

"You can do this," she whispered.

How hard could it be to light one stupid candle? Maybe her hand was shaking too hard. Maybe there was a draft in the kitchen, although she didn't feel one. Whatever the problem was, she refused to let this day end without doing something to honor Mark on the anniversary of his passing.

She ripped another cardboard stick from the souvenir matchbook. They had stumbled upon the bar—*Hernando's Hideaway,* not much more than a dive, really—on their honeymoon in Bermuda seven years earlier.

Back then, she had expected the life of their marriage to be so much longer. Like forever. Because that's what you think when you marry someone you truly, deeply love, don't you?

This will last forever. But 'til death do us part' arrived too soon for them. Without even a whisper of warning.

Thanks to the accident.

They've invented apps for everything else, Verity thought ruefully. *Why not one that warns you of your approaching death? Maybe with a gentle voice, like Siri.*

Beep: One month to settle your affairs, Mr. Cade.

Beep: Three days before your Death Day. You may want to update your will.

Beep: Twelve hours to say goodbye to your loved ones.

Had she foolishly assumed their survival to old age was guaranteed? Perhaps. But not in a bad way. She certainly had never taken for granted her loving, strong Mark. They had created a beautiful place in the world for themselves, defined by their devotion to each other and a shared vision of their future as a family.

Mark had been so certain of the trajectory of their lives he had planned *everything*, month by month, year by year. "Nineteen more months to pay off our debts on the farm," he told her. "Then we can start making babies." He'd waggled a wicked brow at her, his brown eyes luminous, sexy, exciting. As many babies as she liked, he had promised.

Verity sucked in a sharp breath. *Don't go there.*

Fourth try. *Stop shaking, dammit*! She struck the match again. It sizzle-burst into brilliant life.

She willed her hand to remain steady. Slowly, slowly her fingertips moved the fragile flame toward the wick and held it there. A pale radiance blossomed at the candle's tip. The flame flickered and danced, as though reacting to something moving past it, creating a draught.

Instinctively, she looked around the room. No one was there, of course. And no windows were open.

Strange, she thought. It almost felt as though someone was in the room with her, looking over her shoulder. Sharing her grief?

Just when she feared the tender flame would yet again sputter out, it inexplicably licked higher and the blue-white glow brightened. Shadows spooled across the farmhouse's dim room. Success! She breathed out, her work-stiff shoulders relaxed.

Despite the calming fragrance of the jasmine-scented wax, a rough lump lodged in her throat. Tears welled in her eyes. How did anyone keep on doing what normal people do after the loss of someone so elementally dear to them?

"I miss you, my love," she whispered into the flame. "God, how I miss you. I hope you know that."

A floorboard creaked somewhere above her. She tensed for just a moment. After all this time, she hardly noticed the groans, squeaks, and sighs of the 200-year-old Vermont farmhouse. A change in temperature or humidity caused beams, boards and plumbing to complain.

He used to tease her when she expressed concerns about the house's odd noises. "The old gal must like you, Veri. She's talking to you."

Verity wasn't sure how long she sat there, transfixed by the candle's flame. Liquid wax pooled at the candle's tip, rivered down its sides. She ran her fingertips over the waves of warm wax. Exactly one year ago, Mark was 34 years old, the same age as she.

Too young, she thought, *you were far too young to d—*

A distant *thump, thump, thump* interrupted her dark thoughts. This was definitely not a sound made by aging wood or cantankerous pipes. She experienced a little jolt of relief on returning to the world of the living. Someone was knocking on her front door and being ridiculously insistent about getting her attention.

Brushing away mental cobwebs, she swiped at her damp cheeks with a shirt sleeve. The knocking grew louder. *What the hell?*

She scowled at her watch—9:15. No one in a country village like Evansfield came calling at this hour. She considered ignoring them, whoever they were. They'd go away if she waited them out.

Unless...

Someone's car might have broken down and they needed to use her phone to call for a tow. But who went anywhere these days without their cell phone? Whatever their reason for attacking her door, it was just plain rude to bang loud enough to wake the dead.

If only. She sighed.

Verity pushed herself up and away from the long oak trestle table. She snapped on light switches as she dashed through the foyer. The tall antique coat rack and glass-fronted barrister's bookshelves, to her right. Wood banister and staircase gracefully curving upward on her left.

As she reached for the brass knob in the front door her mother's familiar warning rang in her ears. "Never, *ever* open your door to a stranger!"

Verity supposed she really should, at the very least, peek through the glass sidelight to forego exposing herself to the lurking thieves, rapists, and drug-crazed addicts of her mother's worst scenarios. But Evansfield wasn't Baltimore, where there actually was crime.

Besides, she just wanted to put an end to the awful clatter and go to bed. Mornings arrived early for a dairy farmer; she needed to be up before dawn. She flung open the door. And gasped in disbelief.

CHAPTER 2

SIX WOMEN OBSERVED her solemnly from within the amber circle of the farmhouse's porch light.

"We had to come," Denise Delaney said, "even if we woke you." The tomboyish owner of *Denise's Chocolate Designs* wore vivid purple yoga gear in contrast to her spiky red hair. She stepped forward and thrust a gold-foil box into Verity's hands.

"Dark chocolate truffles?" Verity guessed.

"Your fa-vo-rite!" Denise sang out. She hugged Verity then darted into the house without waiting for an invitation.

Willowy blonde Sunny Whitaker moved forward with a smile, her pretty blue eyes soft with sympathy. "You shouldn't be alone tonight, my dear." She held up a plump white paper sack from her Main Street restaurant, The Cat's Cradle Café. The bag exuded fragrances of butter and sugar and cinnamon. "I'll find a plate for these, shall I?" She quickly followed Denise inside.

"We knew if we called ahead," Chaundra Adebe murmured close to her ear, "you'd tell us you were perfectly fine and not to come." Her gorgeous ebony skin glowed against a vintage red-and-yellow flowered sarong. The Ethiopian woman owned the

Antiques Emporium, one of the most popular destinations in their postage-stamp town. "We voted. It was unanimous. Please don't be angry with us for dropping by unannounced. We need to be here for you, Verity."

"She's absolutely right," Martha Humphrey nodded in firm agreement. The portly schoolteacher held up a clear plastic box. "My famous triple-chocolate brownies."

"Thanks. How thoughtful, Martha." A small part of Verity still wished to be alone with her grief. But here they all were, six of her best customers on her delivery route. They'd become dear friends and it appeared nothing short of setting fire to her own house would drive them out.

She sighed and managed a facsimile of a smile. "Come in. Please." Waving Chaundra and Martha inside, she turned to face her final two visitors.

Elvira Evans, local real estate agent and wife to the town's only physician, was carrying on a rather unpleasant-sounding conversation with Mary Beth Loop, wife to Rupert Loop, the town's mayor.

"Don't be daft, Mary Beth!" Elvira whooped. "Of course, it isn't true. You're so gullible! Do you believe everything you see on TV?"

Mary Beth frowned in puzzlement. "No-o-o, not *everything*. But I'm sure they don't put people on television who intentionally lie."

Elvira made an odd choking sound in her throat and threw up her hands in disbelief as she turned toward Verity. "I give up. She's hopeless." She marched into the house in her crimson power suit and trademark four-inch heels, an immense black alligator tote slung over one shoulder.

Verity wrapped an arm around Mary Beth's shoulders and gave her a little squeeze. "Pay no attention to Elvira's moods, MB. She probably lost a six-figure sale today." Mary Beth's business was much less driven. She owned a lovely nursery and landscaping business.

"Thanks, Verity, you're so sweet." Mary Beth shrugged. "Oh, by the way, Kate couldn't get a sitter for her girls. She sends her apologies. And Fumiko had a business meeting in Boston. She said she'd be getting back late. They were disappointed to miss tonight."

Verity smiled her appreciation for the messages and accompanied Mary Beth into the kitchen. She glanced at Mark's candle, now reduced to a stump and puddle of white wax. She tenderly cupped the feeble flame and blew it out.

"Sit, Verity," Elvira ordered, taking charge as usual with a regal wave of her hand toward a chair. "Sunny, locate plates for your pastries and the cake I brought. Denise, silverware. Martha, cups for tea and coffee, if you please." A flurry of activity followed.

Chaundra scooped coffee grounds into a filter and filled Verity's coffee pot with water. Mary Beth brought out the lovely apple-blossom Nippon dessert plates that had belonged to Mark's mother. Delicate pink crystal glasses, another of her mother-in-law's prized possessions, appeared in Elvira's hands and were deftly arranged over a homespun tablecloth.

Years ago, Mark had told her that the massive oak trestle table that claimed a third of their country kitchen had been in his family for five generations. More functional than pretty, it held the scars of wear from a succession of Cade families— badges of love, Verity had always thought of them. The table had become the center of her life on the farm, just as it had been for her mother-in-law and, she suspected, for her husband's grandmother and great grandmother. Verity used it for varied tasks from kneading bread to chopping the veggies she picked from her kitchen garden. She usually sat down to her meals here. Setting a single place in the dining room just felt ridiculous.

From her tote, Elvira produced a box that held a heavenly coconut cake. Then out came two bottles of chilled local white wine. Elvira started pouring.

Verity opened her mouth to object. Turning this day into a celebration felt wrong on so many levels. But her friends had gone to such great lengths to be kind, wanting to cheer her up. She didn't have the heart to turn down their gifts.

As if reading her mind, Sunny picked up a full glass and handed it to Verity. "Sweetie," she said in a tone that brooked no argument, "dear Mark deserves a toast in honor of the good man and generous neighbor he was."

"We *all* miss him," Mary Beth added softly. Nods all around.

Verity drew a breath. *Right.* They had come for her but were honoring him. And wasn't that what she'd wanted tonight? "He *was* a wonderful man." She raised her glass and said, with a firm voice and all the courage she could muster, "To Mark Cade, my love."

"To Mark!" her friends echoed.

In that freeze-frame instant, Verity saw not a dry eye around her kitchen table.

"No more dawdling. Let's eat, everyone!" Elvira barked. She loaded a plate with goodies and pushed it in front of Verity. "Some of us have to work tomorrow, you know." She helped herself to one of Denise's dark-as-midnight truffles.

Verity caught the eyes of each woman and mouthed a "thank you." She obediently nibbled the corner of one of Martha's brownies. The brown square tasted like cardboard. Likely, nothing would taste good tonight, seasoned by her sadness. Returning the remainder of the brownie to her plate, she nudged it away with one finger, hoping no one would notice.

Cheerful conversation circled the table between bites and sips. The scene felt staged for her benefit. Verity tried her best to take part, but her heart just wasn't in it.

"Hmm," Elvira said, eyeing Verity's ignored plate. "I can't believe nothing on this table appeals to your famous sweet tooth. Come on, Verity, you don't want to insult your guests!"

"Sorry," she whispered meekly. "I guess I just don't feel like—"

Elvira shook her head. "Listen, princess, starving yourself isn't going to bring back your man. You get that, don't you?"

Chaundra raised an eyebrow at the realtor's tactlessness. "A little harsh, don't you think?"

"No-o-o, I don't!" Elvira made a face at her. "It's called facing reality."

"Leave her alone, Elvira!" Sunny snapped. "Widows are entitled to be sad. There's no time limit on grief."

"Oh, for crying out loud!" Elvira rolled her exotic lavender eyes. *Liz Taylor eyes*, Verity had always thought. "Stop being so sensitive, all of you. My point is, we went to a hell of a lot of trouble to arrange this special night for her—and she's sitting there moping as if she were at a funer—"

"Sunny's right, Elvira," Denise interrupted, a warning spark behind her stone-cold gaze. She might have built a successful confectionary business, but they all knew there was nothing sweet about Denise when her temper flared. No sane person wanted to be around her then. "Verity can eat or not, as she likes, Elvira. Got it?"

"Oh, alright," Elvira huffed, looking away.

"It's just that I ate such a big dinner," Verity lied, "I can't take another bite." No one looked convinced. "I'm sure my appetite will return tomorrow with a vengeance. Thank you for tonight. Really, it's so wonderful you've done this for me." She chose a glossy chocolate ball topped with tiny pink sugar-flowers, Denise's mark for her famous raspberry truffles, and held it up for all to see. "I'll save this beauty for a special treat tomorrow, between milking cows and feeding my hens."

"If I had to spend a whole day with stinky cows and nasty-tempered chickens, I'd need an entire box from Denise's shop to recover," Chaundra moaned, and everyone laughed.

"Not me!" Mary Beth objected. "Shut me in a barn with livestock any day. Just don't leave me in a classroom with thirty kindergarteners!"

Martha laughed. She taught kindergarten.

Soon, the tension from moments earlier drained from the room. Although Verity felt exhausted and longed for her bed, no one seemed ready to leave. Conversation moved to personal stories about Mark Cade. Every one of her guests had a favorite anecdote to share. A few of the women in her kitchen had known Mark since childhood, sharing classrooms or high-school sports teams and clubs with him.

Verity found herself smiling then laughing as her guests described one hilarious incident after another until she was holding her aching sides.

Sunny gasped and fanned a hand in front of her flushed face. "Oh my, what a hoot!"

Mary Beth fell off her chair in a fit of hysterics, and Denise had to help her get up off the floor.

At last, Martha turned to Verity while everyone else fought to restore their composure. "How did you first meet your darling Mark? I don't think I've ever heard." Her eyes glistened with a romantic's anticipation of a good love story.

Never married, and a few years older than most in the group, Martha often seemed the most serious among them. Verity had no idea why the teacher had remained single well into her forties. She wasn't unattractive but always seemed to wear clothing that made her appear older than she was. Verity couldn't remember Martha ever wearing jewelry. Perhaps her marital status had something to do with her profession. Martha had once mentioned that ninety percent of the elementary school staff was female. She supposed that made finding Mr. Right even more of a challenge.

"You really want to hear how we met?" Verity looked around the room at her audience's hopeful faces. She bit her bottom lip, fearing she might burst into tears if she tried putting those halcyon days into words. To her relief, though, as soon as she began, she could feel the knotted muscles behind her shoulder blades and at the backs of her legs begin to relax.

"We were both enrolled at the University of Maryland, in College Park," she began. "Mark was majoring in agricultural science, and I had a vague idea that I wanted to study French literature. Not the ideal match."

"They say that opposites attract," Chaundra pointed out.

Verity smiled. "Well, we didn't. Not immediately. We met on a blind date. I was convinced it was a waste of time for both of us. There I was a city girl, having grown up in Baltimore. He was a—"

"Country hick?" Elvira studied her polished nails, all innocence.

Sunny shot the realtor a deadly look.

"Oh, no," Verity objected. "Not even then would I have called him that. Mark was more sophisticated and mature than I was or ever will be. He traveled a lot during semester breaks and spent summers as a volunteer, teaching agricultural techniques in Africa."

"So, what changed your mind about him?" Sunny twinkled at her mischievously. "His sexy farmer's bod?"

Verity felt heat flood her cheeks. Yes, well, there was *that*.

She couldn't deny it had been a joy to share his bed. Just the thought of his hands on her…

"Wildflowers," she said quickly.

Denise roared with laughter.

"Wild what?" Mary Beth looked around, confused.

"I feel a punchline coming on," Sunny said.

Verity grinned. "I'm not joking. Mark started leaving bunches of wildflowers at the door of my dorm room. A different kind every day. Pristine white anemones, spikey blue asters, scarlet bergamots, purple thimbleberries, bluebells, and gorgeous blazing stars. He left a little card with each bunch, identifying the flower by both its popular and scientific name."

"Why would he do that?" a still clueless Mary Beth asked. Verity had long ago decided confusion was MB's natural state.

"Because on our first date he mentioned that he was shocked at how many wild flowers he saw in Africa, and I admitted that, although I adored all kinds of flowers, I couldn't tell a rose from a Venus flytrap." She grinned. "So that's how it began for us. I loved his wildflowers. Then I began to love him."

Sunny reached across the table and squeezed her hand.

Mary Beth, Denise, and Chaundra chorused, "Aw-w-w-w!"

Martha blinked away tears.

Elvira crowed, "Oh, God, gag me with a—"

Denise shot out her elbow but missed Elvira's ribs.

Verity laughed at them all. And with them. It was good to be among such wonderful friends, reliving happy times with Mark. A little of the weight she'd been carrying lifted.

"Oh, my goodness, look at the time!" Chaundra groaned. "It's after one o'clock. And at eight this morning I'm supposed to interview a new vendor who's applying for a booth at the emporium."

Mary Beth chuckled, her chins jiggling. "I'm never out this late. The mayor is going to think I've left him for another man!"

"I doubt *that*," Elvira muttered under her breath, but still much too loudly.

"Oh, do shut up, Elvira!" Sunny glared at her. Verity recalled one of her mom's favorite expressions. *If looks could kill.*

Elvira shrugged. "Well, who would want *her*? I mean, let's be frank, ladies." She pulled open her tote and rummaged around inside as she continued talking. "Mary Beth's been snarfing up cookies and pastries all night, like always. She probably tips the scale at two hundred. Talk about having no willpower."

Verity took one look at Mary Beth's flushed face and reached for her arm. "Don't listen to her, MB. She's just—"

"Sh-she's right," Mary Beth sputtered miserably. "I should lose weight. It's just s-so hard. You know how the mayor loves my baking. I do try to resist eating what I make."

"Pay no attention to her," Denise whispered as she stacked up dirty plates and delivered them to the sink.

Sunny moved up behind Verity and tapped her on the shoulder. "I can stay if you need me, sweetie. I'll just flop down on your sofa for the night and—"

"It's not necessary. I'm fine. Really, I am."

"You're sure?"

"Honestly," Verity said. "You've all done more than enough. Get out of here!" She smiled to make sure they knew she meant it in the nicest way. "I'll see you tomorrow when I deliver your eggs and milk."

Once a week she brought dairy items to a list of locals. Most of her clients were professional women who owned or managed businesses in town and had little time in their lives to shop for food, much less keep chickens or cows. Her customers swore they preferred the Cade Farm products over commercial brands available at the local grocery store, even though they paid a little more for farm fresh.

"Oh say, I nearly forgot." Apparently unfazed by the scolding she'd received minutes earlier, Elvira extracted a sheaf of papers from her tote and waved it at Verity. "Just in case you get a chance to look at this, Verity darling, I brought a copy of the sales offer we discussed the other day."

No, thought Verity, *not we. You.* The only conversation they'd ever had about the possibility of her selling the farm was one-sided. Elvira often repeated her wish to buy the land and buildings with the hope of expanding her husband's medical business, primarily by building a clinic, medical offices and parking lot. Verity had made it clear she wasn't ready to even think about selling Mark's farm, *her* farm. To anyone, for any purpose.

Before Verity could respond to the realtor, Sunny swooped in and grabbed the pages out of Elvira's hand. "Oh no, you don't, Elvira. This isn't the time or place and you know it." Sunny's face flushed hotter than the sun's surface. Verity had never seen her friend so angry. "We warned you on the way over here to stop pestering Verity. She's already told you she doesn't want to sell her farm."

"No, she didn't!" Elvira spat furiously. "Last week, before Mark's anniversary memorial service at the church, she told me she just didn't want to make an important decision like this in haste."

Denise stopped tidying long enough to observe the two women, as though anticipating a good fight. And perhaps, an opportunity to join in.

Elvira blinked, as if mystified by the café owner's reaction. "I haven't said a word all week."

Chaundra tossed balled-up paper napkins into the trash and shook her head in disbelief. "Seven whole days. You're giving the woman seven days to decide whether to sell her husband's legacy? You are a cold woman, Elvira Evans."

"Cold," Mary Beth repeated with a demonstrative shiver.

Elvira huffed. "Give me a break! It's been a whole *year* since the accident."

For a breathless moment, Verity feared Denise was going to punch her.

Elvira must have realized she'd gone too far. "Oh, alright. Never mind. Give it back."

Sunny thrust the contract at her.

Elvira swiveled to face Verity. "Sunny's probably right. Bad timing." She shrugged. "I apologize, Verity. We'll talk another time. Sorry if I sometimes come across a little too strong. Honestly, I'm only thinking of what's best for you."

"Not a problem," Verity said quickly.

Everyone gathered their things and headed for the front door. But then Mary Beth had to return to the kitchen for her purse. And Elvira suddenly realized she'd forgotten her scarf and also slipped back inside.

Verity sighed. Some of the warm glow of the evening had seeped away at Elvira's mention of buying the farm. Even a parting hug from each of her friends didn't entirely bring back the lovely camaraderie of the evening. Verity watched from her porch as her friends climbed into Sunny's van and sped off.

She went back inside. The house felt empty again.

"I'm still here, house," Verity murmured, returning to her kitchen to finish cleaning up. "And I love our farm, Mark." Then, with more grit in her voice, she repeated the mantra that always gave her strength. "I'm. Still. Here!"

Yes, you are, a voice whispered so softly she couldn't be sure she had really heard anything at all.

Verity closed her eyes, listening.

Nothing.

She drew a breath, held it. "Mark?" But, of course, there was no answer. Why would there be?

Oh, God, just accept reality! Elvira was right.

And yet, this wasn't the first time she had imagined voices. No doubt as a result of the stress that came with the responsibility for the farm's success. Or failure. Mark had been so very proud of his family's farm. He loved it with the devotion of a father to his child.

"The house is talking to you." Oh, how his eyes had twinkled when he teased her.

Verity laughed and shook her head. Such nonsense. Voices. She was just tired. Her imagination played tricks on her when she was physically worn out. She hoped she would be able to fall asleep quickly.

She spent another fifteen minutes rinsing off the fragile china and antique crystal she dared not subject to the ravages of her dishwasher. By the time she turned away from the sink, her eyes were burning like little furnaces. They focused on a flat, white rectangle on her kitchen table. At first, she didn't recognize it.

Then, suddenly, she knew.

Elvira. The bossy realtor had been the last to leave the kitchen, trailing after the rest of her guests with mumbled apologies for having forgotten her stupid scarf. She had contrived to leave her sales contract, despite her promises to stop bugging Verity. The woman was incorrigible.

Verity briefly closed her eyes. *Oh Lord, maybe it would be for the best.* No matter how much she loved this place and despite her vow to keep Mark's farm going.

Well, tomorrow she would look over Elvira's offer with a fresh eye.

Verity dragged herself upstairs to the king-size bed Mark had insisted they buy when they married—even though it crowded the modest dimensions of their bedroom. He was a big guy, 6'4", and loved to sprawl lazily across it, arms and legs akimbo, eating up extra inches that should have been hers. She never minded. All it took was the lightest nudge and, whether awake or asleep, he withdrew to give her room then pulled her body close to his. They often woke up in the morning entwined.

Maybe it was the stories of Mark, shared with her friends, that made her feel less alone tonight in their bed. She had to admit her friends' raucous company had comforted her. She wedged off her Adidas, slipped out of her clothes. Faded jeans, flannel shirt, underclothes fell to the floor where she stood. Not an ounce of energy remained to pick them up. Barely conscious, she pulled on her nightshirt and collapsed on the bed.

"You are loved." The words seemed to come from a presence other than herself. Impossible, of course.

Silly woman, she mused, *imaging voices again*. Fantasy though it must be, the voice was soothing. *I am loved. Yes, I am*, she thought.

She had wonderful friends. And lovely neighbors in this cozy New England town. She had her animals. Clucking Rhode Island Reds—the best egg layers ever. And gentle doe-eyed Guernseys. She had named each cow, much to Mark's amusement. How very, very lucky she was to be loved by such a fine man.

She pulled the crisp, line-dried sheet, smelling of fresh air and sunshine, up to her chin. A deep sense of contentment came over her—like being swathed in a warm, unthreatening hug. And she slept deeply.

CHAPTER 3

VERITY JAMMED fists on hips and surveyed her kitchen through narrowed eyes. *Now where did the dang thing go?*

Elvira's contract for the purchase of her farm wasn't on the table where she and her friends had gathered the previous night. Neither was it on the two feet of worn laminate countertop beside the original porcelain sink basin. She turned to the granite-topped island Mark had installed to give her additional workspace for sorting eggs and preparing her deliveries to folks in town. The cool stone slab released sticky bread dough more easily than any other surface in her kitchen. But again, no contract.

Squatting in a baseball catcher's crouch she peered beneath her kitchen table, then under the three-tiered wire bin where she stored potatoes, onions, and winter squash from her garden. The blue-and-white floor tiles that always reminded her of photographs of the artist Monet's stunning country kitchen in Giverny also lay bare, except for a light population of dust bunnies.

The envelope Elvira had sneaked back inside to leave for her, unobserved by their friends, had disappeared.

And yet...

Verity tapped the tip of her nose with one finger, thinking. She was absolutely sure she had left it on the table. Was it possible she inadvertently swept the pages into the trashcan along with paper napkins, cupcake and truffle wrappers? As exhausted as she was last night, this was a definite possibility. She dug through the trash. Nothing.

With an exasperated groan, Verity ran upstairs, thinking she might have taken the envelope with her when she staggered off to bed. But no. It wasn't there either. For a moment, she thought she heard something. Laughter? Impossible. No one was in the house with her, and her neighbors' homes were too far away for their voices to carry this far. She shook her head, blaming the house as always.

"It can't have walked off by itself!" she muttered. Another of her mom's admonitions. As a child, Verity had a habit of losing mittens and many other things.

But now, she realized, Elvira's attempt to bully her into accepting an offer for her farm must have upset her more than she realized. Obviously, her traumatized brain had erased any memory of what she'd done with the document. Although, why the real estate agent's behavior should shock her so, she had no idea. Elvira did and said whatever she wanted. The whole town knew that.

But Elvira Evans also helped people. Her contributions to local charities were famously generous. It was just that, well, the woman was so maddeningly unpredictable. She seemed not to understand how hurtful her words could be. Poor Mary Beth! Berating her about her weight in front of her friends. How cruel was that!

"I give up," she groaned. Finding the contract had to wait. Chores called to her.

·   ·   ·

Hours later, Verity felt her energy running low. She had eaten nothing all morning as she sorted eggs; portioned and wrapped slabs of butter she'd churned the previous day; bottled rich milk and cream. She plucked two of Sunny's chocolate-chip-oatmeal cookies and one chocolate-raspberry bar from a plate of last night's leftovers. Not the healthiest of breakfasts, to be sure, but oatmeal was nourishing. Right? And wasn't dark chocolate supposed to be good for you?

Still annoyed with herself for misplacing Elvira's stupid proposal, she plopped down on a kitchen chair and focused on washing down the delicious cookies with a tall glass of cold milk. Eventually the papers will turn up, she told herself. And then she must decide what to do about Elvira's offer. The proposed sale price wasn't the issue; it was a reasonable, if not overly generous, offer. She just couldn't bear to turn Mark's farm into a commercial venture that had nothing to do with its history as a family-owned New England dairy farm.

Elvira's intention to use the land for building a modern clinic with physicians' offices and medical services was, she supposed, laudable. Except, everything she loved—the barns, animals, even her beloved kitchen garden, luxuriant with sweet-smelling herbs and fresh vegetables—they would all go away. Even the lovely old farmhouse Mark had shared with her was destined to be torn down. Losing Mark was hard enough. Losing everything that reminded her of her husband—no, that was too much to ask of her.

She closed her eyes on a bittersweet wave of memories. Without wishing it, suddenly she was back on that horrific day.

Mark had been late returning home that evening. She remembered standing under the wisteria vines on their front porch, looking out into the dusk. Watching for him. A chill breeze blew down the river valley from Canada. She had made his favorite man-casserole—pulled chicken with wide egg noodles and creamy sauce dotted with sweet green peas from her garden. All topped with a salty, crushed-potato chip crust. Yum!

She returned to the kitchen, checked to make sure the casserole was bubbling and cooked through. Turning off the oven she left their dinner covered with foil to stay warm.

He had said he hoped to finish the last of the haying in the north field, half a mile from the house. She pulled on a fleece-lined sweatshirt and started up the road with her pocket penlight, in case they were delayed returning home. If he was close to being done, she could help him. If too much work remained, she'd encourage him to leave it for tomorrow and come home to a hot meal. No use trying to work in the pitch dark.

She knew he had planned to drive his dad's old tractor. Theirs was a small family farm with limited equipment of their own. They budgeted for renting a modern combine, thresher, or plow for seasonal use. The green beast's finnickiness was legendary, but Mark had promised to work only on the flat in case the tractor stalled out, as it tended to do on steep inclines. His two part-timers, the young Grimalski brothers, wouldn't be available until the next day. The twins were skilled at restarting the cantankerous engine, employing a mysterious but somehow effective concoction of throttling the engine, kicks and insults.

Verity walked up the two-lane highway then turned onto the dirt road leading up to the field. The sun still barely peeked above the tree line. Evergreen and birch forest surrounded the field, casting licorice-black shadows against muddy earth and dry stubble. The sweet, heady smell of mown hay filled her nostrils. She could never get enough of that earthy fragrance. Better than any room deodorizer.

As the last of the day's light disappeared, she switched on her flashlight and crossed the dark field, calling out to Mark.

The concentrated glow pricked out a yellow patch of ground just ahead of her boot toes. She began to think it odd that she still hadn't heard the tractor's complaining growl. The machine was due to be replaced as soon as they saved up the money. Mark hated taking out loans.

"Cash on the line from now on, babe" he told her, after they took the financial plunge of using credit to pay for a computerized Robo-Milker system.

Still no sounds. Nothing moved across her line of vision in the gloom.

"Mark?" she shouted.

A breeze tickled her cheeks, carrying with it the scent of pine needles and something else eye-wateringly stringent she couldn't quite place. Above her head, a few stars appeared. No moon tonight.

Had they somehow missed each other? Was that even possible? The only way back home was the same route she'd taken to get here.

Verity frowned, reminding herself to keep her eyes on the rutted ground to avoid tripping or turning an ankle. She mechanically plodded toward the center of the field. Maybe Mark had changed his mind about mowing that day and hadn't thought to tell her. She didn't notice whether his car was in the driveway, or the tractor in the shed. Could he have driven to the bank or the Ag Store in Springfield? But neither made sense. He would have returned to the house hours ago or called to say he'd been held up.

Suddenly, an unfamiliar shape loomed above her. She startled before catching her breath. "Oh!"

A warning tingle zigzagged down her spine. Her heart racing, she stopped abruptly. Her fingers went numb. They released the penlight before she could train its beam on the object and identify it. The little light disappeared between deep, muddy tire tracks.

She dropped to her knees, fumbling around in the muck and sharp grass stubble while keeping her eyes focused on the mysterious shadow. Had Mark left a stack of hay bales in the middle of the field? No. Whatever this was, it felt like...what? The far-too-creative part of her brain imagined a dark monster clawing its way out of the earth. *Don't be childish,* she scolded herself.

"Mark?" she called again.

Nothing. And she still hadn't found the penlight. The smell, the one she hadn't yet figured out, was stronger here.

She gave up uselessly thrusting her hands around in the grass. Standing up cautiously, she planted her feet, prepared to run if necessary. Slowly, her eyes adjusted to the darkness. She stared up at the strange thing that had frightened her.

Metal. Rusty green metal. The tractor. Unrecognizable until now, because it lay on its side like a great wounded dinosaur. Its immense wheels thrust into the air in a pantomime of a dog playing dead. At last, she identified the awful stench— fuel oil.

The truth struck her like a baseball bat swung at her chest. *Oh, God, no!*

Now, a year later, she still couldn't remember what she'd done next. The police told her she dialed 911. They said the operator had stayed on the line with her, asking for details, assuring her that help would arrive soon.

What she did remember was the scream of an ambulance siren. Then an emergency response team bearing halogen lights, earthmovers and an immense machine capable of cutting through steel. It seemed forever before they brought Mark's body out from beneath his tractor and into the glare of the blinding lights.

All she could think at that moment was that he had died alone, under 5,000 pounds of uncaring metal. She hated that fact nearly as much as she hated his dying.

Before the accident, people had told her that farming was a dangerous profession. They spoke in the same solemn, common-sense tone that a parent warns a child to look both ways before crossing a street. She didn't really listen to them. Mark always assured her he was careful around machinery.

Later, she learned that forty percent of all serious agricultural accidents were due to machine rollovers. She told herself she should have paid attention. She should have made him replace the old tractor, even if it put them deeper in debt. She should have been there with him to call for help. She should...

Oh, hell.

CHAPTER 4

VERITY DREW a shaky breath and blinked to clear away her tears and the awful memory. The cookies lay heavily on her stomach. She felt a little sick.

Life goes on, she told herself. And she was behind schedule. Her customers expected her to show up with their eggs and milk. Slowly the sadness ebbed away like a departing tide and she found the strength to stand up from her kitchen table.

One of the things for which Verity felt proudest was the personal, old-fashioned service she provided her customers. They often told her how much they appreciated being included on her weekly egg route. Sunny claimed that the pastries she baked at the café tasted better than anything the big commercial bakery in Brattleboro could supply, thanks to the rich cream-topped whole milk she bought from Verity. Others said they just couldn't buy eggs from a store as fresh as those Verity delivered to their door. The extra cash she earned helped pay her household bills—although most of the farm's income came from the milk she sold to the dairy co-op.

Verity pulled off her turquoise fleece hoodie and walked

back out into the fresh morning. Earlier, the air had been so cool, it had nipped at her face. It was nearly twenty degrees warmer now, and she was glad she'd peeled down to her t-shirt.

For the second time that morning, she checked on her cows and the Robo-Milkers' progress. Some larger farms using the automated milking systems kept their cows indoors, day and night, never to wander lazily across a field. But she and Mark had decided to free-range their Guernsey cows. After the initial four weeks needed to accustom the animals to the machines, her ladies had learned to walk through the open milking parlor and into one of the three laser-controlled pens for milking. Most of the herd volunteered twice a day, but some showed up more often, as if they preferred being relieved of the considerable weight in their udders.

Only one cow in the entire herd of sixty refused the machines. Her dear, sweet-natured, obstinate Molly. And so, Verity milked her fussy girl by hand, talking to her as she drew warm milk from her velvety teats. Molly was an excellent listener.

Verity loaded retro-glass bottles of cream and milk into her little blue Honda Ridgeline truck. She carefully arranged biodegradable egg cartons in the truck bed to ensure not one egg would break during delivery.

Her two farmhands, Jason and Jerry Grimalski, were late that day. Then she remembered the boys—not boys anymore, she reminded herself, since they were 26 years old—had told her they needed to work at their dad's farm for a few hours that morning. They had promised to arrive in time to meet the co-op milk truck and sign the paperwork, if she wasn't back from her deliveries.

Verity took a deep breath of country air—redolent of fodder, animals, and the freesia, stock blossoms, and sweet alyssum growing in the beds alongside the farmhouse. She hauled herself up into the driver's seat of the truck and drove down the gravel driveway.

The egg route had been her husband's suggestion, a way to meet and get to know some of the women in the community soon after she moved in with him. And it had worked! She was welcomed into her neighbors' homes. Offered a cup of coffee or tea—supplemented with the latest gossip. It was lovely, absolutely lovely to be accepted into village life so effortlessly. She soon felt an indispensable part of this small enclave of busy, vibrant rural women. It had been those same women who, after Mark's accident, became her lifeline. An anchor to the living world. She'd never forget how they rallied around her with their loving support.

True, she no longer had her Mark. But she had so much to be grateful for. She must never forget these blessings.

The drive down Main Street and into the center of town took just minutes. She turned into the driveway beside the home of her first customer—Martha Humphrey. Martha's weekly order was small, just one dozen eggs, a pint of cream, quart of whole milk. During the school year, Verity left her order in an insulated box on the porch. But in the summer Martha was usually at home on delivery days.

She reached into the back of the truck for the tote holding Martha's order—the Cade Farm logo stenciled in vibrant green on beige canvas. When she turned, she saw the sturdy figure of the teacher step out through her front door and onto her porch. Waving, Verity walked toward the house. As she got closer, she could see that Martha wasn't smiling. Indeed, the woman's eyes were noticeably red-rimmed and weepy. The flesh of her face, mushroom puffy and pale.

Verity frowned. "Martha, is something wrong?"

"You haven't heard?" The woman sniffled and touched a wadded-up handkerchief to her lips. "You'd best come in, dear. It's terrible news. Just terrible." She waved Verity into her kitchen with two hands.

Verity set her bag on the round table in the center of the little kitchen and waited to hear the news. Martha stood blinking at her, shifting her weight from foot to foot. She seemed too upset to immediately explain what the "terrible news" might be.

Verity decided the teacher needed a moment to pull herself together. She started stowing her delivery into the avocado-green refrigerator that matched the stove and, unfortunately, even the yellowing wallpaper and ruffled priscilla curtains. Why Martha had never renovated her kitchen Verity had no idea. Was a public-school teacher's salary so paltry she couldn't afford to upgrade her appliances?

But now seemed not the time to discuss decor.

Verity turned away from the fridge, folding the empty tote to take with her. "Martha." She reached out and gently grasped the woman's thick forearm to get her to focus. "Tell me what's going on."

"Oh, dear, maybe you should sit down, Verity. I'll make us some tea, shall I?"

A shiver of foreboding crept up Verity's spine. "I'd rather you just tell me what's troubling you."

"I suppose you'll hear soon enough. Better from me than a stranger." Martha pressed fingertips to her swollen eyes and seemed to rally. "Right then. Let's go into the parlor where we'll be more comfortable."

Apparently, no tea then.

Verity could only assume there had been a death in the family. Or perhaps Martha had received an unexpected and worrisome diagnosis of some kind? The woman really didn't look well.

Verity followed her into a claustrophobic sitting room, jammed with old furniture. Heavy wine-colored damask draperies shut out the morning light. She was immediately reminded of her great aunt's home. The woman had lived like a mole, shuffling from one cave-like room to another for decades before her eventual death.

"To keep the sun from fading my good upholstery, of course!" her aunt crowed, sounding as though she thought Verity stupid for even asking.

But Martha couldn't be more than ten years older than Verity. And anyway, the furnishings in this room looked well past protecting. How could a person live without glorious sunlight?

Martha collapsed heavily into a faux-leather recliner. She waved Verity toward a brown couch. Instead of taking the offered seating, Verity pulled a ladderback chair from one corner and sat down facing Martha.

The woman looked away from her and slid the tip of her tongue between thin lips, as if to gather strength. "It's Elvira," she whimpered, "poor thing."

Verity had never heard Elvira Evans referred to as poor with regard to any portion of her flamboyant life. Elvira, who owned one of the largest and most successful real estate agencies in central Vermont. Who, it was rumored, always came out on top of every business deal. She had married a handsome and equally successful local physician. She bore him two children—teenagers now—who, she understood, were cracking smart and bound for college one day.

Despite Elvira's sometimes acerbic nature—and an inclination to occasionally stomp on other people's feelings—she was a respected member of the community. And she was as healthy and svelte as a jungle cat. So it couldn't be that her health was in question. More likely, someone was suing her because of something she'd done or said.

"What on earth are you talking about, Martha?" Verity didn't mean to sound annoyed but she was. The woman was being such a drama queen and making no sense at all! "Just tell me. What has Elvira done?"

The teacher's runny eyes widened in horror. She shook her head back and forth in a disturbing mechanical rhythm. "Oh no, you mustn't say that! I'm so sorry for not explaining this very well." She heaved a mournful sigh and blotted her eyes with the back of one wrist. "It's just that I can hardly believe it's true. You see, Elvira's...dead."

"Dead?" Verity choked on a laugh. Surely, this was a joke! And a bad one at that. "Elvira? That's ridiculous. We all saw her at my house less than twelve hours ago. You were there! She was her usual bossy self."

"It's true," Martha rasped. "Honestly, I just learned it."

"From who...whom?" Martha wasn't above correcting her grammar, no matter how distressed she might be. "Who told you this?" If the usual Evansfield gossip was an earth tremor, this news would have registered at least a seven on the Richter Scale.

"They say she..." Martha's voice dropped to a whisper.

Verity leaned in. "What did they say? Who is *they*?" Verity seized the teacher's hands and squeezed, perhaps a little too hard. Martha winced and shook her off.

"She's killed herself, Verity. Oh Lord! Those poor children. And Doctor John? What will they ever do without her?"

Suicide? Elvira? Seriously?

However, it was clear from Martha's level of hysteria that she believed whatever she'd heard.

"What else do you know, Martha? Concentrate. Do you have any details at all?" Verity prodded.

Martha sniffled and blinked at her, as if the questions surprised her. "I-I, well, I don't know. I saw the sheriff's car race down Main Street earlier this morning. And then...well, you know how word gets around a small town like this."

"Indeed, I do." Often entirely too fast. "Exactly what have you been told?" Verity asked again, holding Martha's tear-filled eyes with her own.

"Th-they say her b-body was found at the bottom of the old granite quarry. Elvira jumped, Verity. Last night sometime. Oh," she moaned loudly, "isn't it just dreadful!"

Verity sat back in the hard wooden chair and thought for a moment. She felt the other woman's eyes bearing down on her, as if hoping she might somehow offer an explanation less horrifying for how Elvira came to be at the bottom of an abandoned quarry.

"Martha," Verity said, forcing calm into her voice. "Let's not jump to conclusions. This can't be right. It must be someone else. Or nobody at all! Maybe this is someone's idea of a prank, or a baseless rumor. I'll bet that's it." She patted Martha's hand. "Listen, I have her order in my truck. I'll stop at her house right now and get to the bottom of this. I'll let you know what I find out."

Martha's face brightened but didn't completely lose its fungi pallor. "Thank you, Verity. That's so kind of you. I'm just...well, you can imagine how upset I am. You may not know this, but I babysat for Peter and Laura and taught both of them in kindergarten. Of course, that was before you married your dear Mark and came to live here. I've just always been close to that family. Such a shock. You understand, don't you?"

"Of course, I do."

Verity moved back into the kitchen, grabbed her tote from

the tabletop, feeling nauseous. *Suicide?* Elvira's inflated ego would seem to eliminate self-destruction as a possibility for her demise—if it indeed had occurred. Then again, maybe everyone had a breaking point.

Do we ever really know what's in the heart of another person? she mused.

CHAPTER 5

BACK IN HER TRUCK, Verity pressed her foot to the gas and sped straight past the next three stops on her delivery route. She felt compelled to quickly sort out this dreadful rumor. Because a rumor was all it could be. Right?

Unless... She pinched her bottom lip between her teeth as she drove.

Was it possible Elvira had been deeply, secretly unhappy? Miserable enough to kill herself? Such sudden desperation wasn't unheard of. She'd read about incidents where successful, supposedly sane people tragically ended their own lives. In today's intensely divisive and competitive world, it seemed to happen more and more often.

If Elvira actually committed suicide, she certainly had worked hard to conceal her despair. None of her friends, to Verity's knowledge, had ever noticed signs of depression. In fact, the realtor looked nothing short of vibrantly healthy and confident the previous night.

Verity frowned at her truck's windshield, barely aware of anything on the other side of it as she drove. Could Elvira's bravado have been an act to hide her vulnerability? Far easier to believe was the possibility that Martha somehow muddled her facts.

Verity turned right, off of Main Street and onto Fairview Lane and a pricey residential neighborhood. Elvira's elegant white colonial, third house on the left, dwarfed its neighbors. Like a queen attended by her ladies-in-waiting, the grand house stood in the middle of a row of New England clapboard cottages in various colonial-replica shades of gray, cream and tan. But what most caught Verity's eye wasn't the homes. It was the sheriff's SUV, its bar lights flashing, and one of his deputies' Range Rovers. Both vehicles were parked in front of the Evans' mini-mansion. A few neighbors stood on their front lawns staring nervously at the big house.

Verity's heart leaped into her throat.

She pulled her truck to the curb on the opposite side of the street. Doc Evans' office and examination rooms, she knew from her own medical visits, were in the wing he had built onto the rear of the house. There was plenty of land on either side for an addition. Presumably the choice had been made to preserve the house's elegant façade. Elvira would have insisted.

Verity sat for another five minutes, nipping at a hangnail on her thumb, trying to decide what to do. Was Martha right? If so, the family would be in crisis. She didn't want to intrude. She should drive away now, be about her business.

On the other hand, if foolish gossip was spreading like a California wildfire, someone really should set the record straight ASAP. With that thought to bolster her courage, she climbed down from the driver's seat. Best to approach the situation as if she had heard nothing.

Verity dropped down the rear panel of her truck bed to retrieve the canvas bags holding the family's usual order. She noticed one of the women from next door moving toward the house.

A sudden rush of movement—like the release of a tightly wound spring—drew Verity's eye to the colonial's lovely wraparound veranda. Her breath caught as Elvira's boy, Peter, trampled down the steps. He stationed himself at the bottom, long legs stiff, arms crossed defiantly over his chest. He glared a warning at the approaching woman.

Verity observed the tense tableau from behind her truck. Peter's baby sister, Laura, lay on a green-and-white striped glider on the veranda and she thought she heard a muffled sob from the girl's direction. Her heart ached for the two kids. Whether or not everything Martha claimed was true, it was obvious *something* was very wrong here.

Verity hefted the two heavy totes, determined to find out what was going on. But she definitely wouldn't ask the two kids for fear of adding to their angst.

She crossed the street, circled wide around the house.

Meanwhile, the neighbor was still marching straight up to Peter. She didn't seem to have gotten the memo that he didn't want her anywhere near them. The woman waved her hand to signal she wanted to talk to him.

Peter snarled at the woman, "Go away, you old vulture! We don't need your pity." Then louder still, for all the street to hear, "Fucking busybodies all of you!"

The woman let out a shocked yip then turned and fled. Verity kept her head down and continued along the flagstone path toward the medical office's door at the rear of the house. She hoped she'd go unnoticed. *Just the harmless farmer lady delivering your milk and eggs, kids.* People still needed to eat, she reasoned, even when facing tragedy. If indeed there was a tragedy.

As she came around the corner, she saw one of the sheriff's young deputies standing guard at the rear door.

"Hey, Henry!" Verity called out.

He looked up from running the tip of a penknife beneath his thumbnail. "Doc isn't seeing patients today, Mrs. Cade."

She held up the lighter of the two bags to show the farm's logo. "Not here for a physical, Henry. I need to leave these for the family—their order for the week. Can I put the milk and eggs in the fridge for them? I don't want things to spoil."

He grimaced as if working out a tricky equation. "Yeah, I guess."

"Is, um, something wrong? Any way I can help?"

His hairless baby face arranged itself into an appropriately stern expression for an officer of the law. But the effort seemed too much for him. He gave her a weak smile. "No offense, Mrs. Cade, but Sheriff says we need to keep this situation under wraps."

"Oh?" She shrugged. "I see." Although she didn't.

By now, Martha would have contacted another dozen friends with her "news." Soon the entire town would be talking about Elvira's supposed suicide, adding their own imagined details. Time was of the essence.

"I guess it's ok for you to put that stuff away." Henry said, startling her out of grim thoughts. "You need help carrying those things inside?"

"No, I'm fine. I'll just nip in and out quickly." She flashed him a reassuring smile. "I promise not to bother anyone. Just need to get these in the fridge," she repeated.

He gave her a little nod.

She let herself inside. The interior door leading from a short hallway into the medical office's waiting room was open. She peeked in. No one was visible inside the reception area. Verity took two steps up to the kitchen door and let herself in. No one in the kitchen. But she could hear voices coming from deeper within the house. First floor, definitely. The living room, she guessed, after listening for a moment to the conversation.

"I just can't wrap my mind around..." John Evans' strained voice trailed off. "You must know what I mean, Sheriff. Elvira would never do a thing like *that*. Ever!"

Verity lifted a bottle of cream-topped milk out of the first tote and set it inside the refrigerator door. *This is none of your business,* she scolded herself. But she couldn't help listening. Even if every word burned in her ears.

"Now, doc—" the unmistakable bass of the county sheriff "—this ain't an easy thing for any man to accept. Only Elvira may ever know why she did it."

"Are you sure you're not mistaken? Maybe the body isn't hers." The pain in the doctor's voice was tangible. "It could be someone who just looks like her."

"Soon as she's over to the morgue, John, we'll have you come on down and formally ID her. Meanwhile, I think I can safely say I'd recognize Elvira anywhere. It's her. No question 'bout it. I am sorry."

Then it isn't just gossip!

An involuntary gasp escaped Verity's lips. The muscles in her chest wrenched tight. Her eyes burned with tears she somehow managed to hold back. The second bottle of milk, on its way to the fridge, nearly slipped from her trembling fingers. She tightened her grip and wedged it safely into the door's shelf.

A third voice spoke—so softly she was unable to understand the words.

"But, Father," John Evans responded, "Elvira is such a strong woman." Ah, she realized, Father Coyne from St. Matthew's. "She's always been so confident." Bossy, Verity silently corrected. "A feet-on-the-ground sort of woman. To think of her flinging herself off a precipice is beyond ludicrous."

Again, the priest's response was impossible to hear.

Verity stood paralyzed, midway between the open refrigerator door and the island where she'd set her delivery bags. *I should never have come into this house*, she berated herself. She didn't belong here. Not today. But now she couldn't seem to move either to finish storing away the butter and eggs or to throw herself out the back door.

"My son, we can never truly know the heart of another," the priest was saying, with a little more volume than before. Wasn't that what she herself had thought at Martha's house? *A cliché, Father. That's the best you can do?*

"But she is...*was* a Catholic," Evans protested. "Isn't it still considered a sin to take one's own life?"

"Yes," Father Coyne said. "To be honest though—we, um, we rarely saw her at mass."

"I know, I know. But when you grow up with a belief like that, you never forget it!" The desperation in John Evans' voice tugged at Verity's heart. "It stays with you. She wouldn't. She just wouldn't..."

Verity was truly ashamed for eavesdropping. She wanted to escape the raw grief flooding this house. But that seemed easier said than done. She felt as though she was straddling an active fault line, the floor beneath her suddenly unstable, on the verge of dropping out from under her. *Oh God! Elvira! Poor John. Poor Peter and Laura.* She held on to the edge of the island for support. Sucked down deep breaths to calm herself before she could finish putting away the family's order.

In spite of her vow to stop listening, she couldn't unhear what had been said or silence the conversation continuing in the next room.

"I need to ask you a few questions, John," the sheriff said, less consoling and more authoritative now. "Father, if you'll step outside for a few minutes so I can speak in private with the doc. You'll have time to talk to him after I leave."

"Of course," the priest said, "I'll wait on the front porch with the children."

I wouldn't do that if I were you! Verity thought, remembering Peter's mood.

"You said before," the sheriff began again at the sound of a door closing, "your wife came home late last night. Maybe as late as two a.m. From a party of some sort?"

"I guess," John Evans responded vaguely. "She didn't tell me what the event was or where. At least, I don't remember now."

"But you spoke to her when she returned from the event?"

"Yes. I mean, no. I was only half awake at the time. I heard her footsteps down the hallway, past the bedroom. I expect she was checking on the children in their rooms. She passed by a second time but seemed in a hurry. She may have been running."

"And would she normally act like that? Running through the house?"

"Elvira? Run?" The doctor laughed. It was as close to a maniacal sound as Verity had ever heard. "I don't believe lighting a fire under my wife would cause her to rush around like that. She always moved, well, at her own pace."

Verity picked up two one-pound packets of butter and stashed them behind the flippy plastic door marked BUTTER. She felt numb, moving in slow motion.

"And then what happened?"

"I heard her leave again. She let the front door slam on her way out. Not like her at all. And no, I didn't see her leave. But you get to know the sounds of your own house, don't you?" The doctor paused, groaned softly. "I thought about getting up to see if anything was wrong. But I didn't. I should have. I guess I assumed she'd be right back, and we'd talk then. I must have fallen back asleep."

"Slammed the door, you said. As if she was angry? Or upset?"

"Yes. Maybe both."

"Did you and she have words, John? And then she left after the argument?" There was something wary, accusing in the sheriff's tone.

"No! We didn't argue. I told you we didn't even speak." Irritation mixed with fatigue and confusion colored the doctor's words. "The last time I actually saw her was around eight o'clock last night, after dinner. I went down to my office to work. She left sometime later for her party, or whatever."

Verity heard what she guessed was the front door of the house opening. Miraculously there seemed to have been no violent outbursts from the veranda, which made her wonder if Peter was still there. She used two hands to carefully lift a carton of eggs from her bag; she didn't entirely trust herself not to drop them. Her fingers felt like nervous birds—all aflutter. She went back for the other dozen and moved them to the second shelf of the fridge. Delivery successful.

"Sheriff, is this necessary?" the priest interrupted the interview. "Can't you see this man is in shock and grief stricken?"

"Alright," the sheriff muttered. "It can wait. You try to get some rest, Doc."

Verity hastily shook out her two empty canvas bags and folded them haphazardly. Her head spun with everything she'd overheard. She suddenly felt less desperate to escape, curiosity having replaced a little of her panic.

She wondered why the sheriff didn't ask more questions. Different questions. Like—was it possible the footsteps John Evans thought he heard were those of one of his teenage children? Or of someone else entirely? An intruder seemed unlikely. And yet...

Verity tucked her bags under one arm and turned toward the door through which she'd arrived.

"Mrs. Cade?"

Startled, she turned to see Dr. John Evans standing in the kitchen behind her. He stared at her with a puzzled expression that was slowly turning to disapproval.

"Oh, sorry. I was just leaving," she mumbled, flustered. "The deputy." She motioned in the general direction of the backyard. "He told me I could leave the milk and eggs for you and the children." She fluttered her empty bags like a semaphore to establish her legitimacy, then felt silly for doing so.

"Oh, yes. Of course. Very kind of you." He blinked as if trying to reorient his brain to the mundane matters of life after having dragged himself up and out of the fires of hell. "I must owe you for the eggs?"

"Please, no. I really don't—" Verity was already backing through the kitchen door "—you don't owe me a thing." Down the steps to the rear door, she trundled. After wrestling briefly with the doorknob, she somehow managed to let herself out.

She shook her head at Henry, who looked as though he might approach her for another chat. Around the back of the house and toward the street she rushed. If she had stayed a moment longer John Evans would have gone in search of her stupid egg money. *How awful!*

By the time she arrived at the front of the house, she became aware of shouting voices. Peter again.

She peeked over her shoulder, afraid he might be yelling at her. But no. He was cursing at a stranger wearing a jacket and tie. The teenager's face shone blood-red with rage. The man's eyes were wide with shock.

"How do you *think* I feel?" Peter screamed. "How would you feel if your mother had just offed herself, you moron?"

"S-son," the man stammered, "I'm from Channel 8 News. I only wanted to—"

Oh no, she thought, *a reporter. Just what this family needs now.*

Before the man could say another word, Peter lunged at him with outstretched hands. He hit the reporter hard in the chest with both palms. Staggering clumsily backward from the force of the assault, the man lost his balance. His feet and legs circled comically—Wile E. Coyote style—barely touching the ground in a futile attempt to regain his poise.

To Verity's horror, he landed flat on his back in the grass and Peter kept coming at him.

"Get the hell out of here! Beat it!" the boy yelled.

Peter scuffed at the grass with one foot, sending clods of dirt flying. For a moment Verity feared the teenager was going to kick the man in the ribs. The journalist, if that was really what he was, scrabbled helplessly, trying to haul himself up off the ground and out of range.

Where the hell is the sheriff? And the doctor? she wondered. Couldn't they hear what was going on?

She took a step forward, ready to intervene if the teen took his belligerency any further. Obviously, the reporter had foolishly asked insensitive questions. But the violence of Peter Evans' reaction seemed out of all proportion to the man's request for information.

Finally, the deputy came running around the side of the house. He gave Peter a warning glare. "That's enough, buddy. Go inside with your dad if you can't control yourself." He put out a hand to steady the journalist, who still seemed to be having trouble finding his equilibrium.

Shaken by the scene, but even more shocked by what she'd learned while in Elvira's kitchen, Verity clambered into her truck and slapped her delivery bags down on the passenger seat.

Dear God! It must be true. Elvira was dead.

CHAPTER 6

VERITY MOPPED AWAY tears with the wrists of her hoodie, working up the energy to drive away from Elvira's house. She stared at the sheriff's SUV across the street from her. Red-and-blue lights, still flashing, flashing, flashing moronically. Advertising tragedy to the world. Elvira would have hated that.

Did the dead have opinions? Did Mark? What would he want her to do about the farm now that he wasn't here? Now that she was struggling to keep it. She wished she knew. And Elvira? Maybe the real estate maven had lost her right to have a say in anything. Didn't she choose to end her own life?

Although...

Like John Evans, Verity found last night's events utterly confusing. Suicide? It seemed inconceivable that Elvira, queen of Vermont real estate—whose ego, not to mention bank account, knew no bounds—would throw herself into a granite pit. What did she have to be miserable about?

At least, that was the way Verity had always thought of her. *Elvira, the woman who had everything*. Verity was quite sure everyone in town would agree with her. Why end your life at the very height of your career? Why, when you had a loving and brilliant husband and two beautiful kids who needed you?

Verity shook her head and sighed in frustration. It. Just. Made. No. Sense.

Finish your delivery route, dammit! You can't sit here all day. Do something!

She looked out from a tangle of disturbing thoughts to see that only two people still stood in front of a nearby house, talking and darting speculative looks at the Evans home. One of them, a gray-haired woman in gardening clothes, whose name she couldn't recall, lifted her hand in a hesitant gesture toward Verity and started moving in the direction of her truck.

Verity hit the ignition button and drove away. She was in no mood for contributing fodder to the neighborhood gossip mill.

A few minutes later, she parked in the Evansfield shopping district—comprised of a half-dozen shops lining the west side of Main Street. The rest of her deliveries would need to wait. She couldn't bring herself to carry on as if this was a normal day.

The truck's windshield faced the village green. Behind her stood the Cat's Cradle Café, Sunny's domain; Denise's Chocolate Designs; Chaundra's Antiques Emporium; Kate Phillips' bookstore A World of Stories; the Evansfield Pharmacy and Fumiko Ota's adorable yarn shop, Knit One Purl. Nestled among the storefronts was the recently restored Historic Vermont Inn. The line of colorful storefronts, reflected in Verity's rearview mirror, all but screamed "quaint Vermont village" to tourists passing through.

In front of her parked truck, two little boys ran across the village green to join their friends. The children tore around in dizzying circles, screaming wildly, waving their arms above their heads in mock horror as a taller boy chased them, roaring. The designated monster.

An old-fashioned white bandstand, looking like something

out of *The Music Man,* stood in the center of lush turf. Her parents had taken her to see the musical at a local dinner theater near Baltimore for her tenth birthday. She had loved every second of it and never been happier.

Today, it was hard to imagine feeling such joy. Verity could remember only one other time when she'd been sadder than she was now. The day Mark died. But Mark didn't choose to end his life.

She swung open the truck door and dropped down onto the pavement, leaning in for her purse, not bothering to lock the door before she walked away. She supposed folks in Springfield, Montpelier, or Brattleboro might. Certainly, drivers locked their car doors in Boston or Hartford. Absolutely, in New York City. But Evansfield had always seemed, at least to her, immune to serious crime.

She glanced across the street at the café with its whimsical wooden sign above the door, a pretty pink and soft green to match the café's interior decor. Sunny Whitaker's cozy eatery on Main Street had become her refuge after Mark's death—a place of comfort, of good friends who shared her grief and plied her with steaming mugs of aromatic coffee, insanely sweet pastries, and hugs. Today, she instinctively sought its soothing atmosphere again. It occurred to her that anyone in Evansfield who had cared about Elvira would eventually step through this green door, drawn to the comfort of neighbors.

Before the end of the day, she needed to complete her deliveries, no matter how dismal she felt. But for just a few minutes she wanted to sit quietly and sort through the rat's nest of troubled thoughts hammering at her brain. Although she couldn't say why, she felt in her bones that something wasn't right about the story of Elvira's demise. *Because there's something worse than suicide?* Was there such a thing? Also, something about the sheriff's attitude bothered her. He had sounded so sure of himself back at the

Evans house. As if there could be no other explanation for Elvira's death than a final desperate act of her own making. And yet, she was sure there hadn't been time for an autopsy. The body couldn't have been discovered until daylight that same morning.

Verity started across the street, barely aware of her surroundings now, her mind firing off possibilities. *Rat-a-tat-tat.*

Maybe slapping a suicide label on Elvira's death was just too tempting for their local law enforcement—an easy solution. Fred Bailey was a man elected to office who seemed to lack experience with fatalities other than those produced by traffic accidents or due to natural causes. Death by one's own hand simplified an investigation that involved neither of those situations. But what if he was missing or just ignoring evidence to the contrary? A witness, a weapon or injuries on the body that couldn't have been sustained in a fall?

As far as Verity could tell, the one thing anyone should be certain of at this moment was that Elvira Evans had died in the early morning hours of that same day. The reasons why she'd died remained, at least to her, as elusive as smoke.

Verity walked slower, letting her mind work over this puzzle. Elvira had apparently rushed off to the abandoned granite quarry in the wee hours of morning after returning home from Verity's house. Why? There must have been an urgent reason.

Was it possible the good doctor kept back information from the sheriff when describing what had gone on at their house? Did he know why his wife might have wanted to kill herself? Maybe he was trying to protect his wife's memory from scandal. (*How Victorian was that!*) And if so, why hide facts that would eventually come out anyway? Everyone had secrets. But in a small town like theirs, they were always discovered. Eventually.

Verity stepped up onto the narrow cobblestone sidewalk in

front of the shops, her head throbbing with each footstep. She winced at the churning in her stomach. Hot, sweet tea—that's what she needed. To relax. But more importantly, to clear her head. There had to be an explanation for whatever had happened last night. No matter how heartbreaking it might be, she needed to understand the truth. Only then would she be able to cope with Elvira's loss.

When she walked through the café door the single silver bell overhead tinkled cheerfully, mocking her black mood. She felt like ripping the stupid thing off its bouncy spring. Heads turned from occupied tables to note her arrival. Conversations stopped. Did they already know?

"Verity," Sunny Whitaker called out softly from behind her display counter of pastries. She came around the glass case arranged with croissants, fruit turnovers, spice-cake slices, and muffins so large two hands were required to hold one. Her lovely features appeared drawn tight with pain.

She gave Verity a hug then led her toward a small bistro table at the rear of the dining area, where Kate Phillips and Fumiko Ota were already sitting.

Verity nearly lost it.

Fumiko stood up, motioning toward the chair she had just vacated. In a flurry of activity Kate and Sunny pushed another table close to the first and dragged over more chairs, just in time for Chaundra and Denise to sweep through the café door, sending the little bell into a paroxysm of jangles.

Hugs of shared sympathy followed words of disbelief and grief. They all sat down, looking at one another, at a loss for anything more to say.

"I have everyone's orders in my truck," Verity announced at last. Her voice sounded scratchy and strained to her own ears. Her throat felt raw. "I guess it wouldn't have done any good to stop at your houses." She gave them each a weak smile. "Since you're all here."

Mostly all. She also had two bags for the mayor's family. Mary Beth Loop always placed a large order each week. And, of course, she had already delivered Martha's milk and eggs.

Sunny excused herself to wait on a customer but quickly returned with a tray of scones, still warm from the oven. "I'd sit with you girls but I have no one to cover for me for another hour. How did you get the dreadful news, Verity? Soon as I heard, I phoned you and Deni, but you didn't answer."

"Sorry." Verity breathed in the delicious buttery aroma of the scones. It seemed obscene to feel hunger, when one of her friends never again would. "I was ignoring the phone this morning. Running late. Martha broke the news to me when I dropped off her order."

"If anyone knows what's going on in town, it's Martha," Kate commented dryly. "I wonder who told her."

"She said she saw emergency vehicles and knew something was up." Verity's stomach gave another warning burble, and she hoped she wasn't going to be sick. Her hand seemed to have a mind of its own. It reached for her favorite raspberry-white-chocolate scone but then hesitated. The cranberry-orange scone she'd tried last week was delicious. And the apricot-cream or almond-cherry were both, well... She stuck with her first choice.

"I bet Mary Beth called Martha," Kate said. "The sheriff would have informed the mayor, and Rupert would tell MB. They compete over who's the first to hear local news." She giggled. "Mary Beth and Martha, that is."

"Have you ever noticed," Denise mumbled around a mouthful of crumbs, "how gossip freaks seem to get a kick out of other people's misery?"

Chaundra sipped her coffee and squinted doubtfully at the confectioner. "That's a little unfair, Denise. We all hurt when we lose someone we care about. Although I will admit that Martha rarely gets emotional over anything."

Fumiko nodded her head thoughtfully, her black shoulder-length hair glistening as it moved. She brushed aside the smooth bangs to better look at them all. "I think she need be tough. Teaching those wild little ones. Ooh! Such patience she must have. Would drive me crazy!" The pretty Japanese woman's English was a work-in-progress.

"Don't we all just carry on the best we can?" Sunny slid a quick look at Verity. "What else can one do in the face of such a tragedy? We mourn. Then we struggle onward and eventually we heal."

"But Martha has always been closer to Elvira's family than the rest of us, don't you think?" Kate said. "She taught both of the Evans children in kindergarten."

Verity nodded in agreement, having heard the same thing earlier from Martha herself.

"Laura was especially fond of Martha, when she was younger," Sunny added. "Quite attached, I seem to remember. Oh!" Sunny jumped up from her seat when a customer signaled her from a nearby table.

"The boy's sixteen now, and a real handful, I understand." Chaundra pinched off bits of her blueberry scone, nibbling daintily. "I've had some trouble with him and his friends at the emporium."

"Aren't all kids monsters at that age?" Verity shook her head, remembering her own teenage years. Not that she had ever done anything illegal, but she definitely gave her parents a run for their money. Then she remembered the pure rage in Peter Evans' voice, the flash of anger in his eyes before he launched himself at the startled reporter. She had been sure he was going to physically attack the man. Well, he had done actually. Didn't pushing someone hard enough to make them fall constitute assault?

"You ok, Verity? You look awfully pale all of a sudden, girl." Sunny had reappeared. She set down a tray of coffees along with cream, sugar, and sweeteners—for Verity, Chaundra, and Fumiko—and a carafe to top off the others' mugs.

"I'm fine. Just thinking about—" She didn't want to say anything that would get Peter into trouble. The kid had enough to deal with, having just lost his mother. "About Elvira. Of all the people I know I would never have predicted she might— well, you know."

"Kill herself?" Denise never minced words.

Verity shrugged. "Where's the logic in it? Elvira. Seriously?"

Sunny sat down with a weary sigh beside Verity and patted her hand. "Just doesn't make sense. Does it, sweetie?" She gave the surrounding tables another quick look to make sure all her customers were satisfied.

The words Verity had never meant to say out loud burst from her lips. "I was at the house. Inside in fact. Just now."

They all stared at her. In fact, the entire café seemed to have gone quiet, as if the air had been sucked out of the pretty little room and no one could breathe let alone talk.

Kate finally whispered, "The Evans house? You were there?" Verity nodded and Kate continued. "I drove past after I heard the rumors. It looked as though the sheriff and his deputies had the place barricaded. No one in, no one out. Just like on TV."

"I tried to stop by, too." Chaundra said. "Before I could even get out of my car, a deputy rudely waved me off. How did you get through, Verity?"

She shrugged. "I guess there's something about a delivery vehicle that looks official. I had the family's dairy order for the week. Young Henry let me in through the back door."

"Oh, my!" Kate put down her coffee mug with a loud clunk, as if it had suddenly become too heavy for her. "Did you see John or the kids? Was it awful?"

Verity flushed with embarrassment. She absolutely had not intended to repeat any of what she'd heard at the house. But sharing a painful experience made even the worst of situation feel a bit more bearable. And today was pretty darn bad.

"It was so sad. I stood in Elvira's kitchen, putting away food she'll never eat and overheard John and the sheriff talking with Father Coyne from St. Matthew's."

"And?" Kate prompted when Verity hesitated.

Just then, the first lady of Evansfield bustled through the café door. Mary Beth Loop was closely followed by Martha Humphrey. The two newcomers quickly spotted their friends, sized up the seating situation and snagged two more of the white-wire bistro chairs from an unoccupied table.

"Guess you've all heard," Mary Beth hooted far too loudly, plopping her generous bottom down in one of the chairs and wiggling to get comfortable.

Denise hushed her and rolled her eyes.

Mary Beth obliged by dropping her voice a couple hundred decibels. "Rupert is being all hush-hush about the details. He says the sheriff told him a body was found in the quarry and it's definitely Elvira. Anyone hear anything more?"

"Not me." Martha squeezed her chair between Mary Beth's and Kate's then busied herself selecting a scone.

"Verity was just about to tell us what she overheard at the doc's house," Denise reminded them.

Everyone looked at Verity.

This is going to sound like the beginning of a bad joke, she thought. *A cop, a doctor, and a priest walk into a bar.*

Verity repeated with considerable reluctance what she

recalled of the conversation between the three men and the events that followed thereafter.

"That's so strange," Chaundra said when she'd finished. "I can't imagine Elvira running out into the night like that, without a word to her family. And have you ever seen her rush anywhere that didn't involve at least a six-figure real estate deal? No disrespect to the woman, but—"

"We all know how motivated she was by money," Kate finished Chaundra's thought in a quiet voice. "I don't think it's speaking ill of the dead if it's true. Anyway, Elvira made no secret of her competitiveness and love of expensive things."

"She once told me that money was sexy," Mary Beth said.

Verity was still hung up on the strangeness of Elvira running. "Come to think of it," she murmured. "I've only ever seen her walk in a regal sort of amble. I always envied her poise."

Fumiko gave a fierce shake of her head. "If she run out of house, I bet it got to do with that boy of hers. Chaundra right. He out of control. I see him with his older friends in their cars, crazy driving. Up and down Main Street. Up and down, like they NASCARs."

"Poor Doc Evans," Mary Beth sighed. "He'll have his hands full without Elvira around to keep those kids in line."

"I'll give him a day or two to catch his breath then go have a talk with him." Martha dusted crumbs off her skirt. "I'm sure Peter and Laura will benefit from spending some time with their Aunt Martha."

"You're related to them?" Verity asked, looking around the circle and finding at least two other confused faces.

"No, no, of course not." Martha made the tittering noise with her tongue that Verity always found annoying. She imagined the teacher chiding her kindergarten students for classroom infractions. "John has always said he appreciated my being at Evansfield Elementary to give his kids such a good start in school." She pinched her lips together and studied the diminishing supply of scones on the tray then snatched up the last lemon-blueberry.

"I just hope that reporter doesn't file a complaint against Peter," Sunny said, referring to Verity's replay of the drama at the house. "Or sue Peter's father if he got hurt when he fell."

"I didn't get the impression the man would be suing anyone," Verity said. "He was out of line and I expect he knew it. Hounding those kids, trying to get them to talk about their mother just hours after her body was discovered."

"Shame on him!" Fumiko snapped.

"If I'd been there, I'd have beat the shit out of the guy." Denise tended to prefer physical solutions to problems and they sometimes needed to restrain her. They ignored her now since the reporter wasn't in immediate danger.

"Did the sheriff question you?" Martha asked Verity.

"No." Verity frowned. "Why would he?"

"Elvira was at your house last night. Hours, maybe just minutes, before she jumped."

Verity drew a sharp breath. "You think he suspects I'm somehow connected with her death?"

Chaundra looked around the group, her eyes dark with worry. "I suppose we all should expect to be interviewed. We were the last to see her alive."

"I don't see why." Kate frowned down at her coffee mug. "All we can tell him is that she didn't act like she wanted to kill herself. Everything seemed perfectly normal at Verity's house. Right? We all left together. We dropped off Elvira at her place. And that—*that* was the last...we...saw... Oh, God!" Kate's chin wobbled.

"Aw honey," Sunny crooned, "it's ok. We all feel the same. It's tough to think she's so suddenly gone."

Fumiko was scowling at the two of them. Verity couldn't figure out if she looked confused or angry. "I agree, yes." The town's knitting expert brushed her shiny black hair away from her eyes. "We all sad. Who cannot be when friend die?" She wagged a finger at Kate and Sunny. "But you forget fight you tell me about."

"What fight?" Kate squinted at her. "Oh, you mean when Sunny and Denise jumped on Elvira for being mean to Mary Beth?"

"It wasn't a fight, Fumiko," Verity said, although she supposed she was arguing a rather fine point here. True, no one had landed a physical blow. But harsh words were most definitely spoken. The tension in her kitchen had felt as thick as a New England sea-fog. "You know how Elvira is...was. She was picking on Mary Beth even before she stepped into my house. Someone needed to set her straight."

"Not sure it did much good," Chaundra murmured between sips of her coffee.

"Anyway," Verity continued, "the sheriff has already informed the family that Elvira took her own life. I suppose he must have enough evidence." Why was she defending him when minutes earlier she'd doubted that any such evidence existed?

"I expect he has to tick off all the usual boxes," Martha agreed.

"What boxes?" American slang sometimes left Fumiko befuddled.

"Well, for instance, legally speaking," Mary Beth's voice took on an authoritative tone, "did anyone have a reason for wanting Elvira dead? Did she have enemies? That's what they always ask on CSI programs. And who would benefit from her death?" They all just stared at her.

"This isn't a TV show, MB," Denise pointed out.

Kate leaned forward, eyes bright. "No, I think Mary Beth is right. What she means is—the sheriff will want to know if anyone might, at least theoretically, have been involved in her death."

"And," Mary Beth added, "maybe there was a witness...but then that person, wanting to protect the killer, made her death *look* like a suicide."

Verity made an effort to stop herself from rolling her eyes. Obviously, Kate had been spending far too much time with Mary Beth. "Sorry but that's preposterous. You're saying two people might have been involved in murdering her?"

Denise crowed with laughter. "Is it any more preposterous than Elvira leaping to her death in a deserted granite quarry at o-dark-thirty?"

"Is that where it happen? OMG!" Fumiko cried.

"That's what my Sarah said." Kate helped herself to another scone. "Her friend Tiffany sent her a text this morning."

"Tiffany Mayhew? How would that empty-headed little twit know anything?" Martha said but then winced at the looks she was getting. "Sorry, but I should know. I taught the girl for two years, and I do not think she ever learned a thing."

"Apparently Tiffany's father and brother found the body," Kate explained. "They were on their way to fish in Browning Creek and took a shortcut through the woods near the quarry."

Verity dropped her head into her hands. "None of this makes any sense. If Elvira wanted to kill herself—and I don't for a minute believe she would or did—why walk half a mile through the woods in the middle of the night to do it?"

"It does seem like a lot of work," agreed Mary Beth, who had an aversion to exercise.

"Not the most efficient way to off yourself either," Denise commented.

Kate gasped. "What a thing to say!"

"C'mon now—it's true," Denise insisted, scanning her friends' faces. "If you intentionally do a face plant off a really high cliff or the fifteenth floor of a building—you're pretty much guaranteed the intended result. Smoosharoo! But if you jump off of some place that's not that high—say only thirty or forty feet like the quarry—you might just end up breaking your nose or an arm—"

"Oh, please," Martha groaned. "Don't be gross."

"She's right," Sunny agreed with a sigh. "Although Denise dear, you might have chosen more sensitive wording. Still, you have a point. Elvira was super-efficient. Goodness sakes, the property didn't exist that she couldn't sell. If she intended to end her life, she'd do it in a way that wouldn't cause her a lot of pain and just end up with her in the hospital."

Kate licked crumbs from her hand, one finger at a time. "Anyway, jumping to her death seems way too messy. Don't you think?" She finished tidying herself up with a paper napkin. "Think about it. Have you ever seen Elvira with a hair out of place or a broken fingernail?"

Verity observed her own ragged nails. She couldn't recall the last time she'd had a manicure. Such was a farmer's life!

Denise gave an odd snort, as though muffling a laugh.

"What?" Martha snapped at her. "If something's so funny, share it with the...us."

Verity winced. Had she actually been about to say, "with the class?"

"I agree with Kate, for once," Denise said. "About jumping to her death being not her style. If you fall any distance and land on a slab of granite, there's bound to be horrid cracking noises from bones breaking and oozing blood and—"

"We get the idea, dear," Sunny cut her off. "I'm sure none of us wants to think about last night in that level of detail."

"But maybe we should." Verity's head was finally clearing, thanks to the caffeine and sugar. "Don't we owe it to Elvira?"

"Owe her?" Martha frowned.

"The truth. About her death." Verity fixed a steady gaze on each of the other women. "I worry that the sheriff has rushed into deciding this was a suicide. Kate and Denise are right. The way she died makes no sense. After all, we should know; we are the people who were closest to Elvira, other than her family."

"That's true," Sunny said thoughtfully. "Plus, if she really did want to end her life, she had easier ways. She had her pick of drugs from John's medical office for a quick and tidy overdose. Job done."

CHAPTER 7

AFTER ANOTHER FEW minutes of discussion that took them no closer to understanding their friend's death, Verity remembered the milk and eggs still sitting in the back of her truck. She helped Kate transfer her order to the bookshop where she had a small refrigerator. The others took away their own bags.

Only two more deliveries remained. Of course, on arriving at her customers' homes, she was asked if she'd heard the news about Elvira. Yes, she told them, she had heard. And, yes, it was indeed a very sad day for Evansfield.

She chose not to repeat the speculation they had shared at the café. Retelling such horrid details just didn't feel right. But she couldn't help continuing to brood over Elvira's demise. Was there something she'd missed? Vital clues of some sort? Had Elvira said or done anything last night at the farmhouse that might have warned her how fragile the woman was?

Oh, God! It was just too awful.

Back at the farm, thankfully, she had no time for flogging herself with might-have-beens. Chores needed doing. She raked out the chicken houses, spread fresh straw, filled water troughs and feed dispensers, all while her hens carried on in a raucous chorus around her.

Checking on her cows felt less like work. The herd of gentle fawn-and-white guernseys were just like those she remembered from childhood picture books. Most of her girls grazed calmly out in the pasture, having visited the Robo-Milkers earlier in the day. Mark had installed the three computerized machines, which the manufacturer had promised would be sufficient for their herd of 60 animals.

She found Molly, her problem bovine, waiting for her in the lower barn, where the old milking parlor had been. "Sorry to be late, pretty girl. This has been one hell of a day."

The cow observed her placidly through liquid-brown eyes as if accepting her apology. Molly never needed to be tied into a stall while being milked. She never kicked and always stood as still as a rock until Verity finished and patted her on the rump to signal their time together was done.

The process of working the cow's udders had become, for Verity, a form of meditation. She talked to the animal in a calm tone, convinced that this relaxed the animal and encouraged her milk to flow. Verity's own joints and muscles immediately began to loosen. Her racing mind slowed, soothed by the cow's soft moos.

These sweet creatures had been so very close to Mark's heart. His animals, this land, and his parents' house—all of this was his legacy. And now it was hers to care for. She loved every creature, every acre and all that grew or grazed upon it.

But maybe Elvira had been right about one thing. As an experienced realtor specializing in Vermont properties, she had warned Verity that managing a working farm on her own would become both a financial and emotional burden. And ultimately, a hardship. "Just think about it, Verity," Elvira had said. "You'll be tied to the place, forever. You can never take long, luxurious vacations like your friends." And she was right. Who would care for her animals, the fields, her beloved kitchen garden? Laying all that responsibility on her farmhands would be too much.

Maybe by the time John Evans recovered a little from the loss of his wife, she would change her mind and offer the property to him. Elvira had claimed he was desperate for land on which to build the clinic and move his practice out of their house.

"If I sell the farm for the right price," Verity confided in Molly, "I could use the money to move back to Baltimore, start my own business." Whatever that might be. "What do you think, girl?"

"And leave us behind?"

Verity's hands stilled. She slowly released Molly's warm teats. She swiveled on the milking stool, curious to see who had entered the barn without her hearing them.

No one was there.

She gave Molly, innocently munching her cud like a teenager smacking bubblegum, a suspicious look. "When did you start talking back to me, Molly girl?" Of course, her imagination must be playing tricks on her. She laughed at herself.

"Please don't go away," a deeper voice whispered. The words came to her from no particular direction. As if they were just molecules in the air around her.

Verity narrowed her eyes and scanned the old milking parlor—dim, pungent with the aroma of animals. Definitely empty. The only movement came from the dust motes floating in the narrow yellow shafts of sunlight that seeped between shrunken barn boards.

But now she was less sure she had imagined the voices.

Verity stood up from her stool so suddenly she nearly knocked over the milk bucket. "Jason? Jerry? This isn't funny, guys." The Grimalski twins weren't by nature pranksters. If anything, they were far too serious for young men in their twenties. She stomped her foot. "I'm not in the mood for foolishness, whoever you are. It's been a truly crappy day."

Was it possible her friends had returned? They'd appeared unannounced last night, a self-ordained rescue party on the anniversary of her husband's death. A gesture of loving kindness. Well, except for Elvira, who apparently had other motives. But she was sure they would never try to frighten her.

More likely the mysterious voices belonged to neighborhood kids. Trying to spook her. What was more fun than faking out an adult?

"Come out, whoever you are," she coaxed gently. "It's alright. I'm not angry."

Still nothing.

Verity lost her patience. "Listen, whoever you are! You may think this is a cute game, but you're trespassing." She reached into her hip pocket for her phone. "If you don't come out this instant, I'm calling the sheriff."

"Oh, now look what you've done, Percy darlin'. You've upset her."

Verity froze. These words weren't whispered. They were clear as a bell and came to her from the space just inches in front of her.

But. Nobody. Is. There! Verity's brain screamed at her.

"She didn't mean it, my love." A man's voice. Now she was sure of it. A woman and a man—hiding in her barn. What the hell! Were they ventriloquists? Throwing their voices from behind a bale of hay?

"I absolutely did mean it!" Verity screamed. "Now get off my damn property before I...before I—"

Molly mooed her distress and nervously plodded toward the door. Verity lowered her voice and spoke between gritted teeth.

"Now look at what you've done. You frightened the poor animal."

A lilting giggle bounced off the barn's walls. "Seems to me, sugar, you are the one who spooked her with all that yellin' and arm wavin'." Was that a southern drawl she detected in the woman's voice? So odd to hear in Vermont. But she still couldn't see anyone in the half-light of the barn.

She took a step to one side, taking care this time to avoid the bucket, and peered up into the rafters. No. The voice had definitely come from much closer. Her senses told her the speaker must be standing right in front of her. And yet, she wasn't. No matter how hard she squinted and searched, she saw nothing.

I'm losing my mind.

"We're so sorry, darlin'. We didn't mean to upset you. We really like you."

"Oh, well, ummm, thank you." Verity shook her head. *Really? Thank you?*

"We've always thought you were special. Ever since Mr. Mark brought you home." The flat New England twang of the male voice was much more familiar to her. "He was a good fella. Worked our farm well and true, just like we would have done. Had we not..." The voice faltered.

"Percy doesn't like to say the D-word," the woman whispered in Verity's right ear, making her jump. "He's very sensitive about our current spectral state."

From deep down in Verity's throat a whimper of disbelief threatened to explode into a scream. *Ghosts? Am I talking to ghosts?* Her hands flew to her mouth and smothered a shriek.

Clearly, a year's worth of grief, too little sleep, and constant worry about the farm had been too much for her. And now this new tragedy had driven her over the edge.

Verity flung her arms out in a gesture of despair. "No!" she shouted. "No, no...no! Just go away and leave me alone!"

"Oh Lordy. She's gone hysterical, Percy. Help me set her down before she faints. Press her head between her knees. Thank goodness she's not wearing a corset. At least she can breathe."

Verity felt hands clasp her shoulders and ease her down on a hay bale. Something pushed softly against the back of her head. She didn't struggle against the strangely comforting sensations. She obediently bent forward and squeezed her eyes shut.

CHAPTER 8

SLOWLY, Verity's head began to clear. The world stopped spinning, and she was able to straighten up without feeling nauseous. She cautiously opened her eyes and saw only Molly's magnificent tan-and-white rump a few feet away. The cow's long tail whipped back and forth, flicking away flies.

Verity drew a deep breath. The familiar pungent odor of barn calmed her. She let her eyes drift shut again as she executed a few unhurried yoga breaths—in through the nose, hiss out through the mouth. In...hiss out. In...hiss, hiss, hiss out.

A waking dream, that's what it had been. Absolutely. There was no other possible explanation.

But then—

"I think she'll be fine now," the honeysuckle-sweet voice murmured.

Verity's eyes shot wide. Her head snapped to the left, automatically tracking the direction of the voice.

A woman in a long, pink muslin gown examined her with concerned, cornflower-blue eyes. Glorious honey-blonde hair was arranged on top of her head but for a few long curls spiraling down to frame her pretty face. She appeared a few years younger than Verity, not yet thirty years old.

Thank goodness, Verity thought at first. It was a real person after all. Relief flowed through her.

But the longer she studied her visitor, the more convinced she became that something was a little off—aside from a floor-length, ruffled dress and multiple petticoats being a little over the top for hiding out in a barn.

Verity needed a moment to put a mental finger on what, in particular, most bothered her about this picture. And then it came to her. The woman appeared—and this was the only word that came to her—*insubstantial.* The lovely stranger stood between Verity and an abandoned milking stall where rakes, shovels, and buckets were stored. Yet, the stall and all of its equipment were visible *through* the woman's body—which, by any law of nature known to Verity, should not be possible.

She blinked once, twice...three times.

The woman was still there. So were the tools, just not *entirely* there-there. She narrowed her eyes and focused on the semi-translucent figure. It was as though she had been fashioned from a wavy piece of blown glass, delicately tinted to represent a woman's image. Almost as if she were a hologram.

"Who are you?" Verity croaked.

"Oh dear, where are our manners?" The figure looked to her left. Verity followed her gaze. A young man in a flannel shirt and canvas workpants stepped to the woman's side.

"Good day, madam. We are the Putnams." He removed his straw hat with two impressively large, strong-looking hands. "I am Lieutenant Percy Putnam, recently of President Lincoln's Army of the North. May I present my lovely bride, Anna Louise. We most deeply regret having frightened you."

"But you see, it was quite necessary," Anna Louise added breathily.

Verity scowled at them. "Necessary to intentionally terrify me?"

"Oh no, never!" the couple chorused.

"Indeed, we have become very fond of you," Percy added solemnly. "My wife, in particular. Having a woman close to her age in our home has been good for her. She was very lonely, you see, before you came to live with Mr. Mark and us."

Us? Verity gulped.

Anna Louise flashed a contrite smile. "As soon as we heard you say you might sell the farm, we had no choice but to beg you to stay. Thus, our appearance before you."

Verity rallied her strength and what little remained of her sanity. The scratchy hay was making the backs of her legs itch through her jeans. She stood up, tugging her pantlegs down.

"I'm not leaving the farm or Evansfield, at least not yet. But you two definitely are! I don't know who—" *or what*, she thought but didn't say "—you really are. Just get out of my barn and leave me alone."

Anna Louise took a step toward her. "But sugar, you must never sell our farm to that doctor. We overheard his wife talking about pulling down all the barns, sheds, even our house and selling the anima—"

"*Your* house?" Verity flashed a warning glare at them. "Let's get one thing straight. Mark Cade legally inherited this farm from his parents. He willed this property and everything on it to his widow. Me!" Tears threatened but she fought them off with her fury.

Why was she even talking to these...these hallucinations? She must have fainted, dreamed them and was still woozy and confused. Any moment now her head would clear. Then these irritating *whatevers* would disappear.

"Oh, my yes," Anna Louise trilled happily. "Our lovely farm, *and* yours of course. The Cades have farmed here—" she drew out the last word into two syllables (he-ah) "—for generations. Your dear Mark's great-great-great grandmother was a Putnam, who married a Cade. It was she, Miriam Putnam Cade, who inherited the farm. Am I not right, Percy dear?"

He beamed adoringly at her. "Exactly so, my love."

"But—" Verity tried to break in.

Anna Louise lifted a finger to silence her. "As you might guess, Miss Verity, I only arrived in this village after the war. Never did I, a southern girl, dream I'd marry a Yankee. But there you are!" She burst into girlish laughter with a dainty shrug.

"But my dear—" her husband turned to take her hands in his "—my family's ancestry is of little importance to Mrs. Cade. Remember, we came out of our shades for a reason." He turned to address Verity, his eyes imploring. "You must not sell this farm. We entreat you, madam. The result may well be disastrous for all concerned."

"And why is that?" She'd be darned if she let her runaway imagination tell her what to do.

"Because we fear what might happen to us," Anna Louise whimpered. She broke away from her husband to pace the barn's dusty floor. Strangely, although her voluminous skirts and petticoats swished around her ankles, the fabric made no sound at all. Stranger still, neither did her footsteps.

Verity frowned, feeling rather ill. What if this wasn't her imagination? Were these really ghosts? *But I don't believe in ghosts,* she reminded herself.

"You see," Anna Louise continued, "we seem trapped in your century, attached in a mysterious way to our dear farm."

"And if the farm were no more," Percy added, "we don't know where that would leave us."

Verity struggled with the logic of this. She understood that they were dressed in 19th-century clothing. That would fit with the female apparition's remark about marrying a Yankee and the war. American Civil War. But hallucinations, if that's what these were, must have an explanation. She'd probably hit her head. Or it was the stress.

She sucked in a deep breath and stared skeptically at the two translucent shapes. "Let me get this straight. You're telling me that you are ghosts. You're both dead!"

Anna Louise sighed and her shoulders gave a delicate shiver. "It does appear so."

"Thank goodness!" Verity laughed, sounding a little unbalanced to her own ears.

The former soldier and his wife looked at each other.

Anna Louise pouted. "You're glad we're dead? That's rather insensitive."

Oh great. Now she'd insulted two ghosts. "Sorry. Of course, I'm not glad you're dead. I'm just relieved to learn I'm still sane."

Percy looked intrigued by her reaction. "You aren't upset that you're seeing departed souls?"

Good point, Verity thought. Shouldn't she be? "Actually, no. I guess I've always wanted to believe that people I cared for might be able to visit me after they passed. You know, to offer comfort or advice." Just the idea of Mark dropping by warmed her.

"We're not sure that's how it works," Percy said gently, as if he'd read her mind.

"What do you mean?"

The young farmer screwed up his face in concentration. "We believe our still being here is a mistake. I think you 21st-century folk might call it 'a glitch in the system?' Anyway, we're not sure why or how it happened. It just did."

"We only know," Anna Louise said softly, "that we're thankful we are together. If I had to leave Percy, I'd just die!"

"You did. You are. Dead, that is," Verity pointed out before she thought better of it. "Sorry. I don't mean to offend." She plopped back down on the hay bale to better ponder the situation. "Maybe the reason you're still together is because you died at the same time. Like in a tragic accident or something. So, you're bound together for eternity!" It did sound rather romantic. Except for the dead part. She expected that had its limitations. Did the dead eat? Laugh? Make love?

"That's just it. We don't know how we died or why we're still here on our farm."

"*My* farm," Verity corrected.

"What we're trying to explain to you," Percy said solemnly, his straw hat clutched in both hands, "is that our fate may somehow be connected to this farm. And, therefore, to you as the current resident."

"Owner," Verity snapped. "It's my farm because I own it... and I happen to still be alive."

"Mrs. Cade. We beg of you. Please don't make us leave until we can be sure of our fate."

Verity sighed then tried blinking again. Very, very slowly, just to be sure. No, the two images were still there.

And I am most definitely awake. Oh, bother.

CHAPTER 9

AFTER VERITY ASSURED her two ethereal house guests that the farm's sale wasn't imminent, they seemed satisfied. She firmly explained that chores needed doing and she didn't have time to help them sort out their eternal lives. To her relief, they apologized for intruding and immediately winked out of sight.

She frowned at the empty space where the two ghosts had stood. The ease with which they'd disappeared was rather unsettling in itself. It occurred to her that if they remained invisible and silent, she'd have no way of knowing if and when they were lurking about, spying on her.

Eeeuuu! She imagined herself stripping down to take a shower.

Well, it was a little late to worry about that. They'd evidently been haunting the farmhouse for decades.

Ghosts were real. Who knew?

She shooed Molly out of the old barn and watched her amble toward the meadow to join the herd. Verity strolled up the hill and into the modern milking parlor. Agatha, Jane, and Tess (Christie, Austen, and Gerritsen, of course) occupied the Robo-Milkers. She had named the girls after her favorite writers, to Mark's amusement. A half-dozen other cows lounged about, awaiting their turn to be milked. All seemed in order here.

Stepping outside again and into the yard, she eyeballed the fence line leading away from the main barn. Good. It appeared no one had knocked down a post, thus enabling a risky escape onto the two-lane highway through town.

The air had warmed considerably since early morning when all had smelled fresh and new, washed in the morning dew. She threw herself into the most pressing of her chores.

By two in the afternoon, she felt satisfied with her progress. The land, now thoroughly warmed by the sun, gave off a musky, baked-grass sweetness. Everywhere she looked—her kitchen garden, the fenced field of chicken coops, the long stretch of meadow leading up to the pine woods behind her house—was lush with every shade of green and the abundance of nature.

She swallowed deep, calming gulps of country air, surprised by how hungry she felt, and only then remembered she'd eaten just cookies for breakfast and nothing for lunch. Slices of Sunny's artisan multi-grain bread with a thick wedge of sharp Vermont cheddar cheese sounded like the perfect solution. Portable and hearty. She needed a walk and some thinking time.

She made herself a hearty sandwich and wrapped it in waxed paper to take with her. Her mouth watered in anticipation as she traded in her work boots for sneakers. Before leaving, Verity fetched a biodegradable trash bag and pair of thin work gloves from beneath her kitchen sink and stuffed them into her jeans' pockets. She set off down the road, away from town.

A brisk walk was the only way she knew to clear her head. Ordinarily, her worries centered on the farm—chores she lacked time or energy to do, equipment she couldn't afford, paying her farmhands what they were really worth. But today she had two new and very serious concerns that couldn't be ignored. First, the mysterious death of a friend. Secondly, a pair of friendly but unnerving spirits who seemed unwilling or unable to leave the land of the living. She mulled over both problems as she chewed her sandwich.

By the time she'd finished eating, she felt revived enough to do more than just walk. She pulled out her gloves and bag. Clearing trash from the side of the road made her feel she was serving her community. It also continued to help her focus on more complicated matters.

She felt a little sad that she had chased away the phantom couple. Even though there was still a chance they were a fabrication of her imagination. For a few minutes she had actually felt a little less lonely. They claimed they hadn't meant to frighten her. She was half inclined to believe them. The pair certainly seemed harmless enough. And rather interesting.

But now that they had delivered their message—*please don't sell the farm!*—they probably wouldn't show themselves again. Why would they? While Mark had been alive, the Putnams had never once shimmered into their lives. Was that because they knew *he* would never sell his beloved farm?

Oh, Mark.

She pressed her hand to the middle of her chest. The pain was sudden, sharp and intense. Making her feel she needed to take shallow breaths. Not a heart attack—she knew that from experience. A form of panic attack, according to Dr. Evans, brought on by stress and grief. The last time she'd suffered the symptoms was nearly six months ago.

She stood still at the road's edge and breathed. Her yoga breaths again. Slowly the pain eased.

Would she ever not feel his loss? Time heals, so they said. How much time? Another year? Five? Twenty?

"I so miss you, Mark," she whispered. "Do you miss me?"

Of course he didn't answer. He never did.

Verity concentrated on the physical act of walking.

Watching the canvas toes of her red sneakers step, step, step—until she turned off the paved roadway and onto a dusty dirt track. Quarry Road the locals called it, although she doubted it actually had a name.

She resumed gathering trash while slowly looping through the woods surrounding the abandoned granite quarry. It was beautiful here—thick with maple trees, stark white birch, frothy green ferns and velvety pockets of moss. Sunlight broke through the canopy in brilliant patches. The forest air smelled intoxicatingly clean.

Between tree trunks on her left, Verity glimpsed discarded slabs of raw granite, all that remained of a once-thriving mining industry. She left the path and cut through the brush toward the edge of the quarry. She looked around for signs of an ongoing investigation.

Nothing.

Where was the ubiquitous yellow crime scene tape? Even in the case of a suicide, didn't the police usually cordon off the scene until they finished combing the area for evidence? Surely, they would search for anything that might indicate alternate explanations for Elvira's death.

She cautiously approached the rough lip of the excavation and stared down into the massive pit. How far was it to the bottom? Hard to tell, really. Forty feet? More? A vision of a woman's shattered body lying below flashed across her mind, and her stomach lurched. But she actually saw no trace of Elvira Evans' demise, at least none that was visible from this height. Just giant shards of broken rock and some trash blowing around in a downdraft.

Evidently, the sheriff's department had completed their work here. Although much faster than she'd imagined possible. In less than twenty-four hours. Whatever they'd left behind they must have deemed unimportant.

She nearly turned around and headed for home, but something about this place demanded her attention. What was it? Why had she even come here when it only made her sad?

Rainwater had collected in a deep, viscous black pool on the far side of the pit mine. The ugly pond was rimmed by a shale ledge where the miners had left off dynamiting. She couldn't recall if she'd ever heard why the quarry was abandoned. Perhaps the quality of the stone had deteriorated, or the company had gone out of business. Maybe the simple, speckled rock failed to compete with more exotic varieties of granite and marble mined in South America or Italy.

She looked down at her sneakers and realized how close she was standing to the crumbly edge. It would be easy to lose one's footing. The place felt lonely. Creepy. Like a ghost town but without buildings. Just cold, unfeeling stone. And that weird manmade pool. Mark had once told her this place was a spontaneous party venue for teenagers. Maybe drawn by that same creepiness, the danger.

Verity couldn't recall where she'd first heard that the water was surprisingly deep. There had been drownings. Kids just messing around, diving in and finding themselves unable to climb back out. So tragic. *Go home,* she chided herself, *rejoin the living.*

As she finally turned to leave, she noticed something odd. Narrow, steep steps had been cut into the stone leading down to the pit's floor. Whatever road had once existed for the mining trucks to reach the bottom was no longer there. Perhaps it had just collapsed over the years, or the departing miners filled it in with rubble to discourage locals from investigating and getting hurt. Then why not destroy the stairway, too? How much more dangerous was that!

She shuddered.

Was that how they had brought up Elvira's body? Probably

not. She envisioned someone rappelling down the pit's wall, attaching some kind of harness to Elvira's body to be lifted up. Verity pressed her palm to her chest but the earlier pain didn't return.

For no reason that she was later able to explain to herself, or to anyone else, she didn't leave then. It was as if something beckoned to her. *Come down the stairs. Take a closer look. You know you want to.*

It occurred to her that one or more of the young people who regularly hung out here might have been around last night and witnessed what happened. Maybe she could find a clue to who they were and talk to them.

Verity twisted the top half of her trash bag, knotting it around a belt loop to free up her hands. She started down the steps.

Without a railing to hold onto, she felt a little unbalanced. She pressed her right shoulder against the crumbling shale wall to steady herself. After inching halfway down, she seriously considered giving up and returning to the safety of the woods above. But to do that, she'd need to turn around on the teeny, tiny step where she stood. The tricky maneuver might make her even more lightheaded. She continued on down.

What if Elvira had attempted this same feat the previous night? It would have been madness in the dark! She might have fallen by accident, not intent. But Verity still couldn't wrap her head around why the woman would have come here in the middle of the night.

Did she intend to meet someone? But why here, of all places? And who?

At last, Verity reached the bottom. She paused to catch her breath and look around. There was even more refuse down here than she'd noticed from above. Fast-food wrappers and napkins, empty potato chip bags, beer and soda cans peppered the rock shelf overlooking the ominous black pool. The local teens who clearly still gathered here, to do whatever young people always did when out of the sight of adults, evidently came prepared to camp out for hours. Perhaps overnight. It occurred to her that Elvira's son Peter was of the age to meet up with friends in a remote spot like this.

*Hmmm...*Her mind spun.

Now that she was here, she felt unable in good conscience to leave all this trash. It was a blight on nature and an insult to the woman who had died here. Verity started chucking trash into her bag.

What if Elvira came to this place looking for her son? she mused. She recalled Denise once saying that Peter was driving his mother crazy, arguing with her about curfews and his allowance money. The word "violent" had never come up. But the young man Verity had witnessed confronting the overly zealous reporter had been out of control. What if Elvira followed Peter to the quarry, demanded he come home, and they fought? What if, in a blind rage, Peter lashed out at his mother while she stood too close to the edge of the pit mine? Or he simply pushed her over.

Verity cringed. No, she couldn't believe that! No matter how upset the boy might have been with his mother, he certainly would have reacted to her differently than he had to an interfering stranger.

Verity continued gathering litter, her thoughts reaching out in different though no less troubling directions. If Elvira left the house not to meet Peter, then who? A lover?

Elvira always seemed too involved in her business to welcome the complications of another man in her life. Men, as lovely as they could be, were time-eaters. Most women knew that. You had to pay attention to them, and that meant time you couldn't spend with your children and husband or your career.

She had seen Elvira in a flirtatious mood when she hosted an open house for one of her properties. Verity had coaxed Mark to come with her to view a house, out of sheer curiosity. She loved picking up tips for décor they might someday use in the farmhouse. Elvira's dazzling smile and seductive lavender eyes targeted a prospective male buyer. But the realtor's behavior had appeared more a performance than an invitation. And although Elvira shamelessly bragged about her real estate victories, expensive shoes, and pet charities—she had never once hinted at having a boyfriend.

Verity became aware of how heavy the trash had become. She should probably go home, but the theories rattling around in her brain were suggesting a nightmarish option to suicide. Or even to an innocent accident.

Murder.

If Elvira hadn't died as a result of mishap or her own intent, someone had killed her. Someone who had been here, in these woods, last night.

The question was—who?

CHAPTER 10

VERITY DECIDED she would return to the abandoned mine tomorrow, bring flowers and finish cleaning up. Feeling drained both in body and spirit, she climbed the narrow rock steps, pressing her left hand against the rough rock wall for support while gripping the neck of the trash bag with her other hand since it had become too heavy to tie to her.

She had nearly reached the top when she felt an odd discomfort, as if someone was watching her. She paused and looked up to see a lanky silhouette at the top of the stairs, pale face framed by a black sweatshirt's hood. Slowly, her eyes adjusted to the glare of the lowering sun behind the figure.

"Peter? Are you alright?"

He didn't answer but shifted his body, planting Vans sneakers shoulder-width apart, across the head of the stairway.

Verity met his eyes. "Could you move aside, please, Peter. You're blocking my way." As if he couldn't see that for himself. Was he intentionally trying to intimidate her?

"What are you doing here, Mrs. Cade?"

"Peter, you need to back away from the edge so I can get past you. This bag is heavy and I'm really tired."

"No!" he shouted. "Not until you tell me why you're here." His eyes fired off sparks. He jammed clenched fists down at his sides, a boy full of bottled-up rage.

The bag of trash was beginning to strain her shoulder, tugging her off balance. She thought about how far down it was to the stone floor of the mine. Her legs started trembling.

"Peter. I'm so very sorry about what happened to your mother." (Not, 'sorry about what she did to herself.' She would never say that!) "I guess I came here to think about last night. But when I discovered that someone—you and your friends perhaps?—had trashed the place, I wanted to clean up a bit." She hesitated, trying to gauge his unpredictable teen mood. "Out of respect for your mother."

He stood firm, flashing furious dark eyes at her.

"I thought I'd bring flowers from my garden tomorrow," she added.

Something subtly changed in the boy's face. His eyes softened. Arms went slack. "What good will fuckin' flowers do her now?" he muttered, spinning off to one side and stalking away.

Her path clear, Verity dashed up the final few steps and onto blessed terra firma. Before she could catch her breath, Peter turned back to face her. She instinctively lifted the trash bag in front of her in a defensive gesture.

"Peter. I'm so very sorry. I truly am. Your mother was a dear friend."

He opened his mouth but quickly closed it in a tight line. What she saw now behind those angry eyes was pain and need. A desire to talk?

"Is there something you want to tell me, Peter? Were you... were you or your friends here last night?" At the horrified look on his face, she immediately wished she could take back her words.

"No!" he screamed. "Of course I wasn't here." His eyes

filled with tears. He immediately pressed away the wetness with the heels of his hands. "Why would you say that?"

"I just thought…" She sighed. "I'm sorry, I don't know why I said it. I'm just very sad, not thinking too clearly."

He shuffled from foot to foot, scuffing at the dry leaves and pine needles. The motion kicked up a musty-sweet scent of decay. Rot. Death. Seconds passed, and she didn't have a clue what to say or do.

At last, he looked around as though just now discovering himself in an unfamiliar place. "Flowers might be nice," he mumbled. "Maybe I'll bring some, too."

Dropping her bag on the ground, Verity stepped closer to the teenager. He stood a good foot taller than her. She reached up and touched him gently on the shoulder. "I think your mom would like that, Peter. I really do." His sorrow-filled eyes and the tightness in his baby-whiskered jaw broke her heart. "I'm leaving now. You can come with me." He shook his head. "Will you be alright?"

"I'm good," he whispered, avoiding her eyes. "Sorry, Mrs. Cade, for being rude. Mom would have had my hide for talking to you like that."

"It's ok. Losing someone is tough. Really tough. Come to the farm if you want to talk. Anytime."

She ached to give him a hug but sensed a gesture that intimate would be off-limits. Maybe from another kid, especially from a girlfriend. But not from her. She took him at his word, that he would be safe on his own. She left him sitting on a boulder in the woods.

On her walk home, Verity was unable to stop thinking about Elvira's son.

He had seemed honestly distressed and disconsolate. Emotions one would expect after the loss of a family member. But her suspicions inevitably returned. Something was bothering that boy beyond the natural grieving process. Did he regret not having been a better son? Did he blame himself for his mother's death? Not directly, of course, but because of something he'd done? Or not done.

She at last climbed to her front porch. Setting the plastic bag beside her green Adirondack chair, she plopped down on it with an exhausted groan and began the process of sorting through her stash. First step—pulling out the recyclables. She was halfway through the bag by the time the western sky dimmed to a rosy-purplish glow. That was when she came across the strange piece of crumpled notepaper that would change everything.

Because it appeared that something was written inside, she was curious. She smoothed out the dirt-smudged rectangle with gloved hands, laid it across her knee and stared at large letters printed in pencil.

Laura, come to the quarry. Gang's all here. Peter

CHAPTER 11

VERITY READ the words over and over, her heart thrashing in her chest.

"Oh, Peter, what have you done?" Laura was barely twelve years old. A wave of nausea rolled over her. If Elvira had intercepted Peter's message...well, Verity could only imagine Elvira's wrath.

This was bad. Really, really bad. She should take the note to Sheriff Bailey. But if she did, what would happen to Peter? She didn't want to make trouble for the boy. He had seemed truly shaken by his mother's death. Was this part of the reason why? Did he secretly blame himself?

Verity stared out into the darkening street. A few fireflies twinkled mating calls. The air smelled pungently country-fresh of cornstalks drying in fields, her neighbors' recently mown grass, pots of spicy geraniums sitting on her porch. Late-summer warmth slowly ebbed away into the stillness of a cooler night.

The scents of her hometown usually calmed her. But not this night.

Was Peter's foolishness the reason Elvira rushed out of their house in the middle of the night? Because she thought Laura—

too young to be out partying with a crowd of wild beer-swilling teenagers—had sneaked out to be with her brother.

Verity sighed. She didn't know Laura well, but she'd always seemed a quiet, sensible girl. Far too sensible to wander outside alone in the middle of the night. And yet, if the big brother she worshipped asked her to come out with him...

Verity scowled at the filthy scrap of paper in her lap. Something didn't make sense. She felt unbalanced, as if she was still on the treacherous steps leading down into the quarry.

John Evans told the sheriff that he and Elvira didn't speak before she left the house. He only heard her closing the door while he was half asleep. So, wouldn't he have been even more aware of the sound of his young daughter leaving the house in the middle of the night? Peter's habit of sneaking out to be with his friends might be one thing as far as his father was concerned. But his baby girl? John Evans seemed a loving and conscientious father. He surely would have stopped her.

But if Laura wasn't at the quarry, the invitation from her brother in hand, how did the note get there? Peter wouldn't have brought it with him. But if Elvira saw Peter's note, she would have been so furious she might not have waited for him to come home to give him a piece of her mind. She would have gone after him.

Verity pinched the bridge of her nose and closed her burning eyes to better concentrate. Damn it! Why wasn't the sheriff or anyone else asking these questions? Why assume it was suicide?

Other thoughts flew at her.

Peter claimed that neither he nor his friends were at the old quarry the previous night. Verity wasn't sure she entirely believed him. Kids his age were often more loyal to their buddies than to the adults in their lives. They protected each other. When *she* had been Peter's age, covering up for her pals had been standard operating procedure.

A part of her wished she had never seen Peter's note. Suddenly, she didn't want anyone else to see it. If she destroyed it now, she might spare the boy untold misery.

No, she told herself firmly. *This is evidence.*

If there was even the slightest chance that Elvira's death wasn't a suicide, she owed it to her friend to help reveal the truth. She had no choice but to take Peter's note to Sheriff Bailey. The consequences be damned.

CHAPTER 12

THE NEXT MORNING, Verity grabbed a quick breakfast then attacked her usual chores. Her two farmhands had already let the cows out into the field to graze and then were off to mow the north field. She had avoided working there, ever since Mark's accident. The twins seemed to understand her reluctance and took it for granted that they should manage that part of the farm for her.

When she entered the milking parlor, one of the three Robo-Milkers was unoccupied while a line of cows waited for the other two machines. She shook her head and smiled. *Crazy cows.*

She walked through to the back of the barn where the collection tanks were located. The larger of the two stainless steel tanks was half full; the raw milk would be drained later that day when the tanker truck from Daisy Dairy arrived again. The dairy would pasteurize the milk and prepare it for sale to local grocery stores. She tested a sample from the latest batch to make sure of the quality and purity, even though the driver of the co-op truck always retested before pumping her cows' milk into his truck. Her smaller tank was now empty, ready to collect milk after the pickup, until she had a chance to flush out the big tank.

Since waking that morning, Verity had begun to have second thoughts about taking Peter's note to the sheriff. What if she did more harm than good by interfering? It might be best to wait. Perhaps ask a couple of her friends for advice. She just didn't want to do anything that would make life any harder for the Evans family.

Finding help with difficult decisions was one of the benefits of frequenting the Cat's Cradle Café. On any given morning many of her friends would stop by for coffee and to catch up on the latest gossip. After her most critical chores of the morning were done, she started walking into town.

The weather was gorgeous—warmed by a brilliant sun, perfumed along the way by bronze and gold chrysanthemums and blue-and-white asters in her neighbors' gardens. The air danced with puffy milkweed seeds. A gentle breeze freshened every breath. After such a traumatic previous day, she felt rejuvenated though no less sad to have lost a friend.

Rush hour, thank goodness, didn't exist in Evansfield. Only an occasional car or truck rumbled past her, usually obeying the posted thirty-mile-per-hour speed limit. She arrived at the row of shops along Main Street in less than fifteen minutes.

When Verity walked into the café, Sunny was standing behind the glass display counter, passing a steam-wreathed pottery mug and plate-size pastry to Kate Phillips. Mary Beth, Fumiko, and Denise had already found seats at the group's favorite table, centered in the bay window overlooking Main Street and the town green.

"Morning, Verity!" Sunny looked solemnly over the top of her antique cash register. The ponderous cast-iron machine still worked and added a decorative 19th-century ambiance to the café.

Verity tried to think of something other than death. The décor of the little café was a welcome distraction. Sunny had furnished her little coffee shop with retro bistro tables and chairs she scored for a song from a popular Brattleboro restaurant that had closed. Most of the furniture was crusty with rust, having been stored in a shed with a leaky roof. The original seat cushions were stained and tattered. Sunny sanded the metal frames, spray-painted them white and reupholstered the chair seats in a pastel windowpane pattern. The result was furnishings that looked as pretty as her yummy fondant-frosted teacakes.

"Good morning," Mary Beth and Fumiko chorused, although with far less than their normal exuberance.

An unsmiling Denise patted an empty chair beside hers. Kate waggled fingers "hello" at Verity as her mouth was full of pastry.

Verity smiled dimly at her friends but didn't trust her voice. The note felt as though it was burning a hole through her pocket. She signaled she would join them soon and made a beeline for Sunny. She ordered a latte and a buttery chocolate croissant.

"You alright, Veri?" Sunny asked, handing her a china plate with her croissant and then her coffee. "We're all sad, but you look like death warmed over, my dear." She winced at her own pun. "Everything ok at the farm? Your critters behaving themselves?"

Verity shrugged. "They're all good. Listen, can you spare a few minutes to sit with us? I really could use some advice."

Sunny's blue eyes studied her with concern. "Sure. The morning rush is over. Amanda can handle any latecomers." She motioned to a teenage girl clearing one of the tables.

As Verity approached her friends, all conversation stopped.

Verity sat down. She took a sip of her latte—delicious and soothing—then wiped the milk froth from her upper lip.

"Ok," she said into the weighty silence. "I have some disturbing news that I think, well, I'm not sure really, but—" She lowered her voice, aware of other customers in the room. Her friends leaned in. "I'm worried that Peter Evans may have had something to do with his mother's death."

Mary Beth laid a plump, beringed hand over hers. "Oh, honey, why would you say such a thing?"

"I know what she's trying to say," Kate said. "Anyone with kids understands the stress they can put on their parents." Kate had two young ones at home. Although both of her girls were well under twelve years of age, they regularly perpetrated dramas within the household, the details of which Kate often shared with the group.

"Stress, yeah. But how is parenting relevant to suicide?" Denise lifted one eyebrow.

"If you had kids, you'd know," Kate said.

Denise huffed. "Give me a break."

"Seriously!" Kate insisted. "Elvira might have been so upset by her son's shenanigans she could no longer deal with them. Parenting leads many a parent to depression. And then, you know—" Kate's hand sketched an arc off the table's edge.

Verity winced at the image but needed to keep the conversation on track. "I suspect the situation was more complicated than that."

"You explain, please?" Fumiko studied her solemnly over the rim of her coffee mug.

"Late yesterday afternoon, I went for a walk. I don't know why I ended up at the quarry, but I did. Kids had left all sorts of trash there. It was a mess and I was shocked."

"That doesn't surprise me at all," Sunny commented.

"Teenagers don't pick up after themselves at home. Why would they act any different out in the middle of the woods?"

Verity drew a deep breath. "I agree. But I decided it was disrespectful to leave the place that way. It was, after all, Elvira's final resting place."

"Only until they took her body away," Mary Beth corrected her. "Her final resting place will be Park Cemetery, after the funer—"

"We all get that, MB," Kate interrupted. "You go ahead, Verity. I think that's a lovely gesture. What were you saying?"

Verity took a bite of her croissant; the buttery layers melted in her mouth and she scored a hit from the rich, dark-chocolate center. Pure heaven! She returned the pastry to her plate, a little annoyed with herself for taking pleasure in food while talking about a friend's death.

She sighed. "I picked up a bagful of litter from the bottom of the mining pit. Nothing terribly surprising except for one thing. I found a note Peter Evans wrote to his sister Laura, suggesting she join him and his friends at the quarry."

"Oh my!" Kate gasped, glancing around the table at the others.

"Not good." Sunny absently wiped a rag across the table's edge.

"I don't get it. What does a little note between two kids have to do with anything?" Mary Beth blinked, looking bewildered.

Ask Mary Beth anything about plants, and you'd think she had a PhD in botany and lectured at Harvard. But people and their relationships were often a mystery to her.

"Think, MB," Sunny encouraged with a patient smile. "Verity is saying that Elvira might have seen the note the night she died."

"And we all know how crazy that would make her, just knowing Peter pulled a stunt like that," Denise added.

"But we don't know whether Laura ever read her brother's note," Verity pointed out. "I think it's very likely Laura never left the house. That just doesn't sound like her. And before I discovered the note, Peter claimed he didn't visit the quarry that night. So, I'm wondering, how did his note—"

"Get to quarry!" Fumiko finished for her with a dramatic gesture of her hands.

"Unless," Denise said, "Elvira had it with her when she went looking for Peter."

"Exactly," Verity sighed.

"Oh, my!" Mary Beth finally got it. "The poor woman. She must have been so upset. Little Laura is far too innocent to be out drinking and doing Lord-knows-what with that rowdy bunch." She took a consoling bite of her blueberry muffin.

"So-o-o," Fumiko said, "it possible our Elvira see son's note at house. She take with her to conflict him."

"Confront him," Denise corrected.

"Same thing!" Fumiko objected.

Denise rolled her eyes.

"The point is,' Verity continued, "*someone* dropped that note at the quarry. It doesn't make sense for Peter to have brought it with him. He must have given it to Laura or left it somewhere in the house where she'd find it."

Kate's eyes were turning pink and watery. She stared dismally at her cherry pastry.

Sunny looked at Verity. "I don't understand. Wouldn't the sheriff or his deputies have found this letter?"

"Maybe not." Verity sipped her coffee, thinking. It was amazing how much clearer things became with the help of a little caffeine. "Sheriff Bailey and his deputies seem to be operating under the assumption there is only one explanation for Elvira's death. She committed suicide. From what I overheard him say to John at the house, his investigation is minimal. And there's something else." Verity hesitated, catching her lower lip between her teeth.

"What?" Sunny nudged.

Verity gazed sadly at the rest of her croissant. Chocolate. Her favorite. But she'd lost her appetite. She swallowed and took a deep breath for courage.

"Before I left the quarry, Peter showed up."

"Oh, thith jus' geth worth and worth," Mary Beth mumbled through a mouthful of crumbs, spraying them across the table.

Denise made a face and thrust a napkin at MB before turning back to Verity. "Why would he go to the place his mother died? Do you think Peter went back there looking for the note? Like, to destroy evidence?"

"I don't know," Verity whispered sadly. "He might have, I guess."

Sunny reached across the table to tap a finger on the back of Verity's hand. "You need to take that note to the sheriff. Seriously."

"Oh, but Peter maybe mean no harm." Fumiko set down her teacup. "It kind of thing teenager do. Yes? Groove with friends."

"What century are *you* in?" Denise laughed. "Groove?"

"It proper American slang!" Fumiko objected, looking confused.

"But his little sister!" Kate whimpered, tears starting to spill from her pretty eyes. "She's not much older than my Sarah."

Verity nodded her head, feeling worse than when she'd arrived at the café. "Exactly. I just don't know what I should do with this information. Peter may have had nothing to do with his mother's death. Not directly. Maybe she found his note and went out to find him but they never met up. When Elvira reached the quarry, it would have been two or three o'clock in the morning. Without any lights in the middle of the woods, it would have been impossible to see much of anything. Unless she took a flashlight with her, she would have been walking blind. She might have just slipped and fallen."

"I hiked out that way once," Denise said. "I found some steps, but they were treacherous. Made it halfway down before I chickened out."

Verity shuddered, remembering her own experience.

"But if you give Peter's note to the sheriff—" Mary Beth brushed a blizzard of crumbs off her lap "—he might think the poor boy really is to blame for his mother's accident." Her eyes widened at her next thought. "Or that Peter intentionally *lured* his mother there—to *murder* her!"

For a long moment, no one said a thing. Even the distant noises of cars passing through town and children playing in the park across the street seemed to have gone silent.

"I think," Kate murmured at last, "we should just keep this to ourselves."

Denise leaned forward, elbows propped on the table, her expression determined. "No way. I agree with Sunny. Verity has an obligation to turn over any information she finds to the sheriff. Withholding evidence is a crime. Right? She could be in deep trouble if she doesn't. And we may be in trouble, too, because now *we* know about the note."

Verity sighed. "I honestly don't want to interfere with the sheriff's investiga—"

"What inves-s-s-tigation?" Fumiko hissed. "Sheriff say suicide. Coroner say suicide. I hear this from customer at my shop. Case closed!"

"I don't even know who the local coroner is." Kate dabbed a napkin at her weepy eyes and looked around the table. "Does anyone?"

Mary Beth beamed with pride. "My husband, our honorable mayor of Evansfield, Rupert J. Loop, is also our town's duly elected coroner."

"You're kidding." Denise stared at her in disbelief. "Somebody, please, tell me she's not serious. A man who is without any medical training is the person who determines whether a murder has happened?"

Verity gave her a weak smile. "My uncle was the coroner in Poughkeepsie. He once told me that's the way it works in many small towns or rural counties. I guess it's not a job many people want. The title often goes to whoever is willing to take it on, and for almost no money. If an autopsy is required, a regional pathologist is called in."

"So, I'm thinking that if you deliver that letter to the sheriff," Sunny mused, focusing on her empty coffee cup as she traced a fingertip around its rim, "he'll be forced to reopen the investigation into her death. Case not closed."

Verity swallowed. She stared regretfully at her delicious croissant. "I suppose I should go see him now, before I lose my nerve."

"Do you want me to come with you to the sheriff's office?" Kate asked, albeit without much enthusiasm.

"No, I'm sure I'll be fine. I'll just turn over the note to him and leave. I need to get back to the farm."

CHAPTER 13

VERITY STRODE ACROSS THE STREET, aware of the thud, thud, thud of her heart—marking time with her footfalls. She hoped she was doing the right thing.

Peter had seemed truly upset when she saw him at the quarry. If what he wrote to his sister had anything to do with causing his mother to go out into the night, he would naturally feel guilty. And that was even if he never saw his mother that night and had nothing to do with her falling.

But, as if losing his mom wasn't enough, life for Peter Evans could potentially become even more difficult. People in a cozy little town like Evansfield were usually caring and supportive when tragedy struck. However, if word spread about the note, well, she could easily imagine the cruel gossip—and how it surely must affect Elvira's children and husband.

Well, she told herself firmly as she marched along the serpentine pebbled paths across the village green, what most mattered was uncovering the truth of what happened that dreadful night. Turning in the note was simply the right thing to do.

Main Street split into two separate roads on either side of

the broad town green. One heading east, the other west. In earlier times—cattle, goats, and sheep had grazed the grassy expanse on market days. Now it was simply a park, bedecked with replicas of antique gas lanterns dangling from ornate wrought-iron poles. Pretty green wooden benches ranged along the paths, providing residents with a place to rest, sit and read, or to enjoy a cup of tea or coffee from the café. She ached to sit down and find a little peace there, but she kept moving forward.

She marched past the Victorian-style bandstand with gingerbread cut-outs along the edges of its bright red roof. A tribe of youngsters ran squealing up and down the steps to the stage where local musicians performed free concerts on Saturday nights all summer long.

The beauty and joy of the scene felt out of sync with her troubled mood and vexing mission. She was on her way, she feared, to cause a world of pain. Not only for Peter Evans and his family. The sheriff, she was pretty sure, would not welcome her information.

Straight ahead was the town hall's sooty red-brick façade. It was the one truly ugly structure in all of Evansfield—jarringly different from the tidy clapboard houses and shops. The result of an imprudent 19th-century architect or misguided town council. Probably both.

Verity yanked open the heavy wooden door and walked inside to a deserted, musty-smelling foyer. In Boston or New York, a guard would have directed her through a security checkpoint before allowing her to enter the building. This was one of the things Verity most loved about her country town. The peacefulness. The trust she felt among its citizens. It had seemed an ideal place to raise a family. Until a freak accident stole her dream.

Verity paused in the vestibule to get a grip on her emotions. She couldn't remember what floor the sheriff's office was on and turned to study the building directory in front of her. Oddly, the little white letters on the black pegboard made no sense at all. Finally, she realized the source of her confusion.

Someone had been messing with the letters and rearranged the civil servants' names into nonsensical anagrams.

REGISTRAR: Jerry Da Jerk – Rm 201
COUNTY CLERK: Mimi Fattypuss – Rm 202
MAYOR'S OFFICE: Loopy da Loop – Rm 105
FISHING LICENCES: I M Underwater – Basement
SHERIFF'S OFFICE: U R Busted – Rms 100-104
SUPERINTENDANT OF SCHOOLS: Evil Dogterd –
Room 230

She smiled. *Definitely kids.* Her mood lightened, for just a moment. She moved past a rack of brochures about local sights for tourists. Then down a creaky old hallway.

She wished she could stop the bizarre thoughts buzzing around in her brain like angry bees. Was Elvira's death an accident, suicide, or murder?

Not your job, she told her brain.

It struck her then that there was a reason why she was struggling so hard to make sense of everything. Ever since her encounter with those two ghosts—specters, haunts, poltergeists, shades, whatever!—she had felt rather unhinged. *Maybe if they've gone away*, she thought, *everything will return to normal.* Or at least what passes for normal after the death of a friend.

Verity stopped in front of a door with a frosted glass pane emblazoned in elaborate gold script: *Frederick Bailey, County Sheriff.* Verity turned the knob and stepped inside.

Harriet Conklin, the sheriff office's gray-haired receptionist, looked up over Benjamin Franklin spectacles and smiled at her. "Why hello, Verity Cade. What can I do for you?"

Verity cleared her throat. "I have something for the sheriff. Possible evidence he'll need to help with the investigation into Elvira Evans' death."

"Oh?" Harriet's brows notched up an inch.

Before Verity could explain further, the door to the sheriff's inner office burst open and the man himself rushed through it. "I'll be out at the Miller farm," he bellowed, struggling to get an arm into his jacket sleeve as he dove past his receptionist's desk.

The flat of Harriet's hand shot out. "Stop right there, Sheriff. Mrs. Cade needs to see you first." Harriet was a big woman and most of her bulk appeared to be muscle. Verity had always assumed she'd been in the military. The woman would have made a formidable drill sergeant.

Bailey flashed an annoyed look in Verity's direction. "Later, ma'am."

"No, Fred, now." Harriet narrowed her eyes and braced her hands on her desktop as though she might at any moment vault over it and physically block his path to the doorway. "You know that Bert's just lonely and wants company." She gave her boss a shrewd look. "And the beer you'll be bringing for the two of you."

The sheriff snorted. "Alright, alright. Mrs. Cade, what is it?"

"I think," Verity said, "we should sit down in your office for this. I need to give you something that might change your assessment of Elvira's death."

He sent her a doubtful look but at another threatening scowl from Harriet he muttered, "Aw hell, come on in then."

Bailey held the door open for Verity and then ambled behind his desk. He sat heavily, crossing arms over his chest then kicked his boot heels up onto his desk and assumed a bored attitude. It was clear to Verity that he'd already dismissed both her and whatever she had come to say.

With a sour taste in her mouth and a sense of futility, Verity nevertheless pulled the note from her pocket. "I found this up at the quarry." She held it out. He didn't reach for it. She laid the piece of paper on his desk.

"Well?" he said. "Go on."

She explained her trip to the quarry and her attempt to remove as much trash from the pit floor as she could carry. She did not tell him she had seen Peter there. Why she left out that detail, she wasn't sure. Maybe because she feared distracting the already distracted man from the evidence on his desk.

"That note," she said, "was among the rest of the trash. It's important. I thought you should see it."

The sheriff puckered his lips almost into a smile. "Commendable," he stated. "Good work, Mrs. Cade."

"Really?" She felt a frisson of hope. Was he actually taking her seriously?

"Keeping our community clean. Picking up after those idiot kids. I wish Evansfield had more conscientious citizens like you!"

Verity rolled her eyes. "You're missing the point, Sheriff. *Read* this." She tapped a finger on the slip of paper then quickly withdrew it. Mary Beth would have reminded her, based on her favorite CSI shows, that she was smudging whatever fingerprints might remain.

The sheriff stared at her then, pointedly, at the door. When he realized she wasn't leaving, he dropped his boots to the floor with a jarring clunk, stood and picked up the note. He focused on it with an expression of less-than-convincing concentration.

"I see. Interesting. So? What do *you* think this means, Mrs. Cade?"

"I think," she began slowly, "it's possible that Peter wrote that on the night his mother died. If Elvira saw it—"

"But," he interrupted her, "it was written to his sister, not to his mother. Are you saying the girl ratted to her mother?"

"No. Or...I don't know." Verity looked away, then tried to regain her focus. She had to make him see how important this was. "Sheriff, we have no idea if Laura ever got the note. But if Elvira realized what her son was trying to do—she would have been frantic."

"Who is 'we,' Mrs. Cade? You and your lady-friends at the Cat's Cradle?" He grinned. "I saw you in the café when I passed by half an hour ago. Heads together. Gossiping."

She stiffened. Not only didn't he believe the note was important, he was also turning this conversation into a chance to make fun of her and her friends.

"Sheriff, please think about this. If Elvira intercepted this note, she very well might have gone out in search of Peter at the quarry. Not in an attempt to kill herself. She just wanted to have it out with the boy for trying to lure his little sister to a stupid party at the quarry."

The sheriff was shaking his head even before she finished her sentence.

"What?" she said, suddenly irritated with his behavior. "It makes sense, doesn't it?"

"No, Mrs. Cade," he said with a Cheshire cat grin. And now she really, really wanted to slug him in the face. "Your theory does not make sense. Because there was no partyin' at the quarry on the night Elvira took her own life."

Verity opened her mouth to speak. Closed it again. She narrowed her eyes at him. What did the man know that she didn't? Moreover, what did he know that none of her friends knew?

"I-I don't understand," she said. "Obviously, all the chip bags and beer cans I found when I picked up this note were left by someone. You must have seen the mess when you—" *Oh, God!* She swallowed at the image. "—when you brought up Elvira's body."

"'Course I did. Fact is, I've been sending my deputies up Quarry Road every few days, to chase off trespassers before someone gets hurt. Some of our high school kids turned up on other nights. But not the night Elvira died. I can assure you, Mrs. Cade."

"Oh." She frowned, confused. "But then why didn't your deputies see Elvira arrive or discover her body?"

He shrugged. "By the time Mrs. Evans got there, after your little get together broke up, my men had already arrived at the quarry. They stayed until after midnight to make sure our young'uns didn't hang around, if they did show up."

She nodded. The man sounded more logical than she'd given him credit for. "Alright. So, if neither Peter nor Laura brought the note, then Elvira must have had it with her when she fell."

"You think? Do you see a date on it?" He held it out to her but she didn't need to see it. The words were imprinted on her brain.

"No," she admitted.

"No, you don't. Because there ain't any. The boy could have written that note to his sis weeks ago, months ago. Obviously, the girl brought it to the quarry one night when my patrol wasn't there."

Verity noticed him stealing another look at the door. She stared down at her hands, thinking. "I don't believe Laura ever hung out with that crowd. They are so much older. It doesn't make sense. She surely has friends her own age."

Bailey tossed the note onto his desk. He stepped forward, hand raised as if he meant to pat her on the shoulder. Mollifying the temperamental child. Annoyed, she pulled away and stood up. Clearly, she was about to be booted out anyway.

He sighed. "Listen here, Mrs. Cade. I get that you don't want to think of your friend as doin' herself in. It's a nasty image to hold in the mind. But those words on that paper prove nothin'."

"But Sheriff—"

"You and your friends are just tossin' around wild theories. No, ma'am. Not even theories—*fantasies*." He walked around behind her and opened his office door. "Thank you for stopping by, Mrs. Cade. I need to get on out to the Miller farm now. Duty calls." He stepped into the reception area, hat in hand, and waved at Harriet on his way past.

Verity hesitated then retrieved the note from his desk and tucked it into her jeans pocket. There was no point leaving it with him. He would just throw it away.

"You alright, Verity dear?" Harriet asked as Verity dragged herself disconsolately toward the hallway door.

"Yeah." To be honest, she felt a bit shellshocked. Disappointed that he hadn't thought the note important, but surprised that he had actually been doing something to protect the town's teenagers from themselves.

CHAPTER 14

THE DAISY DAIRY tanker rattled up the farm's gravel driveway. She exchanged her sneakers for her favorite wellies and met the driver in the tank room behind the milking parlor. He was drawing a sample of the milk from the 1500-gallon stainless steel collection tank. After tapping his readings into his iPad, he held it out for her to sign.

"Ok to email you the receipt as usual?" he asked with a pleasant smile.

"Sure, Terry," Verity said. "Do you have many more stops today?"

"Three. The Waverley farm, John Hansen's place, and Sweetwater Dairy, across the New Hampshire line."

"Busy day," she said, walking him back to his truck.

Terry Lehane was a pleasant guy, married with two little kids whose antics he often described with humor and pride. Her heart always warmed at his words. He clearly thought the world of his wife and little ones. How could she not be happy for him? And yet, his joy sometimes left a bitter-sweet aftertaste in her mouth. The warm family life he described was something she'd never know.

He touched the bill of his green baseball cap with the Daisy Dairy logo and climbed up into the truck's cab. She started back toward the barn.

"Hey, Verity," he called after her, "forgot to tell you. When I was in your tank room before you came out to the barn, I noticed a wad of papers stuffed down behind the cooling pipes."

She turned back, puzzled. "Papers? That's odd."

"Looked like it might be something important. Legal documents maybe? I pulled them out, left them on your worktable."

"Thanks, Terry." Verity pursed her lips in thought. *What the devil?* How had she not noticed them? She marched back into the barn with a new sense of urgency. The Grimalski brothers were far too conscientious to leave anything of theirs behind. And she'd have no reason to bring bills or mail with her to the barn. Maybe an old instruction manual for machinery? Or something Mark had mistakenly left behind that had never been missed.

She crossed through the free-stall area—smelling pungently of sweet hay and warm cow, the ancient wooden timbers arching above her. Brilliant splinters of sunlight shot between shrunken wallboards and across the barn's dim interior. Dust motes sparkled like glitter on a greeting card. She was reminded of the strange, twinkly couple, Mark's ancestors. Thankfully, they had remained out of sight all day. Had they finally found a way to reach their final destination? Wherever that might be. Maybe she'd never see them again. She wasn't sure how she felt about that.

On the small unpainted pine table near the collection tanks, she kept a work log and small card file with contact information for customers, farm suppliers, and repair specialists. Next to the little file box sat the bundle of stained, rumpled papers Terry had left for her. Stuffed behind refrigeration pipes? She frowned, still at a loss for what they could be. She'd take them back to the house after finishing her chores and try to figure out what they were.

Verity flushed out and sterilized the now-empty, larger stainless-steel tank then opened the spigot on the smaller auxiliary tank to transfer the milk collected since the dairy driver had arrived. She cleaned the small tank to prepare for the following day. Each of her cows averaged 8 gallons of milk a day, but her best milkers gave her as much as 10 gallons. Her lovely creatures were busy girls!

The computerized Robo-Milkers located the animal's teats, sanitized them, attached the suckers, and syphoned off the milk then washed the udder area before releasing the cow to wander the barn or return to the pasture. The procedure for each cow took less than fifteen minutes.

The cost of the high-tech machinery was the downside of the convenience to her. Mark had taken out a hefty loan to pay for it. The collateral was the farm. His death resulted in more than the pain of losing her lover, best friend and beloved husband. The farm lost its main source of manpower. Before the accident, Jerry and Jason were just occasional workers. After Mark was gone, she took on as many of his jobs as she could and the twins agreed to work thirty hours a week. Meeting their wages meant she had less money to pay off the loan and buy necessary supplies.

Still pondering over more ways to cut corners, as she endlessly did, Verity nearly left the barn before remembering Terry's mysterious discovery. She returned across the weathered floorboards of the milk room and smoothed out the bunched-up pages on the small desk. Only then did she see the distinctive letterhead.

Elvira Evans Realty, LLC

Serving savvy homeowners and buyers of Vermont prime real estate.

"What are *you* doing out here?" she murmured, as if Elvira's contract had walked itself out of her house and into the barn.

Somehow, she must have brought the contract with her to the barn and completely forgot that she'd done it. Weird!

She had meant to read Elvira's new offer the morning after she'd received it. She hadn't been able to find the thing anywhere in her house because, apparently, it had been out here all along. But this made no sense at all to her. Did she sleepwalk out to the dairy barn? And why jam it down behind refrigeration pipes? Was she sending herself a not-so-subtle message that she didn't want to deal with the decision of whether or not to sell the farm? Perhaps her subconscious refused to accept that she might have no choice.

She rolled the papers into a tube and tapped it against her palm. *Think, Verity!*

If she didn't hide the contract here, who did? Who had access to both her house and to the barn? Her farmhands, yes. But she trusted Jason and Jerry. She was sure they would never tamper with her personal documents or play childish games by hiding things from her. They took their work seriously. In fact, they had become almost too protective of her since Mark's death.

She slapped her palm harder. *Who? Who? Who?*

Verity narrowed her eyes in suspicion. There was someone who might want to sabotage the sale of her farm. Two someones, actually. Seeing red, Verity marched out of the barn, across the open yard and toward the farmhouse.

Her boot soles barely touched the back-porch steps as she flew up them. She wrenched open the door to the mudroom and stomped her foot, fists on hips. "Alright, you two," she shouted, "where are you?"

The house remained silent. One might have said, deathly still.

"If you don't come out where I can see you, I swear I will take this sales contract to Doc Evans and sign it in front of him. He can do what he likes with the land, the barns, animals, house...*and you!*"

Verity's heart felt as if it were ricocheting off her ribs. Her eyes burned with anger. She cursed under her breath, scanned the empty room and waited. Ever so slowly, she felt a change in the air around her. A subtle warmth. Then the room began to shimmer—rather like heat waves rising off of hot asphalt. Her skin prickled. She smelled something sweet. Lavender?

"Talk to me. Now!" Verity shook her paper bat in the air. "What did you think your stupid hide-and-seek game would achieve? It's not as if contracts can't be duplicated."

"I told you it wouldn't work," a deep voice said.

"But darlin', we had to try." Definitely Anna Louise. Although neither ghost was visible. "Lavender is so relaxing, don't you think, Miss Verity? Breathe deeply. Calm yourself."

"Hiding important things from me won't make a difference in my decision. And your spooky aromatherapy isn't going to help either." Although she had to admit the lavender really was quite soothing.

The couple abruptly materialized five feet away in front of her.

"We apologize." Percy bowed from his trim waist. He wore the dark blue uniform of the North, decorated with medals and appropriate insignias of his rank as an officer. "I accept full responsibility, madam."

"Oh no, you don't! It was my idea." Anna Louise smiled sweetly at him, looking pleased with herself in her pretty blue gingham gown. She turned to Verity. "I told my darling Percy to hide those papers somewhere good. But men never listen, do they?"

"Sorry, my love." Percy stared disconsolately at his boots.

"Where or how well you hid the contract is not the point," Verity fumed. "You can't go around stealing things."

"Stealing? Oh, we'd never do that. Borrowed is perhaps a better word." Anna Louise fluttered her long eyelashes innocently. Verity wanted to wring her neck.

Percy stepped forward wearing an earnest expression. "We regret having caused you any inconvenience. In our defense, Miss Verity, we were acting in the spirit of encouragement, not deception."

His wife giggled. "Spirit? Oh dear, Percy. You have the wit of Mr. Samuel Clemens."

"This isn't funny!" Verity screamed, making both ghosts jump. "Snatching a legal document from my kitchen won't discourage me from selling this farm. I need sensible advice and practical ways of paying off the equipment loan and feeding my animals."

Percy stepped forward, arms spread in a gesture of sincerity. "I promise you, Miss Verity, I would offer you my considerable knowledge of farming and raising livestock, if it would help. But I look around our beloved farm—" *my* farm, Verity mouthed "—and so much has changed. My plow was pulled by a horse, while your dear Mark used an immense machine you call a tractor, as do you. My wife and I milked our cows one at a time, by hand of course. With your new ways you don't even need to be in the barn to have your cows milked. So much of this modern era is pure mystery to me."

Verity shook her head miserably. "If Mark had been plowing with a horse, he'd be alive today."

"No, my dear lady, if a horse falls on you, it can kill you as surely as one of your tractor things."

Verity looked up at Percy. "Really? Is that what happened to you?"

Her two specters exchanged looks. "As I believe we mentioned before," Anna Louise said patiently, "we don't know how we died. And we don't understand why we are still here. We just are."

"Well, then, listen up." Verity tossed the tattered contract down on the stairs leading up to her kitchen. She balanced first on one foot then the other to pry off her boots. Knocking off the worst of the barn muck, she set her wellies in the plastic tray beside the steps. "If you're going to continue hanging out here with me, you need to agree to leave my personal belongings alone. That's Rule #1."

"Agreed!" they both shouted, far too enthusiastically.

She slipped her feet into cozy felt clogs and breathed in deeply. Amazingly, the knots in her neck and shoulder muscles felt less...knotty. "And although I hate to admit it, I think your lavender trick is working. Keep it up."

Anna Louise beamed. "It smells divine, doesn't it? I used to sew lavender blossoms into sachets and tuck them in among my unmentionables."

Percy rolled his eyes. "Perfumery? Please. There must be better ways we can assist you."

"Maybe," Verity said. And, indeed, she'd just had an idea. "Come with me."

She led them up the three steps to her kitchen. Anna Louise, followed by Percy, trailed after her, and Percy shut the door behind him. Or rather, the door shut itself. Verity decided she must have missed something. Like, Percy kicking it closed. Or a draft blowing it shut. Because she never actually *saw* him touch the door.

Anna Louise whispered something in his ear and giggled. Her husband's expression wavered between a judge's solemnity and a little boy's smirk, but he finally lost his struggle to fight off laughter. Verity felt like the only one in the room who hadn't gotten the joke. Was she out of her mind to even think she could trust these two?

She swung a hip up onto the tall wooden stool beside her kitchen island. "If you're going to be any help to me, I first need to fill you in on recent events." She received a respectful nod from each ghost. "Today, I visited the sheriff at his office. I assume you both know about the recent death of my friend, Elvira Evans. I found something that might relate to her death."

"Goodness me!" Anna Louise pressed a hand to her throat. "I feared you were going to say that you went to the sheriff to complain about us."

"Not this time." Verity narrowed her eyes at the pair. "Anyway, I doubt he would believe me. And he was in such a rush to see Bert Miller, he nearly didn't let me explain why I'd come."

"Oh, pooh! He only goes out there to drink with his army pal and swap war stories." Anna Louise plucked a strand of straw from the lace trim on her dress sleeve. "The sheriff knows if he, the sheriff that is, sets foot in a bar, friends of his wife will tattle on him. She isn't fond of his love of beer."

"I see." Verity scowled. "And you know this how?"

"We overhear things," Percy said tactfully. "And I've seen him out at Miller's cabin."

"But you told me you can't leave the farm."

"No, dear," Anna Louise corrected her gently, "we said we had no other place to go. No other home." She was investigating the basket of herbal teas on the windowsill.

"We've tested our geographic limits, you see." Percy spun a kitchen chair around and straddled the seat after rearranging the angle of his sword scabbard from his hip. "We have discovered that we're able to move around Evansfield and a few other places, but only if we've already visited them in our natural lifetime. It appears we are unable to venture anywhere that's unfamiliar to us."

"Percy tried to take me home to Virginia for a little visit." Anna Louise sighed. "Sadly, that trip was nothing short of disastrous. We were trapped for hours and hours in a most disgusting place, unable to get home again. I believe it was called a Greyhound bus terminal. You can't imagine the—"

"Best left unsaid, my love," Percy interrupted.

"Oh, my yes. Sorry." She cast him an apologetic smile.

"Interesting," Verity murmured. "So, you have at least local mobility." She suddenly felt excited by new possibilities. "You are familiar with the old quarry north of town?"

"Of course," Anna Louise laughed. "But back then, the quarry was still being worked. When Percy and I were newlyweds, it was our custom on Sundays to carry a picnic lunch to a little pond not far from there."

"I know the place. Buckley Pond. Mark and I loved it, too." Happy memories. She needed to never forget that, although their time together seemed far too brief, they had shared so many beautiful moments together. "Were you near the quarry, the night Elvira—"

"No, sweet thing." Anna Louise reached out to pat her hand. To Verity's surprise she felt the touch as a warm pulse in the air above her skin. "We stayed here to watch over you that night. You needed us."

Verity looked away, struck by a wave of emotion. Anna Louise made it sound as though they really cared about her. She bit down on her bottom lip. *Get a grip, Verity. They're just ghosts, no longer human.* How, or if, they felt anything didn't matter.

On the other hand, she didn't want to hurt their feelings.

"Thank you, both of you," Verity said, the words thick on her tongue.

Percy cast her a benevolent smile. Anna Louise appeared illuminated in an angelic glow. Verity suddenly remembered that on the same night they'd been "watching over her," they'd also stolen her sales contract. She rolled her eyes to the ceiling. *Ghosts!*

"You were saying there is a way we might help," Percy reminded her. "Perhaps in return for continuing our residence on the farm?"

"Maybe. If you can move around Evansfield and not be seen, you might be able to do a little sleuthing for me."

"Sleuthing?" The two ghosts exchanged bewildered looks.

"Information gathering," Verity clarified. "You see, I don't believe Elvira committed suicide. But others in town seem to think she did. Including the mayor, who happens to also be the coroner. He and the sheriff have officially closed her case. But I found a note that...well, you'd better read it." She still had the scrap of paper in her pocket and now fished it out. Unsure whether their ethereal hands were capable of grasping it, she held it up for them to see.

Anna Louise leaned forward, peering at the paper. "Oh, that wicked boy!" she gasped.

Verity nodded. "Peter may be a bad influence—his own mother complained of how difficult he'd become—but I just don't know. When I spoke with him recently he seemed genuinely distressed by his mother's death. Now I'm beginning to wonder if he even wrote this note."

"Oh," Anna Louise breathed, or at least gave the impression that she could. "You want us to find out who penned that awful letter?" To Verity's surprise, the ghost clapped her hands together and did a joyful little jig, her blue gown and petticoats flouncing around her ankles. "Oh, I ever so much love a good guessing game."

"I wouldn't call this a game," Verity said, trying to sound stern. "People's futures are at stake. Can you imagine how awful it would be for a child to blame themself for their own mother's death? Besides, if someone was responsible for Elvira's demise, shouldn't they be brought to justice?"

"Absolutely." Percy struck a solemn pose in his chair, hands braced on his knees. Anna Louise smiled at him rapturously, and Verity couldn't help agreeing with her choice of a mate. The young Civil War officer was strikingly handsome.

"Good." Verity felt better now that she had allies, of a sort. "During your travels around town, I want you to keep your eyes and ears open for any behavior or conversation that might seem incriminating or even slightly suspicious."

"How delightful!" Anna Louise squealed. "Just like Mr. Poe's famous C. Auguste Dupin, we shall investigate a heinous crime."

"Ummm, right." A disturbing premonition made Verity shiver. Maybe setting these two loose on her little town wasn't such a brilliant idea after all. "Anything fishy, you tell me. Don't *do* anything. Just report your observations. Understood?"

"*Oui, madame!*" Anna Louise curtseyed.

"Your mission is in good hands," Percy assured her, standing to perform a snappy salute.

Verity squinted at the pair doubtfully. She was about to provide further ground rules when her cellphone rang. The couple flashed out of sight before she could say another word. Her phone screen lit up: SCAM LIKELY.

Oh, bother! Now she was really worried. What if they forgot to stay invisible? What if someone else saw them?

CHAPTER 15

FOR DAYS, Verity heard nothing from her disembodied sleuths or from the sheriff. She supposed his silence meant he had dismissed her information about Peter. Maybe that was for the better. It wasn't as though she wanted to make trouble for the boy and his family.

Then one morning while she was sorting a freshly gathered batch of eggs in her kitchen her phone rang. She ignored it and eventually the ringing stopped. Nuisance calls had become annoyingly frequent. If it wasn't a window-replacement contractor, a cemetery plot salesperson, or some idiot trying to trick her into giving out her social security number, it was an overly zealous charity volunteer endeavoring to make her feel guilty for not contributing to their particular cause when she simply couldn't afford a donation.

To her dismay, the phone rang again, same number. She worried that the call might be important. She tapped the green "answer" icon.

"Verity Cade?" The masculine voice that responded to her "hello" sounded tentative but possessed an underlying authority.

"Yes?"

"I hope I'm not bothering you. This is John Evans. Elvira's —" The voice went wobbly, sending a panicky wave of concern through her.

"Of course, Doctor Evans," she said quickly. Then, wanting to make the conversation as brief as possible for his benefit, "If it's about your egg and milk deliveries, I can adjust your order any way you like. Or stop deliveries entirely."

"No," he said, "no, it's not that. And please, call me John. We're neighbors after all."

"Of course. John."

"I wonder if I might ask a huge favor of you. If it doesn't interfere too horribly with your routine."

She didn't even stop to think about her answer. "Sure. Anything I can do to help."

"You will tell me if I'm imposing, won't you?"

"Of course. But you won't be, I promise." Although she had more than enough chores to fill her week. The key was choosing which of them to delay without creating mayhem.

He made a throaty sound of indecision at his end. "I'm sure this will sound lame, but I'm finding it hard—no, impossible really—to deal with Elvira's things."

"Her *things*?"

"Yes, personal affects, clothes and such. She has, I mean, she *had* so many dresses, shoes, hats. They're everywhere—in her bedroom, in my room, in the first-floor coat closet, the basement and attic. We can't move without coming face-to-face with a reminder that she's gone." He paused. Sighed. "I know that making decisions about what to do with it all could wait. Perhaps *should* wait. But, you see, it's particularly hard for the children. We need to forget her and—oh, God!" he gasped. "Mrs. Cade, please don't think that I ever want to truly forget my wife. I know it's been less than a week since her death. It's just that moving forward is so very difficult for us when every-where we look there's something of h-h-her—"

"I understand," Verity jumped in, foreseeing the possibility of weeping. "Elvira was such a force to be reckoned with." No, that didn't sound right. She tried again. "Such a vibrant and passionate woman."

"Yes, indeed." He released a forceful whoosh of breath into the phone. "I don't know what to do with it all. Donate everything to charities, I suppose, but which ones? I'm tempted to pay someone to haul it all away, but they might just trash it—and that doesn't seem right. It's over-whelming."

"I'm sure it is," she said in a calming voice.

"You see, I don't dare ask the kids for help. They're pretending to be brave, but I know they're hurting."

"Of course they are. And I'll be happy to help, John." She still had possessions of Mark's that she hadn't the heart to let go, even if she had no use for them.

The boots he wore outside to the barn every day. The leather Stetson he had so loved and wore whenever they went out to eat or visited friends. She had teased him, saying he must have been a cowboy in another life. Seeing him in that hat always gave her chills. The best kind. Woman chills. God, how handsome he had looked with the brim pulled low over his unforgettable brown eyes.

She tugged herself reluctantly out of that sweet memory. "Would you like me to come over and sort through her things for you? I can arrange to donate them, so others will benefit from their use."

"Yes, please. If it's not too much to ask," he added quickly, the relief already coloring his voice. "You could bring along one or two others from your group, if you need more hands for the job. I know all of you were very close to Elvira."

He made her and her friends sound like members in a formal club. *Your group.*

But she supposed, in a way, they were somewhat like a club—her customers. They certainly had become true friends over the years. She just wasn't sure she agreed with him about how *close* any of them had been to Elvira. In fact, when she thought about it now, she realized how little she actually knew about Elvira's personal life.

"When would you like me to come?" she asked him.

"Frankly, as soon as you're able. I know you have your farm and probably as much work as you can possibly handle there. But, like I said, it's been..." He groaned softly. She imagined the poor man slumped over in misery, head in hands. "I found Laura sitting in her mother's room, weeping."

Verity's heart swelled. *Oh, Jeez!* Now she really couldn't say "no."

"I've finished my critical chores for the day," she lied. "I can come over in a couple of hours, if you like. That would give me most of the afternoon to do what I can."

"I'd be so grateful," he murmured. "Truly grateful."

A thought came to her. "Before I get there, would you ask Laura and Peter to choose anything of their mother's they'd like to keep in memory of her. Laura, in particular, might want to save some of her mom's outfits for the future; Elvira had such beautiful things."

"You really think I should? Ask them, I mean."

"Honestly, John, I will feel so much better if the three of you set aside anything that's special to you. That way I won't give away a family heirloom or something that might later be missed."

"Yes. Good idea. Thank you for thinking of that." His voice sounded stronger, less scratchy, as if he'd found new energy now that a plan was underway. "I'll leave a note for you mentioning anything the kids or I want to keep. Please, just let yourself in through the back door when you arrive. I'll leave it unlocked for you. I have patients scheduled for office hours today,"

"Ok." She was already considering packing materials she'd need to bring with her.

"I'll tell Laura and Peter to expect you, although I believe they'll both be at friends' houses this afternoon. Immediately after the funeral I'm driving them to their grandparents' home in Albany. Change of setting and all." The poor man sounded truly wretched. "They'll be staying there for two weeks."

"Oh." She felt a little confused. Why was he telling her this?

"I just thought, you know, if you needed more time to go through everything. Quiet house, fewer distractions and all."

"Of course," she said.

"Anyway...thank you, Mrs. Cade. Ah. Verity."

She stopped herself from responding inappropriately, *My pleasure*. "It's nothing really. Glad to help," she said quickly.

Verity tucked her phone back into her pocket, thinking about how hard it was to let go of the past. She remembered asking her husband why he kept his grandparents' ancient black Bakelite rotary-dial phone, which remained to this day on the upstairs landing. He explained that it had been there for as long as he could remember.

"The dang thing just never wore out, still functions as a perfectly good landline. Even if it stopped working, I don't think I could part with it, Verity." Sadly, the outdated means of communication had outlived his entire family.

I guess that's just what we do, Verity thought. *We cling to the departed through the objects that remind us of them. Talismans connecting us to our past.*

Verity vowed she would make sure each member of Elvira's family had something to remember her by, even if they didn't think they needed that lifeline now. Because someday, they would. And she'd keep Mark's clunky black telephone along with his beloved Stetson, for no other reason than they had once been his.

Meanwhile, she relied upon more modern technology and set about making a few phone calls on her cell.

CHAPTER 16

VERITY ARRIVED before her crew at the house she would always think of as Elvira's. She quietly let herself in through the rear door. The same door the sheriff's deputy had waved her through on the day she learned of Elvira's death. Muffled discussion—a patient and the doctor's receptionist, she guessed —came from behind the interior door to her right, marked with a small, engraved brass plate: John Evans, MD. She walked past and up a couple of steps, into the kitchen.

Verity called out to Laura and Peter but got no answer. If they were already with their friends, she was glad. Kids had a way of comforting each other in times of tragedy that surpassed the awkward attempts of adults.

She made coffee and heated water in the electric teakettle in case anyone preferred tea. Going through Elvira's extensive wardrobe was likely to keep them busy for hours, if not days. The woman's collection of designer duds was legendary. Verity could honestly say she had never seen Elvira in the same outfit twice. She admitted to herself that a part of her was excited about the prospect of rooting through the woman's closets.

By the time the coffee finished brewing and she had set out

teabags, sugar and sweetener packets, milk and cream, she heard a light tapping at the rear outside door. She went to let in her team.

Sunny and then Denise stepped through the door in jeans and faded sweatshirts—perfect garb for a heavy-duty clean-out. To Verity's surprise, a third figure in gray sweats stood blinking at her. Martha shrugged one shoulder, as if to say, "Is it ok I'm here, too?"

"Oh, Martha, hi! Thanks for coming," Verity said. "I didn't call you because I thought this was your tutoring day." It was as good an excuse as any. She was sure John wouldn't welcome a crowd in his house. Three had seemed plenty.

"It is, but my student cancelled. When I overheard Sunny talking to you over the phone at the café, I just knew I should come and pitch in." Martha babbled away as though anticipating a grand adventure. Or maybe she was just as curious as Verity about the contents of the walk-in closets Elvira had so proudly boasted about. "Being closer to the family than any of you," Martha repeated as she pushed past them and into the kitchen, "I'm the logical choice for organizing Elvira's personal affects."

Sunny side-eyed Verity a silent apology. "I know you said we three were enough," she whispered. "But if it's alright with you and the doc—"

"Of course," Verity said. "Many hands make light work, right?"

Sunny looked back over her shoulder toward the medical office's door. "Sounds like the good doctor has thrown himself back into his work. I guess that's a good thing. Although it's sooner than I'd have been able to manage."

Martha turned on the café owner with a reproachful look. "Why, Sunny Whitaker, John's a dedicated professional! He would never let his patients suffer because of his personal grief. Besides, he knows what's best for himself and his children."

Verity frowned, wondering why the woman felt the need to defend the doctor. She opened her mouth to say as much but Martha wasn't done.

"Hard work is the route to healing." Martha sniffed. "Throwing myself into a day's chores has always done well by me!"

Denise snorted. "Yeah, well, personally I agree with Sunny. The man's made a shockingly fast recovery considering it's only been five days since his wife's death."

"Three of those following the funeral," Sunny murmured *soto voce*.

Verity caught a flash of anger from Martha's normally benign gray eyes before the teacher spun away, making it impossible for Verity to see her face. For some reason Verity had never been able to discover, Denise and Martha always rubbed each other the wrong way. Two strong personalities, she assumed. But the last thing she wanted was the two of them squabbling in this house of mourning.

"It's not up to us to make decisions for anyone but ourselves," Verity scolded gently. "Martha's right. The doctor is a busy man with obligations to the community. He's asked for our help. For him and for his children. We're here to do what needs to be done to ease this family through dark days."

"Well said, Verity dear," Martha chirped. She shot Denise a smug look.

Verity rolled her eyes.

Sunny sent her a sympathetic smile. "Let's just get to it, then." Sunny poured herself a coffee. "Where do we start, Verity? We await your instructions!"

Verity smiled at her, grateful that she'd preempted Martha from taking command, as she often did if Elvira wasn't around.

"Right then. Sunny, why don't you take Elvira's bedroom closets. Martha, can you manage the clothing in bureau drawers and cupboards? And Denise, John mentioned a large coat closet that probably has a lot of Elvira's outerwear. I'll take whatever's in the basement."

"I brought a supply of heavy-duty plastic bags." Sunny held up a large tote emblazoned with seashells, colorful fish and sailboats. "We can each take a few to start with."

"I assume we're separating donations and trash-destined items?" Denise said.

"Absolutely. So, label each bag to remind us of where it's going. I'll check Elvira's desk. I'm sure she'll have blank labels with her office supplies." Verity thought for a moment. "If we come across any of her business records, we should set them aside and let John know. Her partners at the realty office will need to handle those."

"Good idea." Sunny paused to take a sip of her coffee then made a face, as if it didn't live up to the impeccable standards of her café. "I noticed that you said *Elvira's bedroom?*"

"Ummm, yes." Verity guessed Sunny was having the same thought that had occurred earlier to her.

"Sexy Elvira and her doc-stud kept separate bedrooms?" Denise notched up her brow and pressed her lips together, obviously stifling a laugh.

"Not that it's any of our business," Verity said.

She knew of other married couples who preferred the privacy of having a room of their own. Her parents, for one. It was her mother's deafening snoring that prompted her father, when all other remedies failed, to warily suggest he move into the spare bedroom. To everyone's surprise, Mom had cheerfully agreed. She immediately usurped his space in their formerly shared walk-in closet.

"This should make things much simpler for us," the always

practical Sunny stated. "We won't need to worry about disturbing John's things."

"Absolutely." Verity selected an herbal tea for her beverage —a blend of chamomile, vanilla, and lavender. The others took their coffees with them and off they each went to their assigned duties.

Verity flicked on the light switch at the top of the cellar stairs. She descended into what was, to her surprise, an unfinished basement.

The air smelled faintly of mold, mothballs, and stale perfume. She was shocked that Elvira had even contemplated storing anything in this less-than-immaculate space. But then she discovered the problem. A massive dehumidifier positioned in the center of the space had evidently turned itself off when the collection pan at its base became full of water. She emptied it into a laundry sink and restarted the machine.

Better, she thought as the air noticeably began to clear.

She wondered why Elvira had never bothered to give the basement the royal treatment she had lavished on the rest of her house. Maybe she ignored it because it was the one part of the house guests never saw.

At the far end of the long, open room stood a bank of industrial-strength steel shelves. Lidded plastic shoeboxes and drum-shaped hatboxes filled the shelves and rose to the ceiling. A row of metal clothing racks, holding hanging items, ran the length of the basement. Verity strolled along one side, peering through clear plastic that protected suits, dresses, loungewear and sporty outfits from even a speck of dust.

Oh, my! She thought. *This is going to take forever.*

She unzipped several of the garment bags and gasped. One chic designer label followed after another: a lavender silk jacket and skirt from Palm Springs, a poppy-red summer dress from a famous Boston boutique, a stunning obsidian-black sheath from a famous New York City salon.

She itched to try on just one. But even the thought of doing so made her feel uncomfortable. She was here to help, not play dress-up like a ten-year-old sneaking into Mommy's closet.

After a hasty inventory, Verity let out a breath of relief. This was actually going to be much easier than she'd imagined. Not one item appeared to show wear, dirt or stains. To trash even one dress or suit would be a crime.

"Some lucky Size 6 is going to hit the jackpot at Goodwill!" she murmured. She'd need way more bags.

Verity transferred everything off the racks into her truck. It did seem a shame that Elvira's daughter wanted none of her mother's lovely things. John had left Verity an IM, assuring her that Laura had turned up her nose at his suggestion that she keep any of her mother's clothing for herself. What did that say about the relationship between mother and daughter? Maybe nothing.

With a sigh and a vow to stay focused on the task at hand, Verity next tackled the dreaded mountain of storage boxes on the steel shelves. The first six turned out to be household supplies, extra sets of glassware, crystal, seasonal tableware and tablecloths. Two others contained old medical textbooks, obviously belonging to the doctor. Another held baby toys and infant clothing. Undoubtedly Peter's and Laura's. Verity left all of these things as she'd found them.

Children never appreciated their own history while they were young, she thought. She certainly hadn't. But her mother had kept a few items from her earliest years, and Verity had come to treasure them.

Then came the hats. Boxes and boxes of them. Elaborate and trendy chapeaux, fedoras, bonnets, fascinators, boaters, bucket hats, turbans, straw skimmers, cloches, and elegant organza styles—beribboned and plumed, beaded or veiled, in every color of the rainbow. Each was lovingly wrapped in clean, white tissue paper and nested lightly within its own storage box. Church hats, Verity thought of some of them. But many would have suited Eliza Doolittle in *My Fair Lady,* for her day at the races. Stitched inside many were posh British hatmakers' labels. Very pricey, she assumed.

Again, she felt a twinge of sadness that such beautiful things would never be worn by Laura. But the doctor had been adamant about clearing away everything of Elvira's. If that gave him and his children any degree of relief, then these hats, too, would grace charity-shop displays and make some woman deliriously happy. She considered keeping just one outfit for herself, or maybe just a single hat or pair of gloves. They were heartbreakingly lovely, every one of them. But where would she ever wear anything so fancy? Her cows and chickens certainly wouldn't appreciate her fashionable new attire. Maybe Anna Louise would.

She smiled at that thought.

Verity made more trips up the cellar stairs and out through the kitchen door with stuffed-full bags. She heaved them up and into the Ridgeline's bed.

On her way back down to the cellar with a fresh supply of bags, she heard loud voices from the floor above. Pausing to listen she was unable to make out the words. Another disagreement between Denise and Martha? But, no, she could hear Denise rummaging through the first-floor coat closet. So, it was Sunny and Martha arguing. *Interesting.*

She considered rushing upstairs to restore order but decided to let the two women work things out for themselves, as long as they weren't disturbing the doctor and his patients.

The remainder of the boxes in the basement contained

medical textbooks, obviously belonging to the doctor. She resealed all of these except for the last one, which included several thin, handwritten journals, each with a different, colorful cover. Curious, she opened a blue leather volume to the first page.

Elvira Gorman Evans.

Even more curious, she read a little of the cursive script in black ink.

Verity's heart clenched. "Oh, my!"

These little books—diaries really—must record years and years of Elvira's life! How very touching, she mused. Her finger-tips buzzed with excitement as she flipped through the little books then arranged them according to their recorded dates.

The first was obviously a child's diary, bound in pink velveteen with a fragile little gold lock that would never deter a snooping sibling or parent. According to its date, Elvira would have been around twelve years old. Subsequent volumes recorded incidents, thoughts, dreams and reactions to life throughout her school years and into the first year of her marriage. Eight slim tomes chockful of memories. Far too precious to chuck in the trash or simply give away. She should ask John Evans what he wanted her to do with them.

But what if he told her he had no interest in keeping them? *Hmmm.* Now that would be a problem. Destroying a lifetime of her friend's intimate memories...well, she just couldn't do that! Surely, someone should preserve these little books as a record of the life of his children's mother. For Peter and Laura, if not for him.

Verity found a smaller cardboard box to hold the diaries and took them out to her truck. She laid it on the passenger seat. If neither John nor her kids wanted them now, she would keep them in a safe place until Laura was older. Just in case she changed her mind.

By the time Verity returned to the kitchen, angry shouts from the floor above had erupted anew. Fearing anyone coming or going from the doctor's offices might hear them, she rushed past Denise, sitting yoga-style on the floor in front of a pile of coats, and up the stairs to the second floor.

"Because, you *can't*, that's why!" The always unflappable Sunny sounded like an entirely different person.

Verity sprinted the last few feet down the hallway toward the combat zone.

"Why not?" Martha demanded. "Elvira and I were very close. BFFs. She'd want me to have some of her pretty things."

"Oh, really!" Sunny huffed.

"What's going on, guys?" Verity leaned against the door-frame, trying to catch her breath and sound nonchalant, but failing.

"*She*—" Sunny pointed an accusing finger at Martha "— keeps pulling dresses out of the donation bags and putting them in one for herself!"

"Just one or two." Martha, to her credit, did look a bit sheepish. "What's the harm? I know Elvira would prefer my having them over strangers."

"You can't know that, Martha." Verity kept her tone calmly neutral. "She often donated to good causes."

"You can't possibly wear her dresses, Martha!" Denise shouted, making Verity jump. She hadn't heard her coming up the stairs behind her. "Get real, girl. Elvira was a size six, maybe even a four. Don't you wear plus sizes?"

Martha's head snapped back as if Denise had slapped her. "Are you saying I'm f-f-fat?"

"I'm saying there's no way any of us could fit into her clothes."

"Martha," Verity began, in her most consoling voice, "if you can't actually use—"

"Oh, alright!" The teacher pulled a handful of silky gorgeousness from a shopping bag and flung the dresses at Sunny, who calmly added them to the donations.

Verity was about to mention the diaries when she saw a subtle change in Martha's disappointed expression. Her eyes positively sparkled. She followed Martha's rapt gaze to an ornately carved wooden chest in the far corner of the room.

Before Verity could ask the teacher what she found so interesting, Martha propelled herself across the room and flipped open the little cabinet's beautiful doors.

"Oh look, her jewelry!" Martha gasped. "I really think we should each take a little something as a memento of our special friendship, don't you thi--"

"No, Martha," Verity said firmly. "Elvira's jewelry should definitely go to her daughter, or whoever is mentioned in her will. I doubt she ever wore costume jewelry. That stuff must be worth a fortune."

Verity crossed the room. She gave a gentle tug on Martha's fleshy arm to suggest she step away from temptation, but the woman stubbornly resisted.

"Martha. Come on," Sunny coaxed. "If her will doesn't mention the jewelry and Laura doesn't want to keep it for herself, her father can sell it all and use the money toward his kids' college funds."

"John should put it all in a safe deposit box until a decision can be made within the family," Verity added.

"Copy that!" Denise said firmly.

Martha glowered.

Verity suddenly felt reluctant to mention the journals to the others. Something felt so very strange about this entire situation. Elvira's obsession with expensive things. Her overbuying to the point of hoarding. Why? And then these diaries. Did John know about them? She felt reluctant to mention them without first talking to him about it.

Then another thought nudged at her subconsciously before growing clearer. If she seriously wanted to find out what happened to Elvira on the night she died, she should learn more about the woman. Who knew what clues might be in hidden in her diaries!

CHAPTER 17

THAT EVENING, after Verity brought her cows in from the field and checked on her hens, she stopped on her way back to the farmhouse to pick handfuls of baby spinach from her kitchen garden. She washed the crisp dark green, deeply lobed leaves in her kitchen sink. Cracking open three fresh brown eggs, she beat them with a fork and cut a thin wedge of the tangy white cheddar cheese one of her neighbors made from Cade milk.

She sat down to enjoy her spinach-and-cheese omelet along with a thick slice of Sunny's whole-grain bread slathered in her own butter. To her, no meal was more satisfying at the end of a busy day.

After a quick wash-up, and still not a peep from her two ghosts (thank goodness!), she was ready to settle in for a quiet evening of reading. Mark's comfy brown leather armchair beckoned to her tired body. She snuggled into the cozy pocket his body had created. If she stretched her forearms along the chair's smooth arms, her elbows reached the hollows where his arms had once rested.

The leather warmed with her body heat. She liked to imagine the chair hugging her. Verity drew a deep breath, leaned her head back, closed her eyes and pictured his arms folding around her. Slowly, the pressure of a busy and emotionally intense day cleared from her mind like the lifting of a summer morning's fog. She reached toward the stack of books on the oak side table and chose the child's pink diary.

When Verity phoned John Evans after she and her crew had finished clearing away Elvira's personal affects, he told her she could do whatever she liked with the diaries. He had no time to look at them and was sure his kids had absolutely no interest in them.

"Are you sure, John?" she persisted. "Elvira may have recorded events that were special to all of the fami—"

His laughter interrupted her. "My wife made sure everyone knew exactly what she thought, don't you worry."

"You wouldn't mind if I read them?"

"Oh, for goodness' sakes, go ahead!" he snapped impatiently.

"Oh, ok," she said, taken aback by his sharp tone.

His voice immediately softened. "I'm sorry. You didn't deserve that. You've done a tremendous service for me and the kids. Can't thank you enough."

Now, sitting in her parlor, her fingertips smoothed across the fuzzy carnation-pink cover. This was a young girl's cherished first diary. Why had *she* never considered keeping a diary? Too busy living life, she supposed.

An inscription appeared on the second page:

To Elvira Ann Gorman.
Happy Birthday, twelve-year-old!
Love, Mom & Dad

The entries began on the following pages. The young Elvira had taken obvious care with her penmanship, forming precise letters in a loopy cursive, more legible than the writing of many adults Verity knew. The language was predictable for a young girl—fanciful, full of dreams and high expectations for her future. A handsome, "very cool" boyfriend, whom she would of course marry. Wealth. ("Like only the best bling and outfits, ever!") An enormous, beautiful home. (Young Elvira used the word "mansion" twice.) Verity smiled. At least she hadn't set her heart on a castle.

The pre-teen writer described with revulsion the modest three-bedroom rancher her family of seven was crammed into. Three rowdy brothers delighted in tormenting their two sisters. Elaine, born eight years after Elvira, was too young to be either companion or protector to her big sister. Verity could only imagine the mayhem in that household. The parents seemed rarely at home. Were they working constantly to support their brood? Or simply living their own lives and ignoring their children? Maybe they, too, felt the claustrophobia of the little house. No wonder Elvira longed for something grander, with at least a bit more space to breathe. She repeatedly wrote that she had no privacy in their home, no ability to control her brothers' rough housing, or to keep them out of the room she shared with her sister.

As Verity mused over the girl's complaints and dreams, she realized that, in reality, Elvira had succeeded in achieving every one of her girlhood ambitions. She was the mistress of a rather splendid home, had wed a handsome and successful man, brought two children into the world, and created a business that had made her a rich woman. Yet, during the time Verity knew Elvira, the woman never seemed entirely satisfied with all she had. Elvira Evans was always reaching for greater wealth, more possessions and recognition.

Was this her way of trying to achieve the most elusive prize of all—happiness?

Of course, there was a lot she didn't know about the woman as she'd only moved to Evansfield seven years ago when she married Mark. But she was convinced of one thing. Elvira needed to be in control of her two worlds—business and personal. Local gossip claimed that her management style made Meryl Streep's character in *The Devil Wears Prada* look like Mother Theresa. And according to a conversation she'd overheard, Elvira was the ultimate helicopter mom, orchestrating her children's lives from birth.

So, Verity mused, if Elvira was all about control, why had she abruptly, and without a hint to anyone, relinquished all control over her own and her family's lives—by killing herself? It just didn't make sense.

Could her sudden and dramatic departure have anything to do with her marriage? Verity looked away from the little pink book in her hands, considering this possibility.

John Evans, in his mid-forties, was still a strikingly handsome man and, by all accounts, devoted to his wife. Their combined income was clearly substantial. Many times over what Verity's little farm ever could earn. And hadn't Elvira stated more than once that she and John possessed sufficient assets to purchase her land and all the buildings on it with cash?

So, what had led this successful woman to take a shortcut to death down a mining pit?

There had to be an answer. And if it was in any of these diaries, she'd more likely find it in more recent volumes. Her weary body and stinging eyes warned her it wouldn't be long before sleep overtook her.

Focus! Read!

And so, she did.

With a sigh, she picked up a book in buttery-soft burgundy leather. All the entries were penned during Elvira's later high-school years in Pittsburgh. Again, the author described in glowing detail her hopes and plans for the future. However, something was different. The actual names of people rarely appeared on these pages. And Elvira lavished much more ink on the school's "losers," whom she was sure would never achieve anything in life, and the "snooty bitches" who refused to include her in their study groups and parties. Because, Elvira wrote:

I don't have the money for preppy outfits. Hand-me-downs don't exactly cut it with girls like them.

Verity's heart ached for her friend. Although she herself had been fortunate to have made good and true friends during her high school years, she knew other students who were virtually ostracized from the popular clubs and activities. Unfair, yes. Cruel, sometimes. But it seemed a fact of human nature that having a social life was easier for some than for others.

Just then, the little Ansonia clock sitting serenely on the fireplace mantel across the room bonged ten o'clock. She blinked at it tiredly. Her eyelids felt as though they were lined with sandpaper. Her neck had cramped. But she longed to continue reading about the life of the murdered woman. She drew a sharp breath at that word. *Murdered.*

When had she begun thinking of Elvira's death as more than just a terrible accident or suicide? Murder. Is that what this really was? Verity searched through the box of diaries for one whose dates indicated Elvira's college years. She needed clues in the past to the woman's mindset closer to the time of her death.

She hadn't been reading for long when she found the first lie.

Elvira always boasted to her adult friends in Evansfield that she'd attended Connecticut College, a posh all-girls school in New London, Connecticut. "My parents only wanted the very best for me." But now that Verity knew how money-strapped Elvira's blue-collar parents had been, she realized they could never have afforded the tuition. Hadn't she just read in Elvira's own words that she was embarrassed her father labored in a tool-and-die factory? And her mother took in laundry from the elite of Pittsburgh.

After reading for another twenty minutes, she at last found her answer.

Elvira had matriculated at spiffy Conn College with a scholarship she'd won from her father's union, covering the cost of her tuition and books. Apparently, she was a good student! She earned her room and board by "slaving away" in the college cafeteria.

Rich girls from pedigreed families, in Verity's experience, could be cruel to their poorer sisters. Was attending as a subsidized student a point of embarrassment or even shame for Elvira? She never mentioned her humble beginnings to her friends and neighbors in Evansfield. In fact, she reveled in her to-the-manor-born act. Maybe she'd modeled herself after her privileged classmates.

Verity couldn't stop turning pages now. The diary read like an exciting novel. The gutsy heroine rises from rags to riches! Even better than a novel, really, because she had known the main character as a real person.

Verity fought off sleep and read on through Elvira's second year at the college. Interestingly, the flavor of her writing changed. Her criticisms of students and professors became harsher, her tone sly and secretive. She sounded less like a dreamer and increasingly determined to get what she wanted— even if it meant destroying the hopes of others. This young woman was beginning to sound more like the obnoxious side of Elvira that Verity and her friends in Evansfield had tried to ignore.

Now, the identities of people she dissed, and sometimes outright plotted against, became disguised in initials or codewords. To shield the innocent? Or perhaps for her own protection, should anyone get hold of her diary. A lustful professor seduced her and took her virginity, evidently to Elvira's delight. She referred to him as Prof Bushy Fro. Sometimes shortened to PBF. His description implied he wore his hair in an afro. Did that necessarily mean he was a black man? Didn't white guys wear afros sometimes? She didn't know.

During Elvira's junior year she entertained a flurry of boyfriends, or at least sexual partners, and she seemed proud of her adventures. Verity found herself alternately blushing and laughing at Elvira's analysis of their personalities, physical descriptions, and the details of their copulation.

And then, early in her senior year, she met a young medical student at a social sponsored by the college. She referred to him only as Slick. Suddenly, Elvira stopped bed hopping. She was taking this new relationship seriously.

I have met the man I shall marry! He is perfect for me in every way. A gorgeous hunk whose papa is a famous Boston surgeon. He is an intern at a hospital in Hartford. And—get this!—he told me today that his mother is the daughter of a U.S. Senator. They are what's called bluebloods—tracing their lineage back to colonial America. My beloved's only fault is a decided lack of ambition. He sees himself as becoming a compassionate country doctor. Shades of James Herriot—OMG! With people instead of animals for patients, of course. He says he isn't at all interested in specializing or practicing in a big city like his father. But I'm sure I can dissuade him from making such a ridiculous mistake.

Later that same year, Elvira admitted a hiccup in her master plan. She hadn't won the heart of the physician-in-training after all. The perfect husband announced his engagement to another woman. Elvira referred to Slick's choice only as Olive Oyl or OO—an allusion to Popeye's bony cartoon girl-friend. Her other descriptions of Slick's fiancée were no more flattering.

I have seen him with this person. The bitch is thin as a rail, no boobs to speak of, and she wears only the most dowdy and cheapest sorts of clothing when not in medical scrubs. Everything bought off the rack at K-Mart, no doubt. I cannot understand what he sees in her!!! They apparently ran into each other while he was interning at his father's hospital in Boston last year. She is a student nurse.

Verity rubbed the back of her neck and rolled her shoulders to ease the throbbing ache. Her mouth had gone as dry as July straw. Every muscle in her body longed for her bed. But she couldn't stop reading. Not when each new entry read like a torrid love triangle!

Elvira hatched a new plan. She befriended the young nurse, and the two young women started spending girl-time together. Elvira then arranged a date for herself with a man who she knew was infatuated with her, and she invited Olive Oyl and Slick to go with them to a movie. By now, Verity was 99% sure of the identity of Slick; he had to be John Evans. The description of the tall, sandy-haired, good-natured medical student fit John to a T. And her theory was all but proven right when Elvira switched to using the initials JE in place of the nickname she'd given him.

The two couples double-dated several times. Whenever the opportunity arose, Elvira flirted with the young doctor. The flirting segued into a seduction game, with Elvira as a seducer.

Verity flipped pages madly.

Until...one evening, Elvira accomplished her goal. She and Slick slept together.

Soon, sex and home-cooked meals and more sex had become the routine. The sham boyfriend was dismissed from Elvira's life. She pitched herself as the woman who could make the young doctor a perfect wife. She even won over his Bostonian parents by demonstrating her social proficiency at a country-club dinner.

JE's mama was clearly impressed with me tonight. She confided in me that she was relieved her son had dropped the little nurse he'd been dating and, more sensibly, chose a bright and attractive young woman of their class. Obviously, I will make sure Dr. and Mrs. Evans never meet my parents.

How a girl from a working-class family managed this coup, Verity could only imagine. Elvira must have learned a lot by watching the Conn College debutants. The engagement with the nurse was officially broken. A new engagement announced at a formal reception—planned by Elvira and the groom-to-be's mother.

Elvira wrote:

oo is heartbroken, or so she claims. Boo-hoo! But I'm doing what is best for all concerned. She is such a drudge, so common. Reminds me of my mother. Little Nursey could never become the partner JE deserves. He needs a wife who will inspire him to achieve his full potential. He is destined to become a renowned surgeon like his father—maybe even more famous with my help. If not in Boston, then in New York, Miami, or LA. We will make an amazing couple!

By that time, Elvira had begun solidifying her own professional goals. After attending free seminars given by a national real estate company, meant to entice graduating seniors to join their firm, she wrote:

I've discovered the ideal moneymaker. Property. Buying it then reselling at a profit. The real estate market can only go up, up, and up. I will never be poor again. I swear to God!

Verity closed the slim leather-bound volume, letting it fall into her lap. She closed her eyes on an image of a ruthless Elvira. A woman who would stop at nothing to get what she wanted. That kind of person must have had enemies.

Sinking into a sea of numbing fatigue, she lay back and drifted in a disturbing netherworld of deceit and dirty tricks.

CHAPTER 18

HOW MUCH TIME passed Verity couldn't have said. But eventually she sensed someone in the room with her. Cracking open her eyes, she peered suspiciously around the room.

Nothing.

Or...maybe not?

"Have you two been reading over my shoulder? Don't you know that's rude?"

A giggle came from close to her ear, followed by a deep voice in her other ear. "I told my darling wife you wouldn't approve. But she was curious to see what you were so interested in. It's quite impossible to dissuade her once she has her mind set on a thing."

"No surprise there," Verity muttered thickly and yawned. The mantel clock started bonging. Midnight. She had to be awake and at work in five hours. She shoved herself up and out of the warm leather chair with a rueful groan.

"Why are you reading about that awful woman?" the still-invisible Anna Louise asked, her tone conveying disapproval. "Imagine stealing another woman's man like that!"

"Yes, well, Elvira has always been very determined. I guess you and she have that in common, Anna Louise."

Percy grunted. "Shameful."

"It wouldn't be the first time two women fought over a man." Verity sighed and laid aside the journal she'd been reading. "I'm for sleep. Off you go, you two."

Verity made quick work of brushing her teeth and washing up. She quickly slipped into her nightgown. As she stretched out on the cool white sheets, every cell in her body settled wearily into the pillowy mattress and sweet-smelling, sun-dried sheets. *Bliss.*

Annoyingly, her mind continued spinning. More people than she'd at first imagined bore Elvira a serious grudge. At the top of Verity's list were two of her victims. The token date Elvira had strung along to get close to JE and, of course, the student nurse Elvira befriended with the clear intent of snatching away her fiancé. But if what Elvira wrote in her diaries was true, she repeatedly seduced and dumped men on a whim. She also used women, although in a different way. The temporary friendships she cultivated in college enabled her to make advantageous social connections, join the right kinds of clubs and gain status.

But that had been many years ago. Surely, anything that happened that long ago wouldn't come back to bite her now. Would it?

Verity decided she needed to talk to people who had known Elvira during more recent years. Like her employees and colleagues in her business world. Did Elvira knowingly trample on some of these people to get ahead? Verity knew little about the real-estate business, but she did understand it was a highly competitive business. A lot of money was at stake in the form of commissions on sales. But at least the individuals involved were adults who knew the game they all played. They weren't innocent, like poor Olive Oyl.

What Elvira did to that woman was unconscionable. Truly shocking. She wondered if OO ever recovered from the loss of her fiancé. Nearly two decades had passed. Surely, the jilted young woman had moved on with her life, found a new love. And yet...

Verity turned over restlessly in bed. She sensed unresolved longing and bitterness—and other emotions just as intense that she couldn't put a name to. Where these feelings came from, she had no idea. But she believed she may have encountered them before—and not just in her own life. She had felt them on the night she hiked to the quarry and encountered Elvira's son.

Peter. Now, the motherless son.

"Poor boy. Poor Peter," she whispered, closing her eyes. "So sad. So very, very s..."

In the dream Verity peered down into the black depths of the granite quarry. She sensed the dark tangle of woods around her, the gnarled bark of tree trunks and thorny shrubs. Leaves rustled. Branches creaked. And yet she felt no wind. A premonition of malevolence sent a chill rippling down her spine.

She was standing so close to the quarry's lip that her bare toes peeked over the crumbling edge. Dirt and pebbles trickled from beneath the soles of her feet and fell with an echoing clatter to the stone floor.

"Get back!" she warned herself. Lest the ground give way beneath her and she fell, as Elvira had fallen.

Abruptly, the forest scene transformed.

She was looking down on a Roman Coliseum. Two female gladiators fought in the middle of the open space below. One wore a crisp white nurse's uniform, the other a carmen-red business suit and four-inch heels. They rushed furiously at each other, brandishing swords.

At the clank of their blades, Verity ordered herself, *Wake up!*

She levered herself upright in bed, eyes wide open, heart pumping. Disoriented, she pressed fingertips into her eyes and shook her head to force away wispy remnants of the unsettling nightmare.

Around her ranged the comforting furnishings of her own bedroom, barely visible in the silver slash of moonlight seeping through her curtains. The oak bureau she'd refinished last winter. The white hobnail-glass lamp on the night table beside her. The bed on which she now sat. Everything appeared perfectly normal. And yet...

A muffled scratching sound came from somewhere she couldn't yet identify. Was that what had generated the weird dream? Sometimes, a raccoon got into the attic; the scurrying of its little clawed feet making her skin crawl. More than once, she had climbed the rickety wooden ladder to chase out a little invader and board up the hole it had gnawed through the eaves. But animal sounds of all kinds were the soundtrack of her life in the country. They were to be expected.

This particular noise, she was sure, wasn't coming from her attic or outside the house. It seemed to originate from one of the rooms beneath her. Even more worrisome, it sounded stealthy, as if whatever was making it didn't want to be heard. She slowly swung her legs over the side of the bed and held her breath. Listening.

Silence.

She was reaching for the flashlight in the drawer of her bedside table when footsteps unmistakably shuffled across the floor downstairs. The explanation struck her and she let out an annoyed breath. *Damn those annoying ghosts!*

"Anna Louise? Percy?" she shouted. "What are you two doing down there?"

No ghostly whispers proclaimed the pair's innocence.

She sighed, deciding to just ignore their mischief and go back to bed. She desperately needed a few more hours sleep before dawn and the start of her workday.

The sound of breaking glass jolted her to her feet.

"What the hell, you two!" Furious, Verity jammed cold feet into her slippers and raced out of the bedroom, down the stairs to the pitch-black foyer.

But what if it isn't them? The possibility came to her, although a bit too late. She hesitated at the foot of the stairs.

Moving more cautiously now, she inched forward. Her flashlight's LED beam scanned ahead of her like the rotating beam of a lighthouse. She aimed its blue-white light through the parlor doorway to her left. Empty. She turned around to check the front door—it was properly closed and locked. Creeping silently toward her kitchen, she hesitated in the doorway then stepped through.

The flashlight beam flicked across a figure in motion. Not a ghost, for sure. She couldn't imagine either of the elegant Putnams in black sweats and a hoodie. Besides, the figure didn't twinkle, even a little.

Verity sucked in a sharp breath and involuntarily flinched, fearing attack.

But whoever it was, didn't rush at her. Instead, the person lurched away and toward the mudroom door. Tucked under the intruder's arm was a box. Verity immediately thought of her mother-in-law's beloved crystal glassware and porcelain collectibles. The only objects of real value in the entire house.

If she'd had time to think through her next move, she

certainly would have followed Mark's advice. "Anyone ever breaks in here, Verity, you don't try to stop them. Let them take whatever they want. Your safety is more important." But she felt an irrational need to control the situation. To *not* be the victim.

"Stop!" Verity threw herself after the retreating figure, the nightgown flying around her body like the robe of an avenging angel. "Stealing isn't...nice!" she shouted.

But, of course, the thief didn't stop.

Verity tackled him from behind, around the knees, and they both went down. Hard. The flashlight flew from her grasp, chattering metallically across the floor tiles. At least that gave her another hand with which to grab hold of clothing. Her adversary lost their grip on the box. In the dark, Verity could just make it out, sliding across the floor tiles and under her kitchen table.

What now?

If she let go of the kicking legs and reached for her phone to call 911, the thief would get away. Then she remembered her phone was still upstairs. *Stupid, stupid...stupid!* What had she been thinking, leaving her only lifeline with law enforcement on the bedside table?

While she tried to figure out Plan B, she held on tight to the squirming intruder and hoped all the thrashing around would exhaust him, before it exhausted her.

He kicked backward, digging the heel of an athletic shoe painfully into her stomach. When she curled up to protect herself, one of the captured legs escaped her grasp. Another fierce kick smacked her hard in the nose and chin. She tasted the saltiness of blood and suspected she'd bitten through her lip. The room spun. Her arms automatically released the remaining leg.

Nauseous and dizzy from the pain, Verity sprawled on the floor, her face throbbing as she helplessly watched a shadow stagger out through her kitchen door. She tried to push herself up onto her hands and knees but the effort made her head pound so violently, she felt her skull must surely split in two.

She collapsed back down onto her kitchen floor. The cool tiles soothed her burning cheek. The room spiraled around her, turned upside down and then...

Nothing.

CHAPTER 19

HOW LONG SHE LAY THERE, she hadn't a clue. Only when she became aware of distant voices did she attempt to open her eyes.

Apparently not so distant, she realized on looking up to see a pair of faces hovering inches above her. One face, a young blonde woman's, belonged to a stranger. The other one, she knew.

"Peter?" she whisper-rasped. "What are you doing here?" Her first impulse was to accuse the teenager of breaking into her house. Except. Hadn't the intruder worn a black hoodie?

Peter was outfitted in a green windbreaker bearing an emergency response team patch on its shoulder. His gal-partner, not much older than him, wore a similar uniform.

"Please, just lie still, Mrs. Cade," Peter said. "We're going to get you to the hospital."

Peter Evans was an EMT? Her brain seemed to be working at half its normal rate.

She opened her mouth to refuse the offer but her throat felt raw. She attempted to sit up. Her head thundered at her, which must have shown in her face.

Peter's partner pressed down gently on her shoulders and murmured, "Let us take care of you, ma'am. You look pretty beat up and may have a concussion."

"Oh bother," Verity moaned and gave up trying to fight them.

"I'm Sandy, by the way. We're volunteers with the Evansfield Fire Department, in case you haven't already guessed." She smiled and tapped a finger on her shoulder patch.

"Oh, ummm, hi." Verity managed a weak smile. She gently rolled her head to one side to view the room.

Now that someone had switched on all the lights in her kitchen, she could see, for the first time, the destruction of the room around her. Her lovely white pottery canister lay in shards amid a blizzard of flour. The wall rack holding her metal spatulas, ladles, spoons and tongs had come crashing down—which was probably what had awakened her. Broken glass from an as-yet-unidentified source glittered on the far side of the room. Thank God she hadn't been rolling around in it when she wrestled with the thief.

"Ah!" she breathed on seeing the box the thief had been carrying before she tackled him. It lay on its side beneath her kitchen table, looking like a frightened animal hiding from the mayhem. She met the kind eyes of Peter's partner and gestured toward it.

"You want me to get that for you?" Sandy asked.

"Yes," Verity croaked. "Please."

The EMT scooted under the table on hands and knees and retrieved the box for her. Verity rolled cautiously onto her side and reached inside. To her surprise, her fingertips didn't encounter the porcelain or glass she imagined the thief had come for. Inside the box were six of Elvira's diaries.

Verity blinked in relief. The rest of the journals were still upstairs in her bedroom where she had taken them to read.

Good, all accounted for. She gave the box to the young woman to set on her kitchen table.

"Can you tell us what happened here?" Peter asked, scanning the room with a worried look.

She told them about finding the person in her kitchen and trying to stop him taking anything.

Peter and Sandy exchanged looks.

"I know. I should have just let him go but I was just so mad—"

"You're safe now," Sandy said, laying a soft hand on her shoulder. "It's over. You just rest, Mrs. Cade." And Verity nearly wept at the girl's gentle words.

The two young EMTs expertly shifted her onto a stretcher and strapped her in.

"Do you need anything from home in case the ER doc wants to keep you the rest of the night?" Peter asked.

It hurt far too much to think. "Ummm," Verity murmured, groggily. She hoped she wouldn't pass out again. "My purse. It has my medical insurance information. And my cell phone. Upstairs. First bedroom on the left."

"I'll get them," Peter volunteered and dashed off.

"How long was I out?" Varity asked his partner.

"Probably no more than ten minutes. It took us less than that to get here, after your call."

Verity grimaced, trying to force her whirligig mind to focus. "I called you? Are you sure?" Had she somehow crawled up the stairs to her bedroom, dialed 911, then come back down again before passing out? And if she had—although she could remember none of it—why not bring the phone down with her?

"Of course you called. How do you think we got here?" The girl gave her a compassionate smile. "The 911 operator contacted us before you hung up. Don't you remember? She asked you to stay on the phone and keep on talking to her until we arrived. I guess you must have lost consciousness just before we arrived." Apparently, it hadn't yet struck the girl that the only phones in the house were on a different floor from where her patient lay helpless.

"But I d-didn't," Verity stammered, "I didn't call the—" But then, standing behind the EMT, Verity saw two shimmering images.

A solemn-faced farmer in dungarees held a pitchfork in one hand, its tines pointed toward the ceiling. Beside him posed an equally serious woman in a calico apron. *American Gothic*, Verity thought, *the famous Grant Wood painting*.

"Very funny, you two," Verity muttered hoarsely. She ached to demand why her two resident ghosts chose to wait until *after* the intruder had kicked her senseless before showing up.

Peter bounded into the kitchen with her purse and phone. "What's funny?" he asked.

Verity sighed. "Just talking to myself. Guess I'm still a little dazed."

"You'll feel better soon," he assured her. "The on-call doc is waiting for you in ER."

The two EMTs carefully maneuvered the stretcher down her back steps and into the back of an ambulance then climbed in after her. The driver—bless his heart!—refrained from turning on the woo-woo-siren.

Despite her pounding head, Verity tried to sort through events since she had been awakened by the obviously incompetent thief. What kind of burglar made such a racket while burgling? And why break into her farmhouse anyway? She never kept much cash in the house. She owned no expensive jewelry; only her wedding band was real gold. And of all the things to steal—why diaries?

Her expression must have appeared anxious to Sandy. She clasped Verity's hand in her own and leaned in from the pull-down seat beside the stretcher. "Don't you worry, Mrs. Cade. We'll take very good care of you—as will Dr. Evans. We just heard when we called in that he's on duty tonight. He's the best."

Verity glanced sideways at Peter, who was diligently filling out paperwork. If he had heard his father's name mentioned, he didn't react and continued noting information on an iPad. Perhaps, she thought, there's more to the boy than people realize.

CHAPTER 20

"WELL NOW." Dr. John Evans was studying a screen attached to the beige wall of the hospital room. "Let's see how those tests turned out."

"Good news, I hope." Verity laughed, nervously. She dangled bare legs off the edge of the hospital bed, feeling ridiculously self-conscious in the flimsy mint-green hospital gown she'd been given to wear the night before.

"I'd say it is," he murmured after a moment. "The CT scan and x-rays show no swelling in your brain, no fractures anywhere. Your labs have all come back and appear normal." He looked down at her thoughtfully. "Still, I think it was appropriate to keep you overnight. You can't be too careful with head traumas."

"And this?" Verity reached up to touch the bulky bandage across the back of her head. Beneath layers of gauze were thirteen stitches, required to close a wound she received during her scuffle with the thief. She must have hit her head on the granite countertop's edge, or something else equally hard, though she couldn't remember it happening. "Can I take off the bandages at night for sleeping?"

"I'm sure your pillow covers are clean, but I'd prefer you leave the bandage on for at least a few days. A week would be even better, just to keep out any dirt, dust, bits of barnyard straw and such. I assume you'll be out in your cow barn and around the henhouses to care for your animals."

"Yes. Of course."

"Then definitely keep the wound covered until it's had time to heal. The stitches I put in will hold that nasty gash closed, but bacteria are sneaky."

Verity sighed. "When can I go home?"

She had hated the idea of staying even one night. But he insisted on moving her into a room, for observation. Like the EMTs, he suspected she had a concussion. It was then that he'd given her "the look." The one she hated and all but shouted: *I feel sorry for you because your husband died and now all you have is a shit load of work and a farm that everyone knows will fail.*

Being pitied was the worst.

Verity looked up out of her thoughts to find him still talking to her. "Sorry, Doctor. What did you say?"

He entered a few more notes into his tablet then tapped off and looked up at her. "As soon as the nurse completes your paperwork you can check out and go home. Promise me, though, you'll take it easy for a few days. Lots of rest. Yes?"

"Sure," she lied. What was the man thinking? There was always too much to do on any farm, particularly during this time of year. The seasons were turning. With fall came the last of the harvesting and preparations for cold weather. The weather-channel pundits were already promising Vermont a particularly harsh winter.

Evans started toward the door but then hesitated and turned back to face her. For a moment, she feared he was going to give her that dripping-in-compassion gaze again. But someone knocked on the door, distracting both of them. *Thank goodness!* She could hear a clamor of high-pitched voices from the hallway.

"Come in!" Verity shouted. She'd hardly gotten the words out before the door flew open. As if a dam had broken, a flood of bodies spilled into the room. Sunny, Mary Beth and Chaundra rushed forward nearly trampling the startled physician.

He dodged out of their way. "I see your fan club has arrived. Ladies, she's all yours."

Her three friends mobbed the bed.

"Verity. Oh my God!" Mary Beth cried. "We would have come sooner but no one knew a thing until Sunny heard your news at the café this morning."

"And by the time we all reached the hospital," Chaundra added, "the floor nurse told us that you were having tests done."

"She was worse than Nurse Ratched in that movie," Sunny grumbled. "Wouldn't even let us wait in the room for you."

Verity smiled at her wonderful friends but felt momentarily confused about something. "Sunny, who told you about my being hurt?" She'd heard of criminals bragging about their misdeeds, but the thief would have been pretty stupid to boast about attacking her hours earlier, while in a coffee shop full of her neighbors.

"Peter Evans sometimes comes in for coffee and donuts when he gets off duty from the firehouse," Sunny explained. "He's part of the group of high school volunteers."

"Peter?" Chaundra's said. "Elvira's Peter?"

"Not everyone knows," Sunny said. In fact, Verity couldn't have been more surprised when she had found that out the previous night. Sunny continued breathlessly, "I overheard him talking to the Gifford girl who was with him, also an EMT, and he mentioned your name, Verity. Something about an attack, for gosh sake! He acted embarrassed when I tried to get him to tell me what happened. Patient privacy rules and such. He finally told me to call the hospital if I wanted information."

"Attacked? Sunny, you didn't tell me that part!" Mary Beth danced in place, eyes popping, her bountiful bosom heaving. "Oh my, oh my! What happened, Verity?"

"I'll tell you the whole story, I promise," Verity assured her friends. "But first, please help me find my things so I can get dressed and out of here. The nurse said everything I came in with is in that locker over there." She pointed and gave Sunny the pink bungee from around her wrist that held a key.

Sunny retrieved the bag and dumped its contents on the bed. Purse, slippers and a thin cotton nightdress speckled with dried blood. "Is that all?" She looked at Verity.

"I totally forgot I was in bed when I heard the intruder," she stared in dismay at her pitiful belongings. "I can't walk out of here in a bloody nightgown and slippers."

"No worries," Sunny said. "Chaundra had the foresight to make us stop by your place before we came here. Your farmhands let us into the house. By the way, the twins were so cute in their concern for you. Absolutely furious about what that guy did to you."

Mary Beth giggled. "The taller one—you know I never can tell them apart—he offered to 'make the bastard pay.' He's such a cutie."

That had to be Jason, Verity thought. He was a mafia-movie aficionado.

Chaundra held out a pretty Vera Bradley bag covered in brilliant purple and red poppies. "Change of clothes inside. And you get to keep the bag. It's a welcome-home gift from the group. They'd all love to be here, but the receptionist warned us, no more than three guests at a time."

"It's gorgeous!" Verity hugged the bag. "You shouldn't have, but I love it!" She flashed her friends a wide smile, which tugged uncomfortably at the adhesive holding the bandage to her head. "But I haven't been in the hospital even twenty-four hours."

"It still counts," Mary Beth insisted.

"Ten minutes in any hospital counts, as far as I'm concerned." Sunny wrinkled her nose and shimmied her shoulders. "Hospitals—ugh!"

"Well, at least I got a few hours' sleep," Verity said. "Until an orderly woke me up to take me to radiology."

Mary Beth looked like she was jogging place. She pulled a handkerchief from her purse and fanned her pink face. "Wow-o-wow! Imagine that—one of my closest friends, the victim of a home invasion. This is the most excitement I've had since the mayor brought home a parrot!" They all stared at her in puzzlement. No one dared ask for an explanation for fear of encouraging her. MB's ramblings about just about anything could run on for hours.

"Well, come on now," Chaundra coaxed Verity gently. "Get dressed then tell us what happened. We're dying to find out."

"Not much to tell." Verity pushed up and off the bed, pausing with bare feet planted on the floor to test her balance. Good. No dizziness. "It happened so fast. One minute I was sound asleep. The next I heard sounds from downstairs."

She dove into the adorable poppy bag and pulled out a handful of clothes. Bra and panties slipped on easily beneath the loose hospital gown. Sunny tossed the discarded gown into a bin marked for that purpose while Verity tugged on a clean pair of jeans and t-shirt.

"And then?" Sunny prompted. "You heard sounds and called the police?"

"Actually, no," Verity sighed. "I should have, of course." How could she explain that she was, at first, sure the culprits were two ghosts? "I guess I just wasn't thinking clearly. I grabbed a flashlight, went downstairs to investigate and found someone in my kitchen."

"Did you get a good look at them?" Chaundra asked.

Verity shook her head and winced at the ripple of pain through her skull. *Best not do that again!*

"No. It was too dark and—" she smiled. "Funny, I was thinking about just that while I was lying in the CT tunnel. I tried to remember anything at all that might identify the person. But they were wearing the sort of cat-burglar outfit you always see in movies. You know—black pants, hoodie and gloves."

"And one of those balaclavas? Robbers *always* wear them," Mary Beth announced with authority. She shaped an opening between her hands and peered through at Verity. "All you can see is their spooky, evil eyes."

"Stop it, Mary Beth," Sunny snapped. "This isn't a game. Verity could have been killed!"

"I don't think that was the person's intent," Verity admitted. "They seemed to be looking for something."

"Like what?" Chaundra said.

"I don't know. But the only thing he was holding before I tackled him was a box of Elvira's journals."

Sunny rolled her eyes and mouthed to the other two women: "Tackled?"

"No way!" Mary Beth looked impressed.

"Diaries? Seriously?" Chaundra scowled at her. "You risked your life for—"

Verity waved off her concern and stepped into her slippers. They'd have to do until she could exchange them for her sneakers or wellies. "I didn't know that's what was in the box when we started scuffling on my kitchen floor. I must have rattled him enough that he didn't try to retrieve the books in the dark."

"Veri dear, I think that head injury has muddled you."

Chaundra patted her arm. "Why would anyone think someone's diaries were worth stealing?"

"Unless they'd been written by a Kardashian." Mary Beth smirked.

"Well, someone obviously wants to get their hands on them," Verity pointed out. "They risked breaking into my house to snatch them."

"Didn't you say that John gave you permission to hold them for his children?" Sunny widened her blue eyes suggestively.

"What?" Verity said.

"I was just thinking. Maybe if we read them, we'll find out why anyone would think they are valuable enough to steal them."

"I think they should be read for another reason." Verity looked at each of her three friends in turn. "It's possible Elvira wrote something that might explain, um, why she—" she swallowed over a sudden burning sensation in her throat "—why she, you know..."

"I agree," Chaundra reached for Verity's hand and gave it a sympathetic squeeze. "There might be a clue to why she took her own life. For instance, something recent that happened to her. Or even an incident from her past."

Verity sat down heavily on the edge of the hospital bed. "Or maybe a mention of someone who hated Elvira enough to want to kill her." She felt sick at that returning thought but forced herself to continue. "Actually, I've already started skimming a few of the diaries. I don't want to talk about anything specific yet. I'm thinking it would take me forever to read all of them, on my own. Maybe we should split them up, each take one to read then we can compare notes."

"I like that idea," Sunny said. "As long as we have permission from John to read them."

Verity nodded in agreement. "Of course. What I don't understand is how anyone knew I even had her diaries."

"Oh, oh…oh!" Mary Beth was agitatedly hopping from foot to foot, which Verity thought quite impressive given her opulent size. "What if the burglar *knew* that Elvira stashed something valuable in her diaries? Like she sewed gold coins or diamonds or stock certificates inside the bindings!"

"MB, you do have the most delicious imagination." Sunny shook her head while Verity and Chaundra just looked at each other, fighting back smiles.

"You're right, Verity," Chaundra said. "To save time, we can divide them among us. Then report any clues we've discovered to the group."

Sunny nodded in agreement. "Perfect. The café closes early tonight. Why don't we all meet in the Cat's Cradle at seven-thirty." She hesitated and glanced at Verity. "Unless you want us to come to your house, sweetie. If you'd be more comfortable staying at home."

Verity cringed at her last memory of the farmhouse's kitchen. "My place won't be company-ready after last night. We'll meet at the café. I'll bring the diaries with me."

Plans having been made, Sunny left the hospital to prepare for her café's dinner crowd. It was Fried Chicken Night. Vermont style. Chicken fingers with maple-chipotle dipping sauce.

"I need to go, too. I have to make a few important phone calls. Family stuff." Mary Beth did a too-da-loo two-finger wave as she whisked out the door in her neon-bright flowered caftan.

Which left Chaundra the honor of driving Verity home. The antiques expert huffed. "Family stuff, my Aunt Fanny! You and I both know, she can't wait to tell everyone in town about your intruder and how bravely you fought him off."

"I wish she wouldn't," Verity admitted. "I don't have time to answer questions from everyone in town. Besides, I'm not sure how brave it was. More like a lapse of common sense."

"Everyone means well. We all love you, Verity."

"Not the sheriff, I'm sure."

"No, not him," Chaundra laughed. Before Sunny and Mary Beth left, Verity had filled in her friends about Bailey's reaction to Peter's note.

Chaundra waited with Verity until her paperwork arrived. They stopped at the hospital pharmacy to pick up a prescription for Tylenol, the hi-test kind laced with codeine. Every muscle, ligament, and joint in her body felt stretched and strained. Her head was booming like a bass drum now that the painkillers Dr. Evans had prescribed during the night were wearing off. As soon as they reached Chaundra's van, Verity popped a capsule in her mouth, swallowed it dry, then cautiously leaned back against the seat and closed her eyes while the drug did its thing.

By the time Verity opened her eyes, they were off the highway and back on country roads, overhung with the leaves of crimson maples and yellow ash. Green vistas of the lush river valley peeked between swaying branches. As the pain lessened, Verity felt her body begin to relax, like a slowly loosening spring.

"You're sure there's nothing you need help with?" Chaundra asked. "I can make you a late lunch, feed the chickens, help tidy up your kitchen. Anything?"

"No, I'm good. Really. Just a little sore. The medicine helps. You have the emporium to manage. How many vendors do you have now?"

"Over twenty, and more artisans and artists apply every day." Chaundra laughed, dark eyes shining. Her close-cropped, curlicue hair formed a neat black cap over her head. Verity wished she could wear her hair like that; it looked so stylish and cool, perfect for summers. "They're a talented crew, my vendors, but a challenge to keep up with. There's always something—items disappearing from displays, competition over stall locations, petty vandalism. But everyone seems to be making money, which is why they like being under my roof. Their stall rentals are a fraction of the price for opening their own storefront."

The van slowed to the thirty-mile-an-hour limit through town. Village shops wheeled past.

"Your place is amazing." Verity smiled. Ever since Chaundra came to the United States and Vermont, Verity had wanted to ask her about her birth country. But her friend always found a way to change the subject. Maybe this time would be different. "Are there similar co-ops for crafters and artists in Ethiopia?"

"It would be a very good idea if there were. Especially for the women." Chaundra sighed. "There are many talented artisans in my country. But creating something like my emporium would be a full-time job. I have no desire to return to Ethiopia." The corners of Chaundra's lips pinched downward and she turned away to focus on the road.

"Maybe you could teach someone back in your country to use your model. Then you might only need to stay for a few weeks to help set up the business. Your protégé would take over and run it."

"No," Chaundra said quickly. "Impossible." She shook her head vehemently.

Verity thought she glimpsed an expression of revulsion flash across the woman's lovely face.

"Ah, look! The Brothers Grimm are waiting to greet you."

Indeed, Jason and Jerry Grimalski stood beside the farmhouse. The townsfolk had given them the nickname for their habitually serious demeanor, but their expressions at the moment were even more solemn.

"Do you need help getting into the house?" Chaundra sounded relieved for the distraction as she steered into the driveway.

"No. Seriously, I'm fine. Thanks for the lift. See you tonight?"

"Of course. Get some rest. You've been through a lot."

As the emporium van drove away, Verity turned toward the farmhouse but couldn't stop thinking about her friend's odd reaction to her suggestion. Chaundra was such a generous and talented person. It seemed totally out of character for her to not even consider helping her sister Ethiopians. But perhaps she was more like Elvira than Verity had realized. The consummate businesswomen. Focused solely on her own professional goals.

She looked up from these thoughts to see Jason and Jerry Grimalski loping toward her. Without a word, Jason took the poppy bag from her. Jerry shyly offered his arm, as though he expected she'd need help walking.

"Hey, I'm not an invalid, you guys."

"But you are the talk of the town," Jerry said. "Such fame rates an escort."

Verity groaned and humored him by looping her arm around his. "Talk of the town? Please, no."

"You just missed the sheriff," Jason reported. "He came by to take your statement about the incident last night. I guess he tried to catch you at the hospital, but your medical team was keeping you too busy."

"Are you alright?" Jerry asked, eyeing her up and down doubtfully.

"I'm fine. Honest." She knew her face was horribly bruised from the thief's kick. She was lucky her nose hadn't been broken.

However, she limped a bit and felt as though she was moving a little slower than usual. "Has the milk truck been by yet? Did you feed the chickens and shift their coops like we discussed?"

"We'll take care of the milk pickup and everything else for the rest of the day." Jason gave her a look, way too stern and mature for a Gen Z'er. "You are going to rest. Doctor's orders."

"How do you know what my doctor—"

"Doc Evans' nurse called and gave us strict instructions for your care."

"Did she now." She allowed her two farmhands to guide her toward her house, then frowned. "Why are we heading for the front door?" Front doors, as everyone knew, were for guests.

"The kitchen is out of bounds," Jerry explained. "Sheriff Bailey taped it off as a crime scene."

"Oh." Reminded of the invasion, she suddenly felt nauseous. She knew she wouldn't feel comfortable again in her home until she'd thoroughly cleaned her kitchen and put everything to rights.

"We can help you with the cleanup, soon as he says they're done in there." Jerry moved up her front steps at grandmother speed, keeping a lock on her arm. She had to smile. Normally the boys bounded up steps like gazelles.

"Thank you. Some help with the clean-up would be much appreciated."

"We've already scoped out the whole house," Jason informed her, opening the porch door for her. "Checked closets, under beds and stuff—you know, just to make sure the jerk didn't come back."

She couldn't help smiling at their efforts on her behalf. Not for a minute did she believe the thief would return. Wouldn't it be foolish of him to target the same house twice? There were so many other homes with more expensive things to steal. *Unless the diaries are really all he was after.* But that made no sense.

As soon as they stepped into her foyer, Verity turned to her farmhands. "I'm fine, guys. Really, I am. But if you can cover my afternoon chores, that would be wonderful."

"No sweat," Jason said.

"Absolutely," his brother added, "we're on it. You sure you're...it's just you don't look all that great."

"I'm tired that's all—already took the pain medication the doctor prescribed. I'll climb into bed. Probably sleep straight through the rest of the day." She didn't mention going out later that evening.

At their insistence, she promised to call if she needed them. Verity closed the front door after them, locked it and immediately crossed the foyer to the kitchen doorway. Yellow plastic tape crisscrossed the opening. She peered between strips. In the light of day, the devastation looked even worse than what she'd been able to see from her position on the floor the night before.

Tomorrow, she'd throw herself into the job of tidying up, so long as the sheriff gave his permission. She'd ask the twins to do any of the heavy work.

By the time she reached her bedroom, she had already decided against trying to sleep.

What she really wanted to do was dig deeper into Elvira's life before she met with her friends at the café. She reached for the three diaries on her bedside table then stared in surprise at the small white paper bag. Written on its side in black marker were the words: *Eat Me!*

She chuckled.

Inside the bag was a sandwich (tuna salad on sour dough bread with lettuce and tomato), a bag of Kettle Chips, an apple, and a fudgy brownie the size of Rhode Island—all from the café. She grinned. There was also a bottle of water. Her boys had thought of everything. Bless their little hearts.

But she didn't want to eat in bed, so she gathered up her food and reading material.

Going down the stairs was worse than going up. Every muscle in her body tugged painfully with each step. Since the kitchen was currently a no-man's land, she cut through her parlor which connected to the living room. She settled on the couch, stretching her legs up along the seat cushions, and unpacked her meal. There was more than enough food for both lunch and dinner. She ate half the sandwich and the apple then returned the rest to the bag for later.

Verity opened one of the journals. "Tell me your secrets, Elvira Evans," she whispered.

CHAPTER 21

VERITY BLINKED herself awake at the sound of a car grinding its way up her gravel driveway. An open diary lay in her lap. She must have fallen asleep on the couch while reading. Voices drifted in through the parlor window she'd opened to let in a breeze and cool the house down. The air was redolent with the scent of the lavender and hydrangea bushes she'd planted beneath the windows along the side of the house.

Mark's parents had never considered installing air conditioning in the old farmhouse. In fact, very few people in Vermont saw the need for it, since temperatures reached as high as 85 degrees for only a few days each summer. But Elvira had claimed, "You can't expect to get a decent price on a house these days if it doesn't have central air! Mark should have installed AC years ago." Verity didn't understand why the realtor cared, when she had already admitted she'd tear the house down to make way for John's clinic.

If Verity sold the farm to her. Which was no longer Elvira's concern. Because she was dead, Verity thought morbidly.

Anyway, if John Evans pursued the purchase she would put off making a decision for a while. Between puzzling over Elvira's accident/suicide/murder—whatever!—and the break-in last night, she didn't have a single brain cell left to think about anything else. Had crime finally come to peaceful little Evansfield? She sighed. Perhaps it was inevitable. Was there any place in today's world where violence didn't exist?

She closed the journal at the sound of a slamming car door. The back door screeched open. Boots stomped across the floor planks in her mudroom then grew louder as they crossed into her kitchen. So much for not contaminating physical evidence!

Jerry poked his head into her living room. "You good to talk to the sheriff now?"

"Good as any time," she said, unable to hide the reluctance in her voice.

After her last conversation with the sheriff, she felt wary of his reaction to the break-in. Maybe he'd claim the intruder was a fabrication of her imagination. Or he'd suspect she was using the incident to make him to change his mind about Elvira's cause of death. Although how she could have beat herself up seemed a stretch—even for a man as stubborn as Fred Bailey.

"Mrs. Cade." The sheriff stepped into her living room, hat pressed to the front of his chest with both hands, like a mourner at a funeral home. Perhaps the gesture of sympathy was an encouraging sign? "Your boys tell me you're takin' it easy, under physician's orders. I promise not to keep you long. Just need to ask you a few questions about what went on here last night."

"Of course, Sheriff." She folded her hands over the blue leather volume in her lap and waited for him to retrieve something to write on from a pocket. "The light is better over near the window, if you need—"

"It all sticks right...up...here." He tapped his forehead in time to his words then gave her a wink. As if, between the two of them, they were acknowledging his superior memory.

Verity cleared her throat to camouflage her laugh. She

recapped the night's drama, giving the same information she had shared with her friends at the hospital. She tried to leave nothing out from the moment she first heard suspicious noises to her scuffle with the intruder. Throughout her tale, the sheriff's ruddy face remained emotionless.

"And your injuries?" he prompted.

"I don't honestly remember if he bashed me over the head with something or just pushed me and I accidentally struck my head," she admitted. "All I know is—I blacked out. The EMTs said I might have been unconscious for only ten minutes, but it sure felt a lot longer."

"I see." He scowled. "Sorry for needing to ask you all these questions when you're not feeling well." He explained that, by law, neither the EMTs nor the hospital staff could share medical information with his office without her permission.

"You said," Bailey continued, "you were in a deep sleep before you heard the noises that alarmed you?"

"Yes."

"I'm wondering if—" *here it comes*, she thought "—you mighta been disoriented in the dark. Fell down or tripped over—"

"No," she interrupted firmly, "I didn't just fall down. Someone was ransacking my kitchen. I saw the person. We fought."

"Ransackin'," he repeated, as if the word amused him.

"Yes, and rather loudly, too. I didn't imagine the clamor, sheriff. And I didn't just dream about wrestling with someone on my kitchen floor. I have the bruises to prove it." She pointed at her own face then rolled up one sleeve to display a Rorschach pattern of purple-and-green mottling on her upper arm.

He bobbed his big head and had the decency to look sheepish. "Right. Makes sense, 'specially with the condition of your kitchen." He looked over his shoulder. "Should have realized last night when I saw the damage."

"You were here last night?" She tipped her head, thinking about this. "I only recall seeing the two EMTs."

"By the time I got here the ambulance had already taken you off to hospital. Gotta say, that room in there looks like a war zone." He chuckled.

"Well," she sniffed and threw him a look, "it kinda was, Sheriff."

He must have realized his reaction was just a smidge inappropriate. "I'm real sorry this happened to you, ma'am. As I'm sure you're aware, things like this just don't happen hereabouts. Not attacks on a person in their own home. But prob'ly the only reason you got hurt was 'cause you tried to stop—"

"You're saying, this was *my* fault?" She narrowed her eyes at him.

He flapped his hat in the air, as though waving away her words. "Not at all! I'm just sayin', Mrs. Cade, that tryin' to capture the bugger was ill-considered. Had the miscreant been armed, the outcome could have been far worse."

Verity snorted at his scolding, but almost immediately thought he was, sorta, right. Allowing the thief a clear escape route would have been the wiser move. Mark certainly would have agreed.

"You got any idea what the thief was after?" he asked. "Keep a lot of cash in the house, do you?" She shook her head. "Valuables left to you by your husband or from your mother-in-law's estate?"

"She had some nice glassware and collected china figurines, but whether they are worth anything—" She shrugged. "I've no idea of their value. The only thing the thief was holding when I knocked him to the floor was a box of books. Diaries actually. Elvira's."

"Huh?" He scrunched up his face—the image of a man hard at work thinking—then shook his head. "Diaries? That don't make much sense. Just a bunch of girlie gossip and fantasies. Not like he could sell the things."

"Girlie?" He must have seen the outraged flush on her face.

"No offense intended," he said quickly. "Never known a man to keep a diary. Anyways, after an experience like you had last night—you're probably confused 'bout what you actually saw. Maybe he *was* holding a box. Maybe he intended to dump out the books and load it up with something else."

"I guess." But she didn't believe it for a minute. She looked up from the couch, trying to set aside her irritation with him and get a grip on her thoughts. "Listen, Sheriff, if you don't need the diaries for evidence, my friends and I would like to look through them. Just to see if we can find out why anyone might think they have value." She didn't add her real motive—to discover a reason why anyone might want to kill Elvira Evans. He'd only repeat his assumption that all evidence pointed to suicide. "That is, unless you or your deputies need to study them for clues to my break-in, which I'm sure would take hours, if not days."

His eyes shot open in horror. "Good Lord, no, Mrs. Cade! My department is understaffed and overworked as it is. You ladies go right ahead."

She smiled. "Good. I promise I'll let you know if we find anything important."

"You do that." He jammed his hat down on his head and turned to leave.

"Sheriff, do you think you'll find whoever broke into my house?"

He hesitated before turning back to face her. "My guess is some youngster did it on a dare. Part of a scavenger hunt or hazing prank. Only thing makes sense to me."

"Ah," she said. *Just like it makes sense to you that a wealthy woman in the prime of her life jumped to her death.* But she didn't say that. Instead, she said, ever so sweetly, "Thank you for stopping by, Sheriff. Oh, and is it alright if I clean up my kitchen now? I don't want to destroy any evidence in your crime scene."

"You go right ahead, Mrs. Cade. I've seen all I need to see. Might I suggest you commandeer a few of your girlfriends to help out? Since you're s'posed to be resting and all."

"I will," she promised. But already, her mind was spinning off in far darker, although more interesting, directions.

CHAPTER 22

VERITY EASED BACK against the soft sofa cushions as soon as she heard her rear door clack shut. She took a long swig from her water bottle and listened to the sheriff's SUV depart, engine revving, tires grinding up her driveway. Smoothing one hand over the book in her lap, she returned to thinking about something that had been bothering her since she returned home from the hospital.

She had a bone to pick with someone, and it wasn't with the sheriff.

"Anna Louise. Percy. Come out where I can see you."

She waited.

No incandescent figures appeared.

"I'm honestly not angry with you two." Hadn't she read somewhere that when a person used the word "honestly" in a sentence, it meant they were hiding something? "I just need to ask you about something important." At least that much was true.

Nothing.

"If you're going to hang out in my house, *like forever*, you need to stop being rude by going all invisible and silent when I'm trying to talk to you!"

Anna Louise, in all her antebellum glory of petticoats and blonde banana curls, sparkled into sight. "Never let it be said that a southern lady lacks manners," she cooed. A second later, her husband appeared in full military uniform. Something in the way his gaze shifted back and forth between her and his wife made Verity wary.

"Where have you two been?" Verity asked, trying to sound as casual as possible.

"O-o-oh, here and there." Anna Louise gestured loftily with a white lace glove.

"Very busy," Percy responded, avoiding Verity's eyes. His wife nodded vigorously, sending her curls jiggling.

"Busy? Let me remind both of you. You. Are. Dead! What obligations could you possibly have?"

Anna Louise played with the ruffles down the front of her robin's egg blue gown. "What my darlin' husband isn't explaining very well is—we felt rather guilty about not being here when you were so ruthlessly attacked. We decided it might be best if we made ourselves scarce. At least, for a little while."

Percy added, "We'd like to help now, though, if we could."

"Cleaning up the mess in my kitchen would be a huge help." It was a long shot, but worth a try. So far, the pair had seemed pretty useless. Were they even capable of performing mortal chores?

"Oh, sweet girl," Anna Louise sighed, "housework is simply not my forte. That has always been—um, best left to someone else."

"I see. And who were those someone elses? Slaves?" Verity didn't even try to keep the accusation out of her voice. Just reading about that cruel and sad part of American history always made her furious. To think that people believed you could own a person as if they were a piece of furniture!

"Oh no!" Anna Louise objected. "You see, we were far too poor to afford any kind of domestic help. I just meant my sisters were better at cleaning and cooking and...well, just about anything. Mother always said I was hopeless, just a little daydreamer."

Percy gazed fondly at his wife before turning to Verity. "We're truly sorry we weren't here when you needed us last night. By the time we returned from our sleuthing, we found you lying on the floor."

"I was just beside myself with guilt," Anna Louise whimpered, tears suddenly springing to her pretty lavender eyes. Who knew a ghost could cry actual tears! That is, if they were real. "I feared you were...were—"

"Dead like you?" Verity said, perhaps a bit too bluntly.

"It seemed a definite possibility." Percy's pale face suddenly reddened. "Forgive me, but I must apologize. I—ah, I *touched* you. On the throat. To feel for your pulse." He demonstrated by positioning his fingertips on his own neck. "It was most reassuring to know your heart was still beating."

"It would have been reassuring to me, too," Verity laughed, "if I'd been conscious."

"But then we didn't know what we should do!" Anna Louise dabbed at her eyes with an embroidered hanky that had appeared out of nowhere.

Percy nodded. "Until I remembered hearing Mr. Mark tell a little neighbor boy that he should call 911 on a telephone if there ever was an emergency. And we knew that's what he called the black machine on the stairway landing—a telephone."

"You called 911 to get help for me?" How sweet was that! Verity felt truly moved.

"Percy asked me to do the talking part." Anna Louise had stopped sniffling, the tears miraculously gone. "I gave your name when a woman in the telephone asked who was calling. I do an excellent imitation of you, Miss Verity, if I do say so." The ghost beamed with pride.

So, Verity realized, *that was why the two emergency techs thought I made the 911 call!*

"Well, thank you for that," she said. "I trust, Anna Louise, you won't abuse your talent in the future?"

"Oh no, Miss Verity." Anna Louise windshield-wipered a gloved finger to emphasize her sincerity. "I would never do that."

Percy stood silently at his wife's side, studying his feet, which wasn't exactly reassuring.

"What were you two off investigating in the middle of the night?"

"We visited Dr. Evans' house," Percy explained. "I believed it might be useful if we listened in on the family."

"And what did you find out?"

"Most of the time, they didn't talk to each other at all." Anna Louise pulled down a blonde corkscrew of hair and examined it closely, which made her look a little cross-eyed. "Do you think I would be prettier with red hair? Red hair is so passionate!" She batted her eyelashes at her husband.

Verity ignored the change of topic. "But when they did talk what did they say?"

"Dr. Evans stayed in his surgery most of the time," Percy said. "When he didn't have patients, he was reading medical journals late into the night. His daughter gossiped with her friends for tedious hours on her telephone without wires which, by the way, I find even harder to make sense of than the big black contraption. I believe you call the little ones 'cellphones?'

Although they have very little in common with a jail." Verity smiled and acknowledged her agreement with a nod. He continued, "The boy was only at home for part of the night. He changed into a costume that looked like pajamas."

"Peter was probably on emergency duty again," Verity said. "You must already know that he and another young volunteer responded to your call and took me to the hospital. Peter seems to take his job very seriously." Verity frowned.

"Is something wrong?" Anna Louise asked.

"Maybe. I'm not sure." Verity started to shake her head but stopped herself, afraid of making her bandages pull again. "I was worried that Peter might have had something to do with his mother's death. But now I wonder if that's even possible. I think his grief over losing his mother was sincere. And he seems genuinely good-hearted, civic-minded. Not the type of person who would kill his own mother."

"But that's good, isn't it?" Percy observed her solemnly. "He appears a decent lad, if a bit quick tempered."

"Yes," Verity agreed. "But I think the sheriff is wrong about Elvira having committed suicide. That leaves either natural cause, an accident, or murder. And if someone other than her was involved in her death, well, *who* was that someone? And does that same person have anything to do with what happened last night in my house?"

"Yes, these are important questions." Percy frowned down at his hands. "But I wish you would be more careful when you are doing your investigating." His eyes snapped up to meet hers. "I sense an evil force at work in our town."

"Oh, Percy," Anna Louise whispered, "do stop! You're frightening me."

The lieutenant took his wife's hands in his own. "My dear, we are past harm now. But our benefactress is most vulnerable.

Witness what has already happened to her." He turned back to Verity. "Heed my warning, madam, take care lest you cross this wicked person."

Verity shuddered. Somehow, the ghost's words made everything feel so much more real. And dangerous.

PARKING SPACES directly in front of the café were already occupied by Kate's adorable cherry-red Mini and Sunny's white van with the Cat's Cradle Café logo on its side. Verity parked her truck in front of Chaundra's Antiques Emporium. She slid off the driver's seat, wincing when her feet hit the pavement. Pain ricocheted through every muscle in her body. Dr. Evans had warned her to expect feeling stiff and achy after her tussle with the intruder. She just hadn't realized the discomfort would worsen in the first few days. She carefully reached across to the passenger seat for the red poppy bag into which she had loaded Elvira's journals.

When Verity stepped through the café's door to the tinkling of the little silver bell, Fumiko, Kate, and Denise were already seated at three tables they'd pushed together to give everyone enough room to spread out and work. Pads of lined paper and pens were arranged at each seat—probably Sunny's doing. A glass bowl on the center table, brimming with Denise's irresistible chocolate truffles in colorful foil wrappers, beckoned to Verity's sweet tooth. Flowered pottery bowls, one with pretzels, the other with assorted nuts, sat on the end tables.

Good, Verity thought, *no potato chips. Too greasy.* Hopefully, the individual wrappings for the truffles would prevent chocolate fingerprints from smudging pages. She felt responsible for keeping the diaries in good condition since she was sure Laura would eventually change her mind and want them someday.

"Looks like you've thought of everything, Sunny," Verity said.

The café's proprietor laid a stack of napkins beside the snacks. "I'll get coffee for anyone who wants it." She got a "yes, please" from everyone.

"I hope the munchies will help keep everyone awake," Verity sighed. "It could be a long night." Then again, the painkiller she'd taken earlier made her eyelids feel like little lead curtains. Maybe the power of drugs was beyond the influence of caffeine and sweets.

"Sugar always does it for me." Kate popped a truffle into her mouth. "Mmmm. Denise, you've outdone yourself. These are melt-in-the-mouth sinful."

"They're called Chocolate to Die For, my newest flavor—salted caramel and milk chocolate."

"Oooh," Fumiko said, "I must try one." She took two.

"Who else is coming?" Verity asked, looking at the arranged chairs.

"I called Chaundra, MB, and Martha; they all agreed to come and help," Sunny said. "Since you said there are nine diaries and there happen to be eight of us, I figure we can each take one, that is if everyone shows up and wants to take part. The extra one can go to the fastest reader."

"Good idea," Verity agreed. "I don't mind taking a second diary if someone doesn't have time to read. I need something to occupy my enforced rest time." She pulled the books out of her bag, each cover a different color and material—fabric, faux or real leather. Their mismatched appearances had at first surprised her. She doubted Elvira ever set foot out of the house without coordinating her clothes, shoes and purse. Verity fanned out the diaries on the center table.

"Oh, they look like a rainbow! Pret-ty, pretty!" Kate giggled, then looked embarrassed. "At least, that's what my girls would say."

Verity settled into a seat, anxious to get started. "The beginning and end dates of the entries are written inside each front cover. When Elvira filled up one book, she started a new one, even if it was in the middle of a year."

"Anyone see a favorite date they'd like to read?" Sunny asked.

Kate picked up the pink velveteen volume with the tiny lock that Verity had already perused. "How sweet is this! It must be her very first diary, when she was—what did you say yesterday, Verity? Twelve years old?"

"Yup. You'll probably like it. I read a little last night."

"Before you were so rudely interrupted by some criminal breaking into your house," Sunny huffed in disgust.

"That'll mess with anyone's plans for the night!" Denise threw back her head and laughed. "Sorry. I know that's not at all funny. Must've been awful."

Verity nodded. "That it was." Through the front window of the café in the fading light, she saw two people approaching the door. A third joined them from the other direction along Main Street. "Looks like Chaundra, Mary Beth, and Martha have arrived."

Although it was nearly 8:oo pm, the sun hadn't completely set. Verity loved summers. They gave her more daylight to get chores done. Before long, it would be dark by five o'clock; she'd be bookending her days with work by electric light. Even her animals seemed to feel less energetic as fall arrived, perhaps sensing the arrival of another cold, snow-covered winter.

The bell over the café door jangled cheerily again. Verity looked up to see Chaundra in leggy blue jeans and a jeans jacket decorated with tiny seed pearls and beads, sequins, and hand-painted images that reminded her of Native American symbols. Clasped around her throat was a chunky turquoise beaded necklace.

"Oooo!" Verity breathed, suddenly wide awake. "I love your jacket—and jewelry!"

Chaundra performed a fashion-model twirl. "I have Sunny to thank. She tipped me off to a crafter she knows in Putney. The woman recently moved from New Mexico. After one look at her stuff, I asked her if she'd like to join my vendors. Told her I had a free booth just waiting for her at the Emporium. She creates original Southwestern jewelry and wearable art."

"Spectacular!" Sunny examined the jacket's beadwork with her fingertips.

"And don't *you* look all dressed up!" Verity said when she noticed Martha in a navy-blue wool coatdress, standing back as though waiting to be noticed. "Have you come from somewhere special?"

In fact, Verity had rarely seen the kindergarten teacher wearing makeup, much less a dress that wasn't washable denim or corduroy. She supposed that anyone teaching kindergarteners soon learned to wear indestructible clothing. The kind that didn't matter if it became spattered with finger paint, glue, applesauce or snot.

Martha stepped toward the tables and shrugged as if the compliment was barely worth responding to. But the corners of her lips tugged ever so slightly upward into a suggestion of a smile. "Nowhere special, no. I just don't usually fuss over my appearance the way some people do."

"Of course," Verity said. Was she referring to someone she knew? Elvira? Chaundra? "You just look nice, that's all."

Unfortunately, as Martha came closer to the tables, Verity could see how heavily her makeup had been applied. She might have slathered it on with a butter knife. *Poor thing*, Verity thought, *she just doesn't know how to do it*. She wondered if Martha would allow one of her friends to coach her.

Verity was a minimalist, where makeup was concerned—a little tinted sunscreen or nothing at all. The cows never complained when she greeted them in the morning with a naked face. Sunny's makeup always looked flawless and subtle. Maybe she'd ask her to take Martha aside and provide a few tips.

"Alright, everyone," Denise said, clapping her hands loudly to get their attention. "Time to get to work. Verity has brought all Elvira's diaries. If you haven't already chosen one, now is the time."

Martha scowled. "You mean you didn't wait to choose until all of us were here? That's not fair. MB, Chaundra, and I only have the leftovers to pick from."

"Really, Martha? Does it matter?" Denise groaned.

"We'll each report to the rest of the group anything that we think is important, so you won't miss anything." Verity tried not to let her irritation show. She didn't want the evening to spiral into a competition over who got to discover the juiciest moments in Elvira's life.

"Is there special one you want, Martha?" Fumiko asked gently.

"We're all looking for the same thing," Denise reminded them with clipped impatience. "Clues that will help explain what happened to Elvira the night she jum—" Sunny flashed her a warning look. "—uh, passed away."

"And who might have wanted to harm her," Verity added.

"Or why she didn't want to go on living," Kate whispered.

"Alright, yes, all of that," Sunny agreed. "So, let's get started."

"Come on, Martha," Verity coaxed. "We'll put all the diaries back into the center of the table if it's important to you. You can even choose first. Do you know which one you want?"

Martha hesitated as if she'd been asked a trick question. "Well, um, I had hoped to read about her college years and just after graduation."

Verity reached for a distinctive leather-bound book with hand-tooled decorations on the cover, one of the diaries she had started reading the previous night. She handed it across the table. "It's yours, Martha. Enjoy."

The teacher's eyes glowed in anticipation. "Oh, I'm sure I will." Apparently satisfied, she immediately plopped down onto the nearest chair, scooped a handful of pretzels onto a napkin and stuck her nose into the book. Verity had to smile at the woman's enraptured concentration.

"Choose your prize, everyone." Verity made a sweeping gesture toward the remaining journals, á la Vanna White.

"What *exactly* are we looking for? You said clues. But what kinds of clues?" Mary Beth waved plump fingers in the air like confused butterflies. "I still don't understand what we're supposed to be doing. I mean, I'm not even sure we *should* be doing this. I told the mayor, and he said we had no business snooping into Elvira's personal correspondence. Diaries are meant to be private. Well, aren't they?"

Kate wrinkled her nose and sighed. "She may have a point."

"We will honor Elvira's privacy. Nothing we discover in her journals will leave this group," Verity stated firmly. "If there's any chance that Elvira didn't commit suicide, her family will want to know. And if someone made her fall, either intentionally or by accident—shouldn't the law decide if they are guilty of murder or manslaughter or, I don't know, just carelessness? I just don't like the way the sheriff and coroner, without doing a lick of real investigating, decided she must have ended her own life!"

Denise tossed a palmful of nuts into her mouth, chewed and quickly swallowed. "Besides, if Elvira was murdered, no way would she want her killer to go free."

"If it were me, I'd sure want the truth to come out," Sunny said.

"O-o-oh, I don't kno-o-ow," Mary Beth moaned. "I don't want to get in trouble."

Fumiko squinted, scanning the room as if checking for assassins lurking beneath tables. "If killer not caught, killer kill again. No?"

"Oh my goodness, don't say that!" Kate shuddered and wrapped her arms around herself.

"But what if Fumiko is right?" Chaundra in a much calmer voice. "We can't let a murderer run free to hurt others. Look at what happened to our favorite dairy farmer." She nodded toward Verity. "Whoever broke into her house might be connected in some way to Elvira's death."

"Verity dear, do you really think Elvira might have been murdered?" Sunny asked.

Verity shook her head. "Let's just say it's beginning to appear less like suicide or even just a really unfortunate accident. I've never believed she intentionally killed herself, and now I'm having a hard time imagining Elvira simply falling into that quarry without...well, without help." She sighed, feeling a bit sick at the thought. "Elvira once bragged that she could weave her way through a busy construction site on 4-inch heels while juggling cell phone, clipboard, and contracts—and never even turn her ankle."

"I remember her saying that, too." Denise smiled. "We used

to run together some mornings before I opened my shop and she left for her office. We'd talk the whole three miles. She had some amazing stories about her business. It's funny but I don't think she ever doubted herself. Everything was Elvira's way or no way."

"Oh, Denise—" Sunny began.

"Seriously. I don't mean it in a bad way. She set a goal for herself and stuck to it, no matter what. I admired her. She wasn't swayed by what others thought. She never backed down. You could see that aggressiveness in the way she ran, too." Denise's short red hair appeared electrified. "I agree with Verity. Stumbling into the quarry? No way! I can see that happening to a klutz like Katie or Martha, sure. But not to Elvira."

Kate shrugged. "She's right. I trip over my own feet. Constantly."

Martha didn't even look up from her reading.

Sunny took over. "It sounds as if most of us feel we should at least try to look into our friend's death since the sheriff isn't. If anyone is uncomfortable doing a little investigating, they can leave now and no one will think any less of them. I promise. We're all friends here." She smiled. And waited.

No one moved.

"I'm staying," Kate said softly.

"Me, too." Mary Beth leaned back in her chair, arms crossed. "I don't have to agree with everything the mayor says, even if he is my husband."

"Atta girl!" Denise boomed.

One after another, they all nodded their assent. It was unanimous.

"Good." Sunny rubbed the bridge of her nose, looking relieved but a little tired. "Verity dear, is there anything you want to add, since you've already gotten a peek at some of the diaries?"

Verity's gaze wandered wistfully across the room toward the glass display case of pastries. They looked a lot more scrumptious than pretzels and nuts. Although Denise's chocolates weren't anything to sneeze at. She regretfully blinked away the image of a glazed bear claw. After all, they were here to work.

"Yes, actually. Although I don't know whether it's important." She blew a strand of hair from over her eyes. "In her earliest diaries, Elvira mentions classmates, friends and family members by name. But as soon as she left high school, she switched to using initials or codenames."

"Whoa. How mysterious is that!" Kate cried.

Sunny frowned. "I wonder why."

"To protect the innocent?" Mary Beth stared at the book in her hand.

"Or the guilty." Denise chuckled.

Chaundra leaned in across the table. "Maybe Elvira was afraid that someone she wrote about would get hold of her diary and read what she thought of them."

Verity recalled several entries that had been particularly harsh. "I came across some things she wrote about people close to her that definitely seemed cold or even hurtful."

"Sorta like the way she acted?" Mary Beth said, and Verity couldn't help thinking about the way Elvira had treated their plump friend at the farmhouse.

Sunny pursed her lips. "Exactly. If she was trash talking people in her diaries, she would definitely want to keep what she wrote to herself."

"I think it was even worse than just talk," Verity said slowly. "If what I've already read is true—not an exaggeration or stories she made up for her own entertainment—Elvira used people to get what she wanted."

"Ah," Fumiko made a face, "that not nice."

Martha looked up from the diary open on the table before

her, her expression bland. Verity wished she knew what she was thinking. As close as Martha had been to Elvira's family, by her own admission, maybe she knew something the rest of them weren't aware of.

Of course, others in the group had also known Elvira longer than Verity, the relative newcomer to Evansfield. So, it made sense they might be aware of events or relationships she herself was unaware of. Was it possible her friends were holding back information from her? From each other?

An itchy sensation, like spiders scampering into the short hairs at the back of her neck, made her shiver. Verity squeezed her eyes closed and tried to ignore the spiders. But the sensation didn't go away. It felt a lot like fear.

CHAPTER 24

THE SUPPLY of munchies dwindled over the next two hours as they read. Traffic noise from Main Street faded to an occasional soft rumble as a car or truck passed. The night beyond the café's windows felt like another world. Invisible except for whatever lay within the circles of blue-white light beneath streetlamps.

Anything could be out there, Verity thought. *Or anyone.*

"Who's ready for more coffee?" Sunny chirped, returning to the tables with a steaming pot.

"No amount of caffeine is going to keep this girl awake much longer." Chaundra rubbed her eyes then turned to study Verity's face. "Honey, you look close to falling off your chair. You've had a rough few days. Go home and get some sleep."

Verity pulled herself up straighter in her chair, closed the journal she'd chosen and yawned. "I think the meds Doc Evans gave me are fighting with the coffee." She laughed. "Maybe not a great idea to do codeine and caffeine at the same time."

"I'm going cross-eyed trying to read Elvira's handwriting when she was in seventh grade," Kate groaned. "It's beautiful penmanship, but the letters are so tiny. I don't see how anyone can write that small."

Fumiko leaned across the table to peer at the open pages in front of Kate. "Oooh, so bad for eyes."

"Anyway, I don't see what good this will do," Kate said, "reading about what happened a decade or more ago. How can it have anything to do with her death?"

"I'm with Chaundra," Martha said wearily. "I can't keep this up another minute." She slapped the diary she'd been reading shut, shoved it into her purse and stood up.

Fumiko and Kate also pushed away from the table preparing to get to their feet.

"But we haven't compared notes," Verity objected. "I'd love to call it a night, but don't you think we should share anything important, while it's still fresh in our minds?"

As an example, she told an abbreviated version of the Olive Oyl story, and how Elvira had contrived to steal the young woman's fiancé. Before she had finished, they were all back in their chairs, eyes wide.

"That's just so mean and selfish," Kate commented.

"And you're sure her sexy Slick is Doctor Evans?" Chaundra shook her head in amazement.

"Whether or not John Evans is Slick is beside the point," Sunny said. "The way Elvira used that poor nurse was mean. Cruel, really."

"More than cruel," Martha added darkly. "Evil."

Verity felt suddenly chilled. Evil was the word Percy had used. She looked around the nearly empty café to assure herself the two ghosts weren't hovering nearby. Then again, if they didn't want to be seen, they'd remain invisible.

"Well," she said in summary, "that's the most important takeaway I've discovered while reading. That young nurse certainly had reason to hate Elvira. Although whether she'd ever consider murdering her after all these years seems questionable. Has anyone else come across a possible suspect?"

"I don't know if this is a suspect." Denise tapped her pen on the journal page in front of her. "But maybe, like they say on the news, 'a person of interest?'" Everyone looked at her.

"Well?" Chaundra made a rotating "come-on" gesture with one hand. "Let's have it."

Denise took a deep breath. "So-o-o, I came across something about a girl in Elvira's high school who was badly bullied. Elvira wasn't the only one to pick on her, but our realtor-to-be certainly added to the kid's misery."

"Do you have a name?" Sunny asked.

"Elvira refers to her only as ND. Maybe Nancy Something?"

"Nancy Drew? I'm kidding. Sorry." Kate reddened.

"Bullying can be so damaging, especially at a young age," Mary Beth stated solemnly. "It's like depriving a young tomato plant of light when it's just a seedling. It may never recover, leaving it forever stunted."

Verity smiled. "An interesting comparison, MB." Leave it to the owner of a nursery to analyze human tribulations from the perspective of a plant. "But does social shunning in high school necessarily create a killer decades later?"

"Who knows what turns a person into a murderer," Sunny mused. "Is the desire to murder in the genes or something a person learns? Nature or nurture."

"Now that's deep," Denise teased, digging an elbow into Sunny's ribs. "Anyone else find someone suspicious?"

Chaundra nodded slowly. "I have a journal that Elvira wrote during her early years in the real estate business. So far, I've come across two possible Elvira-enemies."

Verity recognized the volume as one she'd sampled the night of the break-in. She was pretty sure she knew what Chaundra was about to say.

Chaundra continued, her voice strained. "Before Elvira

received her real estate license she was working as a clerical assistant at a Boston realty firm. She sounds determined to move up in the office. When I read this part, it gave me a really creepy feeling."

"This is so suspenseful!" Mary Beth giggled.

"Shut up, you silly woman," Martha snapped. "This is serious."

"Sorry." Mary Beth stared down into her lap.

Chaundra cleared her throat. "It seems an intern in the same office was soon to be licensed and, according to office gossip, he was a shoo-in for the only opening as a full-time agent." Chaundra ran her finger down the page until she found what she was looking for. "Elvira writes: 'I'm not about to sit on my hands while he takes the job that should be mine. I'm ten times smarter than he is!'" Chaundra quirked a meaningful brow. "She goes on to admit that he'd been with the firm much longer than she had and she still needed to finish her real estate courses before she could even apply for her own license. But by then she feared the opening would be filled."

Sunny passed the bowl of remaining truffles. "Go on."

"Elvira started a rumor about the guy, hoping to kill his chances of getting the position." Chaundra looked up from her notes, disapproval in her eyes. "She knew the owner of the firm was biased against homosexuals."

"She outed the poor guy?" Denise gasped.

"Oh. My. God." Kate's eyes widened to doll-size frisbees.

Fumiko just shook her head.

"She doesn't say here whether her co-worker actually was gay," Chaundra pointed out. "I don't think it mattered to her. It was just a way to get under their boss's prejudiced skin."

"So, did he lose his job because of her meddling?" Martha said.

"According to Elvira, the next day the owner accused the

guy of having 'unprofessional conversations in the presence of clients'—whatever that means. His boss claimed the man was giving the agency a bad reputation. Said he had no choice but to let him go. Two months later, Elvira received her license. She moved into the guy's desk and took over clients who would have been his."

"If I were him, I'd sure want to kill her," Denise snarled. "But why wait all this time to get back at her?"

"I know. It doesn't make sense, does it?" Chaundra flipped through her notes to another page she'd marked with an empty sugar packet. "But there are other incidents. A receptionist left the office six months later. I think this time it was a case of pure jealousy on Elvira's part. The young woman had caught the eye of the agency's owner, and he frequently flirted with her. Elvira sounds here—" she poked a finger at the journal page "—as though she resents someone other than herself being considered the most attractive female in the office. She reacted by mentioning the flirtations to the woman's fiancé when he came to pick her up one day. The woman quit the next day."

"How petty is that!" wailed Martha. "And what if the poor thing refused to leave the job she loved? What then? Her boyfriend might have dumped her, that's what!" The school-teacher suddenly seemed overwhelmed by emotion, her eyes brimming with tears as she dug frantically in her purse for a tissue.

"It's ok, Martha," Verity said gently. "We all sympathize with these people."

"Sorry, everyone," Martha apologized, dabbing at her eyes with the tissue. "I don't usually get so emotional over other people's lives. I...I guess I didn't know Elvira as well as I thought I did. How could she do such things?"

"It is rather shocking," Denise agreed. A mischievous glint

crept into her eyes. "Can you imagine what she might have written about us if she'd continued keeping a diary?"

There was a long, weighty silence while that possibility sank in.

What indeed? Verity mused. "Do names ever come up for either of these people, Chaundra—the intern and the receptionist?"

"No. Not even initials. Just stupid nicknames she made up for them. Golden Boy for the intern and Princess Leia for the receptionist." Chaundra threw up her hands in a gesture of futility. "This is a waste of time. How can we possibly track down these people without names?"

"We'll worry about that later. Who's next?" As challenging as putting faces to these stories was, something told Verity they needed to push on. The truth taunted her like an annoying mosquito buzzing in her ear. She couldn't ignore it.

"I have victim...I mean suspect," Fumiko offered. "Sorry. I get confuse."

Sunny patted the top of Fumiko's sleek black head. "It's ok, sweetie. We're all confused at the moment. Go on."

Fumiko blinked at her notes and pinched her bottom lip between tiny, pointed white teeth. "Elvira, she move to larger real estate company. This happen years later, maybe five but still Boston. Big-time agents there. Elvira, she calls business 'blood sport.' Sometimes senior agents, they try push cheap-o houses on her. 'No!' she say. 'F-you!'"

"Because of the low commission on those properties?" Chaundra asked.

"Yes. See?" Fumiko pointed to a page.

Sunny and Chaundra leaned in from opposite sides to read.

"Elvira writes here," Sunny said, "any commission less than five figures isn't worth her time."

"*That* must've ruffled some feathers," Denise hooted, "if a real estate agency is anything like a law office. My father wanted me to study law and join his firm. I used to hang out there on weekends, do some junk like filing. If a junior member of his firm refused the grunt work and took such a high line, they didn't last long."

"Well, I say good for Elvira," Mary Beth stated firmly. "She was standing up for herself in a man's world." Which seemed, to Verity, a very strange remark coming from Mary Beth Loop, whose opinions rarely varied from those of her husband. Mayor Rupert Loop wasn't known as a supporter of women's rights.

"But it's *how* she protected herself, don't you get it?" Sunny said. "She achieved her goals, but often at the expense of others. Like Verity said, she was using people. I know she was our friend. And no one's perfect. But this—" she waved a hand over the journals scattered across the tabletops "—this is very dark stuff. We can't let our loyalty to her stand in the way of uncovering the truth."

"She's right," Kate whispered shyly. Murmured agreements circled the table.

"I guess I'll go next," Verity said, then sensed Martha turn sharply to look at her. "Unless you want to go first, Martha."

The teacher shook her head and held up her notepad. "I took plenty of notes but couldn't find anything to report as suspicious. Guess I pulled the boring book."

"Alright then," Verity paused to gather her thoughts. "Apparently, Elvira left off writing her journals thirteen years ago. This is the last one."

"Unless we haven't found all of them," Sunny interjected.

"Well, yeah." Was it possible Elvira had continued writing to the very end of her life? But if so, where were the other diaries? "But we went through tons of boxes at her house. These were all we found, and they were all in the same place."

"Makes sense for her to keep them together," Martha said. "I would."

"It's getting late. Get on with it, Verity. Most of us have to be at work early," Sunny urged.

"Right. This journal covers the first few years Elvira lived in Evansfield, just after she married John." Verity sensed nervous movement in the room but when she looked up everyone seemed settled and focused on her. "Ummm, in this diary there are lots of codewords for people. No names or initials like before, just crazy nicknames."

Sunny looked around the table. "Some of us were already living here at that time. Maybe we are in there."

"Not Fumiko or Verity," Martha said. "You and your dear Mark only married—was it seven years ago?" She gave Verity a sympathetic smile.

At the mention of Mark's name Verity's throat turned raw and threatened to close. She blinked, ordering her tear ducts to shut down.

Martha's plump hand curled softly over hers on the table.

"I wasn't here either," Chaundra reminded everyone. "I purchased the old Fabric Factory store five years ago."

"That's right, you did, sweetie," Sunny recalled. "You gutted the interior to make room for your studios and sales booths. It just feels as though you've always been part of our community. We're so lucky to have you here."

Chaundra's dark-cocoa complexion glowed with delight at the compliment.

"As I was saying," Verity croaked then cleared her throat, determined to speak even if she did sound like Kermit the Frog. "Several entries refer to a child in her daughter Laura's nursery school class. The girl's mother threw a birthday party for her daughter. Most of the class was invited." She looked up from her notes to meet a circle of curious eyes. "But not Laura."

"Oh, the poor kid," Sunny groaned. "She must have been so disappointed."

"Probably not as much as Elvira was. Little Laura wasn't much more than a toddler. Anyhow, Elvira's reaction was off-the-scale ballistic. She writes: 'No daughter of mine will grow up a social outcast!'"

"I never!" breathed Mary Beth.

"Oh my," whispered Kate.

"What Elvira *do*?" Fumiko asked anxiously.

Verity laughed at the ridiculousness of the realtor's behavior. "She blackmailed the woman into inviting her daughter."

"No!" A chorus erupted from the group.

"Yes," Verity assured them. "She called the birthday girl's mother and told her that by not inviting the entire class she was setting a bad example for the children by picking favorites. And if she didn't immediately correct her error, she, Elvira, would not only be unable to support the woman's election for president of the PTA, she'd make sure no one else would support her."

"Well, that gives a whole new meaning to dirty politics!" Denise laughed.

Verity did not laugh. She rubbed her stinging eyes. Every part of her begged for her bed. The last pain pill she'd taken had worn off hours ago. "We might have a better chance of finding out who that mother is, since the family is local. Anybody have an idea?"

The only response was a lot of head shaking. Verity was sure everyone else was just as brain dead as she was.

Sunny suggested, "Let's call it a night. I think it's safe to say, Elvira has engaged in business and personal relationships that have emotionally or otherwise hurt innocent people."

"Although," Martha added, "most of these took place a long time ago. I can't believe they'd be relevant today."

Denise tossed her head in dismay. "I freakin' can't believe I ran with the woman almost every day, and I never guessed she was this ruthless. I mean, sure I knew she was a wheeler-dealer. She killed at sales and got the better of the good-ole-boy types. Cool! But now...I just don't know. Life sounds like just a game to her."

"It's after midnight," Sunny pointed out. "I say we take our notes and diaries and go home. Think about what we've found. Any one of these provocations might have resulted in long-term hard feelings."

"But murder?" Martha blinked. "I still can't imagine it. If she didn't take her own life, I'm sure it must have been an accident."

"If we can match these codenames with real people," Chaundra proposed, "we may be able to discover if any of these people have recently contacted Elvira. And then we could find out which of them, if any, were near Evansfield at the time of her death."

Verity frowned down at the extensive notes she'd taken while reading and listening to the disclosures of others around the table. Her exhausted mind came up with only one coherent thought: *This list of suspects is going to grow much, much longer.*

Because, it appeared, Elvira Evans was a nasty piece of work.

CHAPTER 25

ALL THE NEXT DAY, Verity labored under a soul-crushing cloud. The routine activities of caring for her garden, home and animals normally had a calming effect on her. But not today. She couldn't stop thinking about the troubling things she'd learned about the woman who had been one of her closest friends.

It was all so disturbing.

Evidently, Elvira Evans had spent much of her life scheming against people who, she believed, stood in the way of her happiness or financial success. This made Verity wonder about recent years. Just because Elvira stopped documenting her exploits, it didn't mean she'd had a change of heart. If a mysterious person had a hand in her death, wasn't it reasonable that this individual was one of the realtor's more recent victims? Even a sane person might act in the heat of the moment. Lash out at Elvira without intending to kill her.

Who had Elvira recently crushed beneath her steel will and spike heels? If there was a murderer, it stood to reason this was the person they should be looking for.

Unable to get all of this wickedness out of her mind, Verity still managed to push through the tasks of her day. She loaded sacks of feed onto the little Bobcat tractor and hauled them out to her chicken runs. She filled the bins in each coop then cast a handful of grain in a wide arc across the ground. Watching her pretty Rhode Island Reds frenzied scampering for the grain, one would think that they hadn't been fed in a month. But her Reds were dedicated foragers, pecking at little grass shoots, gorging on bugs, beetles, and worms throughout the day. Funny little creatures, chickens were. She smiled and clucked at them. They clucked back at her in friendly response. For a moment she was at peace.

As the day wore on, her mind returned to the questions surrounding Elvira's death.

She had read somewhere that the criminally insane were incapable of empathizing with the pain of others. They felt no guilt. Even found pleasure in hurting others. In real life, Elvira sometimes made light of her unkind antics and, in her diaries, she even sounded proud of her cleverness and trickery. But did she actually enjoy her victims' pain? Or was she just oblivious, too self-absorbed to care while wrapped in her cocoon of success?

Although the sheriff had scoffed at the mere idea of murder, it now seemed to Verity a miracle that someone hadn't plotted Elvira's demise sooner. From her teenage years until her recent death at 38, Elvira had made herself richer, pushed herself higher in society, and burnished her ego at the expense of others. In a world where a teenager could be beaten to death in the street over a pair of Air Jordan Retros, why was it so difficult for the sheriff to believe that someone hurt by Elvira had confronted her, resulting in deadly consequences?

Verity just didn't understand him.

By the time she finished her morning chores, violent images had left her in a truly black mood. Yes, she believed in justice.

But what was the point of seeking justice for a woman who cared so little about other people?

Still, there was the issue of closure for Elvira's family. If the death of John's wife, and Peter and Laura's mother, turned out to be just a tragic accident, at least they would know she hadn't willingly left them. The same could be said if she'd been murdered. Knowing the truth was important.

And if it turned out that Elvira really did choose to end her life?

Then I'll know I've done due diligence.

Verity checked in with Jason and Jerry in the milking barn, to make sure they wouldn't need her for the next few hours. They assured her they had everything under control and urged her to go back in the house and rest. But resting wasn't all she had in mind.

She made herself a toasty grilled cheese sandwich on her homemade oat bread. Sliced a crisp red apple. Poured herself a tall, iced tea. Then arranged her lunch on a wooden tray painted with Monet-style golden sunflowers. Carrying the tray, a notepad and pen, and the diary she'd brought home from the café, she walked out the front door of the farmhouse to her sunny front porch.

While she ate, she read more about Elvira's dramatic scheming but was most intrigued by the mysterious Olive Oyl. Of all the people Elvira had run roughshod over, this was the one person from her past that Verity wished she could find and talk to.

But how could she even begin to search for John Evans' former fiancée without more information? Lots more! Elvira and the doctor had met in Boston while he was an intern. That much she knew. Was Boston where Olive Oyl lived? Maybe, still lived? So far, the woman's real name hadn't been mentioned; without a name there seemed little hope of tracking her down. All she knew about the woman came from Elvira's description. She was a nurse, excruciatingly thin and, according to Elvira, not very attractive.

"You should add a sprig of mint to that tea, darlin'," a lilting voice suggested.

Verity jumped. Then sighed. "I don't like mint in my tea, Anna Louise." She looked down at her notes. Useless doodles really. A stick figure of a woman wearing an old-fashioned nurse's cap. Another of a man with a stethoscope around his neck. A third figure in towering heels. Everything she drew looked like the work of a kindergartner. So much for artistic talent.

"Lemon?"

"Go away, Anna Louise," Verity grumbled.

"Oh dear, are we in a sulk?"

"I told you to leave her alone," Percy chided his wife. "She's obviously traumatized. Still recovering from that brutal attack."

"I am not traumatized," Verity insisted. But honestly, her bandaged head still hurt, and she was a little nervous about being alone in the house at night. "I'm just thinking."

"About dead moths and wilted weeds?" Anna Louise murmured sweetly, indicating the sketches on her notebook page with a translucent finger.

"No. About who killed Elvira and why." Verity felt movement in the air then turned her head to see two barely visible forms shimmering behind her. "I wish you two wouldn't do that."

"Do what?" Anna Louise asked.

"Creep up on me like you do."

"I do not creep. I move with southern elegance. Do I not, my love?"

"You do, my dearest. You are the epitome of grace."

Anna Louise gave an extra twinkle of pleasure.

"Well, if you must pester me while invisible, or nearly so, the least you can do is announce yourself. Although, I'd much prefer to see you clearly. This glittery stuff is very distracting."

"Shall we, my dear?" Percy said.

"Hardly seems worth the energy. But if we must."

The two insubstantial clouds that had been hovering near her chair grew decidedly denser until they appeared nearly as solid as a living person.

"What did you and your friends find in the diaries last night?" Anna Louise perched a hip on the arm of Verity's green Adirondack chair. The ghost arranged a bevy of marshmallow-y white skirts around her.

Verity blew out a long breath. "A lot. Too much actually. It seems my dearly departed friend was a bit of a bitch."

"She was a dog?" Anna Louise's confusion might have been amusing had Verity been in a better mood.

"Perhaps a 21st-century aphorism?" Percy guessed.

Verity nodded. "She wasn't a very nice person."

"Oh, I see." Anna Louise lifted a lace shoulder in a delicate shrug.

Verity found herself wondering if there was any way she could borrow one of Anna Louise's frou-frou gowns. Anna Louise seemed capable of conjuring up an unlimited assortment of delicious garments on a whim.

"Have you decided to give up trying to find out who killed the bitch?" Anna Louise asked innocently.

Verity winced, wishing she hadn't called Elvira that. Anna Louise delighted in learning new words but tended to employ them with little restraint. Much like a pet parrot.

"No. I've decided to continue searching for clues. She may have treated people badly at times, but no one deserves to be taken forcibly from their family. My friends and I just want to know the truth behind what happened to her."

"Well, I suppose that only makes sense." Anna Louise tapped her on the arm with one graceful finger. "In your case."

"In my case? What does that mean?"

"Your name. Verity," said Percy. He stood at attention in his handsome Northern blues, saber at his hip. "It means 'truth.' You are a seeker of truth."

She smiled at them. "Funny. I remember my mother telling me that when I was a little girl. I haven't thought about it in a long time."

"Do you know why she chose that name for you?" Anna Louise stood up and waltzed around her chair, humming a song Verity didn't recognize.

Percy looked toward the road as if worried his wife's performance might attract the attention of a passerby.

Verity thought for a minute. "My mom said that names always have meanings. Like beauty, wealth or luck. A name presumes to tell the future or make a promise. But of course, that's impossible. Who can say if a baby will grow up to be beautiful, rich, or attract great luck?"

"Ah, but anyone can seek the truth if they want to," Percy said. "She was a smart lady."

Anna Louise pirouetted the length of the porch, apparently unconcerned with philosophical discussions.

"Yes, she was very wise. I miss her so very much." Verity drew a deep breath. "Enough of this. I need to concentrate. I'm beginning to think I'm just not clever enough to figure out this puzzle."

"I wish *we* were clever enough to understand why we are still here." Percy scowled as he leaned against the porch railing.

"Well, I can't help you with that. Sorry. But maybe you can assist me in finding out who this Olive Oyl is."

"Olive oil?"

"A woman. Spelled O-Y-L."

"I declare! Such a strange name." Anna Louise flicked open a lace-and-ivory fan and twirled to a stop. "I've never heard the likes."

"You wouldn't unless you saw old cartoons. She was Popeye's girlfriend."

"Was he an Evansfield farmer?" Percy said.

This was going to be a challenge. As far as Verity was aware, only political cartoons existed in the 19th century, and those appeared in newspapers and broadbills. TV and motion pictures certainly weren't around back then.

"No," she said, "Popeye and Olive Oyl were cartoon—ah—story characters."

Anna observed Verity with alarm, over the curve of her fan. "You think a story character murdered Elvira?"

Verity closed her eyes and counted to ten. *I can do this!* When she opened her eyes the two ghosts were still staring at her.

"In Elvira's diaries she gave people funny names or used their initials to hide who she was writing about. She called one woman Olive Oyl, because she was very thin like the story character."

"Oh." The ghosts smiled, but Verity still wasn't sure they understood.

"The woman was Dr. John Evans' fiancée, before he met Elvira. Did either of you know his first fiancée?"

They gave each other a blank look. Maybe the young doctor hadn't yet brought Olive to his hometown.

"Why don't you just ask the doctor who she was?" Percy asked.

Verity clipped her pen onto the notepad. "I thought about that. But it seems super insensitive to bother the man. He's still grieving."

"It may be the only way to find out," Percy pointed out.

Oddly enough, Verity thought, this made sense.

"I could help you," Anna Louise offered brightly. "Subtlety, you know, is one of my virtues."

Verity thought she saw Percy roll his eyes.

"I can't let you talk to Dr. Evans. Revealing yourself to him would be a really bad idea."

"Perhaps we might help you in other ways, then you could help us with our problem?"

"You mean, your inability to move on to the other side?" She frowned. "I have no idea how I'd do that."

"We need more information," Percy explained. "The boundaries between the world of the living and the world of the dead are confusing."

"Like all that Mason-Dixon Line nonsense," Anna Louise interrupted. "It's not like people paid much attention to lines drawn on a map." She fanned the air. "Two of my older brothers fought for the South. My youngest brother joined Lincoln's army, much to Papa's disgust." A shadow passed across her pretty face.

"That must have been difficult for your family," Verity said softly. "Dare I ask if they all—"

"Only my middle brother came home." Anna Louise's gaze lowered away from Verity's. "We don't often talk about those days."

"I'm so sorry." Verity whispered.

Percy circled a strong arm around his wife's waist. "It was a long time ago."

Indeed. Over 150 years.

Still, she could only imagine how hard it would be to lose two brothers in one of the bloodiest wars in American history. Maybe you never got over something that dreadful. She was thankful Anna Louise had found her Percy.

Anna Louise touched her fingertips to the moist corners of

her eyes. "You're right, it would be unwise for me to try and talk to the doctor. But I can go with you and whisper in your ear if you're at a loss for words. He won't see or hear me, I promise. I'll just be there to make suggestions, if you need me." She flicked her fan closed and grinned. "That's another of my gifts. I'm *very* good with words."

Verity narrowed her eyes at Anna Louise skeptically. She wasn't at all sure this was a good idea.

CHAPTER 26

OVER THE NEXT FEW DAYS, the farm kept Verity busy. But she kept thinking about the possibility of approaching John Evans and asking about his former fiancée. She also was itching to find out if her friends had any luck tracking down names for victims from Elvira's ignoble past.

Was it fair to call them victims?

True, Elvira hadn't actually *murdered* anyone. But she had left in her wake a trail of emotional and financial damage. The more Verity read and considered the calculated ways by which the woman had taken advantage of others, the angrier with herself she felt. To think she had known Elvira Evans since the day she moved to Evansfield with Mark, and she'd never grasped how truly appalling the woman was!

Verity supposed she had simply modeled her own opinions after the reactions of her Evansfield neighbors. When the flashy, charismatic Elvira behaved most outrageously, people either ignored her or reminded each other of how generous she was with her money. Donating a rumored $50,000 to the Catholic church's organ-restoration fund. Locating and paying for temporary housing for families whose homes were destroyed when

Otter Creek overflowed its banks. Creating an endowment for a new maternity wing at the Central Vermont Regional Hospital.

All well and good, but didn't those donations come from dirty money? Ill-gotten gains from her lies, trickery, and back-stabbing. Maybe her generosity was an attempt to assuage her guilt. If Elvira was even capable of feeling guilty.

On her egg-route day, Verity could hardly wait to start on her deliveries. The perfect opportunity, she thought, to find out if anyone had found a new lead. And a chance for a private talk with John Evans when she dropped off his family's milk and eggs. She had been practicing their imagined conversation.

However, an unexpected scheduling conflict arose at the last moment.

"This morning is simply impossible," Anna Louise told her. "I have a prior commitment."

"You're dead," Verity huffed. "How can you have anything to do but haunt my farmhouse?"

"Our farmhouse," the ghost corrected with a dismissive flick of her beribboned fan. "You need to visit him when I'm free. Asking a man about his love life requires a delicate touch, and you promised I could come to coach you."

Verity dared not ask what this commitment might be. A fitting for a new ethereal gown? A job interview in heaven? Was she getting a mani-pedi? But she finally promised Anna Louise to make her stop at the doctor's home the last on her route so Anna Louise could go with her. After all, the Putnams had summoned help for her after the still-unidentified thief knocked her senseless. She owed them.

Anxious to be off on her route, Verity got busy packing orders into Cade Farm canvas bags. As often happened when late summer nudged into a Vermont fall, the temperature had dropped precipitously overnight. By mid-morning, the sun was making a valiant attempt to warm the air but suddenly disappeared behind ominous ashen clouds. The temperature struggled to make it to 50 degrees, and a biting wind whipped down the river valley from Canada. When the rain started just before Verity was ready to hit the road, it sliced sideways in icy needles, making an umbrella useless.

Unfazed, Verity broke out storm gear from her sailing days. After living in Baltimore for years, her parents had moved to Annapolis, Maryland and lived there until her mother passed away. Like many area families who could afford summer camp for their children, her parents registered her for sailing lessons. Verity learned to navigate a temperamental 14-foot Laser on the Chesapeake Bay—on sunny days or in squalls. Later, in college, she sailed on a race team and loved every minute of it. Fortunately, her well-used Helly Hansen hooded jacket and pants still fit and would keep her dry no matter how vicious the weather.

She checked in with her farmhands to make sure the brothers wouldn't need her for a few hours. Her problem girl, Molly, would have to be satisfied with one of the guys milking her, unless they were more successful at coaxing the obstinate cow into a Robo-Milker than she had been. She backed up her truck to the rear porch of the farmhouse and loaded the bags of eggs, rich cream-topped raw milk, and home-churned butter.

Verity stopped first at Kate's house and let herself in through the rear door. After leaving her dripping outer garments on a hook, she heard Kate call out from the kitchen, "I hope you can stay for coffee and homemade blueberry muffins. Please don't tell me you've already eaten."

"I haven't." Verity stepped through to the sunny yellow kitchen, took one look at Kate and raised a brow at the petite brunette's expression. "Why do you look like the cat that swallowed a canary?"

"Do I? Maybe I'm just glad for time to talk with a friend." Kate's eyes positively glowed. "Or may-be-e-e-e I have news for you." She poured coffee then pulled two flowered dessert plates from her cupboard and set a gorgeous, high-domed muffin on each.

"You've discovered the identity of one of our mystery victims?" Verity split her muffin—moist and overloaded with purply-sweet blueberries—and buttered both halves. She took her first bite and savored its rich gorgeousness.

"Not only that, I *spoke* with him over the phone."

Verity nearly choked on her coffee. "Seriously? You really are a good investigator, Katie. Don't keep me in suspense. What did you find out?"

Kate stirred sugar into her coffee. "Do you remember the young real estate intern in Boston that Elvira spread a rumor about? She called him Golden Boy."

"Of course. She claimed he was gay."

"Right. And no, I didn't ask him if it was true. He volunteered the information. He was...and is. But in no way should that have cost him his job."

"Of course not," Verity agreed. "So, what did he say about Elvira? You told him that she has, ah, passed away?"

"I did, but he already knew." Kate sipped her coffee. "He's no longer living in Boston. Moved to New Hampshire years ago, only about an hour's drive from here. He read her obituary in a local newspaper."

"Interesting," Verity said.

"Anywhooo, he was more than willing to admit he wasn't at all sad to hear of her death. But he claimed he hasn't seen her in years, not since the day he was booted out of the Boston office as a result of her meddling."

Verity dug her little notebook and pen out of her jeans pocket and quickly found the page where she had taken down the details from Kate's earlier report at the café. "Then you must know his name since you somehow got hold of his phone number."

"Oh, yes. He's Gerald Kelly."

Verity had to stop herself from bouncing like Mary Beth. This could be the break they needed to find Elvira's killer! "And when you talked to him, did he sound like someone capable of murder?" She wasn't sure how a killer might reveal their homicidal inclinations through tone of voice. Maybe by an outburst of fury or string of cuss words at the mention of Elvira's name?

"Well," Kate said thoughtfully. "I don't know about his being capable or not. He sounded like a calm and rational guy, although I guess anyone could fake that. But—" she lifted her coffee mug toward her lips then put it back down again without taking a drink "—here's the thing. He's still in real estate—"

From somewhere in the house came an earsplitting shriek then squabbling voices. Kate cast a mother's alert gaze toward the kitchen ceiling, as though she could see through it to the floor above. After a moment of gauging the level of combat overhead she seemed satisfied that no one was injured and returned her attention to adult conversation.

"As I was saying, still in real estate but now he has his own office. *And* he sounds *very* pleased with how business is going."

"So, you're thinking," Verity guessed, "why would Gerald Kelly wait until he becomes successful to kill his tormentor."

"Exactly. But there's more. He was on vacation in Hawaii with his partner on the day Elvira died. They had rented a beach house on Kauai for two weeks."

Visions of coconut palms, pristine white beaches and pina coladas interrupted Verity's thoughts of murder. "Must be nice." She sighed, and gave herself a moment to enjoy an imaginary vacation before forcing herself back to reality. "Well, good work, Kate. At least we've eliminated one potential suspect."

They chatted for a little longer while finishing their muffins. Then Kate's daughters called down to her, begging release from bedroom-cleaning duties.

"I'd better get up there and check their work." Kate pushed away from the table. "Last time they cleaned their room, I found dirty clothes kicked under the bunkbed and months'-old Halloween candy buried in the toybox. I spent hours pulling sticky lollipops off stuffed animal fur."

"I need to go anyway." Verity licked the last delicious crumbs from her fingertips. "Plenty more stops today."

At Martha's house, Verity placed a dozen eggs and quart of milk in the fridge while the teacher went upstairs to fetch her notes. "I'm sure you'll want my report," she sang out, already halfway up the stairs.

Verity wandered into the living room. When she'd visited before, she hadn't paid much attention to the décor because she'd learned then of Elvira's death. Now, she looked around wondering how she hadn't noticed so many things here.

Martha was in her late-ish forties, about ten years older than Elvira. Not a huge difference in their ages, less than a whole generation, but their homes couldn't have been more different. Elvira's taste in furnishings ran to expensive-modern—sleek and minimalist. White and black, with stainless steel and silver-toned accents. The kindergarten teacher's living room over-flowed with a hodgepodge of what appeared to be a mishmash of family hand-me-downs and thrift-store bargains. A thread-bare Persian carpet in murky mauves and browns covered the entire floor. Macrame cords held back swaths of heavy burgundy drapery from the windows. The couch and uphol-stered chairs seemed far too big for the tiny room, as though they had been shifted from a much larger house and crammed in to fit.

To Verity, the room felt claustrophobic. It reminded her of Great Aunt Lucy's dark old Baltimore townhouse. As a child, she had been convinced it was haunted. The irony wasn't lost on her that she now inhabited an actual haunted house.

However, there wasn't a speck of dust anywhere in Martha's living room, and it smelled like a lemon grove. Martha obviously cherished and regularly polished each piece of furniture. Verity's mother had been a bit of a packrat, too. So, she understood the teacher's unwillingness to part with a single item, even if giving away a few things bought her a little more breathing space.

Verity had a different attitude toward housekeeping duties. She gave away anything she wasn't actually using on a regular basis—clothing, kitchen or garden tools, furniture or bric-a-brac. She liked to think of dust bunnies as a decorative touch; her smudgy windowpanes as frosted glass. She *did* clean her house. Really, she did! But daily dusting, vacuuming, and the dreaded window cleaning took a distant place to ensuring the barns and chicken houses were clean and organized. Her animals depended upon her. Their health and welfare were her responsibility. And although she had the twins to help with chores and maintenance, everything ultimately came down to her.

Martha finally returned, shuffling along in slippers like a much older woman with her notepad and a leather-bound diary in hand. Although it was nearing noon, she still wore a fleecy housedress zipped up the front that looked more like a bathrobe than daytime clothes. Verity assumed the casual attire was Martha's norm while on summer vacation from school. After all —why not relax? Frankly, she envied her. Having no schedule, no commitments, seemed pure luxury. When was the last time *she* had stayed in her PJs all day?

Martha's eyes widened at seeing Verity standing in her living room. "Don't you want to sit in the kitchen for coffee?"

"I'd better pass. I've already had two cups." She noticed a framed photograph sitting beside a ring of keys and several pieces of mail on a small oak table. "Your parents?" she asked, pointing.

"Yes." Martha smiled, for an instant looking years younger. "This house was theirs, but most of the furnishings came from my grandparents' home in upstate New York. I grew up here, you know, in Evansfield."

"Oh," Verity said, wondering if Martha thought that living as an adult in her childhood home was a good or a bad thing. Some people treasure their past; others want nothing more than to escape from it.

"I guess I should feel fortunate to have inherited this place. Not many single teachers these days can afford to purchase a house on their salary."

"It's very, ummm, sweet," Verity said, while thinking "depressing." "So, tell me about your investigations."

"Oh yes!" Martha immediately brightened. "This is so very thrilling. Come on back into the kitchen and sit with me." She seized Verity by the hand and dragged her into the kitchen. "Sit," she ordered, sounding exactly like a kindergarten teacher addressing her class.

Verity obediently sat. A thought nicked at her mind but was immediately gone as soon as Martha spoke again.

"I think I may have a lead on a suspect." She moved a chair closer to Verity's and plopped down in it, bunching her fleece tent around her. "Oh my, don't I just sound like one of those CSI actors on TV?" She giggled, then looked stunned at the sound. Martha wasn't the giggling type.

"Go on," Verity prompted, grinning at the woman's inability to contain her enthusiasm.

"Well, alright. I have verified one fact you mentioned in the café the other night. Elvira had a string of lovers. Shameful really." She made a tut-tut sound with her tongue. "I found remarks about two of her romantic interests in the volume I'm reading. She was dating both men at the same time, and I don't think either gentleman knew about the other."

Verity made a silent 'O' with her lips. "You think she was playing them off against each other?" she asked. Martha nodded. "Why?"

Martha threw up her hands as if to say, "Who knows!" "Her entries were vague, to be sure, but they implied rather strongly that she was seriously considering marrying whichever one of them proposed first. So long as he was able to provide her with a sufficiently elevated lifestyle." Martha cleared her throat, as though in preparation for a dramatic finale to her discovery. "MH, as she referred to him, was Melville Hunt, according to my research. He is the great-grandson of Henry Hunt and heir to a canning-industry business that's worth millions. Elvira must have drooled over the prospect of marrying into *that* family."

Verity thought for a moment. "Did he propose to her?"

"He did. But she soon turned him down." Martha flipped through the diary then slid her finger down the page until she reached the spot she was looking for. "The only reason she gave was, and I quote: 'Guess he wasn't as well-endowed as he led me to believe.'"

Verity giggled. "So, either his inheritance turned out to be far less than she'd assumed, or once she saw him with his clothes off, she couldn't bear sleeping with him." She wiggled an eyebrow. "Well endowed?"

Martha shot her a stern look. "Verity, please! This isn't a joke."

"Sorry. So why should we suspect Mr. Hunt of wanting to kill her?"

"Isn't it obvious? She dumped the man, and he was quite upset." Martha shot her a don't-you-get-it glare. "He *cried*, Verity. I'm not making this up. Elvira wrote that he telephoned her constantly, sobbing. In her words, 'the man wept like a little boy who doesn't get his way.'"

"Oh, dear." Verity leaned back and let this discovery sink in. *The poor guy.* But then it struck her. "Why would a man with so much at stake—his reputation and at least a modest inheritance—risk going to jail to knock off an old flame years after they split?"

"Oh." Martha looked deflated. "I see what you mean. But he might have hired someone to do it."

"That still doesn't seem logical. Too much time has passed. Who else do you have?"

Martha blew out a long breath and searched her notes. "There is this other fella. No initials this time. Elvira called him Mr. Whiskers."

"Oh, gosh!" Verity couldn't stop a laugh from bubbling up. "That sounds like something you'd name a cat."

Martha shook her head solemnly. "I think it was her way of poking fun at him. His real name was Anthony Savage. And he was a senior partner in the Boston law firm where she worked as an intern one summer— Clough, Savage, & White. I looked them up and called. Sure enough, one of the law clerks who has been there a long time remembers Elvira. She also remembers that Mr. Savage and Elvira were *very, very* close."

"And I'll bet partners in law firms usually don't get chummy with their junior interns unless—"

"Precisely," Martha cut her off before she could add anything more descriptive about what an older man might want from a beautiful young woman. "Elvira must have been only nineteen or twenty. He, on the other hand, was no spring chicken. She mentions his gray hair and beard."

"Thus, the nickname, Mr. Whiskers?"

Martha shrugged. "I suppose."

"And why do you suspect him?"

Martha's smile was almost wicked. "Because their breakup makes her dumping the canning heir sound like a child's birthday party. This man wasn't just hurt, Verity. He was furious with her. According to her entries, Mr. Savage threatened her. Warned her that he'd come after her if she tried to leave him. 'You can't hide from me!' That sort of awful male bluster." Martha looked up from her notes to meet Verity's eyes. "I believe she was really frightened. She seriously thought her life was in danger."

Verity sucked in a breath. "Oh my God! That's terrible."

"Elvira was playing with fire." Martha might as well have said, "She deserved it, didn't she?"

"Of course, she was. But again there's the problem with timing. Why would any man wait almost two decades to make good his threats? Did you find out anything else about him, Martha? Like, does he have a criminal record? A history of violence toward women? Anything that might prove he was so emotionally unstable he might track her down, after all this time, with the intent to harm her?"

Martha squinted at her, as if stupefied. "This isn't enough? She *dumped* him, Verity. She made fun of the man. Mr. Whiskers! Lord above, how cruel is that! And he threatened her."

"Yes, but we've already established that was ages ago. And we have only Elvira's entry here—" she tapped the diary in Martha's hands with one finger "—claiming that he reacted badly and might be dangerous. I wonder if she mentions him in later volumes. Continuing threats over the years, phone calls or face-to-face confrontations with him."

Martha tossed the diary on the table and stared dejectedly at it.

Verity reached over and touched her on the shoulder. "You did a great job. Really. Don't feel as though you've wasted your time. It's just as helpful to eliminate suspects." Maybe she'd been too quick to squash the teacher's discoveries. Martha seemed truly hurt by her criticism. "Listen, I think these two guys cry out for more research. Remember, we can't be sure how much of what she writes is true. You know Elvira always had a flair for the dramatic."

"True." Martha's eyes remained downcast.

"And we all know how charming Elvira could be when she wanted something. She could talk her way out of any situation. She may have found a way to diffuse Savage's anger, back at the time when all of this was happening." Another thought struck her. "Do we know how old he is now?"

Martha looked up, eyes widening. "I hadn't thought of that. Let's see, if he was at least fifty back then—considering the gray hair—then around twenty years later...hmmm. He could easily be in his seventies by now."

"And Elvira was a physically fit and tough woman of thirty-eight when she died. Is there any chance he could have over-powered her?"

"Probably not. But you never know," Martha added hopefully.

Verity glanced at her watch. "Oh no, I need to get moving. Thank you, Martha, for doing such a good job tracking down these two men. Just finding their names is amazing."

"I'll keep on reading," Martha murmured with a weak smile. "I'm only halfway through this volume. There may be other possibilities, I guess."

"That's the spirit!" Verity stepped into her rain pants and pulled them up over her jeans. Martha held Verity's storm coat open for her to stick in her arms. Verity imagined the kinder-garten teacher providing the same assistance for her little students before letting them out on the school playground.

"If this isn't enough for the sheriff to consider these men as suspects, what do I have to do?" Martha grouched. "Get a full confession?" Her improved mood apparently hadn't lasted long.

"Of course not," Verity soothed. "But if we want to take our suspicions to the sheriff and get him to reopen Elvira's case as anything other than a suicide, we need real proof. Solid physical evidence. Not just hearsay from a diary."

Martha made a pouty face.

"If you feel uncomfortable carrying on," Verity suggested, "you can give me your diary and I'll finish reading it." In fact, she was beginning to wonder if the diaries would ever give them a suspect worthy of serious consideration.

Martha fell back a step, shaking her head. "No, no," she said quickly. "I'm sorry to make such a fuss. I'm not a slacker. I'll do it. It really is my responsibility."

"You're sure you won't find it too distressing to do a little more digging?"

"I'll be fine," Martha assured her. "I want to do my part. Really I do."

CHAPTER 27

VERITY STOPPED NEXT at Fumiko's yarn shop, Knit One Purl, then at Mary Beth's house. Unfortunately, neither of them had useful information to share.

After completing her other deliveries, except for the Evans family's order, Verity stopped at the Cat's Cradle. She waited five minutes while Sunny finished boxing an order for a customer and instructed her assistant to take over while she took a break. Chaundra came in and joined them at their usual table in the bay window's alcove. Verity shared Kate's and Martha's recent reports with them.

Chaundra listened intently and asked a few questions, but Sunny seemed distracted, her gaze constantly roaming the café, as if she had trouble focusing on what Verity was saying.

"Is something wrong?" Verity asked.

"Maybe." Sunny made a face. "Or not. It's just that...I don't know. I was getting kind of ugly vibes while we were reading last night."

"How so?" Chaundra asked.

"The dates of the journal that I'm reading were about seventeen years ago. Most of Elvira's entries are about the doctor she referred to as either Slick or JE."

"I think we pretty much agree that has to be John Evans," Chaundra said. "It's too much of a coincidence otherwise."

Verity nodded in agreement. "For Elvira to have become involved romantically with two doctors both of whose initials are JE—well, that's about as likely as my finding a pearl in one of my chickens' eggs."

"Right!" Sunny laughed. "But here's what's really strange. I've kept on reading and something very different was happening in Elvira's life. She sounds terribly upset. Heartbroken."

"Why? What happened?"

"She doesn't say, exactly." Sunny folded her hands on top of the table and frowned. "She writes that she hasn't slept, isn't eating, cries herself to sleep every night. She complains that she is prettier, smarter, and a much better match for Slick than Olive Oyl. And then she stops writing entirely."

"Whoa! That sounds like her plans for him fell through," Chaundra said.

"Right. And here's what I think," Sunny continued. "Although she never comes right out and says it, I suspect she gave her young doctor an ultimatum. Choose one of us—her or me!"

"And he chose his fiancée?" Verity studied the paper napkin she'd mindlessly folded into an origami bird. Or maybe it was a dog. She looked up at her two friends. "That's why she must have been in such a state. She'd gambled and lost."

"It makes sense." Sunny watched as a young couple came through the café door and was greeted by her helper Amanda.

"But how can that be?" Verity said. "We know that Elvira and John married. If he chose the nurse, what happened to her?"

Sunny threw up her hands and leaned back from the table. "I don't have a clue. There's no explanation and no further mention of Olive Oyl. She disappears from the diary. When Elvira begins writing again, months later, she's bragging about her diamond engagement ring."

Verity's mouth dropped open. She stared at Sunny, then Chaundra. Were they thinking what she was thinking? Was it possible that Elvira somehow got rid of her competition all those years ago? Not by killing her, of course, but she was clever at getting her way. If she somehow manipulated John Evans into marrying her, might he have regretted his decision years later? Did he also feel guilty for whatever happened to the nurse he'd loved?

Sunny lowered her voice to a more intimate volume. "Do you think we should consider the doc a suspect in his wife's murder?"

Verity stared at the napkin that now lay on the table in shreds near her fingertips. She couldn't recall dismembering whatever creature it had been. "We can't eliminate a person from suspicion just because we like them. It's not our job. So, I guess the answer is yes. He's a suspect."

"It's not our job to capture a killer either," Chaundra pointed out. "I'm beginning to think we're in way over our heads. What if John Evans actually did kill his wife? If we are the ones who finger him—"

"Finger him?" Sunny yipped. "What 1930's movie did you get that from?"

Chaundra waved her off. "You know what I mean."

Verity felt torn at the thought of any physician being capable of murder. Didn't they take an oath to "do no harm?" Doctors were trained to *save* lives. Then again, that same education also made them aware of how lives might be intentionally ended.

"Ok. He's a possible suspect," Sunny decided for them. "Verity's right. We can't eliminate the man just because he's a neighbor and our local physician. Plus—" she held up a finger to emphasize her point "—on true-crime shows, they say that murder victims often know their killer. It's a spouse, partner or other family member. And the police always question them first."

Oh God! Verity shook her head, feeling miserable. John had always seemed like such a lovely man.

No one said a thing for long, uncomfortable minutes.

Finally, Chaundra broke the silence. "If we're including people closest to Elvira—" she clicked her long, glossy red nails on the tabletop "—I'd say *we* need to be included. Don't you think?" She looked at Verity then Sunny for confirmation.

Sunny winced. "Come on now. Seriously? None of us ever would have hurt her, Chaundra. You know that!" But there was more weariness than conviction in her voice.

"Not intentionally, I'm sure," Verity added. *One of us, a killer?* It was just too horrid to contemplate. She wedged her hands under her denim-covered thighs to stop herself from further demolition of napkins.

"Ok. Fine," Chaundra allowed. "Her killer doesn't have to be one of us. I hope it isn't. But wouldn't it make more sense for someone in her recent life to react violently after being provoked by her?"

"I hate to say it, but she's right," Verity whispered. She'd removed her bandages and been headache-free for days, but now her head was throbbing again. She leaned her elbows on the bistro table and massaged her temples. "But then everyone in this town should be considered a suspect. I doubt anyone in Evansfield has escaped a lashing from Elvira's sharp tongue."

And just like that, the cheery little café felt a lot less friendly. Or safe.

CHAPTER 28

VERITY SAT IN HER TRUCK, outside the home and medical office of Dr. John Evans. She did not get out. She was too busy arguing with herself. She felt as though she had become stuck in a revolving door. Round and round her thoughts went, going nowhere. Nothing made sense since the night Elvira died.

She had promised Chaundra, Sunny, and herself that she'd interview the Evans family. But asking the questions she needed to ask just felt wrong. She thumped the heels of her hands on the Ridgeline's steering wheel in frustration.

"I can't do-o-o this!" she moaned.

Unfortunately, learning what happened to the woman formerly known as Olive Oyl seemed a critical key to understanding John and Elvira's past. Verity didn't really believe the doctor was capable of intentionally killing anyone, let alone his wife. Yet she understood how crazy Elvira could make a person. She couldn't imagine living with her! Just the idea spiked her blood pressure.

She stared through the windshield at the steel-gray sky. Silver droplets raced in chilly rivulets down the glass. It had rained all day, showing no sign of stopping. The weather didn't do her mood any good.

Verity slowly became aware of a presence hovering over the passenger seat next to her. She hadn't heard the door on that side of the truck open. Could ghosts really pass through solid steel?

"So good of you to finally join me," Verity muttered. "Cleared your social calendar, did you?"

"My-oh-my, Miss Verity! You *are* in a tither," Anna Louise sighed. "I take it you're not looking forward to our chat with the good doctor?"

Verity tried not to snarl. "I am not."

"Even if this is the only way you'll find out who your Olive Oyl is? The doctor's spurned fiancée surely must be a prime susperson."

"Suspect," Verity corrected. She just wished she hadn't allowed Anna Louise to come along, although she had to admit she needed emotional support. But Sunny was short-handed at the café, so she wasn't available. And Chaundra had to head back to the emporium to relieve her assistant.

"Now, darlin'," Anna Louise coaxed, "puttin' off a chore won't get it done."

Verity sat glued to the driver's seat. Her finger itched to hit the ignition button. If she simply drove off, who would know? She could just say she'd talked to the doctor but found out nothing new.

She startled when the door beside her swung open, spilling a gust of cold mist onto her face. Something whacked her on the shoulder. Hard!

"Oh, alright, you don't have to get physical," Verity complained. "You're turning into Denise. That hurt!"

Anna Louise giggled. "I should have made Percy come along and carry you to the door."

"He could do that? I mean, I'm sure he was strong enough when he was, like, alive but —" She found the complicated rules of the non-living even more confusing than the two ghosts did.

"You'd be surprised what a ghost can do when he puts a mind to it."

"I don't even want to think about it," she murmured.

Verity dragged herself up the flagstone path toward the house in her dripping rain gear, the family's order of milk and eggs secure in the canvas sacks looped over her shoulders. She hated the very idea of asking personal questions of a man who was mourning the loss of his wife. It seemed beyond rude. Cruel really. But real detectives and investigative journalists asked tough questions to get to the truth. And the truth was important to her.

Get a grip, Verity. You can do this!

Resigned to her fate, Verity forced herself forward, back to rehearsing what she would say, step by soggy step. By the time she reached the rear door of the house she felt only a little less wretched. At least she had what passed for a practiced speech. And she was expected.

Verity had phoned Evans' house before leaving on her delivery rounds that day. Her hope had been that she could avoid having to face John by asking her questions over the phone. At a safe distance. Admittedly, it was the chicken's way out. If he refused to answer her and hung up—well, that wouldn't be so horrible, would it? At least she would have fulfilled her promise to the group by trying.

Alas, the home line automatically rang over to his office phone, and his receptionist answered. When Verity asked if the doctor could come to the phone to answer a quick question unrelated to her health, his receptionist Cindy said, "Not at this moment, dear. He's chockablock with flu cases. Come on by later in the day. I'll pull him out between patients to speak with you."

And so, in pursuit of Plan B, Verity pressed the button on the intercom beside the rear door, announced herself, and waited. The rain suddenly stopped. Perhaps a good omen? She pulled down her hood and shook herself like a wet dog. She could neither see nor hear Anna Louise now, not even a glimmer. She wondered if the ghost had changed her mind about venturing inside.

Good, she thought. She was beginning to feel more nervous with the ghost's so-called support than without it.

Cindy's sing-song voice called out through the intercom. "Come straight through, Verity. Your timing's perfect. His next appointment is running late."

Which meant John might have time for more than a hit-and-run question. He might demand to know why she thought it was her business to poke her nose into his personal affairs. He might even complain to the sheriff about her questioning him. *Oh, crap!*

"Relax, darlin'," Anna Louise whispered in her ear, making her jump. "Everythin' will be fine. You'll see."

"Like you would know." Verity glanced longingly back toward her truck. It wasn't too late to change her mind and make good her escape. Something whacked her between her shoulder blades. "Hey! What's that for?"

"Stop stallin'. Move!"

Who knew ghosts could be so bossy? Verity stepped in through the door and hung her wet jacket on a hook in the dim entryway. She set the canvas bag on the steps leading up to the kitchen, planning to put the family's order in the refrigerator on her way out.

She opened the door into the reception area. Tidy and bright, it provided just enough space for Cindy's desk, two upholstered chairs for patients—presently unoccupied—and a narrow table wedged between the chairs, amply supplied with magazines.

Verity nodded a greeting to Cindy, who was talking softly on the phone, and sat down to wait. Five minutes later, Annabelle Guest breezed through the door leading out from the examination rooms.

"Morning, Verity. I hope you're not feeling poorly."

"Oh no, Mrs. Guest, not at all. Just a routine visit," she improvised.

"Oh good. I expect I'll see you Sunday in church?" She patted her gray permed hair, as though already on her way into the service.

"Absolutely," Verity assured her.

John Evans stepped into the waiting room a moment later. He wore a blue button-down shirt, the collar casually open, and navy chinos. His easy-going attire made him seem less intimidating than if he'd opted for a traditional white lab coat. His smile was, as always, kind and reassuring. His recent bereavement showed mostly in his eyes, which seemed a bit sunken, the tiny red capillaries across the whites a little more obvious than she remembered from earlier times. Not a lot of improvement since Elvira's funeral.

"Good morning, Mrs. Cade. Cindy tells me you need a word?"

"Yes, yes I do," she said breathlessly but couldn't seem to make her body lift out of the chair.

"Come on in. Cindy, could you give Raymond a ring and make sure he's on his way?"

Verity reluctantly pushed herself to her feet and moved at a death-march toward the door he held open for her. "Thank you, Dr. Evans," she murmured in passing.

She wanted nothing more than to turn around, race back

out the door and across the soggy yard to her truck. But her friends were taking their assignments seriously. Just as Martha had promised to do her part, so should she.

The doctor waved her through another door on her right. The small consultation room with pale green walls held only the basics of a medical practice—desk, computer, two chairs, three-drawer filing cabinet, a light box on the wall for studying x-rays, wall charts displaying the human anatomy. He waited for her to sit. Leaving the door open, he leaned one hip on the front corner of his desk and looked down at her.

She was struck again by how handsome a man he was. A perfect physical match for Elvira. They had made a truly stunning couple. However, their personalities were polar opposites. He exuded warmth, compassion, a desire to help and heal. Elvira—well, as Verity was learning, the successful business-woman hadn't understood the meaning of compassion. Elvira looked after Elvira, and the rest of the world be damned.

On the night she died, did the doctor's wife foresee the danger she was in? Had she finally crossed the wrong person?

Verity surfaced out of the muddy waters of her grim thoughts to realize John Evans had been speaking to her. "Sorry, doctor. What were you saying?"

He tipped his head and looked at her a little strangely. "I said, I don't think I've thanked you enough for all you've done for my family in recent days."

A nervous laugh escaped her. "Oh, bringing your dairy order is noth—"

"I meant—the massive job of sorting through my wife's things and delivering the donations to appropriate charities."

"Oh, it was my pleasure." *Wrong word. Pleasure?* Who in their right mind would call packing away a deceased person's clothing fun? "I had lots of help," she added quickly.

He checked his watch then lifted a cupped hand toward

her. "Well then, Verity, how may I help you? You told Cindy this visit isn't related to your health."

"Right. Yes." Verity looked around and felt a moment's relief when she saw nothing to indicate Anna Louise had followed her into the room.

"The last time I was at your house," she began, "the sheriff came to, ummm, tell you..." She could see from his solemn expression that she didn't need to finish the sentence. "Anyway, I overheard you express your belief that Elvira would never have committed suicide."

"Yes." His body language altered subtly, becoming less relaxed. "I certainly hadn't foreseen her decision. But both the sheriff and coroner are satisfied with their conclusion. You sound, Mrs. Cade, as though you're still unconvinced."

"I'm not the only one. Others of Elvira's closest friends are having a very hard time accepting—"

"It's always difficult to accept the death of someone dear to us," he interrupted gently. "We naturally want to deny the end of a life that was once so vibrant. We were all shocked by my wife's actions."

Verity shook her head. "It's more than shock or denial," she said firmly. "I have proof...well, not actual proof yet but suspicious information that—"

"Mrs. Cade, that's enough." A flush crept across his face. "You're looking for an explanation where none exists."

"Doctor, please. You knew Elvira better than anyone. She wasn't a woman to willingly choose death over the life she shared with her family and community. To think otherwise isn't logical."

Something pinched her arm.

"His fiancée!" Anna Louise hissed in her ear. "Ask about his —" Verity slapped her hand over her right ear.

A sharp elbow jabbed her in the ribs. Verity bit her lip to

stop herself from squeaking in protest. This wasn't coaching, it was abuse!

"The point I'm trying to make," she said, "is that we believe someone might have held a grudge against Elvira. Well, more than a grudge. Let's say, a serious resentment because of something she said or did to them. If their bitterness turned violent—"

"You're saying you think someone *murdered* my wife?" He pushed himself away from the desk and stood staring down at her.

"Yes. Yes, that's exactly what I'm saying. It's at least a strong possibility that shouldn't be ignored. Not to speak ill of the dead, but we all know Elvira could be more than a little harsh."

"Of course, but murder?" He shook his head. "We all search for explanations of events we don't understand. I've questioned in my own mind the events of that night. When I heard Elvira rushing out the door, why didn't I ask her what was going on? Why didn't I follow her outside? The simple answer is, I was exhausted and didn't want to get out of my damn bed. But I need to put all those questions, and the guilt, behind me. If for no other reason than for my children's sake."

"Of course," Verity said meekly, standing up to leave.

But as soon as she did, strong hands pressed down on her shoulders from behind her.

"Oh, alright, don't be so pushy!" Only when she saw the surprised look on the doctor's face did she realize she had spoken out loud.

"I beg your pardon?" Now he was studying her with a clinical eye she found unnerving.

"Just talking to myself. Sorry." She steeled herself to complete the task she'd come to do. "Please, I need to ask you just one important question."

"Go on," the doctor said with a weary sigh.

"In Elvira's diaries, she mentions you were engaged before you married her. What was the woman's name?"

"What?" He glared at her. "My personal life is not your concern."

"I know. But it may be important. Please, can you tell me her name?"

The doctor's eyes darkened in a most alarming way. His lips pressed into a hard line, making them nearly invisible in his flushed face. "*That*, Mrs. Cade, is a *most* inappropriate question."

"I'm so, so sorry," she stammered. "But you see, we are considering all possible suspects from Elvira's past including Oli—" Oh God! She'd nearly said Olive Oyl! "—including the woman who once believed she would marry you. You see, we think that would give her quite a strong motive—"

"Suspects? A motive? This isn't a game of Clue, Mrs. Cade!"

"N-no, of course not. But if we could just talk to her and eliminate her as—"

"This is ridiculous!" he bellowed.

Verity was sure she had never seen a human face turn that particular shade of puce.

For some reason, she couldn't cease jabbering. Words spewed from her mouth as unstoppable as lava from a volcano. "Honestly, we j-just want to talk to her. In the most tactful way. Please, John...Doctor. If you can help me to contact her, I promise we'll be ever so p-polite."

The man's complexion grayed from its virulent hue to the color of wet cement. "Absolutely not! I most certainly won't give you and your busy-body friends the name of anyone I've dated." He flung an arm toward the door. "I'll thank you to leave. *Immediately*. And please let your friends know I don't appreciate them sticking their noses into my family's affairs."

"I-I—oh, God. I'm so very sorry I've upset you." She staggered to her feet. How could the conversation have gone even worse than she'd feared? Her eyes swam in hot tears, making it hard to see the doorway.

She sensed Anna Louise hovering beside her. As soon they were out of the examination room, Verity hissed, "I thought you were going to help me!"

To her horror, Evans must have heard her. "If by helping you," he raged at her retreating back, "you mean supplying you and your friends with gossip fodder, you can damn well forget it!"

Verity scrambled past an open-mouthed Cindy at her desk. An older man seated in the waiting room dropped a magazine on the floor and stared at her.

Horrified, Verity fled.

CHAPTER 29

IN SEVENTH GRADE gym class Randy Michaels told everyone he'd seen Verity's bloody panties. In reality, he'd noticed (before anyone else including Verity) the red, dime-size blotch that had leaked through her gym shorts when her period started unexpectedly.

Then there was the day she'd failed her driver's license test by sideswiping the testing officer's personal car in the MVA parking lot. Nearly as awful was her performance in The Mikado, her junior year of high school. She'd stepped onto the stage as Pitti-Sing and every one of her lines evaporated beneath the glare of the footlights.

But never, *never* had she felt as humiliated as she did that afternoon as she fled Dr. John Evans' office. She hadn't even thought to tell him that his eggs and milk were sitting on the kitchen steps.

Verity found herself parked in front of the Cat's Cradle, with no memory of having driven there. She flew out of her truck, exploded through the café door and threw herself bodily at the glass pastry case.

"I need whatever you have in there with the highest possible sugar content and a double espresso. Now!" she shouted.

The teenage part-timer, whose name Verity suddenly couldn't remember, shot an alarmed look at her boss.

"It's ok, Amanda, I'll take care of her." Sunny flicked muffin batter from her nitrile-gloved fingers. "She's not upset with you, dear. Or dangerous. At least, I don't think so." She narrowed her eyes speculatively at Verity. "Why don't you finish getting the blueberry muffins into the oven."

Sunny removed her gloves and stood, hands on her hips, glaring at Verity. "Don't abuse my staff!" She shook her head. "What's going on, sweetie?"

Verity remembered visiting her grandparents in Los Angeles when a 5.0-Richter earthquake rattled the city. The tremors rose up through the sidewalk, the soles of her shoes and all the way up her body, shaking her like a ragdoll. That's how she felt now, trembling head to foot.

"I'm serious," Verity groaned. "I need something strong—oh, jeez!—why don't you have a liquor license?"

"My best herbal tea is what you need. We'll talk later about food that might be less like rocket fuel, given your current condition. Now go sit down and I'll bring your tea."

Verity made a face at her, sniffed and obeyed.

After she had been forced to take at least three long swallows "not sips" of the honey-vanilla chamomile tea, Verity blotted her eyes with a napkin and managed to explain how her conversation with the doctor had imploded.

"I made a total mess of it. I must've sounded so incredibly rude and insensitive and stupid and absurd and—"

"I'm sure it wasn't as bad as you think."

"It was a nightmare! The kind you try to wake yourself up from and you can't. It just gets more and more scary." She covered her face with her hands.

"Drink. Breathe deeply."

When Verity peeked out from behind her hands, Sunny was observing her with concern. Verity drank a little more and did her best to breathe, as instructed. She felt as though no oxygen was getting to her lungs.

"Now then," Sunny said encouragingly, "you did what you went there to do even though it was tough going. That was very brave of you. Did you get the mysterious Olive Oyl's name?"

"Of course not. He refused to tell me anything about her."

"Why?"

"Because we are meddling, gossiping women. And he's right," she mumbled miserably.

"We aren't meddling. We're concerned that a friend may have been murdered. We have every right to ask questions about what happened to Elvira." Sunny frowned, looking thoughtful. "I wonder why he didn't want you to have her name."

"Because it's none of our damn business?"

"Maybe," Sunny agreed. "But what harm could it have done? Whoever the mystery woman is, she's not someone from around here. It's not like we're going to look her up and interrogate her."

But wasn't that the point of finding out who she was? Verity thought.

Just then, Kate and Mary Beth pushed through the café door to the jingly tune of the overhead bell. Chattering away, they ordered their pastry and coffee at the counter, then joined Verity and Sunny at their regular table, commanding a gray, storm-drenched view of Main Street. The rain that had stopped earlier now splashed loudly against the curved window.

Kate took one look at Verity's face and shot Sunny a questioning look.

Sunny promptly brought the newcomers up to date since

Verity still wasn't past the mumbling and moaning stage, and her eyes threatened to flood again whenever she tried to speak.

"Well, I never," Mary Beth snorted. "The nerve of that man."

"That doesn't sound like John at all," Kate said. "I've never seen him lose his temper, even when I've brought him sick and screaming children, one of whom—not to spoil anyone's appetite —vomited on him."

"Oh, lordy." Mary Beth made a face and put her pastry back down on the plate.

"It's all my fault," Verity whimpered. "I tried to tell him how concerned we all were about the sheriff's less-than-thorough investigation. At first, he seemed calm enough. Maybe he was just humoring me. Then he suddenly erupted and threw me out of his office. Even his receptionist looked shocked."

"Motives." Sunny pronounced the word with a raised finger as though it conveyed everything that needed to be said.

"Huh?" Verity wrinkled her nose.

"Did we miss something?" Kate blinked, looking confused.

Sunny nodded. "Before you and MB arrived, I was wondering why John would refuse to divulge his former fiancée's name."

"Oh." Mary Beth returned her attention to her almond croissant. She took a big bite and closed her eyes in bliss then licked sticky filling from her fingertips. "I know why! He probably doesn't remember her name and was too embarrassed to admit it."

"Who doesn't remember the name of someone they were ready to marry?" Sunny shook her head.

"Oh, right. Sorry."

"Maybe he just sees no purpose in naming names," Kate suggested. "I can see why he'd be furious that we're snooping into his personal life."

"We aren't snooping, we are investigating." Sunny solemnly observed them over the rim of her coffee mug. "There's a huge difference. Really, there is!"

Verity was no longer sure of that. Miserable, she dropped her face into her hands again and tried to ignore the sour feeling in her stomach. When she looked up minutes later, half of Kate's blackberry scone sat on a clean napkin in front of her.

"Thanks, Katie," she murmured and broke off a nibble. *Delicious.* At least her taste buds still functioned. She could almost feel the rich mixture of butter, sugar, and juicy, dark berries doing their work. Energizing her. See? She did need sugar!

"Maybe his reaction isn't because he's offended by our looking into his private life," Sunny mused, a suspicious twinkle in her pretty eyes.

"Ok. Then what is it?" Verity said.

"Guilt!" Sunny set her coffee mug down with a clunk as emphatic as a judge's gavel.

Verity looked across the table at Kate and Mary Beth, who appeared clueless. Doc Evans had mentioned feeling guilty for not going after Elvira that night but that had nothing to do with his former love life.

"I know why he feels guilty!" Kate beamed at them. "Because he's rekindled his romance with his former love and he doesn't want anyone to know since it's so soon after Elvira's death."

Like less than two weeks, Verity thought. *Talk about a brief interlude of mourning.* But she couldn't believe the doctor would look up an old girlfriend so quickly, if at all. He just didn't seem the type. Did he?

"Oh, I know." Mary Beth rolled forward in her chair and brushed croissant flakes off her lap. "He blames himself for an argument he had with Elvira the night she died, which made her so distraught she couldn't bear to go on living."

"MB," Sunny said. "Good thinking really, sweetie. But when has Elvira ever lost an argument? Or, for that matter, when has she let anything or anyone upset her perfectly organized world?"

"Good point." Kate pushed her coffee mug aside to make more room for her elbows on the table. "How about this. Let's say that Elvira showed John the note she found. The one Peter wrote to his sister, attempting to lure her out into the night. Maybe John blames himself for not stopping Elvira from rushing out of the house. He'd definitely feel guilty about that."

"Or maybe—" Sunny lowered her voice to barely a whisper, as though whatever she planned to say next was just too terrible to announce out loud "—he doesn't just *feel* guilty. He *is* guilty." She widened her eyes.

Kate shook her head. "Oh, no, I don't think h—"

"What if he didn't stay at home in bed like he claims?" Sunny continued. "What if he lied and he followed Elvira to the quarry. And that's where they argued until things spun out of control and—"

"—and he pushed her!" Mary Beth yipped.

CHAPTER 30

VERITY'S CELL phone rang just as she was finishing work in the chicken coops. She pulled off her poop-caked gloves before plucking the phone from her pocket. Her poor Samsung had seen better days. Its screen got cracked months before when she dropped it in the milking parlor and one of the cows—Emily, she seemed to remember—stepped on it. Remarkably, the instrument still worked although the screen was spiderwebbed and plastered with a permanent layer of fine sticky dust.

Chaundra Adebe's name came up on her caller ID.

Just thinking about the Ethiopian antique dealer made Verity smile. "Hey, lady, what's up?" She tried to sound cheerful although she hadn't stopped thinking about the possibility that their town's physician might just be a murderer.

"We need to call an emergency meeting. Right now!" Chaundra's normally clear voice sounded like she was talking through the wrong end of a megaphone. Verity's stomach flip-flopped. "Can we have it at your house tonight, Verity? I don't want to impose on Sunny and ask her to host us again at the café. I think it means extra work for her."

And it doesn't mean more work for me? "Sure," Verity said, rubbing the aching small of her back. "What's going on?"

"There's talk around town. People are saying Dr. Evans murdered his wife."

"Oh, Lord," Verity muttered. Someone must have overheard their conversation at the café. Or maybe it was just the usual vicious rumor mill at work. Either way, this was bad.

Verity changed phone hands and tugged at the coop's fencing to make sure it was secure. Last week, in the middle of the night, a fox dug under the edge of one of the wire enclosures. Thankfully, she'd heard her hens' frantic squawking and raced outside. As quickly as she acted, she still lost two of her hens—one carried off to be dinner, a second bloodied and dead in the straw. The survivors of her poor flock were a hysterical mess.

Chaundra was still speaking excitedly. "I overheard two tourists talking as they browsed my stalls. 'What an idyllic New England town this is,' one woman said. 'You wouldn't say that,' responded her friend, 'if you knew about the local doctor who brutally murdered his wife just days ago.'"

"No-o-o!" Verity groaned.

"Yes! We need to stop this kind of talk before someone gets hurt. I'm sure John can weather the storm, but think about his kids! And not to sound selfish, but this can't be good for the town's business."

"You're right." Verity rubbed a spot on her forehead that had started to ping painfully. "We should meet. All of us. I'm afraid this may be partly my fault." She explained her impromptu meeting with their friends at the café.

"I see," Chaundra said grimly. "Personally, I think it would be totally out of character for John Evans to lash out violently at anyone." Although Verity couldn't help thinking he sure sounded violent when he was throwing her out of his office.

Fumiko and Mary Beth were the first to arrive.

"I so sorry." Fumiko dipped her head, her black eyes apologetic. It had been decided they should make the meeting a potluck since some in the group might not otherwise have time to eat. Fumiko was wearing one of her hand-knit sweaters. Verity was instantly envious of the summery shades of the yarn —raspberry, orange, and lemon—like scoops of icy pastel sherbet. "Have no time make food," the Japanese woman muttered. "I pick up pastries at café. If Sunny bring, too, we maybe got too much."

"Can there ever be too many pastries?" Mary Beth crowed joyfully.

Verity laughed. "My waistline might argue with you."

Mary Beth elbowed her as she passed by. "Like you should worry. Skinny thing that you are."

Verity smiled. Farm work definitely burned calories. "Whatever you've got in that casserole dish smells amazing, MB," she said.

"Beef Stroganoff. The mayor's favorite. I had to spoon out a portion for him before I left." She giggled. "Or he might not have let me out the door. Can I rewarm it in your oven?"

"Here, let me have it. I'll put it in with my mac-and-cheese." Verity peeked under the foil of Mary Beth's dish. Beef chunks, vegetables, and thick egg noodles swam in luscious dark brown sauce. "M-m-m-m. How did you find time to make this gorgeous thing? I thought this afternoon was your choir practice."

Mary Beth plopped down on a kitchen chair and eyed the taped-shut box of pastries Fumiko had brought. "I always make two or three of anything. We eat one, freeze the others for emergencies or days when I need to stay late at the nursery."

Verity grinned. "Smart woman!"

Everyone else, except Martha Humphrey, arrived soon after. To Verity's relief, Denise brought paper plates and cups. At least there wouldn't be a sink full of dishes to wash at the end of the night.

They found seats around the table and dug into the hot dishes and cold salads.

"Martha said she'd be late," Chaundra commented between bites. "She's tutoring this summer. Her last student for the day won't finish until six o'clock, and she has to drive back from Springfield."

"Unfortunately, I think we need to start without her," Verity said. "I hope she'll understand. We can fill her in when she gets here."

"I'll begin since I called for this meeting." Chaundra went on to explain. "We must either be much more careful about how we discuss Elvira's death and our theories—" she sighed "—or we need to stop investigating. The latter might be best. Playing detective has been fun. But we've found no real proof that anyone was actually with Elvira the night she died."

"I agree," Denise said, "we need to find more than a note and Elvira's cryptic diaries to convince the sheriff she was murdered. But I don't want to stop trying."

"I think we should just stop," Kate said sadly. "We're getting nowhere. There may be nothing more to discover."

"We *can't* quit," Denise argued. "Elvira wasn't perfect but she was our friend. We just need to get serious about this investigation. Stop treating it like a hobby. We have to find better ways to get solid evidence and learn the truth."

"If we not find evidence, then what?" Fumiko looked around Verity's kitchen table at the others.

"Then we stop this nonsense," Chaundra stated firmly. "End of story. Case closed."

Fumiko nodded her head slowly. "I take so-o-o-o many notes in diary. To be honest, they not bowl me off."

"Bowl you over," Verity gently corrected her. "Fumiko is right. Although there are plenty of suspicious-sounding incidents, nothing cries out 'murderer.' We do know, however, that some of her dirty tricks caused serious consequences. I think we should focus on those and dig a little deeper."

"Like that realtor-guy she screwed out of a job." Denise scowled. "That's not something I'd ever forget."

"But he had an alibi!" MB reminded her. "He was on a trip to Hawaii. Remember?"

"He owns his own real estate firm now. He could have paid someone," Denise insisted.

"Don't forget the woman who left her job to save her marriage," said Mary Beth.

"I wonder if Doc Evans even liked her," Kate added timidly. "Elvira. I mean, why would he? She tricked him out of marrying the woman he loved. And we've all heard her bullying him in little ways, like she does...*did* to everyone."

"But would he murder her just because she was a..." Verity hesitated and poked at a tomato slice on her plate.

"Bitch," Denise supplied.

"Right. Anyway, it's easy to see how broken up John is about her death."

"Is he?" Denise leaned back in her chair, arms crossed over her chest and stared at her empty plate as if trying to decide whether to go for seconds. "It's not that hard to pretend you're grieving." She burst into a dramatic torrent of tears and wailing.

"Ok, ok. You've made your point." Sunny laughed and flicked a hand at Denise to make her stop her caterwauling. "Let's get down to business. I'll summarize. We started out with three suspects. The young male realtor who lost his job years ago, the dumped fiancée known as Olive Oyl, again many years ago, and the receptionist Elvira manipulated into quitting. But both the realtor and receptionist have alibis. And the nurse-fiancée seems untraceable since we don't even know her name."

"And Doc Evans himself, our fourth suspect," Chaundra reminded them. "He claims he never left the house the night of his wife's death."

"Claiming you were somewhere isn't really an alibi." Denise, always the skeptic. "I hate to say it, but I think we're only seeing the tip of the iceberg that was Elvira's life. Who can say how many more enemies she made that we don't even know about."

"Then, there's *us*," Kate whispered.

The clatter of cutlery and clink of glasses fell silent. They looked at each other.

Denise spoke into the sticky atmosphere. "Don't be ridiculous. Us? What could we possibly have to do with Elvira's death?"

Verity swallowed over a boulder-size lump in her throat. "I don't think I can go there. You are all such wonderful friends. I can't believe any of us—" she gulped "—would ever, you know."

"And we feel the same about you, sweetie," Sunny said. "But Kate's right. We've all had reasons for wishing we could dropkick Elvira off her high horse. Even you, Veri. You were just as determined to keep your lovely farm as Elvira was to snatch it out from under you. I don't know how many times I heard you begging her to stop hassling you about buying your place."

Mary Beth bobbed her head emphatically. "Sunny's right. The night she died, when we met at your house, you looked so angry you might have mur...well, you know."

Verity's eyes welled up. "I know. The last words I said to her were in anger."

"Enough," Chaundra said. "We need to make the most of what we've learned so far and move on from there." She reached into the leather purse hanging from her chair back and pulled out a folder. "I've arranged all our reading notes into a big chart to help us visualize the possibilities. Look—here, in Column 1 are the suspects we've already agreed should be eliminated because each of them has a solid alibi. And in Column 2 are names of people who are still viable suspects."

They all leaned over the food-cluttered table to study Chaundra's colorful chart.

Impressive! Verity thought. "What's this sidebar in red writing mean?"

Chaundra pursed her lips. "I didn't know where to put those people, because we don't have enough data to help us identify them. Plus, there are generic people, wild cards." She pointed.

"Oh, I see," Kate said. "Tourist. Stranger passing through. Escaped convict. Druggie."

Chaundra shrugged. "I was just brainstorming. It's possible that someone Elvira didn't even know came across her at the quarry by chance, making it a random killing."

"You are so well organized," Mary Beth said admiringly. "Just like the CSI guys on TV!"

Verity rolled her eyes. "Except this is real life. If we accuse the wrong person, it could be a disaster. For them, and for us."

"Are you going to add us to your chart?" Kate asked with a little wobble in her voice.

Chaundra shook her head. "No, dear. I agree with Verity. I can't believe any of us would do anything so awful."

"Good," Kate murmured, staring down at her hands. Verity thought she looked relieved. *Why is that?* But the idea was a fleeting one and gone in the next second.

They all settled back into their seats. Food remained on plates but everyone's appetite seemed to have disappeared.

"Right," Sunny said at last. "So, we agree that we'll move

forward, carefully. Exactly where was everyone on the night Elvira died? Are there witnesses to people's alibis?"

"Oh, oh...oh!" Mary Beth popped up and down on her chair seat like a berserk jack-in-the-box. "We should definitely follow our main suspects. I want to go on a stakeout!"

"Oh please," Denise groaned.

Verity held up a hand. "Wait. MB may be right. Except for the doc, these people don't know what any of us look like. While we're watching them, we might see or hear something incriminating."

Denise laughed and slapped the table. "Like a killer is going to say, 'Boy, did I ever enjoy seeing her bounce off that quarry floor.'"

"Denise!" Kate cast a horrified look at the candymaker.

"Sorry," Denise mumbled. "But let's be honest here, we're not professional investigators. I fail to see how we can do actual surveillance on a possible coldblooded killer."

"We can't just forget about something as terrible as this," Verity insisted. "What if this person kills again? We must do everything we can to make sure that doesn't happen."

"I agree," Sunny said. "It's our civic duty."

"Count me in." Mary Beth, of course.

"Me, too," Chaundra added solemnly.

"And me, I guess." Although Kate sounded less sure of herself.

"All for one and one for all!" cried Denise, who didn't have a Musketeer's sword but held up a palm for a gang high-five.

"What's all the noise about?" The voice had come from the kitchen doorway.

They all turned to see Martha smiling expectantly at them.

"Martha, come sit down," Verity said. "You must be exhausted. And famished. Let me get you a plate. Chaundra will explain everything."

"So, has everyone already drawn straws or whatever we do to decide who follows who?" Martha asked after Chaundra briefed her.

"No, you're just in time," Kate assured her.

Martha dug into her food with gusto. "Oh my, this mac-and-cheese is amazing!"

Verity smiled. It had been one of Mark's favorites. She still couldn't make it without remembering the expression of pure male pleasure on his face as he took his first mouthful.

"I'll write out slips of paper with our suspects' names on them," Sunny said. "Two slips for each suspect. That way each of us will have a partner for safety's sake and to corroborate evidence. So, it won't be just one person's word for what a suspect says."

"Oh, this is absolutely thrilling!" Mary Beth squealed.

"Knock it off, MB. Don't you get it?" Denise scolded her. "This is serious."

The joy in Mary Beth's eyes died. Her face turned as solemn as a nun's prayer.

Whose mood changes that fast? Verity couldn't help thinking. Criticism normally had little effect on the forever cheerful Mary Beth. Verity exchanged a puzzled look with Sunny who shrugged. Admittedly, Denise had been unusually harsh.

They took turns drawing slips and comparing assignments.

"Oh good! Kate and I get the realtor guy," Denise said. "He's in New Hampshire, so a little drive. But hey, maybe he'll be a hunk! I haven't had a date in Lord knows how long."

"Isn't he gay? And anyway, I'm not sure I'd want to date a possible murderer," Verity commented dryly.

Kate patted Denise's arm. "Sorry."

Verity plucked a strip from the vase and stared glumly at it. "Who else has Dr. Evans?"

"I do." Sunny waved her slip of paper in the air.

"I need to trade with someone," Verity said. "I can't face that man again."

Sunny made an offended face at her. "You don't want to be my sidekick on a stakeout?"

"It's not that. I just don't want to give him a reason to go off on me like he did the other day."

Sunny put an arm around her shoulders. "I'll run interference, throw my body between the two of you, if necessary. If we are sneaky enough, he'll never see us. Anyway, he likes my almond Danish way too much to yell at me. I might ban him from the café."

"You can *do* that?" Mary Beth looked alarmed.

Sunny laughed. "You have nothing to worry about, sweetie."

Denise leaned over to whisper in Verity's ear. "MB's pastry purchases alone have financed the café's new van."

Verity stifled a giggle.

Mary Beth and Martha drew the receptionist. Chaundra and Fumiko got the dumped fiancée.

"Not fair," Chaundra protested. "She's the hardest one of all. We don't even know who she is!"

"I guess you need to start by doing a little more research," Verity said. "Sorry."

"If you can locate your subject, try to watch them without being noticed," Sunny advised everyone. "It's been less than two weeks since Elvira died. If any one of our suspects actually is responsible, they'll probably still be extra vigilant."

"Criminals always make a mistake that gets them caught," Mary Beth announced authoritatively. "Or they do something stupid—like bragging about what they did."

Denise laughed. "That would sure simplify things! Let's all hope for a stupid killer."

CHAPTER 31

THE MORNING after the emergency meeting of the amateur investigators Verity scrunched down low in the passenger seat of Sunny's car, staring at the unraveling tears in the knees of her blue jeans.

"You've been awfully quiet What are you thinking about?" Sunny said.

"Books. Mystery stories I've read."

Sunny closed the gourmet magazine she'd been reading to pass the time while they were on stakeout in front of Dr. John Evans' home. "What about them?"

"There's always a moment when someone says, 'had I but known...' or 'why didn't we see *that* coming?'"

Sunny laughed. "You worry too much."

"No, seriously. I have this awful feeling we're missing something really important." Verity looked up at the beautiful white colonial with its graceful wrap-around porch and blue tile roof that matched the shutters. "Elvira loved this house," she sighed.

"I know, sweetie. Say what you will about the woman—she had great taste."

"I still feel terrible about upsetting John; he was so furious with me the other day. I don't think I can bear another scene like that."

Sunny opened her mouth, no doubt to say something soothing.

Verity held up a hand to stop her, knowing nothing would make her feel better. She chewed the tip of one nail and slid down another inch to make sure most of her head was below the side window. Sunny planned to disappear behind her magazine if anyone came too near the car.

"There's something else that bothers me about the way the doc went berserk," Verity said.

"Other than the fact you'd been literally thrown out of a medical office in front of witnesses and totally humiliated?"

Verity winced at the memory. "I can't shake the feeling that John was, I don't know, intentionally yelling loud enough for the whole neighborhood to hear him. He wanted to be heard. He wanted others to know he thought we were crazy."

Sunny tapped the magazine against her chin. "You think he was belittling our investigation for a reason."

"Yeah. Maybe. Like, our questioning him, the grieving husband, was so absurd it was laughable. He's one of the most respected people in town. Folks listen to him. He was proclaiming his innocence for all the world to hear." She wondered if his kids had been at home then. Could his rage have been for their benefit? Anyone upstairs in the house certainly would have heard him yelling.

"Well, we *are* being just a tiny bit presumptuous," Sunny laughed, "playing detective like this. By labeling us as busybodies and snoops he makes anything we uncover less credible."

"Exactly." Verity stared down at the ragged fingernail on her index finger and forced herself to stop attacking it. She was just making it worse. Like a lot of things these days.

"On the other hand," Sunny said, "considering what the

poor man has been through—losing his wife and being left with two teenagers to raise—it's not surprising he'd be on an emotional precipice. You could have been the last straw that tipped him over the edge."

"Now that makes me feel so-o-o much better." Verity wrinkled her nose and poked her head up to scowl out through the car's windshield.

"Listen, Veri, the man would have reacted the same way to any of us asking about his love life. I'm sure you were as discreet as possible."

Verity felt a little bilious. If memory served, discretion hadn't been her strong point. And then her eyes widened. "Oh, here he comes! He's walking toward his car."

Sunny smacked the steering wheel with the heel of her hand. "The chase is on!"

"Looks like he's in a hurry. Probably a medical emergency."

"I think he does morning rounds at the hospital." Sunny started up the car. "This may be a waste of time but we should follow him anyway. Good thing I didn't bring the café's van with my logo splashed all over the sides." She laughed. "Some private investigators we'd be then!"

Indeed. "If he's not on his way to the hospital, maybe he's making a house call. I think he still visits a few patients who are housebound."

Sunny's blue eyes lit up. "Hey, I have an idea! We could casually bump into him. You apologize about the incident at his office, and I'll smooth everything over while sneakily fishing for information."

"Ooo-kay," Verity said, although simply following at a distance and remaining incognito was much her preference.

They soon passed beyond the Evansfield town limits. The doctor's dark-blue Mercedes turned toward the highway on-ramp.

"I didn't know he had patients outside of town," Verity said.

Sunny flicked on her turn signal and followed the sedan onto I-91. "I think he still stops in to check on Alma Smith."

"Who's that?" Verity asked.

"You probably wouldn't know her. A Vermont old-timer. She must be in her nineties, at least. Never leaves her house. It's probably hard for her to find a driver to bring her to medical appointments."

Not what one might expect of a typical killer.

Sunny slid her a look as if she'd read her mind. "You're right. He *is* a nice guy. Unfortunately, you experienced the one percent of the man that wasn't so nice. We all have a breaking point."

"Of course," she admitted, "but most of us have the common sense to take a step back and cool down. He went ballistic."

She shivered, remembering the rage she'd seen in John Evans' eyes. So much like his son's rage with the reporter. The sense that their confrontation might become physical at any moment had terrified her. She was still trembling an hour after she rushed out of his office. What might have happened if his receptionist and a patient hadn't been there?

An image flashed in her mind. Elvira arguing with John at the lip of the quarry. Fire sparking in Elvira's eyes as she refused to let him have his way. About what? Buying the property she wanted for his clinic? Something to do with their kids? Was one of them having an affair?

"He's pulling off the highway," Sunny said, snapping Verity out of her daymare.

"Don't follow too close. He might get suspicious."

Sunny let the car drift back a few more car lengths to make them less noticeable. After another half mile, the Mercedes turned into a residential community. Sunny's brow wrinkled.

"What's wrong?" Verity asked.

"I'm pretty sure Alma lives much closer to Evansfield."

"Maybe he's visiting a private clinic or nursing home?"

"I guess."

After three more turns through the neighborhood, the Mercedes pulled up to the curb in front of a trim cream-colored Cape Cod with dark green shutters. The pretty little house boasted an immaculately manicured front lawn. Late-blooming rose bushes heavy with red, pink, and peach blossoms ranged beneath the windows along the front and side of the house. Sunny drove past, hung a U, and parked a couple houses farther down, on the opposite side of the street.

Verity frowned as she watched the doctor step out of his car and lope up a flagstone path toward the Cape Cod's front door. "He doesn't have his medical bag with him. Wasn't he carrying it when he left his house?"

"I don't remember," Sunny admitted.

The front door opened and a woman who appeared to be in her thirties stepped out onto the cement stoop before he reached the front door. She was wearing tan chinos and a faded sweatshirt. Gardening clothes, Verity immediately thought. They hugged warmly and exchanged a few words. She kissed him on the cheek.

"She was expecting him," Sunny murmured. "I wish we could hear what they're saying."

Verity sighed. "I wonder who she is. Patients aren't usually that familiar with their physicians."

"Take down the address. We should be able to get the name of the homeowner from town records."

Verity dug a notepad and pen from her purse. When she looked up again, the woman was stepping back through her door.

"He must be leaving," Sunny said. "Duck."

They both slid down and waited for the Mercedes' engine to roar to life.

After a few minutes of silence, Verity said, "One of us needs to risk looking."

Sunny rose up an inch to peek through the windshield. "His car's still there and he's not in it. He must have followed her inside."

"Oh, wow!" Verity breathed.

After sitting outside the little house for nearly an hour, Verity had contemplated every scenario she could think of that might bring John Evans to this attractive woman's home. She looked at Sunny who had found three new recipes in the magazine to try at the café and was now playing video games on her phone.

"How long should we wait?" she said.

"I don't know." Sunny gave her phone a frustrated look and clicked out of her solitaire game. "In stakeouts on TV, police officers watch a perp for hours. Sometimes days."

"Perp?" Verity rolled her eyes. "You're beginning to sound like MB with her CSI jargon."

Sunny sighed. "That can't be good. Anyway, I should get back to the café before the lunch rush starts."

Verity wiggled to get more comfortable in the worn vinyl seat and caught herself biting her nails again. She dropped her hand into her lap and remembered the woman they'd seen smiling and standing so close to John Evans. She had kissed him —albeit on the cheek—and he had reacted as if this was not unexpected.

"You know what I said before about us having missed something?" Verity said.

"Yeah."

"Well, I have the strangest feeling I know that woman from somewhere."

Sunny frowned. "I'm sure I've never seen her. Could you have noticed her at the funeral?"

"I don't think so. You were there, too. One of us would remember her. Does John have a sister?"

"No. He told me years ago that he was an only child."

"There's just something awfully familiar about her." Verity narrowed her eyes. "She looked really slim, didn't she?"

"One might say, *skinny*." Sunny chewed her bottom lip in thought. She blinked, as if struck by a new thought. "You think it might be *her*?"

"I do." Verity grinned, suddenly excited. "Hello, Miss Olive Oyl!"

CHAPTER 32

NOT TEN MINUTES LATER, Verity saw the front door of the little house open. She straightened in her seat, alert.

"No! Scooch down." Sunny crab-clawed the back of her shirt and shoved her into a crouch on the car's floor.

"How can I see anything if I stay down here?"

"Just try not to be so obvious." Sunny peered out from behind her Fabulous Food magazine.

Verity winched up a little and stared across the street at John Evans and the mystery woman. "I think he's leaving. She's saying goodbye."

"Oh, bother," Sunny said.

"What?"

"We should be taking photos. My phone's got a lousy camera. Like 200 pitiful pixels."

Verity fished her sad little cracked-screen phone from her purse. Fortunately, the camera was a decent one and its little lens had somehow survived bovine destruction. She held it discreetly just above the dashboard. "He's standing in the way. All I can see is his back. I can't get her at all."

"Bummer. We really need a picture. MB or one of the others might recognize her."

"Yes-s-s-s-s!" Verity hissed. "He's moving." She clicked a shot. Then another just as the doctor started to turn away from the pretty blonde. And one more as he stepped off her stoop, turning back to face her. The woman said something that made him smile. "Ooooh! This is frustrating. I wish we could hear what they're saying."

"If we were any closer, they'd notice us for sure. Did you get a good shot of her?"

"Yup!" Verity dropped back down to flip through the photos. "One is from far enough away to show both of them. The other two are closeups of her face."

"Perfect!" Sunny cautiously peeked out. "And just in time. I think she's going back inside."

Not until the doctor turned his car around and drove off the way he'd come did Sunny begin to follow him from a distance.

Verity snapped on her seatbelt, so excited she could hardly breathe. "Let's see if we can locate the local town hall and find out who lives in that little dollhouse."

"Wish we could," Sunny said. "But I really need to get back to the café. Shirley is my helper today. She's sweet and tries hard, but she's not up to handling a crowd on her own. It's always a hot mess on Saturdays. Sorry."

"Oh, well. I have a lot to do, too. Another day." But Verity couldn't hide her disappointment.

"Hey, we accomplished a lot. The best part is—I think we're getting close to catching Elvira's killer."

"Really?" Sure, they now had a promising lead, but Verity wasn't as confident.

"Absolutely. You said it yourself." Sunny hummed a happy little tune as she drove. "That skinny gal must be Olive Oyl. She and the doc have linked up again. Do you think they could be in it together?"

"In what?"

"The plot to murder Elvira, of course." Sunny waggled an eyebrow at her. "It's just like MB said—they've slipped up, made a mistake by being seen together so soon after the murder."

Verity considered this. "I don't know…"

Sunny squinted at the street sign when they came to a corner. "Hmmm. I think we took a right turn when we came, so returning we must turn left here. Anyway, they've obviously reignited their passionate relationship. But before they could be together, they needed to get Elvira out of the way."

Verity squinted out through the side window doubtfully. "And how does the note Elvira found, signed by her son, fit into their scheme? I can't believe Peter would conspire with his Dad to kill his mother!"

"So maybe Peter didn't send it. The doc and Olive Oyl could have written it, hoping to lure Elvira to the quarry." Sunny tapped her carnation-pink fingernails on the steering wheel, looking pleased with herself. "Then one of them was waiting for Elvira and pushed her over. Lordy, just saying those words gives me chills. How cold-hearted is that!"

"Ruthless," Verity agreed. *If* Sunny was right.

Verity returned her phone to her purse as they drove onto the highway, no longer following the Mercedes. A niggling uneasiness teased her stomach.

"I don't know," Verity murmured softly, more to herself than to her partner. "Something about your conspiracy theory doesn't feel right."

"Why not?" Sunny sounded as if she was sulking. "It would explain everything. Name one reason—other than John Evans' reputation as a respected physician—why he couldn't have been involved in his wife's death."

"Ok. There was the kiss."

"What about it?" Sunny shrugged. "You admitted it was weird, not to mention inappropriate for a patient to greet her doctor with a hug and kiss. And, if she's not a patient, why did he come all this way to see her?"

"Didn't that little show of affection seem a bit chaste for two lovers?"

"Oh my God, Verity! Of course they'd tone it down. They were standing outside where any of her neighbors might see them. We have no way of knowing what level of passion erupted as soon as they were snuggled up behind closed doors."

Verity tipped her head side to side, weighing alternatives. "Maybe you're right and I'm just trying to make excuses for John. I hated the scene he made in his office, but I really don't want him to be a murderer."

"They were in that house a-lo-o-one," Sunny sang out. "For a long, long time."

"Too long for a doctor on a house call," Verity agreed. So, if they weren't making love, what were they doing in there? Before she could come up with a reasonable explanation, the off-ramp from the interstate appeared. "Why do return trips always seem to take less time?"

Sunny winked at her. "Anticipation of the unknown adds minutes to any journey. Didn't Einstein have a theory about that?"

"I doubt it. Anyway, I'm glad I'll get back before milking time."

"Aren't your Robo-Milkers working?"

"For everyone except Molly." She lifted her hands in a what-can-I-do gesture.

"She still refuses the intimate touch of stainless steel?"

Verity laughed. "Wouldn't you prefer warm hands on your teats?"

"I'd like warm hands anywhere at all on me!"

They looked at each other and broke into hysterical laughter, unable to stop until, gasping and wiping tears from their eyes, the car rolled to a stop in Verity's driveway.

That night Verity transferred the three photos she'd snapped to her PC. She printed 8x10 blowups in the hope they would jolt her memory. She still believed she had seen the pretty blonde woman somewhere before. But where and when?

If it had been at the funeral, Sunny surely would have remembered. Sunny had a gift for names and faces. How often had she watched the café owner recall a customer's name, even if they'd only visited the café once before? And although virtually everyone in Evansfield had attended the funeral, they all knew each other. A stranger would have stood out.

Then again, if you murdered someone, why would you show up among the mourners at your victim's funeral?

She shut down her computer and ambled into her living room with the printed photos, still thinking. She'd need more information about the woman and Dr. Evans before she and Sunny showed the photographs to the sheriff. Without supporting facts, he'd laugh them off and claim (again!) they were sticking their noses where they didn't belong.

Verity plopped down into Mark's leather chair and stared at first one, then another of the pictures she'd taken earlier that day. They blurred together before her tired eyes. Slowly she became aware of a subtle breeze drifting across her face. She turned toward the living-room window but the curtains weren't fluttering, even a little.

It occurred to her she hadn't seen her two ethereal house-mates recently. Oddly, the thought brought her no joy.

"Hey, Mr. and Mrs. P., are you there?" she called out.

For a long moment, she felt only the heavy silence of an old house around her and her own breathing. Outside, she heard the scurrying of a squirrel attacking the birdfeeder suction-cupped to her window, a tractor grumbling as it rolled past her house, the chirps of house wrens from their nest in her eaves. And then—the soft rustle of taffeta and clump of boots.

She blinked at an empty space in the middle of the room. Two figures dimly materialized.

Verity's eyes flew wide. "Oh, my! Look at you two!"

Anna Louise wore a stunning midnight-blue velvet gown, a choker of sparkling sapphires around her throat. Percy sported a Civil War officer's dress uniform, a thin red stripe down the outside of each dark blue pant leg. The heel of his hand rested at his left hip on the hilt of a long sword in an ornate scabbard.

"Are we going somewhere special tonight?" Verity said.

Anna Louise wrinkled her nose prettily. "I do so wish we were, Miss Verity. Sadly, our social engagements of late have been extremely limited. No one in the entire county is hosting a ball. Or even an intimate soirée, potluck supper, or barn raising. Darling Percy and I are bored to tears. We just felt like dressing for dinner."

"Even though you don't eat?" Verity asked, trying not to chuckle.

"Just to lighten our spirits." One corner of Anna Louise's pretty lips lifted in a playful smile.

"Spirits. Very funny," Verity agreed. "Well, you could always dress up for church tomorrow. Coffee and doughnuts after the service in the church hall. It's as close to a soirée as we have around here." She wasn't even sure she knew what a soiree was.

Anna Louise gazed down at her voluminous skirt and swept it side-to-side along the carpeting. "I fear I might be over-dressed."

Percy made a sympathetic sound in his throat. "And my uniform is woefully outdated, as anyone familiar with your modern military might realize."

"True." Verity smiled at them affectionately. Her ghosts, although frequently annoying, could be so cute. "But since you can't let people see you, just wear whatever makes you happy. I think you both look amazing."

Anna Louise pouted. "I can't say that I'd enjoy eating nuts with my coffee. Why do they not serve cakes?" She fluttered in front of her face a particularly attractive lavender fan that nearly matched her extraordinary eyes.

Verity laughed. "Not nuts—doughnuts. You've never had a doughnut before?" She tried to remember when one of her favorite guilty pleasures was invented. Perhaps in the south they had other names for fried dough. "You haven't lived until you've eaten a Krispy Kreme!"

Mark had argued that the golden, sugar-glazed gems she so adored weren't real doughnuts. He insisted she taste Vermont cake doughnuts spiced with just a touch of nutmeg and rolled in cinnamon sugar. She had to admit they were delicious. But they failed to satisfy her childhood memories of KK's.

"Verity," Percy said, interrupting her sweet fantasy, "we have something for you."

She forced herself to refocus. "Yes?"

"Some evidence, a clue as you say, possibly related to your investigation." He pursed his lips, looking a tad smug.

Anna Louise stepped closer to her husband and took his arm. "Stop stalling, Percy. This is serious." She turned to look at Verity, her lavender eyes luminescent. "Someone stuck a letter under your back door." She held out what looked like a sheet of white printer paper, folded in quarters.

"Did you see who left it?"

"No, we were too busy getting all fancied up for you," Anna Louise said. "We thought you might be amused. You seem in need of cheering up lately."

"Well, thank you for the effort." Verity smiled at them and accepted the letter that floated in her direction at the tips of Anna Louise's slightly translucent fingertips. Verity tucked the paper into her pocket.

"Aren't you going to read it for us, so we'll know what it says?" Percy asked.

"You mean you haven't already read it?" Perhaps it was a bit mean to test them.

"Oh, heaven forbid!" Anna Louise objected with an agitated quivering of her fan. "We would never interfere with your private correspondence."

"Of course you wouldn't." Verity squinted dubiously at one ghost then the other. Percy had the decency to blush. Anna Louise just hid behind her fan.

Her customers sometimes left a voicemail or emailed her a change in their weekly order, but it seemed a lot of trouble to hand-deliver a request. She unfolded the paper.

There were three lines of handwritten printing, barely a dozen words—but they came down on her with the weight of a grand piano.

Verity let out a gasp and jumped from the leather chair to her feet.

Percy looked confused. "We thought it no more than a foolish joke!"

"Aha!" She shook the note at him. "I knew you'd read it."

"Mercy me," Anna Louise whispered, looking ready to disappear at any moment.

"We apologize," Percy said. Then quickly, "You believe it's a serious threat?"

"I do," she said.

"Well then, perhaps it can be useful? I understand that today much importance is ascribed to the marks from fingertips in crime solving."

Verity indulged herself in a full minute of hyperventilation as the words on the paper ricocheted through her head. She waited for her pulse to return to normal. "No, I don't think it's a joke at all." She paced the room as she read aloud the words.

What are you—stupid?
Can't you take a hint?
Stop messing about or die!

"I told you it was terribly rude, Percy." Anna Louise sighed.

"If this isn't someone's idea of buffoonery, it is more than rude," Percy stated firmly. "Miss Verity, you must be careful. You should take that message directly to your sheriff."

Verity shook her head. "He hasn't believed a thing I've said before. I'm sure he'll just tell me this has nothing to do with Elvira's death or our investigations."

"But if the same person who wrote this is the person who killed your—"

"I know, I know, Percy!" Verity said. "Whoever they are, they've already proven themselves capable of murder. They may do it again, if only to protect themselves." She rubbed her forehead with one hand, still holding the awful note in her other. "Elvira was my friend. Not always a good friend, but she had her moments. At the very least, she deserves justice."

Anna Louise drifted closer in her floaty sort of way and tucked an arm around Verity's shoulders. "Then you must show your friends that disgusting letter. They should be forewarned, too."

"At least make a copy of it and leave it with the sheriff," Percy insisted. "The worst he can do is ignore it. But if something later happens to you or one of your friends, he will then realize he should have taken the threat seriously."

Would it take another violent break in, more threats or another death to make Fred Bailey do his job properly? She picked up the three photographs that had fallen from her lap when she stood up so suddenly.

"Alright. I promise I'll do at least that much. Tomorrow. Meanwhile, I'm exhausted. I'm going to bed." She turned back to face the pair. "Maybe you two should hold your own ball, right here in the living room. You're certainly dressed for it." She smiled. Perhaps she was beginning to get used to them. A little.

That night Verity dreamt that the person who broke into her house returned. The faceless figure in black sweats confronted her and demanded to know why she hadn't stopped interfering with his plans. *What plans?* she thought murkily. *Elvira is already dead.*

In the nightmare, they struggled again, toppling to the floor and thrashing about. Strangely, Verity was more interested in identifying her attacker than escaping from him. With a boldness that surprised her, she reached up and tugged the hood off his head.

To her shock, the face revealed was a woman's.

And not just any woman. It was the pretty blonde who had stood in front of the sweet little Cape Cod house and kissed Dr. John Evans on the cheek.

CHAPTER 33

VERITY GROANED and cracked open her burning eyes. She stretched in bed. Her neck felt stiff; her back ached. Crouching for hours inside Sunny's car the day before had added to the lingering painful aftereffects of her real wrestling match with the thief. The nightmare of a rematch had left her unable to relax and get back to sleep.

She tossed off the sheet and comforter, sat up in bed and waited for her head to clear. But the memory of the disturbing dream cast a grim fog over her day.

John Evans and Olive Oyl—or whatever the woman's real name was—partners in crime? Really? She honestly couldn't believe that. And yet...

Even if the couple was innocent of conspiring to murder Elvira, their being together so soon after Elvira's violent death seemed foolish on their part. An invitation to speculation and gossip by anyone who knew the doctor. Did John Evans' indiscreet hooking up with his old love mean he'd done away with his wife? Or were the two events totally unconnected?

Just thinking about these new developments made her head spin.

How did private detectives get to the truth when investigating a suspicious death? Mary Beth often cited examples from her favorite TV shows. But Verity wasn't sure how accurate that information was, seeing that CSI plots were conceived by the show's writers. She had tried asking the doctor about his past—and that had gotten her nowhere. Worse than nowhere. Good grief! Now she needed to find herself a new physician. Returning to him as a patient would be way too embarrassing!

Unable to make any sense of things, she decided she had no choice but to get on with her day. It was Sunday—the one day in the week that called for a change in her usual routine.

She looked forward to attending Sunday service at the Congregationalist Church in Evansfield. She had met so many kind and generous people there. And not all of them lived in their little village. Throughout the year, families often came from surrounding cities and towns to participate in the service at the historic church. During the early fall when a panoply of vibrant red, gold, and orange leaves painted Vermont hillsides and country lanes in gasp-worthy tapestries, the church literally overflowed with visitors.

Leaf peepers were good for everyone's business. They sipped samples of apple cider from Murphy's Cider Mill and purchased gallon jugs of sweet or hard versions of cider. They nibbled tangy Vermont cheddar at Homer Peterson's roadside stand and then bought wedges cut from huge wheels of aged cheese to take home with them. Tourists and locals alike snatched up brown paper sacks of old-fashioned cinnamon-and-sugar coated doughnuts, still warm from the fryer at the Cat's Cradle. Few left Main Street without stopping to pick up maple sugar candies and buttery-smooth fudge from Denise's Chocolate Designs.

Verity often wondered how many of their purchases made it home if they had a long drive.

The Congregationalist Church was one of the oldest, continuously active houses of worship in the entire state of Vermont. The beautiful, classic structure had been built from the stones pulled out of the surrounding fields by plow horses back in the 17th and 18th centuries. In the 21st century, worshippers were attracted by its colonial ambience and the traditional New England hospitality of the town's residents. Others returned week after week for Pastor Tom Sanders' colorful sermons.

On beautiful clear days like this one, Verity always looked forward to a stroll into town to attend the eleven o'clock service. Dress was casual but never slovenly. Some women wore Sunday-best but most favored clean jeans or slacks and a favorite blouse. Only a few men bothered with a suit or sports jacket, but whatever they appeared in wasn't their work duds. Their wives saw to that. Sundays were Verity's days to store up human contact, since she spent most of the week alone on her farm, or with her farmhands for occasional company.

Today, however, Verity admitted to herself that she felt apprehensive about venturing out among people—familiar or strangers. The more time passed since Elvira's death, the more convinced she'd become that someone had played an active role in Elvira's death. Was it possible that one of her neighbors might be a cold-blooded killer?

Yes, she answered her own question.

Why? Because an outsider who commits murder doesn't hang around to break into homes and write threatening letters— they get the heck out of town. That seemed so obvious to her. Thus, maybe she and her amateur sleuths should be looking for Elvira's killer closer to home. Very close.

The note Percy gave her warned continuing her investigation would result in the writer *killing* her. Well, not precisely but pretty much the same thing. It had said she'd die! You don't argue semantics when your life is at stake! Since the letter writer—presumably the killer—was now majorly pissed at her, it seemed common sense to lie low and avoid intentionally annoying them.

There was one problem with that. Verity, by nature, was not a quitter. She felt compelled to uncover what really had happened to Elvira and set things right.

As she carried out her early morning chores before showering and dressing for church, she imagined how nice it would be if, like in the movies, the sheriff provided her with police protection. Fat chance of that with Bailey in charge of the town's law enforcement! The Grimalski brothers would watch over her if she asked them to, but Sunday was their day off. Jason and Jerry deserved time with their family. And she certainly couldn't ask them to stay overnight during the week if she got the willies again.

Working alone in the dark barn that morning, she felt vulnerable and kept looking over her shoulder. Maybe Percy was right; she shouldn't wait to call the sheriff's office and report the note. But would anyone be there on a Sunday?

Two hours later—chores accomplished and back inside the house, doors locked—she showered. To cheer herself up, she chose the brightest dress in her closet to wear. The sunflower-yellow dress had been one of Mark's favorites. Knee length with a full skirt gathered into a fitted bodice and wide fabric straps over her bare shoulders, it screamed vintage summertime. She added a short-waisted white cardigan and white flats to match the delicate lace edging at the dress's neckline. Hats weren't her thing, except for warmth during the coldest months of the year. She clipped her hair back over one ear with a tortoise shell comb she'd bought at a craft show. During the week, she rarely wore makeup. But today she took time to apply tinted moisturizer, pale pink lip gloss, and a stroke of eyeliner to highlight her hazel eyes. Only one small bruise on her cheek remained after her scuffle with the intruder.

She always walked into town on Sundays. Stepping out her back door she envisioned herself strolling serenely down the country road. In movies, that was always when a black sedan came screaming over a hill to run down the heroine. The Ridgeline was parked on the gravel between the dairy barn and house. If she drove to church, Elvira's killer couldn't smoosh her to roadkill. She turned and marched across the yard toward the reassuringly solid metal cab of her truck.

Verity stopped before reaching for the vehicle's door. "Oh bother!" Changing her Sunday routine felt like giving in to her fears. Letting evil win. Anyway, stuff like that didn't happen in quiet New England towns. Right?

Two weeks ago, a voice inside her head reminded her, *you didn't think someone would murder one of your friends.*

"Argh!" Refusing to be intimidated, she stepped away from the truck, spun around and marched toward the road. After church, she would follow Percy's advice and show the sheriff the threatening letter. What he did about it was up to him.

I can't believe I'm taking the advice of a ghost.

Shaking her head at what her life had become, Verity picked up her pace to get some gentle exercise without working up a sweat and ruining her makeup. She spared only an occasional backward glance at the sound of a vehicle approaching her from behind. The longer she walked along the two-lane highway, the more relaxed she felt.

"Yoohoo, Miss Verity!"

She whipped her head around. No one was behind her but she immediately knew it was Anna Louise. Her tenant...or landlady. She still couldn't figure out which.

Just what I need, she thought and lengthened her gait.

"Ma'am. Miss Verity." Now it was Percy's deep baritone. "I believe I advised you to notify—"

"Yes, I know, Percy. I will inform all the right people about the stupid note. Soon. See, I even have it here with me." She patted the pocket of her skirt. "Now please, both of you, go away." She rolled her eyes toward the cloudless blue sky and murmured a silent prayer that they'd obey.

Another thirty feet along, she could still hear them behind her, whispering to each other. She turned to walk backward along the side of the road and was surprised to find they'd become visible. He, in military dress. She, in a red velvet gown and jewels. Showoffs.

Verity scanned the road anxiously. No cars. Thank goodness!

"Lieutenant and Mrs. Putnam, what do you think you're doing?"

"Don't worry, darlin'. Only you can see us," Anna Louise assured her. "You said we could go to church with you."

Verity did remember saying something of the sort, probably in a weak moment of sympathy for the pair. "You'd better sit near the back of the church; the last two or three rows of pews usually remain empty. We don't want people plopping down into your laps."

"No indeed!" Anna Louise giggled.

A red sports car zipped past heading north. The driver shot Verity a puzzled look. She didn't blame him. If she'd seen someone walking back-to-front down the road while talking animatedly to herself, she'd be inclined to worry.

"Excellent idea!" said Percy.

"And stay invisible. Totally. Not even the faintest glow."

"We wouldn't have it any other way." Anna Louise twinkled at her.

"Because I don't think my quiet little town is ready for a full haunting."

Percy leveled a solemn gaze at her. "Oh, ma'am, we absolutely agree."

They seemed entirely too accommodating. She narrowed her eyes suspiciously at the pair. "Why did you choose to go to church today? You've never mentioned attending before." Of course, she thought, that didn't mean they hadn't been there—in their spirit forms.

Still walking backward, Verity tripped over a rock the size of a small cantaloupe and staggered into the weedy verge before catching her balance. She turned around to walk in a safer manner.

Anna Louise linked arms with her. "We're going with you today because we know that awful letter frightened you." She patted Verity's hand.

"We're quite worried about you," Percy added. "We've decided to be your protectors."

Not exactly the bodyguards she'd imagined, but... "And how do you propose to do that? Protect me, that is."

The ghosts grinned at each other.

"Oh, we have our ways," Anna Louise purred. "First of all, we will—"

"Never mind." Verity waved her off. "I don't think I want to know. Just, whatever you do, please don't make a scene." Although why they'd intentionally draw attention to themselves, she hadn't a clue.

Verity stepped into the cool interior of the old stone church and felt a familiar serenity flow over her. Lilies graced the altar, their scent fighting with a mad blend of perfumes and aftershaves of worshippers and the aroma of coffee already wafting up from the community room downstairs. She scanned the rows of pews on either side of her for familiar faces as she walked up the center aisle, nodding to friends and neighbors as she passed. At last, she spotted Chaundra seated on the right side of the church, beneath a vivid stained-glass window—Jesus and the Apostles. Sunlight cast brilliant bands of red, blue and gold through the glass and across the church's interior. She looked quickly behind her but didn't see her spectral housemates.

Good.

She didn't know why she felt so edgy about them being here. They seemed genuinely concerned for her. It was really rather sweet that they thought they could protect her.

Chaundra turned to look up at her as Verity stepped into the row where she sat. Her dark skin glowed in contrast to the retro ivory knit suit she wore. She studied Verity's face and patted the oak bench, inviting her to sit. "You alright, Veri?"

"Fine. Just tired." She settled against the seat's hard wooden back that never quite fit the natural curve of her spine.

For years, red cushions had softened the church's seats. Eventually they became tatty and needed replacement. The foundation committee decided since bare wood was good enough for their Puritan ancestors' tushes, modern tushes also must make do.

Organ music began with a flourish of chords that rumbled in her chest. The hymn's familiar melody worked its magic on her. She closed her eyes, rested her hands in the yellow cotton fabric over her lap and felt the muscles in her shoulders relax. Soon, the lingering fear from the night before had all but disappeared. Here, among her friends and neighbors, she was surely safe. Elvira's killer wouldn't dare attack her in public. Right?

Verity felt inside her skirt pocket for the threatening note. She'd decided Percy was right. She should show it to her friends as soon as possible. After all, they were doing as much investigating as she was.

She slanted a look at Chaundra. Although Elvira had sniped at the Ethiopian woman as she did nearly everyone when she was in one of her moods, Chaundra never seemed to hold a grudge.

Verity elbowed her gently and slipped the note into her hand. *Read it,* she mouthed. Chaundra blinked in amusement at the request but unfolded the sheet of paper and studied it, her brow puckering as its meaning sank in.

"When did you get this?" she whispered in Verity's ear, barely making herself heard above the organ's soaring crescendo.

"Last night."

"How awful!"

Verity nodded. Out of the corner of her eye she caught a disapproving look from Mrs. Grimalski, her farmhands' mother. She felt like a high school kid, about to be reprimanded for talking in class.

Pastor Sanders opened the service with his usual warm greeting to the congregation. Verity faced forward and tried to look suitably attentive.

"Has anyone else seen this?" Chaundra whispered.

"Not yet." Verity held out her hand for the note. When she didn't feel the paper against her palm, she side-eyed Chaundra and saw her tapping the shoulder of the man in front of her.

Before Verity could stop her, Chaundra shoved the note at him with a wave toward Kate, who was sitting with her husband and their two little girls another row forward.

"Oh, no!" Verity gasped.

Mrs. Grimalski poked her in the back with a rock-hard finger.

"What?" Chaundra whispered.

"I didn't mean for you to—" Verity lifted her hands helplessly. By the time she turned away from Chaundra again, Kate was passing the note along their pew toward the center-aisle, where Martha Humphrey sat.

Verity covered her eyes with both hands and stifled a groan.

"Sorry," Chaundra whispered in her right ear. "I thought you wanted me to show the others."

Not now! But she didn't say it out loud, and anyway it was too late. Three other people in the row peeked inside the folded paper before passing it along.

"Are you ill?" Anna Louise breathed in Verity's other ear, making her jump. "You don't look at all well, darlin'."

"The note," Verity rasped, pointing toward Martha.

"You don't want her to read it?"

"Right." Although she was whispering as softly as she possibly could, this earned her another poisonous glare from Mrs. G.

Chaundra glanced at her with concern, as did others in the congregation. If chatting with a friend during the service was bad form, talking to no one at all was apparently worse.

"I shall retrieve it for you!" the ghost announced gleefully.

"No!" Verity's shouted, which brought one of the ushers running up the side aisle from the rear of the church.

Mortified, Verity murmured, "Sorry. Sorry, so sorry!" to everyone around her. She pantomimed "lips-zipped."

"Asperger's," a woman somewhere behind her pronounced far too loudly. "They can't help themselves."

Flushing from embarrassment, Verity looked around frantically. Where were those ghosts? It was good, of course, that they were staying invisible. But she had to see them to make sure they did nothing more to disrupt the entire service.

She looked behind her. The usher was now halfway up the aisle, hurtling toward her, as unstoppable as a comet. She imagined him hauling her out of her seat by the scruff of her neck like a naughty child. In front of half the town. She felt sick to her stomach.

And then a miracle happened.

Two miracles, actually. The first was ok as miracles go. The second, not so much.

Miracle #1: The usher tripped. Or *was* tripped, as she later discovered. He disappeared behind a wave of worshippers who had just been asked by their minister to rise for the singing of the first hymn.

Verity stared in shock. While nearby people rushed to assist the man scrambling on the floor, and the rest of the congregation burst into song, she used the precious few minutes she'd been given to figure out what to do before another usher could get to her.

Her heart racing, Verity desperately searched the crowd for any sign of Lieutenant and Mrs. Putnam, deceased. She couldn't see them anywhere.

That was when Miracle #2 happened. The white square of paper that had been passed, hand-to-hand moments earlier, now fluttered with the grace of a swallow from the far side of the church toward her.

Oh. My. God! She felt dizzy, probably from lack of oxygen. She'd definitely stopped breathing.

Verity watched, mesmerized by the mysterious twirls and leaps of the note that might just have been possible had there been a particularly strong and erratic breeze wafting through the church. But the air wasn't moving at all. The paper never descended low enough for anyone to grab it, although a few did try.

Oh no! No, no, no! But this time she kept her lips pressed together even though the robust hymn-singing voices surely would have drowned her out.

A small red-and-white sign to the right of the altar caught her eye. *Exit.* She prayed the door wouldn't be locked.

The note floated slowly down within her reach. She snatched it out of the air, pushed past Chaundra and the other five people between her and the side aisle, and made her escape.

CHAPTER 34

VERITY RUSHED INTO HER MUDROOM, breathless from having run all the way home. Before she even made it to her kitchen, her phone started ringing from inside her purse. She unzipped the side pocket; wrong one. Unzipped another. Felt around inside. No phone.

You'd think the thing had a lead sinker attached to it. Somehow it always ended up at the very bottom. Giving up, she pulled the shoulder strap up and over her head and dumped out the entire contents of her purse on the kitchen table.

Denise's name flashed on caller ID. She punched "answer" just as the ringing stopped.

"No!" she screeched, throwing her hands up in frustration.

"Verity, are you alright?" Miraculously, Denise was still there.

"I'm fine," she gasped. *Liar.* She hadn't stopped shaking since she made her humiliating retreat from the church. She was sure the entire congregation had been staring at her as she disappeared out the door.

Verity collapsed on the closest chair. Her chest cramped

with every breath. In college she used to have painful anxiety attacks before tests. This felt annoyingly similar.

God! Would she need to change churches, too?

"You took off like maple sap in the spring," Denise barked at her through the phone. "We looked for you after the service. Katie said you'd volunteered to help clean up after coffee and donuts."

Verity moaned. "Sorry. I had to leave without telling anyone."

"You looked like you'd seen a ghost."

Imagine that! she thought.

Although…she hadn't actually *seen* either of her two resident spirits. They'd remained invisible to everyone, including her. She clenched her jaw and scanned the kitchen. No electric-blue sparkly shades hovered nearby. They were probably hiding, having seen her reaction and realizing how furious she would be with them.

"Deacon Adams looked fit to kill, sprinting up the aisle after you started shouting." Denise sounded less angry than amused. "My grandma once made me watch a silent movie with her—Keystone Cops, I think she called it. You and the deacon were far more entertaining."

Verity imagined Anna Louise—or was it Percy?—floating above people in the church with her note. How could it not occur to the ghosts that the air in the church was as motionless as a cemetery headstone? A self-propelled letter was bound to look suspicious.

"Verity? You there? Oh my God, the killer!" Denise's voice dropped to a tense whisper. "Has he come back? Is he there with you now? Just say 'present and accounted for' if he is."

"No, not present!" Verity said. "Really I'm fine, Denise. I was just so embarrassed when Chaundra passed that stupid note around for the world to see."

"I'm sorry. I guess she must have misunderstood. For her eyes only." She chuckled. "James Bond. Get it? For Your Eyes Only?"

"I get it," Verity groaned. "Was Deacon Adams badly hurt when he fell?" She guessed Percy had something to do with that. Which meant Anna Louise must have been the note fetcher.

"Oh, I doubt it. He stood up right away...well, with a little help. And after the service, we all trooped downstairs for coffee like nothing had happened. I saw him helping himself to a whole plateful of doughnuts. That man sure loves his junk food. Although I shouldn't complain, he's one of my best customers at the chocolate shop."

"Your amazing creations aren't junk food, by any stretch of the imagination." Verity sighed, wishing she had a big ol' hunk of Denise's dark-chocolate almond bark to take her mind off the catastrophic day.

"Thank you," Denise said. "Listen, I called the EPI members and—"

"The who?"

"EPI. Evansfield Private Investigators."

"We have a name now?" Verity raised an eyebrow.

"Why not? As I was saying...only part of the group was in church and read that threatening note. Now the rest want to see it. We also need to make some important decisions."

Verity frowned. "What kinds of decisions?"

"You'll see," Denise brushed off her question. "Sunny asked me to make sure you're at home now, and safe. Are you?"

"Yeah."

"Doors and windows locked?"

"You betcha." Why was she channeling her father's Midwestern dialect?

"Good. Stay there. We're coming right over." And she hung up.

Fifteen minutes later, two cars pulled up to the farmhouse's back door in a cloud of dust and screech of brakes. Women exploded out of the vehicles like kernels of popping corn. Verity stood on her back porch, counting heads. It looked like everyone was "present and accounted for."

Mary Beth was carrying a small brown paper sack, which she handed to Verity.

"What's this?"

"The after-service doughnuts you missed. You need your strength. I saved you two of your faves—chocolate cake, glazed."

"You're an angel, MB." Verity smiled. "Thanks. I didn't eat breakfast and probably should opt for something more nourishing. But if I drown my coffee with milk, I can count that as a serving of protein. Right?"

"Absolutely. And I'm sure there was an egg in the batter for those donuts."

Sunny took charge immediately and led the group through the farmhouse's rear door then into the living room. Verity barely had time to nuke a mug of water for instant coffee. No time to perk her favorite brew. A sacrifice, but needs must.

"First off," Sunny was saying to those already seated by the time Verity joined them, "you should know that Verity and I followed Doctor Evans. We haven't had a chance to report what we discovered until now. And we have photos." She nodded to Verity who spread out the photographs she'd printed.

"Does anyone recognize this woman?" Sunny pointed at the best closeup of Evans and the mystery woman.

"Oh my, they look friendly, don't they?" Chaundra

narrowed her eyes. "You're thinking this might be the Olive Oyl from Elvira's diaries?"

Sunny nodded and soft gasps filled the room.

"No," Chaundra said after a moment, "I don't think I've ever seen her." Everyone else agreed.

"Right. Then obviously, we need to get these to the sheriff." Sunny turned to Verity. "We can't wait any longer to act, now that the threats have continued."

Verity nodded reluctantly in agreement.

"Next, who hasn't already seen the letter Verity received?" Two hands went up. "Ok. So that's Fumiko, Denise, and me. Verity, if you please, may we see what we've missed?"

Verity slid the now thoroughly rumpled sheet of paper out from the pocket of her sundress skirt and handed it to Sunny. The room fell silent as she read aloud the menacing words.

No one moved or made a sound for a full ten seconds after she finished. Then, mayhem broke out.

"I can't believe this!" Mary Beth shouted, bouncing up off the sofa. "Who would do something like that?"

Denise laughed. "You believed Elvira was murdered but you can't believe someone would write a menacing letter?"

"That's not what I meant."

"We can't let someone get away with stuff like...!" Kate waved her hands in the air, in lieu of finding the right words. "First killing Elvira then attacking poor Verity. And now, terrorizing her or worse, if they mean what they say."

"The sheriff ought to be replaced—useless slug of a man," Martha muttered.

"It's not his fault a crazed killer has targeted our town," Kate whispered, tears in her eyes. "I bet he's...he's just..." An attack of hiccups got the better of her.

"Lazy?" Fumiko suggested.

Chaundra laid a hand over Kate's and looked up at Sunny.

"Maybe we should do what the note says and stop poking around."

"No!" Verity stated firmly. "We can't give up now. Obviously, our investigation has made whoever killed Elvira nervous. That means we must be getting close to the truth."

"She's right," Sunny said. "Now that Verity and I have found the mysterious Olive Oyl—"

"And so, apparently, has the good doctor," Denise waggled a brow.

Sunny shot a warning glare at Denise and continued. "I believe it's becoming more likely John Evans had something to do with his wife's death. But exactly how, we don't know. He could have acted alone, had the help of his lover, or even paid someone to cause Elvira's death."

"He's definitely acting suspicious, I'll give you that much," Denise agreed from her seat on the carpet, her legs tucked under the coffee table. "But whether Elvira jumped or we've got a killer is in our midst, we're not the ones who should be tracking him down. It's the damn sheriff's job!"

"You can't blame Sheriff Bailey if some drifter wandered into town and killed our friend," Kate protested in his defense.

Verity smiled affectionately at the young mother. How lovely it must be to always think the best of people.

"Drifters don't hang around after murdering someone so they can break into a house and then write nasty letters," Chaundra stated, echoing Verity's earlier thoughts. "Unless they're imbeciles."

Martha muttered, "Bailey ought to be removed from office. He's doing nothing."

A burst of seconds prompted Sunny to stand up and place two fingers between her lips. Her earsplitting whistle created abrupt silence.

Verity looked around her living room at the distraught faces of her friends, feeling a sour tension in the air that hadn't been there before. They had always gotten along so well as a group, but now she sensed the beginning of a rift. Fear was pulling them apart.

Sunny resumed speaking. "Ladies, this is getting us nowhere. Let's at least agree that what has happened in our town is unacceptable. Our friend has died, possibly was murdered. Verity has been attacked in her home. Now someone is threatening her life. And whether or not the sheriff is doing his job properly, can we at least agree that we need to give him another chance and let him see this note?"

Murmured responses ensued. "Absolutely." "Sure." "Of course."

"I'll deliver the note to him tomorrow," Verity agreed. "But honestly, I'm convinced he'll find any excuse to do nothing. He might even accuse me of having written it myself."

"We know you never do such crazy thing!" Fumiko cried.

"Even Fred Bailey will know that," Martha said. "But he still might not take the threat seriously." She gave Verity an anemic smile, no doubt her best attempt to reassure.

Denise banged her fists down on the coffee table. "We need to be proactive!"

Verity feared for her poor table's survival.

"Expecting Verity to just sit around and wait for another attack isn't a solution," Denise said. "At the very least, I think we should take turns staying with her at the farm."

"Like bodyguards?" Kate scoffed. "Oh, my God! What good can we do? Then *two* of us will get murdered!"

"Katie's right," Mary Beth said, glumly. "We're not cops or even professional detectives. We haven't been trained to handle this sort of thing."

"It's worse than anyone here is admitting." Martha interrupted in her most strident school-teacher voice. Everyone stared at her.

"What do you mean, dear?" Sunny said. "How can it get worse than this?"

"Whether or not we try to protect Verity, we're already in danger. All of us. Not just Verity. This killer—if he exists, and we seem to agree he does—is furious with us for trying to catch him. And you know what they say about a cornered animal being dangerous." She shook a finger at them for emphasis. "That's what we're doing, forcing him to protect himself. Forcing him to kill again." She lowered her voice and squinted at each of them in turn. "Think about it! He could pick us off, one at a time. Nothing is stopping him. Certainly not our idiot sheriff!"

"Oh, do you really think so?" Kate whimpered. She dropped her head into her hands.

Chaundra shifted in her seat, looking nervous. "I can't believe I'm saying this but—I think I agree with Martha. We've taken our investigations as far as we can. Maybe too far."

"But we can't stop now!" Sunny sounded suddenly desperate. "Verity's right. We've obviously made the killer nervous—that's a good thing. Now they will be more likely to make a mistake. We just need to be patient and hold our ground."

Kate shook her head, her eyes red-rimmed. "I have two little kids. I'm sorry, guys, but my first allegiance is to them and to my husband. Tony never wanted me to get involved in this. I promised him we were just doing book research and I'd be perfectly safe. I don't think that's true anymore."

"Does anyone else feel they need to drop out?" Verity asked in as calm a voice as possible with her heart racing. "I promise, I won't be hurt if you do." She gave Sunny an apologetic look. "It's only fair that we each do what we think is right."

Sunny nodded with obvious reluctance.

Mary Beth held up her hand. "Sorry, gang. But I'm with Kate. It was fun playing detective. But, as the mayor pointed out to me the other day, we may just be inviting trouble. There's no telling what this horrible person might do to avoid being caught."

"Anyone else?" Sunny asked, looking a bit like a deflated birthday party balloon in her candy-floss-pink, going-to-church dress.

They looked at one another solemnly.

Denise groaned. "Ok. I guess I'll hang in for another week. My boyfriend—former boyfriend—told me before he broke up with me last night that he thought I was loony for doing this stuff." She chuckled. "Maybe he's right. The Evansfield Private Investigators. What a laugh!"

"I'm definitely in," Verity stated. "I can't stop now. I feel as though I'd be letting down Peter and Laura if I passed up the chance to give them the truth about their mother's death."

"I'll stay, but not much longer," Martha agreed, looking solemnly out the window. "Things are getting a little too scary, even for a kindergarten teacher."

"Fine. Let's give it another week," Sunny said. "Kate and Mary Beth are out, though. That leaves six of us. Chaundra, Verity, Denise, Fumiko, Martha, and me." She faced Verity. "Sweetie, I'm not a quitter, but the others may be right. If we're really in danger, we need to let the pros take over."

"But that's the problem, isn't it?" Verity insisted. "What do we do if professional law enforcement continues to refuse to step up? Just quit?"

"So far, the rusty cog has been Fred Bailey," Sunny pointed out. "Going over his head will cause all sorts of grief, I'm sure. But we may need to do just that. Maybe that means seeking the help of the state police."

"Or the FBI!" Mary Beth shouted with far too much enthusiasm.

Did the FBI even concern themselves with supposed suicides? Verity didn't think so.

"Oh, good grief, MB," Chaundra snapped. "Next thing you'll be calling on the Secret Service or NSA."

Mary Beth beamed dreamily. "Do you think they'd come?"

Sunny rolled her eyes. "We need a serious plan of action."

"First—we protect our Verity," Fumiko insisted.

"Absolutely," Sunny agreed. "And we'll do that by making sure she's never alone."

Verity opened her mouth to speak but Martha beat her to it.

"Seriously? We're all busy with our own lives. Are you saying we need eyes-on-her 24/7?"

Sunny turned to Verity with a look of concern. "How well do you trust your hired help?"

"Jason and Jerry? I'd entrust them with my life. Absolutely!"

"So, when they are here on your farm, you need to stick close to them. Show them the note. They'll understand and want to help by watching over you."

"But the boys leave at five pm," Verity objected. "And they're off on Sundays." The nighttime, it seemed to her, would be the obvious choice for the killer to strike, if the threats weren't empty.

"That's when one of us comes to stay with you. Or," Sunny added brightly, "you could spend Sundays and nights at one of our houses."

Verity prickled at the thought of being uprooted from her own home.

Sunny sighed. "Sweetie, it's for your own good. Martha can work out the assignments. She's good at organizing things."

Martha nodded, looking pleased with the compliment.

Mary Beth reached out to grip Verity's hand. "We would

feel just terrible if anything happened to you." Her eyes glistened, but not, Verity thought, with tears. Excitement? The woman looked a little manic. But then, Verity thought, she often did.

Denise harrumphed. "That can't be all there is to our plan. Shack up with Verity and wait for the killer to strike?"

"You're right. That was just Part One." Sunny's blue eyes glowed the way they did when she tried out a new recipe at the café—and then stood over you waiting for you to taste it. Heaven help you if you said you didn't like it. "Part Two: Verity and I deliver the note along with the photographs we took of Dr. Evans and his lover to the sheriff. As soon as he arrests them, Verity will be safe!"

"And what if the doctor wasn't involved in Elvira's death?" Chaundra said.

Sunny looked pensive for a moment. "Obviously, we'd have no choice but to move on to Part Three: Setting a trap to force the killer out into the open!"

Verity stared at the café owner in disbelief. In movies, setting a trap for a criminal often ended badly for whoever was the bait. And like it or not, that's what she was. Bait.

CHAPTER 35

"YOU HAVE no proof this woman is anything but a patient!" Sheriff Bailey pushed the photographs back across his desk.

Verity threw up her hands in disgust. "You can't just ignore—"

"This *is* evidence!" Sunny wailed.

"No, it isn't." Bailey tucked in his chins, the image of stubbornness.

"Bullshit!" Denise growled under her breath, earning her a poisonous glare from the sheriff.

Sunny and Denise had volunteered to accompany Verity to the sheriff's office for moral support when she delivered the photographs and death-threat note to Fred Bailey. Although Verity had already emailed him copies of the photos she had snapped of John Evans and the attractive blonde woman, the sheriff had failed to respond. Cornering the man in his cluttered office, which was not much bigger than a closet, seemed the only way to make him listen to them.

The three women sat in creaky wooden folding chairs facing his massive oak desk. What space remained in the room was taken up by bookshelves overflowing with law books, journals and magazines, many of which appeared older than the sheriff himself. As much a part of the building as the very walls.

While Sunny calmly explained witnessing the romantic rendezvous in front of the woman's house, Bailey had listened calmly, nodding his big head occasionally, never once interrupting her. But then he held up a hand the size of Rhode Island, signaling he'd heard enough.

"I understand you ladies are upset," he said. "Why, that note is enough to rattle anyone's bones. But imagining the woman in these pictures is the doc's mistress and there was some kind of conspiracy to murder his wife, that's just—" his gaze wandered as if searching for words to pluck from the air "—pure romantic fantasy. In a town this size, don't you think someone would know if the doc had a lady friend? You gals been readin' far too many o' them Harlequin paperbacks."

Sunny slid her sunglasses down her nose and peered over them at Bailey, her blue eyes dark as a stormy sea. Denise lowered her chin like a bull preparing to charge. Verity restrained herself from saying, *I told you so.* Hadn't she warned her friends he wouldn't listen to them?

"Which one of you dreamt up this insanity?" Sheriff Bailey stared at Sunny. "You're usually the sensible one of this crew, Sunny Whitaker." His gaze shifted toward Verity. "Naw, it's more likely Mrs. Cade's doing."

Verity glared at him, refusing to be cowed. "This isn't our imaginations. Just look at these pictures!"

"I saw the woman with my own eyes," Sunny objected. "She *kissed* John. Patients don't go around snogging their physicians."

"Kissed him?" he grinned, his anger slipping away to amusement. "I doubt it's the first time a woman's done that. John is a good-looking man. Even while Elvira was alive, he generated plenty of female interest hereabouts. Why do you s'pose so many of his patients are women?"

"Maybe because he is the only doctor in town and he's capable?" Verity stated dryly.

The sheriff closed his eyes as if pained. "The woman probably just wanted to show her sympathy, losing his wife like he done."

"Ok, forget about the mystery woman," Denise snapped. "What about that threatening note left for Verity? Whoever wrote it didn't intend just to spook Verity so she'd stop looking into Elvira's so-called suicide. Can't you recognize a death threat when you see one?"

"All I see is a kid's prank. Just look at that writing." The sheriff jabbed a fat finger at the page lying on his desk blotter. "Looks like it's written by a ten-year-old with a crayon."

"Red pencil," Verity said. "Maybe blood was hard to come by."

The sheriff gave her a hard look. "Listen, ladies, everyone in town knows about the break-in at Mrs. Cade's house." He heaved himself up and out of his double-wide seat with surprising alacrity. "Some numbskull thinks he's bein' funny by tauntin' her. There's nothing more to it than that. But just to make you feel more at ease, Mrs. Cade, I'll tell my guys to keep an eagle eye out for any unusual activity at your farm."

A sudden movement caught Verity's attention and she turned to her right. Denise's face had gone blood red, her eyes bulging, jaw clamped tight enough to contain the steam.

Verity reached toward her. "No, Deni—"

Denise lunged toward the sheriff, fortunately stopped by the substantial desk between them. Jamming her fists down at her sides she glowered at the man. "This is crap, John Bailey, and you know it! It doesn't take a criminal expert to see someone doesn't want questions asked about Elvira's death. Why are you covering for them?"

Bailey was around his desk in two thudding strides and

plowing toward Denise. All three women jumped from their seats. Denise braced herself, arms crossed defiantly over her chest. Sunny teetered back on her heels.

"Now, I'll say this once, so I hope you gals pay attention." Verity had never seen the man so angry. His entire body was quivering with rage. "I've sworn to uphold the law and protect the residents of Evansfield. I intend to do exactly that."

He observed them for a moment, as though hoping to see less resolve in their expressions, then sighed. Some of the heat drained from his face. His big shoulders lowered an inch.

"Please, let me do my job, ladies. I promise you, these incidents are totally unrelated. Elvira either jumped to her death or she chose to go for a walk alone at night in a very dangerous place. Bad decision on her part. We'll probably never know what she was thinkin'." He drew a rattly smoker's breath. "As to the break-in at Mrs. Cade's home, it's got nothin' to do with Elvira Evans. Thief just thought he might find something he could sell for drug money."

"What about her diaries? *They* are the connection," Verity insisted. "The thief was trying to steal them! Obviously, we weren't supposed to see something written in one of them."

She hated the way her voice had risen a whole octave, making her sound like a little girl complaining about a bully. She swallowed and forced herself to continue.

"Elvira made enemies over the years," she stated firmly. "Lots of them. My friends and I have read, *in her own words*, how she used and hurt people. Surely that's motive enough for someone to want to kill her."

Bailey looked down his red-veined nose at her in exasperation. "No one breaks into a house to steal books. Money, computers, jewelry—yes. Not books. Never books. The idiot must have picked up the wrong box in his panic when you confronted him."

He sighed as though resigned to the fact nothing he said was going to satisfy them. "In good police work we avoid jumpin' to conclusions or creatin' connections where none exist. All I'm sayin' is, nothin' you brought me changes or proves a thing."

He stomped forward in his Size-13 boots, arms spread wide like a sheepherder. Verity shuffled back toward his office door, Sunny and Denise bunching in close to her.

"You—you're doing zilch?" Denise stammered in disbelief. "Is that what you're saying?"

"I will find out who your mystery woman is," Bailey said. "But if she turns out to be a patient, and I guarantee she is, you're not getting her name." He held up a warning finger before they could respond. "*And*, if it turns out she's the doc's girlfriend, you don't get anythin' about her from me. Their relationship is none of your damn business."

"Just one more thing, sheriff," Verity begged weakly then jumped back again as he continued herding them out his door. "Please?"

"Go home, all of you," he grumbled. "Stop interferin' in your neighbors' lives. Leave the goddamn police work to me."

Verity had intended to tell him about their trap. But clearly, any chance of gaining his help had passed.

CHAPTER 36

THAT NIGHT, the Evansfield Private Investigators, diminished in number by Kate's and Mary Beth's resignations, met again at the Cat's Cradle Café. Sunny's aromatic, dark coffee ('drop two dollars in the jar, please') and free day-old pastries ('I can't sell them tomorrow anyway') rewarded those still willing to pursue the mystery of Elvira's death. Verity guessed from the frequent glances toward the window, everyone was probably thinking the same thing.

Was Elvira's murderer lurking somewhere in the shadows, waiting for them to step outside? And here they were, calling attention to themselves, sitting in the window of a brightly lit café. From out in the dark street, they'd look like helpless little fishies on display in an aquarium. Easy targets. A shiver ran up her spine.

"Verity." Sunny's sharpish tone let her know it probably wasn't the first time she'd called for her attention. "Will you fill in Chaundra, Martha, Fumiko and Katie about the sheriff's reaction to our visit?"

Verity winced. It wasn't an experience she particularly wanted to relive. Reluctantly, she related their presentation of the photographs and threatening note to the sheriff. She also mentioned his angry reaction to their Lovers-From-the-Past-Turn-to-Murder theory.

"He refused to even question the doctor or the woman about their movements on the night of Elvira's death?" Chaundra made a bewildered face.

Denise rolled her eyes. "When Verity dared suggest that the doc and his former fiancée might have anything to do with Elvira's death, Bailey just blew her off."

"Well, it is a bit of a stretch," Martha said looking around at the others. "Isn't it? I mean, seriously. Doctor Evans?"

"Sound like Japanese *dorama*," Fumiko giggled. But when she took in their blank faces she added, "Like bad American soap opera."

"The likeliest explanation," Martha said, "is the simplest one. Elvira was looking for Peter and when she stepped too close to the edge of the quarry, it just gave way."

"I have to admit that does seem the most plausible explanation." Sunny sipped her coffee thoughtfully. "Verity, when this all started you were at the quarry when you found the note signed by her son. Did the ground surrounding the pit look unstable to you?"

"It did seem sort of crumbly near the edge." She tried to recall details. "But I didn't notice a major disturbance in the ground like you might expect to find if a person had lost their footing and they were scrambling for their life before falling over."

"Well," Chaundra mused, "it's probably too late to see signs of that by now. We've had a few days of rain since then."

Denise made an exasperated sound deep in her throat. "We need to focus on how to spring our trap instead of arguing about all this other stuff."

"Right," Sunny said. Although she didn't sound as if her heart was still in it.

Chaundra and Martha looked at each other and shrugged.

"So-o-o," Verity said, "any suggestions how one goes about designing a trap to catch a killer?"

For a long moment no one spoke. Verity finished the lemon Danish she'd selected from Sunny's leftover pastries. Denise chose a second chocolate éclair. Fumiko ran her fingertip around the rim of her mug of tea, appearing deep in thought.

"I have an idea," Martha said at last. "Verity can announce she has new evidence and she's taking it to the state police."

"Going over Bailey's head? Oh, he's gonna love that!" Denise laughed.

"What new evidence?" Fumiko yipped. "What I miss?"

Martha grinned. "She doesn't really have anything new. Do you?" She glanced sideways at Verity, who wished she could read the strange expression that had just crossed the teacher's face. Was it hopeful, concerned, or something Martha was making an effort to conceal?

"No, of course not." Verity sighed. "If I did know anything more, I'd have told the sheriff. And he'd still have thrown us out of his office." This getting tossed out of people's workplaces seemed to have developed into a weird pattern in her life.

"It doesn't matter," Martha insisted. "All you need to do is mention to a few people that you've discovered evidence which will change what everybody thinks about Elvira's death. Do it during lunchtime right here in the Cat's Cradle. Word will spread like wildfire." She grinned as if pleased with herself.

"Why me?" Verity said.

"Because you are the one who has been reporting what we find to the sheriff. You're our spokesperson. And you received the threat."

"She's right," Sunny agreed. "In his office, you made it clear you were frustrated because he refused to act on the note that threatened you. So, it's logical you'd take new evidence to a higher authority."

"And once the killer hears what you're doing, he'll of course want to stop you," Martha said.

Verity rolled her eyes up at the pressed-tin ceiling. "So, to stop me from going to the state police, the killer will have to come after me. Fantastic. Dare I ask what will stop this maniac from murdering me?"

"We will, sweetie. All of us," Sunny said in her most reassuring voice. "During the day you'll be on your farm with your strapping young farmhands to protect you. The Grimalski brothers will be thrilled with the idea of playing bodyguard and getting a chance to snag a murderer. It's only during the night when you'll be vulnerable."

Verity shuddered. "Exactly. I'm the sacrificial lamb. I love it." *Not!*

"Don't worry." Sunny gave her arm a consoling double pat. "We'll take turns staying with you at night. When Elvira's killer shows up, whoever is on guard duty will simply call 911 and report an intruder. The sheriff's department has to respond to emergency calls."

For the next two days, life seemed almost normal to Verity. Maybe even better. She found Jason and Jerry's added vigilance comforting. She enjoyed working alongside them in the barns or fields, and they made an extra effort to stay close by when she needed to be off by herself in the house. She couldn't help feeling, if she ever had a son, she would be thrilled if he grew into someone as kind, hardworking and smart as the twins.

When the boys left for the night, her assigned sleep-over buddy showed up. She cooked omelets for Sunny and herself the first night. Denise insisted on making tacos the next night. Verity and her bodyguards talked about everything—their childhood, plans for the future, favorite TV shows and books. Verity felt safe, happy and closer than ever to the two women. She had friends who cared enough about her to set aside their personal routines and watch over her. By the third night, the threats and break-in seemed less real and no more than what the sheriff claimed—unrelated incidents, nothing worth worrying about.

Day 3, Martha was on night duty. Dinner was spaghetti with marinara sauce and a salad of fresh greens and ripe tomatoes from Verity's own garden. They played Scrabble to pass the evening. Martha was an excellent player and won all but the last game. Verity couldn't make up her mind whether the schoolteacher was just tired of playing or had intentionally let her win because she felt guilty for having beaten her so badly three times in a row.

"You know," Verity admitted, brushing the Scrabble tiles off the table and back into their box, "I feel rather silly for fussing so about that stupid note."

"It probably was just meant to scare you," Martha said.

"Maybe," she admitted.

Martha yawned and stretched her arms over her head. The belled sleeves of her white peasant blouse fell to her elbows.

Verity frowned and pointed at Martha's left arm. "Where did you get that scratch? It looks infected."

Martha lowered both arms and smoothed down her sleeves. "Caught myself on the rose bush in my backyard when I was trimming it. It's fine," she retorted, looking a little annoyed. "I know how to take care of little scrapes."

Verity laughed. "Of course you do. I'll bet your young students bring you all sorts of injuries from the playground."

Martha gave a stiff nod. "Indeed, they do." She rubbed her

eyes. "I hope you don't mind if I go upstairs and have a lie down. I'm used to early nights."

"Of course not," Verity said. "I'll be glad to get a good night's sleep, myself." She stopped herself from adding that Sunny and Denise had kept her so well entertained she'd been up hours later with them. They'd also diligently watched over her, sitting outside her bedroom door until dawn when her farmhands reported in.

"Don't worry," Martha said sleepily, as if she'd read her thoughts, "I'm a very light sleeper. At the whisk of a mouse tail, I'm on my feet. My phone will be right beside me. But I doubt it will be necessary."

"You may be right," Verity admitted. After all, it had been days since she started the rumor about taking new evidence of Elvira's murder to the state police. Surely the guilty person wouldn't risk waiting to stop her.

As on previous nights, Verity provided clean sheets for the guest room. Martha retreated upstairs with a mumbled, "G'night."

Verity tidied the kitchen in preparation for the morning. Upstairs, she undressed for bed, brushed her teeth, moisturized her face and hands then closed her bedroom door. She grabbed the mystery novel at the top of her reading pile and stretched out in bed to read herself to sleep. After fifteen minutes she gave up. Although she'd enjoyed the story the last time she picked up the book, this time she felt unable to focus.

Turning out the light, she lay down on her left side as she did every night. But this put her back to the bedroom door, and tonight that somehow felt creepy. Eyes on the door, even if they eventually drifted shut, seemed somehow safer.

Idiot! she chided herself.

She clamped her eyes shut and eventually felt her muscles relax, her body sinking deeper into the soft mattress and bedding. Her mind swam with the vertiginous sensations she recognized as the precursor to a slow, blissful slide into deep sleep.

That was when she heard the dull click of a door latch.

Still adrift in a semi-conscious state, she kept her eyes closed. *The house is talking to you, Verity.* But the sound of feet padding softly across the floor came to her.

Verity's eyes flicked open. The moon's silver glow filtered through her gauze curtains.

From close to her ear came an urgent whisper, "Wake up! Now!"

Ghosts! she thought ruefully. She needed her sleep. Why couldn't they leave her alone?

"Get out of my room!" she roared, bolting straight up in bed.

That was when she saw someone standing in the shadows just inside her open bedroom door. The door she definitely remembered shutting before getting into bed. And the figure was not a glittering apparition with blonde curls bouncing at her cheeks. Neither was it a Civil War veteran turned farmer.

Verity's hand shot out. She switched on the bedside lamp. The etched-glass globe cast delicate flower shapes against the walls. Martha Humphrey stood in her bathrobe, blinking at her. She held a knife in one hand, lips locked in a firm line. She stared wide-eyed at Verity.

Verity swallowed. "Martha? What the—"

Just then a vehicle ground its way up the farm's driveway. Headlights flashed across the bedroom window from outside. Martha's eyes darted to the window then back to Verity.

"I just came to tell you." She held the knife out in front of her, as if she thought Verity might not have seen it. "I-I heard someone outside. I didn't know what else to do other than grab a weapon from downstairs then warn you."

"Ummm, thank you." Verity swept back the bedcovers and rushed to the window.

With her eyes still blinded by the lamp's light, she couldn't make out anything in the darkness outside. Then, coming around the back of the barn, she saw the beam of a flashlight tracking across her yard. The light disappeared as it came closer to the house. She heard the side-porch door rattle.

"Oh, God!" Martha cried. "They're trying to get into the house!"

The whispers in Verity's ear returned but she brushed them away like annoying mosquitoes. "I'm going out there to find out what's going on," she said, "and put an end to this nonsense."

"Oh, Verity, no! You...you should stay here."

"No! You call 911 like we planned." Verity reached under her bed for Mark's shotgun, already loaded like always. No kids in the house to worry about, and there was always a chance of a marauding fox, wolf or, tonight, something on two legs.

Martha's eyes saucered. "I didn't know you h-had... You wouldn't shoot—"

"I would. Now get on the phone. Use the old landline on the stair landing. The police will immediately know our location."

"Oh, oh, oh my," Martha panted, looking ever more pale.

An adrenaline cocktail of fear and excitement coursed through Verity's veins. She rocketed down the stairs barely feeling them beneath her bare feet. She raced through her dark kitchen, into the mudroom.

There was no window in the door that opened onto the rear porch, no way to know who might be on the other side. She didn't want to fling wide the door and open fire. The sheriff might be right. Teenagers just messing about. But she refused to continue hiding in her own home, playing the victim.

She stood back from the closed door and listened. She heard

the scuffle of boots on the wood planks of her porch. Then the scratch of a struck match. *What the hell?* Who stopped for a smoke in the middle of a B&E?

"Get the hell off my property!" she shouted and raised the shotgun to her shoulder, as if the person on the other side of the wall could see her and know she meant business. "The police are on their way. If you don't move this instant, I'm going to unload this shotgun through you."

"I would 'preciate you not doing that, Mrs. Cade."

She blinked. She slowly lowered the shotgun, her finger still quivering over the trigger. "Sheriff?"

"Yes, ma'am."

She hesitated then stepped forward and opened the door. "What are you doing here?"

"I knew you were scared the day you and your friends invaded my office." He puffed on his cigar and observed her with what might actually be concern. "I been stoppin' by each night, just to check on you." He gave her a smug look. "Bet you didn't even know."

"I didn't," she admitted sheepishly. "But thank you. I think."

"You look disappointed to see me. Who was you expectin'?"

She shook her head. "Never mind."

"Let me guess. Elvira's killer?"

She looked down and remembered then to take her finger off the trigger. Damn guns, she hated them.

"I think you'd best put that blaster of yours away for the night. No one's lurkin' around your outbuildings. All's quiet. I'll be 'round a little longer while I finish my cigar."

She gave him a meek nod. It didn't seem fair that her skittishness should cost the man his sleep. "I do appreciate your concern," she said. "I know my behavior probably seems ridiculous to you."

"I'm not one to judge," he said. She nearly laughed at that.

Just then, Martha burst through the door and onto the porch, puffing out breaths like an old steam engine. "They're on their way!" she shouted. "The police, I mean. Uh, Sheriff?"

"Don't worry, I'll call off the cavalry." He waved at them with his cigar hand, clumped down the stairs and off the porch. The beam from his flashlight picked out his SUV, parked around the corner of the driveway and tucked in beside the hay barn.

Verity looked at Martha, who appeared deflated, the wrinkles around her mouth and shadows beneath her eyes cavernous in the dark. "Thanks for waking me, Martha, even if it was a false alarm."

The teacher seemed miles away. She scowled into the dark as if she hadn't even heard her.

"Martha? Are you alright? I'm so sorry if all this drama has frightened you."

"Yeah, it really has," she mumbled. "I'm, uh, I think I'm going home now. If it's alright with you."

Verity wrapped her arm around the teacher. "You poor thing, you're trembling. I don't blame you. I'm sure you'll be able to sleep better in your own bed. Thanks to the sheriff, I know I will."

CHAPTER 37

ALL THE NEXT DAY, Verity worked to catch up on chores she had let slide since learning of Elvira's death. Most critical among them—tallying the farm's profit/loss statement for the month of August. She often felt lucky to break even, but this month the farm had miraculously made a small profit. Mostly due to a lack of veterinary bills and the exceptionally good weather with enough rain to avoid irrigation. Cause for celebration!

And yet, as she worked through the pile of bills and receipts at her kitchen table, she didn't have the heart for rejoicing.

She couldn't help thinking she'd missed something critical about the night Elvira died. Reading diaries and tailing suspects —what good had that done? Then there was the EPI's so-called trap, which had failed miserably. In spite of her very public announcements in town that she would be going to the state police with evidence that proved Elvira had been murdered, the killer still hadn't made a move.

It all seemed so very silly to her. Their amateurish attempts at uncovering a crime where one might never have existed. Maybe Elvira really did commit suicide.

However, Verity had learned something rather surprising about Sheriff Fred Bailey. He wasn't as useless as she'd once believed. The man turned out to be concerned about her safety. Enough to sacrifice his own sleep, drive to her farm and make sure she was safe. She smiled at that thought and felt an unexpected warmth in her heart for the old curmudgeon.

Who knew?

She closed her ledger and reached both arms over her head, stretching the stiff muscles of her shoulders and neck. Her lower back twinged, on the verge of cramping. She needed to move.

Seizing her favorite harvest basket of woven reeds, she stepped through her back door and loped across the lawn to her kitchen garden. Out in the chickenyard, she could see Jason and Jerry dragging a coop frame behind the tractor to its new location. By shifting the position of each coop twice a month, even just a few feet, they provided her hens with a fresh patch of grass to munch. But what her feathery brown ladies really loved was the new supply of juicy bugs and worms hiding among the blades.

Verity waved to the boys so they'd know where she was and knelt in her kitchen garden to pick late-season bush beans for her supper. As she worked her way along the row, she paused to yank out weeds, prickly thistle and long, woody strands of wiregrass that seemed to fight back the harder she pulled. How deep were these stupid roots anyway?

More of the beans were long enough to pick than she'd expected. Beans needed to be removed from the vines before they went to seed and signaled the plants to stop production. Any beans she couldn't use for her meal that night, she'd blanch and freeze. They'd last straight through the winter.

The work was mechanical, mindless. She used her picking time to revisit their failure as investigators. Maybe, like the sheriff said, they never would know why Elvira ventured out alone into the night. Or what caused her to end up at the bottom of the granite pit. She mused over Mary Beth's claim that criminals always made a dumb mistake that gave them away—at least they did in her beloved television series. Unfortunately, in the case of Elvira's death there had been no obvious giveaways.

If indeed someone had played a role Elvira's death, Verity feared that person was far too clever for them. They had gotten away with murder.

Verity stood up and stepped across two rows of red romaine lettuce heads to her tomato vines. She plucked a ripe tomato the size of a softball from its vine with a twist of her wrist. She tenderly nestled the tomato into her basket among the mound of jade-green beans.

Her brain continued churning out troubling messages. Endless questions.

Notes, she thought. Those damn notes. Two of them.

The first one, presumably, had fallen with Elvira at the quarry. The second was left intentionally at her house. They looked nothing alike. The first, written with an ordinary pen in blue ink. The last one, dashed off in angry-looking, two-inch letters in red pencil. Was it possible that two different people wrote them?

But she sensed something else important about those notes. And although she couldn't yet put her finger on exactly what it was, the not knowing made her skin crawl. Maybe Katie and Mary Beth had felt it, too. The threatening letter delivered to Verity by the two ghosts had so frightened her two friends they'd given up investigating. She didn't blame them. They believed their lives were at risk. They might well be right.

Last among the issues pummeling her brain was the break-in.

An intruder in black. A box of diaries. A desperate wrestling match on her kitchen floor. Verity had ended up bruised and concussed. Did the thief escape that night without injury? The memory of that night still rattled her, like a jigsaw puzzle with pieces missing. Making it nearly impossible to work out a pattern.

She wiped droplets of sweat from her forehead with the back of a dusty hand and stood in the middle of her garden, blinking up into fierce, blinding sunlight for a long moment. She had an idea. A very little one. But maybe, just maybe a good one.

Her basket full, she left the pulled weeds in a heap on the ground to deal with later and hurried back toward the house. It's a long shot, she warned herself. But sometimes those were the moments in life you had to seize or regret later.

Verity waved at the Grimalskis, shouting to them that she was going inside. She raced around the outside corner of house and through the mudroom to avoid tracking dirt into her kitchen. Hopping on one foot, she pulled off one gardening boot, then the other. In stocking feet, she rushed through the kitchen and foyer, then up the stairs to the second floor.

On her bedside table lay the envelope into which she had slipped copies of the two mysterious notes along with comments she jotted down while reading Elvira's revealing journals. Somewhere in this messy exposé of the woman's life, Verity was convinced, lurked the incident that had doomed Elvira Evans to an early death.

She shook everything out of the envelope and onto her daffodil-yellow bedspread. She clicked on the etched glass lamp on her bedside table. It created a bright splash of light across the scattered pages, as if they were witnesses undergoing interrogation. Sitting cross-legged in the middle of her bed, she reread every page. Every word.

And that was when things finally began to make sense.

Verity found Sheriff Bailey at home, just sitting down to his dinner. Not the ideal circumstance, considering how much the man loved his food.

She stepped into the dining room behind his wife, Penelope, known by all as just Penny. "We have a visitor, Frederick," she announced, casting Verity a warning glance.

The sheriff scowled. "Well, Mrs. Cade, what is it now?" He gently placed his knife and fork on either side of his plate as if the two utensils were his most prized possessions. Piled high on his plate were generous servings of pot roast, mashed potatoes smothered by a sea of thick brown gravy, and corn on the cob glistening with melted butter. The rich, beefy aroma made Verity's mouth water.

She held up the two notes. "I need to show you something important."

"Seriously? I've already seen those things. My dinner's gonna get cold. Believe me, you don't want to still be in this room if that happens."

"I can vouch for that," Penny's voice held not a hit of humor.

"I promise. I'll be quick." Verity shifted serving dishes and a water glass aside to make room then placed the letters side by side on the flowered tablecloth. She turned the writing toward the sheriff and took a deep breath. "Sheriff Bailey, do you agree that these are true copies of the two notes I left with you on previous days?"

Bailey rolled his eyes. "You aren't displaying evidence before a jury. Get on with it, Mrs. Cade."

"Of course." She smiled nervously. "Well, one thing we've already discussed was how different these notes look, so maybe they were written by two different people."

"Or maybe not," he said. "It's obvious the paper and the

writing instruments are different. The writing itself is another matter. But I'm no handwriting expert."

Penny came to stand behind her husband. She stared for a moment at each of the notes. Verity realized from her horrified expression that this must be the first she'd seen of them. "Oh, my, how awful! Fred showed me Peter's message to his sister. But not that one." She pointed to the one Verity had received. "It's absolutely menacing! Aimed at bullying you, Verity?"

She nodded in answer. "I needed to see you right away, Sheriff, because I think I've found a way to prove they were written by the same person. And that may change the way you think about Elvira's death."

He gave her a skeptical look but she pressed on before he could stop her. "Look at the lowercase 'e' in the note left at my house. Do you see how the center line is curved rather than straight? And the 'r' looks more like a 'v', as though the writer was too rushed to bother with precision."

"So what?" The sheriff picked up his fork and stabbed a chunk of pot roast.

"Just humor me, please. Now, look at the note I found at the quarry. Who wrote that one?"

"Her son of course. Peter." Bailey waved the tines of his fork at the signature. "The boy may be the reason she went wandering that night—to have it out with him—then she accidentally fell. Or she might never have seen his note and I've been right all along. Suicide. End result is the same." He tucked another bite of pot roast into his mouth.

Penny shook her head sadly. "Poor thing." She turned to Verity with a puzzled expression. "Fred told me you don't believe she committed suicide."

"I don't." Verity tried to catch the sheriff's eye between bites. "I've just now realized that the note left at my house arrived *after* Peter and Laura were sent off to their grandparents' in New Hampshire following the funeral." Verity bent over the table and glared at Bailey until he made eye contact with her. "So, it doesn't make sense that the second note came from him. Wouldn't you agree, Sheriff?"

"I s'pose," he mumbled through a mouthful of what sounded like mashed potatoes.

"You're saying that if they were written by the same person, and Peter didn't write the one meant for you...then he also didn't write the note that's signed with his name?" Penny frowned at first one then the other scrap of paper. "Fred, I think she's right. Look closely at the shapes of the 'e' and 'r' in both letters."

The sheriff laid down his fork with an air of resignation. He studied afresh the two notes. Slowly his eyes hardened. "Well, I'll be damned. It just might be somebody forged that letter to little Laura to make it look like it had come from her brother. But I can't for the life of me see why."

"Because, just maybe, Laura was never meant to see it." Verity paused to gather her thoughts. "It had one purpose. To lure Elvira to the quarry."

Penny covered her mouth with one shaking hand and stared at Verity.

"Still might've been an accident, her fallin'," Bailey hedged, but immediately winced sheepishly. "Right. What else you got? You know who wrote these? Got a name for me?"

"No," she admitted. "I wish I did. But at least you'll now admit Elvira's case should be reopened, right?"

He did an up-and-down, side-to-side motion with his head. He did not look happy.

Verity felt more than happy. She felt triumphant. "And may I respectfully remind you that I've located two suspects who, in my humble opinion, should be questioned."

"Humble?" He smiled dolefully.

"I know I'm not a professional law enforcement officer like you, Sheriff. But you must admit Dr. Evans and the woman he's hooked up with are more than a little suspicious."

"Verity, that's a bit of a leap, isn't it?" Penny interrupted. "Fred told me about your little adventure with Sunny Whitaker. Why would you assume the woman you saw was his former fiancée? It was such a long time ago."

"Because we know she couldn't be a patient," she groaned in exasperation. "If you'd seen them, well, it was obvious from the way they behaved. Plus, she matches the description in Elvira's diary, at least her body shape does. Very slim—plus she's the right age. And why wasn't she at the funeral paying her respects to the family like all the doctor's other patients in the county? That in itself is suspicious."

"Hmmm." The sheriff frowned down at his plate. His mashed potatoes had turned a noxious shade of gray. The gravy was congealing and looked more like recently poured cement than anything edible. "Alright, Mrs. Cade, you can leave this with me." He looked up at her. "I'll noodle around and see what I can find. I'm not officially reopening the investigation into Mrs. Evans' death. But you and your friends have done enough to convince me there are unanswered questions about what happened that night."

"Oh, thank you, Sheriff." Verity felt near tears with relief. All their hard work might still pay off and bring Elvira's killer to justice.

"No more playing Nancy Drew though. And I mean it this time. Promise?"

"Promise." But she didn't cross her heart. And she certainly didn't hope to die.

CHAPTER 38

THE NEXT DAY Verity felt as though a weight had lifted from her shoulders—an Airbus A380 kind of weight. Everything had changed.

Based on the evidence she'd given Sheriff Bailey, he would pursue new motives, interview suspects. He was seriously investigating instead of clinging to his first impression of death by suicide. She knew this because she'd seen the man's dull, apathetic eyes spark with curiosity and a need-to-know that hadn't been there before. He looked like a bulldog, its eyes locked onto a particularly juicy bone. Nothing would stop him from getting the answers now.

She couldn't wait to share the news with her friends. The EPIs had made a difference. Justice would be served. It was only a matter of time before the sheriff discovered the truth, she was sure of it.

Free of the time-consuming pursuit of a mystery killer, Verity tackled a job she'd put off for over a year. Her mother-in-law, Karen Cade, had collected delicate Lladró porcelain pieces since the 1950s, buying up dozens of the whimsical little figurines when they must have been relatively cheap. Farmers and their wives rarely had extra money for anything that wasn't necessary, as Verity well knew. So, she supposed they were worth even less now. Mark held on to them after her death, although he once admitted to Verity that he'd never really liked the delicate statuettes.

When Verity asked why he kept them, he shrugged. "They meant a lot to Mom." Then he laughed, nearly choking. "One time, I suggested she box them up and give them to the church charity sale. I thought she was going to disown me."

Although neither the subjects nor the style were to her taste, Verity could see their appeal to some people. Unfortunately, the highly glazed ceramic surfaces were dust magnets and she had no time to care for them. It seemed a shame to keep them when someone else might love them as much as her mother-in-law.

"I'm sorry, Karen," Verity murmured as she wrapped six figures in bubble wrap, including a shepherdess with a lamb, a little boy carrying a fishing pole, a pirouetting dancer.

Verity brought the box out to her truck and drove to the Antiques Emporium, calling Chaundra on the way to ask if she was free to look at some knick-knacks she'd inherited.

———

"Sure," Chaundra Adebe repeated when Verity arrived at her workbench in the rear of the emporium, "I'll be happy to give you an evaluation."

"If they're worth anything at all," Verity laughed. Even fifty or a hundred dollars for the whole collection would help a little with the feed bill. "I only brought you six as a sample."

"Well, let's take a look, shall we?" Chaundra carefully started unwrapping the first piece. "Oh, this one is a Lladró!" she exclaimed. "When we spoke on the phone, you just said they were assorted knick-knacks."

"Well, they are but I think they are all Lladró-type knick-knacks. At least they look similar to me, but what do I know?" She laughed. "Anyway, I think that's the term Karen used to describe them."

"Well, I'll need to do more research before I can give you firm estimates but, for example, this little piece with a mother and baby is so sweet. I saw one exactly like it on eBay a few months ago and watched as the bids kept going up. It sold for $400."

"Really?" Verity was shocked. Did people really pay that kind of money for kitsch like this?

"And you have how many Lladró pieces?"

"In total, I think there are about twenty. All different sizes and subjects."

Chaundra stared at her. "You're kidding."

"No. They're in the dining room in a glass-fronted cabinet. You've probably never noticed them since we're usually in my kitchen." Verity hesitated, not wanting to sound greedy. "Can you, well, give me a little idea of what the whole collection might be worth?" Paying off even a small portion of the loan for the Robo-Milkers would be a relief.

"Hmmm, let me see." Chaundra started unwrapping the rest of the figures. "The larger, more elaborate pieces like this one are usually priced higher than your little mother-and-child. Originally, they were made in Spain, in the 1950s. They were intended to mimic the elegant porcelain of the 18th century—with soft, lustrous glazes and elongated shapes for the people. Rare pieces have been auctioned off for as much as $70,000 dollars."

Verity gulped. "Each?"

Chaundra laughed. "Uh-huh. To the right collector, they are priceless. If it's alright with you, I'll hold onto these for you, do some research and get back to you with better estimates. I have a place to display these in my own booth, and I can put some up on eBay or other sites favored by collectors, if you want me to try and sell them for you."

"I do. Oh, Chaundra, thank you so much. I can really use the money. And someone should get a chance to enjoy them, don't you think? I haven't even glanced at them in months." Verity eyed the graceful porcelain pieces sitting on Chaundra's workbench. "It's sad, though. Karen really loved these. And here I am selling them."

"Each to her own," Chaundra said lightly. "Besides, I'm sure she'd want you to use her legacy to help you keep your property. The Cade Family Farm meant a lot to her, too."

"Thank you, Chaundra. I feel so much better." Verity gave her a warm hug. She breathed in the comforting aroma of cedar wood, lemon oil, and potpourri that permeated the vendors' stalls.

She left the antique shop with her head spinning pleasantly. If Chaundra was right and she was able to sell at least some of Karen's beloved collection for a good price, she might walk away with a thousand dollars or more. It wouldn't be like winning the lottery but—hey!—a few more loan installments paid off would be amazing.

"Thank you, Mom Cade," she murmured as she swung wide the emporium's door and stepped out onto the sidewalk, dollar signs dancing in her head.

"Hey there, watch it!" a voice shouted a second after she'd collided with someone standing in her path.

Jarred her out of her daydreams of imminent wealth, she looked up into the scowling face of Dr. John Evans. "Sorry," she muttered automatically. Deciding not to stick around for a lecture about paying attention to where she was going, she turned and dashed for her truck.

"Mrs. Cade!" He sounded angry. Of course, he did! After

their confrontation in his office, she'd be forever on his blacklist. But she'd already said she was sorry. What more did he want?

You can yell at my back as easily as in my face! she thought, leaping into the driver's seat. She slammed the door, started the engine.

"Wait! I need to talk to you." The doctor lunged off the curb and was suddenly standing next to her window before she could back out of the parking space. His face red, eyes wide and urgent, he pantomimed with one hand: *roll down your window.*

She shook her head firmly "no." She wasn't going to let him rant at her and spoil her good mood.

She shifted into reverse and started backing up her truck, expecting him to move away. To her frustration he jogged alongside her window, continuing to shout at her. His words were muddled by the engine's growl.

She ignored him and checked the road to make sure no traffic was coming but caught a glimpse of his face. Or rather of his mouth. She thought she read his lips: "You must be crazy!" Or was it: "You must be careful!" Then: Something...something "dangerous."

"Leave me alone!" she screamed, her heart racing. The nerve of the man, accusing *her* of being dangerous.

She shifted into "drive."

Unbelievably, Evans continued running alongside the truck as she picked up speed. He yelled, "She's not who you think she is!"

Ah, so that's it! She realized he must have found out from the sheriff that she'd followed him and found out about his girlfriend. Well, he could deny it all he liked. She knew what they'd seen.

She pressed her foot on the accelerator, and saw him falling back and away in her rearview mirror. Thank goodness! But then she frowned. What was he doing now? He had pulled out his phone and was frantically punching it with one finger. Her phone rang from inside her purse.

You've got to be kidding! If he thought she would pick up and endure another of his tirades he'd have to wait until eggs rained from the sky. She ignored the phone and kept on driving north and out of town. Eventually, the ringing stopped.

Verity drove the Ridgeline straight into her garage and hit the button on her dashboard to bring the door down. She sat for a moment in the dark, catching her breath, letting her pulse return to normal, then laughed out loud. She'd always thought John Evans a calm, rational man. Proved wrong twice! What a ridiculous scene he'd made in the middle of town.

The thought came to her that she probably should call the sheriff and tell him about the incident. After all, the doctor was one of the suspects Bailey would be looking into.

Well, at least she was back home now. Jason and Jerry should still be finishing up their work for the day. And her volunteer bodyguard for the night was due to arrive at any moment. Sunny kept track of the rotation schedule; Verity couldn't recall whose turn it was today. The important thing was—she was safe.

Thinking she heard an ominous rumble as she stepped out of the garage, she looked up at the sky. It had been clear all day but the forecast mentioned possible thundershowers. Iron-gray thunderheads were indeed stacking up in the west. Her cows hated heavy storms. Rain wasn't too bad but hail and high winds frightened them.

She called the twins on her phone to tell them to bring in the herd.

"Already on it!" Jason responded.

Good. One thing less to worry about. Her hens would seek shelter on their own. She decided to grab her wellies and go help the boys.

Before Verity reached the house, a familiar car turned into her driveway. Martha's gray Ford sedan cut a U-turn in her driveway then stopped facing the road. The teacher climbed out, grinning at her.

"Martha, you just had your shift two nights ago," Verity reminded her. "And you're almost an hour early."

"I know, I know." Martha shrugged her wide shoulders and glanced toward the twins' truck, parked between the house and cow barn. "Your farmhands are still here?"

"They're out in the field, bringing in the cows that haven't already come in on their own."

"Oh, good."

"Good?"

The teacher shrugged. "That way you don't need to do it. Must be an awful chore."

"Not really. If I get the A-cow started in the right direction, the others follow along."

"Huh?" Martha was looking around her as if she expected something had changed since she'd last been there. "Oh, you mean sort of like the leader of the pack. Only not with wolves, cows instead?"

"Sort of." Verity frowned at her. "Martha, why are you here? Isn't it someone else's turn to sleep over?"

"Oh, I told Fumiko I'd take her place. She's preparing for a big sale at the yarn shop."

"Oh, I hadn't heard about it." Verity turned to walk toward the house. She still wanted to help Jason and Jerry. It was nearly time for them to leave. It didn't seem fair to expect them to stay any later and hold up their family's dinners.

"Wait!" Martha called out, chasing after her. "Where are you going?"

"Inside to get my boots. You can go along inside and get

settled for the night, if you like. I've already made up the spare bedroom."

"No, no, you can't go yet."

"Why not?" Verity laughed. "I'll be perfectly safe in the field with two strong guys. Stop fussing, Martha."

The older woman stopped dead still and took a deep breath as if realizing how frenzied she must have sounded. "I only meant, I brought something special for you. It's in my car but it's too heavy for me. It will only take a few minutes if you can help me carry it into the house. Please?"

Verity smiled in spite of her preoccupation with her animals. "What is it?"

"A surprise!" Martha looked thrilled with herself. "Honestly, it's so special. Something I found at the emporium for you."

"Alright. Fine." Verity followed her to the back of the car, still looking over her shoulder past the cow barn and toward the pasture.

The first of her docile beauties were just coming into sight. Her farmhands would be bringing up the rear of her herd in a few minutes. She glanced up at the sky again while Martha popped open the Ford's trunk. The clouds looked blacker by the moment, suspiciously plump with rain. Out of the corner of her eye, she saw Martha reach down into the car's open trunk.

"Let's see what's gotten you so excited," Verity said, turning to look down. The trunk was empty. "Martha?"

Something hard came down on the back of her head and with such wicked force she was sure it had split open her skull. The blow stunned her, stealing away her breath and making it impossible for her to cry out for help. She retched, staggered up against the car's bumper and braced herself with both hands against the hard metal as lightning bolts of pain, complete with colorful pyrotechnics, shot through her head.

Before she could recover her breath and cry for help, hands grabbed her hips and pitched her forward into the open trunk. She tried to fight herself free—but her body refused to function, instead going limp, useless. The best she could do was roll onto her side.

She squinted up into the plump, white face looming over her. For a second her vision cleared enough to see a hand holding a tire iron. *Probably what she hit me with*, Verity thought woozily.

Then everything disappeared with the bang of the trunk lid.

"N-no!" she sobbed. "Please!" She tried to scream for help but her voice produced only a weak mewling sound. A memory flashed through her mind. In a movie, a kidnapped teenager had kicked out a car's taillight to escape from a car trunk. Was that even possible? But she couldn't lift her leg, let alone kick anything with destructive force.

The interior of the trunk smelled of gasoline, sour milk, and grubby carpet. Verity allowed herself only shallow breaths, afraid of inhaling the fumes. She tried to lift her head but a sudden wave of vertigo threatened to make her vomit. She gripped the sides of her head with both hands but it didn't help. A moment later it didn't matter. Because everything simply... was gone.

CHAPTER 39

UNITIL SOMETIME LATER...

She breathed in fresh air that smelled of pine trees and the clean mustiness of damp earth and woods. Something wet splattered her face. Rain? Her next thought was: *The storm! I hope my cows are alright.*

Probably not what most people would consider their highest priority if they had been beaten senseless and kidnapped, she realized.

Where was she? And where was Martha? Crazy, sick Martha. Because a person had to be insane—didn't they?—to clock a person with a tire iron, or whatever, and stuff them into a car trunk.

Rain fell in large, generous drops through tree limbs hanging over her. Refreshing against her face but doing nothing to soothe the thunderous pounding in her head.

Somehow, she must have escaped from the car's trunk. Or somebody had freed her. Because now, it appeared, she was no longer trapped, lying here on the ground. She could feel the prick and crunch of pine needles beneath her back. The air smelled of a woodsy-clean, almost antiseptic aroma. It was intensely dark out here. Wherever here was. How many hours had passed? How long had she been trapped in the car, unconscious?

Moonlight filtered down through a web of tree branches. The pine needles made quite a comfortable bed. She wasn't tied up. So, that was good. *I could lie here forever*, she mused. Which might actually be her only option because her head hurt so horribly, she didn't dare move. She was getting pretty wet from the rain, but a little water had never bothered her.

Something shifted above her, blocking out the moonlight. The stocky silhouette reminded her of another time. When? It came to her almost too easily. The night of the break-in. The intruder.

"Martha? Is that you?" Verity whispered.

"Oh, fuck. I thought you were dead."

So much for friendship. "You're officially banned from my egg route."

"Oh, shut up. I guess I didn't hit you hard enough."

"I guess not." It hurt to talk. Moving her jaw made every other part of her skull ping and jab. Little knives. Everywhere. She tried to sit up, but the trees danced around her. She'd never be able to stand on her own. Running? Fat chance.

Martha bent over and wrapped her fingers around Verity's ankles. She started dragging her over pine needles, rocks, tree roots, granite shards. And then it struck her: *Oh God, she's brought me to the quarry!*

And, of course, she knew why.

Because Elvira had died here, probably in much the same way. Except she had been lured to this place with a note signed with her son's name but written by Martha. Elvira was stronger than Martha but, taken by surprise and off-balance, anyone could be pushed over a ledge.

Why did Martha Humphrey kill Elvira? She might never

know. What she did know was that the woman was going to kill *her* tonight. Because she had discovered the diaries and, more earnestly than any of their other friends, she had insisted on getting to the truth. And the truth, it seemed, was something Martha Humphrey didn't want the world to know.

The teacher had played along with the group's investigation —probably just to keep track of what the amateur investigators knew or might soon discover. She'd already managed to scare off two of their number. By murdering another member, she undoubtedly hoped to frighten the rest and close down their investigations.

What Martha didn't know though, the previous night Verity had finally convinced the sheriff that Elvira had been murdered. And, say what you will about Bailey's competence, he wouldn't be scared off by a second death, even if it appeared to be accidental. The man's law gene had been titillated. He would stick to it until he'd found Elvira's killer...and now, hers.

"Stop!" Verity shouted, although it came out as barely a squeak.

She wriggled on the ground, testing her muscles. The little nap she'd taken in the trunk must have helped. She found she could at least move now. She kicked her legs, hoping to dislodge the woman's grip on her ankles. It didn't work.

"Please stop. M-Martha, why are you doing this? It makes no sense."

"Can't be helped," Martha muttered. "You were spoiling everything."

Verity thrust her left foot into one of her captor's wrists. "For gosh sake's what did Elvira do to deserve—"

Martha's pale eyes flared with icy fury. "Elvira was...*mean*. She used people. She was wicked!"

"But she had her good days." Verity couldn't believe she was defending the woman, after all she'd learned about her true character. "And even if being mean was an acceptable reason for killing a person—*which it's not!*—I've never been mean to you." Verity tensed and prepared herself for the pain her next move would cost her. Gritting her teeth, she quickly rolled onto her stomach, reached out and grabbed the low branch of a sturdy looking shrub with both hands. "Dammit, Martha, this is crazy!"

"Is not!" Martha grunted, taking a firmer grip of Verity's ankles and leaning into the job of pulling her free of the under-growth. "It's your fault. You leave me no choice. You and your stupid...ugh!...prying friends."

"Do you plan to kill them, too?" Verity's palms felt sticky with pine pitch. In a way, the goo made it easier to hold onto the rough wood. She was literally glued to the tree. "Martha, I'm your friend. So are Kate and Sunny and Chaundra and—"

"They pre-*tend* to be my friends," Martha snarled. "But all they really care about is Elvira. Why couldn't you mind your own business? You chose her over me. Just like *he* did." She gave a hard yank on Verity's ankles that sent pain shooting from her heels all the way up her spine to her poor head.

"Ow!" Verity screeched. Then, suddenly, everything fell into place. Or nearly so.

"Doesn't! Matter!" Martha was shouting. "Once you're dead, everyone will stop asking questions."

Verity hardly heard the woman's raving. She felt light-headed, almost joyful. She knew why Elvira had to die. She knew how she'd died. And she knew who had killed the wealthy real estate agent.

But what good would any of that do if the knowledge died with her?

And she was pretty sure, if Martha had her way, she was most definitely going to die.

"From the very beginning, you've been sabotaging the investigation, haven't you?" Verity said, already knowing the answer. "You told us you'd found nothing important in the diary you were reading. The one you insisted on keeping to yourself. Because you knew from the dates when it was written there likely would be something in it you didn't want us to know. Why didn't you want us to read about that particular part of Elvira's past?"

"Because it's my past, too!" Martha seethed, tossing her head wildly as she continued trying to dislodge Verity from her branch.

And there it was. The truth that meant Elvira had to die. Which Verity had finally come to understand a minute earlier.

Tears flooded the teacher's ruddy cheeks. "She took *everything* from me, you ninny!" Her words reverberated off the quarry walls in eerie doublets and triplets. *Ev'ry...ev'ry...ev'ry... nin-nin-ninny.* "You saw in her diaries how she lied and cheated and used her nasty tricks to get whatever she wanted. And what she wanted was mine. *Mine!*" Martha stomped her foot so hard it seemed to Verity the ground should have trembled.

Fueled by her anger, Martha gave a tug so hard she finally ripped Verity free of the little tree, leaving her hands raw and gummy with pitch.

Verity twisted onto her back to face Elvira's killer. "*You* were Olive Oyl!" Even as she said the words, knowing they were absolutely true, her eyes widened at the sight of the thick-wasted, dowdy kindergarten teacher.

Martha must have seen the look of disbelief on her face. "You don't believe John could have ever loved me? Well, he did! I didn't always look like this. We were in love. Happy. Planning a family and life together. Then *she* came along."

"But you followed them to Evansfield?" This made no sense to Verity.

"To be near him!" Martha screamed. "If I couldn't marry

him, I would at least be able to watch over him. And the children, when they came. I was more of a mother to them than that bitch ever was," she hissed. "I loved Peter and Laura. I never blamed John for leaving me. It was all her doing. She tricked him into marrying her!"

"Oh, Martha. I'm so sorry." Verity could only imagine the suffering the woman had endured at the loss of the man she loved. And, obviously, still loved.

Somehow, Martha and John had kept their past relationship a secret from the rest of the town. Now Verity understood why he'd gone ballistic in his office when she insisted on knowing the name of his former fiancée. He was protecting Martha (a.k.a. Olive Oyl)—even though she, eaten up with grief and jealousy over the years, had become a different person from the thin, attractive young nurse he had fallen in love with. No doubt because he was well aware of what the town gossips would do to her. And Elvira, for some reason, had honored their arrangement.

The rest of their story she'd probably never know.

"Martha, what the hell!" Verity redoubled her efforts to break free. "Think! What happens after you kill me?" Martha leaned into her work, ignoring her. "What will John think if he learns you've killed two people, one of them his wife?" Of course, she thought grimly, the doctor must already suspect the awful truth about Elvira's death.

"You said it yourself." Martha stopped to catch her breath. "Sheriff Bailey is lazy idiot. He'll take the easy way out. A second suicide. Maybe someone will suggest you killed Elvira and then took your own life, unable to live with yourself." She grinned, looking pleased.

"It won't work!" Verity screamed.

But the woman was no longer listening. "John loves me."

She smiled dreamily. "He always has, you see. He will under-stand what I had to do for us to be together."

Good grief, she's mad as a fruitcake!

"We know," a familiar voice answered from nearby.

Verity was almost certain she hadn't spoken out loud. But her heart gave a leap of hope. "Percy?"

CHAPTER 40

"WE'RE HERE, MISS VERITY!" Anna Louise cried triumphantly.

Verity looked around. The night was so black the trees rising up around her were only visible when the bright half-disk of moon slipped out from behind clouds. "Where are—I can't see you!"

Martha swiveled her head and rubbed against her shoulder to brush raindrops from her eyes. "I'm right here, you idiot. Just shut up." She shuffled backward with renewed strength, in spite of Verity's gyrations and attempts to grasp low-hanging tree limbs. "Another two feet and over you go!"

"You horrid woman!" Anna Louise shrilled with ghostly fury. "We'll see who gets pushed off a cliff."

"No!" Verity shouted. "Don't kill her."

"Why not?" Anna Louise suddenly became visible to her.

Verity smiled at the innocent pout on the ghost's pretty face. "Because she's a sick woman who needs help. Have some compassion. Just help me get away from her!"

"Who in the blazes are you talking to?" Martha shouted. "Never mind. Let's get this over with." She dropped Verity's feet to the ground and stepped around to her side, sandwiching Verity between herself and the pit's edge.

Unable to stand or even sit up on her own, although she did try, Verity could only wait for the inevitable.

"You're about to join your dear, dead Mark." Martha held her arms stiffly in front of her, hands lined up with Verity's shoulders and hips—and lunged toward her.

Helpless, Verity squeezed her eyes shut and waited for the inevitable tumble over the edge. Although she felt a whoosh of air, this apparently wasn't caused by her falling. Wonderfully solid ground remained beneath her. Then she heard a woman's shocked wail.

Martha? Oh God, no!

Verity's eyes flew open. But the teacher hadn't been pitched over the edge of the quarry as she had feared. She was doing just the opposite. Martha rose above the forest floor, her legs cycling madly, arms flailing.

Percy materialized behind the teacher in his field uniform of Lincoln's Army of the North. His arms were wrapped around the woman's thick middle, pinning her to his chest as he floated away from the quarry pit and Verity.

Anna Louise flickered into view again. Verity hadn't taken much notice of her clothing earlier, as she'd been preoccupied with surviving. But now she admired her glorious riding outfit— fitted jacket, jodhpurs and sleek knee-high leather boots. Free of the interference of her customary voluminous skirts and petticoats, Mrs. Putnam moved swiftly toward Verity, scooped under her arms and slid her away from the quarry's dark mouth onto a cushion of pine needles. She leaned her gently against a wide tree trunk.

It was the expression on Martha Humphrey's face that told Verity her ghosts had become visible to her. The crazy woman hung limply in Percy's arms, staring wild-eyed at the beautiful ghost standing protectively over Verity, then up into the face of the soldier who had captured her.

"Who, wh-what are these—"

"It's alright, Martha. They're my friends." Verity looked at Percy, then Anna Louise, in that moment forgiving them for everything they'd ever done to annoy her. She cautiously tried to flex first one leg then the other. "We should get her to the sheriff. But I'm not sure how to do that without his entire department seeing you two in your present very visible form."

"Sheriff Bailey is already on his way," Anna Louise said. "When he arrives, he'll tell you that Jason called him to report you were kidnapped by Martha and taken to the granite mine. By the way, sugar, I think you need to see a doctor. Did you know your head is bleeding—again?"

Drat! Another concussion on top of the one she experienced during the break-in. No wonder she felt so woozy. Verity blinked, distracted by another thought. "Jason? How did he know where I...?"

Anna Louise peeked at her from beneath long eyelashes. "I know I promised not to. But Jason has such a lovely tenor voice, I couldn't resist."

"I can see I'll have some explaining to do after all this is over," Verity said. "Can you help me up? I think I can stand with help."

Anna Louise obliged, looping an arm around her waist.

Sirens were approaching from the direction of the main road, their woo-woo wails growing louder as they raced at speed down the dirt lane toward the quarry. "Time for us to depart, my love," Percy said.

"Wait!" Verity imagined Martha escaping through the woods or attacking her again.

"She won't move in inch from this spot," Percy stated, lowering Martha to the ground and giving her a moment to find her footing. He spun her around to face him. "Because if she even thinks about running, I shall draw sword and slice her from crown to heel before she takes a single step."

Martha stared at him, open-mouthed, for all of five seconds before her knees gave out. She accordioned to the ground in a lump.

"That should do it," Verity agreed.

CHAPTER 41

TODAY, she was yanking dead tomato vines out of the ground. She had planted sweet little cherry tomatoes for salads; Big Boys for slicing into sandwiches with bacon, lettuce and mayo; and Italian plum tomatoes full of savory pulp for pasta sauce. Although unripe fruits remained on vines, the days were growing shorter and cooler, signaling the plants that ripening time was coming to an end. The larger of the green tomatoes she tossed into her wicker basket. Fried green tomatoes for supper. Yum!

She heard a soft pad of footsteps in the cultivated dark earth. The tips of polished brown oxfords made her look up with a jolt.

Dr. John Evans towered over her, his expression solemn. She glanced nervously toward the farmhouse's rear door.

"Please, Mrs. Cade, I just want to talk with you. It's important we do this in person."

She flinched when his arm shot out toward her. He held his hand, palm up. An invitation to help her to her feet? She narrowed her eyes at him, felt her heart thudding against her ribs.

"I'm not here to berate you, I promise," he said.

She rose to her feet allowing him to assist her as her legs were still a little weak after her tussle with his old girlfriend. She brushed dirt from her palms. He looked at his own hands, which now carried a share of her garden.

"Sorry," she mumbled. "Occupational hazard."

He laughed awkwardly, pulled a handkerchief from his pocket and dusted himself off. She used the sides of her jeans for the same purpose.

"I'd offer you a few end-of-season tomatoes but they're all pretty green and hard as golf balls."

"I'll pass." He smiled, and she was reminded of one reason both Elvira and Martha must have fallen in love with the man. That dazzling smile carried all the way up into his eyes.

"So, doctor, what brings you out my way?"

"I think," he with a touch of nervousness in his tone, "I owe you an apology and an explanation for my recent behavior."

"Oh?" She agreed. But it felt satisfying to prolong his obvious anxiety, just a little. "Why is an apology necessary?"

"I'm sure you already know. I was out of line that day in my office when you asked me about my past."

She shrugged, giving in a little. "Well, I wasn't doing a very good job of being tactful."

He smiled. "No, you weren't. But that doesn't give me an excuse for shouting at you, or lying to you."

"I don't remember a lie."

"A lie of omission." He shifted on his oxfords, as if trying to find one foot that was more comfortable than the other. "You asked about the woman Elvira called Olive Oyl in her diary—very cruel of her, actually. And yes, I've since started reading some of her journals after you returned them to me. But even then, in my office, I knew exactly who you were referring to and I panicked. You see, when I broke my engagement to marry

Elvira, I didn't handle it well. My fiancée, as you discovered, was Martha Humphrey, a nurse I had been dating and then proposed to."

"I see." That much Verity had figured out that night in the quarry with a crazed Martha. But she hoped to learn more now.

John scrubbed the toe of one shoe across a furrow of dirt. "Martha was a very different person in those days. Just as serious as she is now but quite attractive and at least sixty pounds lighter. Not that the latter should matter. She was, I thought, a very good match for my personality. Medicine meant everything to us. We were devoted to using our skills to helping others."

"Quite different from Elvira's me-first attitude," Verity said, then wished she hadn't when she saw the man's face fall. "Sorry, that was rude. I shouldn't talk about her like that. She's not here to defend herself."

"It's alright. My wife was very much enamored with the better things in life. Luxuries. Status. But she shared her wealth with our community."

"Her donations to flood victims, the hospital, and church."

"Exactly." He looked away. A cloud of despair fell over his eyes. "But Elvira had a mean streak. I didn't understand that until we'd been together for more than six months. She kept that part of her personality hidden, at least from me. By the time I began to have doubts about our future together, she was pregnant with our son."

"Oh my!" Verity breathed.

"I worried that I'd made a horrible mistake—too bedazzled by the showy Elvira to see her negative side. But I'm not the sort of man who'd ever ask a woman to abort a child or walk away from their baby. So, I stayed. But I let her know I was serious about opening a medical practice in my family's hometown. I absolutely would not follow in my illustrious father's footsteps.

Surgery wasn't for me. I would be a small-town doctor; it was my dream."

"She was very disappointed?"

"I think she probably considered leaving me. But she wanted that baby. And I think she decided to make the best of things. She is...*was* a very strong and willful woman, as you know. I expect she believed she could still have her way most of the time."

"But how did Martha end up here in Evansfield? She said something about that on the night the sheriff arrested her for kidnapping me, but if it were me, having lost the love of my life —" And here, he winced so she paused.

"No, no. You're right. Martha said those exact words to me when I broke up with her. 'You are the love of my life, John. I'll never have another.' But I was swept away by all that Elvira offered me—her beauty, her charm, her worldliness. My parents just adored her and actually seemed relieved when I told them my engagement to Martha was over. As attractive as Martha was in a simple, homespun way, she didn't have Elvira's social polish or ability to charm."

Verity nodded her head. "When Elvira walked into a room, she definitely made a statement. I loved just watching her sometimes." Verity cleared her throat. "What I was trying to say a moment ago is—if I'd been dropped by my fiancé for another woman, the last thing I'd want to do was move to the town where he and his wife lived."

"I agree. But one of the things Martha and I had in common was that we both had roots in Evansfield. She didn't grow up here, but her grandparents lived here and she visited them often as a child. I grew up in this town, in an old farmhouse. The Ivey's farm on the road to Springfield."

"Yes, I know the place." She picked up her basket and

looked up into the blazing sun. "Come, walk with me. Let's sit up on my porch where it's cooler."

They were silent for the short walk and quickly settled into the green Adirondack chairs on the shaded porch.

After a moment Doc Evans continued his story. "When Martha proposed moving into her grandparents' old place, I tried to discourage her. She asked if she could be my nurse but I told her how hard it would be, for both of us, seeing each other every day. I told her no. She claimed she could do something else in town, but all I could think of was teaching. I knew public schools had trouble keeping teachers. So many of our county's young educators want to live in exciting, big cities."

"That's how Martha got the job as a kindergarten teacher?"

"Yes, she'd always loved children and she took the necessary minimum of courses to get certified. But I feared what Elvira would do to her. Nothing physical, of course. Emotionally." His gaze drifted away, his eyes troubled. "You see, Martha had a mental health crisis immediately after we broke up. She spent nearly a year at an in-patient facility in Massachusetts. She was so fragile, so close to the edge of...well, killing herself. Elvira could have destroyed her."

"But she didn't," Verity said. "In fact, Martha told me, all of us really, that she babysat for your kids. And for years, I never heard Elvira say a mean word about her."

"Because I made her promise that she wasn't to do anything to hurt Martha. I told her if she did—just one word, one insult or mention of her engagement to me—I'd ask for a divorce."

Emotional blackmail. Interesting. "She must have believed you. Would you have? Left Elvira that is?"

"I never needed to make that decision. Shortly after Martha moved into her grandparents' house, Elvira became pregnant with our daughter. To leave two children...well, even if I could, I knew she'd fight to keep them and find a way to stop me from seeing Peter and Laura."

Verity sighed. "And when Elvira wanted something, she got it."

"Yes." He blew out a long breath. "The thing is, I was convinced that Martha had healed. She appeared to have moved on in her life. She seemed content with her teaching and home here in Evansfield. It wasn't long before she fell into the role of surrogate mother when my kids were young. I believed she was even happy."

"Maybe she was for a while."

"Yes." He stared down at his hands, and she thought he looked incredibly sad. "But I think as the kids grew older and needed her less...well, that broke her heart. And might have driven her to do things I never could have imagined her capable of."

"Like luring Elvira to the quarry and—"

"Yes, like that."

"But once she'd committed murder," Verity mused, "her problems became worse. She had to protect herself. She couldn't let anyone suspect what she'd done because what she really wanted was to step into Elvira's shoes and reunite with you. To be a real mother to your children. And the wife she believed she should have been all along."

He dropped his head further and for a moment she was sure he might weep. "What I hope you can understand, Mrs. Cade, is this. After Elvira died, and you and your friends started digging into the past, I was still so shocked and confused by events, I just didn't pay attention to anything else. I don't believe I was thinking about anything really."

"Understandable," she said gently.

"So, when you asked to read Elvira's diaries," he continued, "I entrusted them to you without even considering that Elvira might have written anything about Martha. Why would she? The only person Elvira found fascinating was Elvira." He gave a low chuckle. "But when you mentioned my having a relationship before Elvira, an engagement that was broken—well, as you saw—I panicked and just lost it. I had vowed to protect Martha from embarrassment and gossip. Never in a million years could I have imagined her hurting anyone. Not my wife, my children, me—certainly not you, Verity."

"If it makes you feel any better," she said, "none of her friends suspected her either."

"I'm afraid that doesn't help me feel any better. I knew she'd been sick before. But I should have stayed alert to warning signs."

"What will happen to her?" Verity whispered.

"I don't know. A doctor, not me of course, will determine through various examinations and conversations if she's able to stand trial. I expect not. I'll do all I can to make sure she gets the care she needs, but she may never be able to return to Evansfield."

Remembering how close she had come to being Martha's second victim, Verity couldn't help feeling at least a little bit grateful for that gift.

CHAPTER 42

WITH THE FALL tourist and hunting seasons fast approaching, everyone in Evansfield was busy. The usual jet stream of gossip had slowed but didn't prevent people from discovering Martha Humphrey's arrest even before events made it to the local newspapers. And once the shocking details of the murder were out, it was all anyone talked about.

Verity IM'd her fellow Evansfield Private Investigators about the dramatic events leading up to Martha's arrest at the quarry. (Although she chose to leave out certain particulars involving her timely rescue. Namely those involving Lt. and Mrs. Putnam, deceased.)

The EPI members agreed to protect the privacy of Dr. John Evans and his children by never disclosing what they discovered in Elvira's diaries. At first, Mary Beth refused to keep mum, saying she was being denied her right to free speech. But she came around when Sunny threatened to bar her from the café (i.e., her pastries). And *that* was that.

The Evansfield Sentinel ran a brief article mentioning an assault on an unnamed community member resulting in Martha Humphrey's arrest. The paper reported that the sheriff's department planned further investigation into the death of Elvira Evans.

Sunny Whitaker called for a formal debriefing of the EPIs at the Cat's Cradle Café. She hung a sign on the window announcing the café would be closed to the public that evening for a private reception.

Everyone arrived promptly and in good spirits, exchanging hugs and cheek kisses. Only after everyone was seated with a beverage and their choice from Sunny's day-old (but just-as-good) pastries did the mood change. Eyes turned solemn. Talk ceased.

Verity looked around the two tables pushed together to accommodate the seven amateur detectives; she noticed the others doing the same. They were down another member. This year, they'd lost two friends. One to murder, the other her killer.

"Thank you, all, for coming," Sunny's words broke the silence. She had asked Verity if she wanted to run the meeting, but Verity passed on that duty with great relief.

Kate reached over and rested her hand on Verity's. Verity didn't dare look at her; she knew Kate would be teary-eyed. If she saw her crying, her own flood gates would open.

Sunny straightened and drew a deep breath before continuing. "I think I can speak for everyone by saying that in spite of what Martha did—"

"Allegedly did," Mary Beth murmured under her breath.

"—we will miss her and hope the best for her. I want to thank everyone for honoring the sheriff's recent request that we avoid encouraging gossip. More details will come out soon enough, I'm sure, but as unofficial investigators into Elvira's death, we owe it to Dr. Evans and his family to keep our findings to ourselves."

Mary Beth's hand shot up, waving wildly. "Rupert, ummm, Mayor Loop says talking about what we've found out might damage Martha's chances of a fair trial, if her case even goes to trial."

"I'm confused. Will there be one or two trials?" Chaundra asked. "Wouldn't she be tried for Elvira's murder but also for her attempted murder of Verity? How does that work in this country?"

"I don't think anyone knows the legal ins and outs yet. Last I heard, Martha was still being evaluated by a psychiatrist." Sunny turned to Verity, who nodded her head in response.

John Evans seemed to think he owed Verity regular updates, after failing to warn her of Martha's mental health history. To be fair, he had tried, when they collided in front of the emporium and she'd driven off in a panic. It was then that he became seriously worried and contacted the sheriff with his concerns. When Jason (or rather Anna Louise pretending to be Jason) reported Verity's kidnapping, a search immediately ensued.

"Martha was wrong in what she did," Verity added. "We shouldn't make excuses for her. Even if Elvira might have seemed to deserve punishment for all the harm she did. Taking another person's life is never ok. But can we set aside discussions of right or wrong for tonight? I asked Sunny if we might meet to make a few decisions for the future."

"Like no more butting into other people's business?" Denise laughed. "Good luck with that!"

"Actually, I was thinking just the opposite." Verity couldn't decide whether what she was about to propose was a great idea or a very bad one. "When I've made deliveries to my dairy customers, several customers have expressed concern over the increase in local crimes and community controversies. For some reason they think I, ah, *we* might look into these issues, as support to the sheriff's office."

Kate wrinkled her nose and turned to Sunny. "We looked

into Elvira's death for one reason—to give her justice. And we've accomplished that."

"That so true!" Fumiko agreed. "Job done. Over and out. Kaput! No?"

"Yes," Verity said. "That task is finished. And I think we can feel good about what we did." She sighed. "We made some mistakes, but eventually we discovered the truth."

"More like it smacked us upside the head when Martha kidnapped you," Denise guffawed.

"Well, yes. But the point is, if the community needs us, why not play an active role in trying to sort out problems?"

"The sheriff is *not* going to like this," Kate said firmly.

"Maybe," Verity agreed. "But I think he will become much more open to listening to our observations. And after John Evans filled him in on his past relationship with Martha and the strained friendship between her and his wife, Bailey admitted he should have delved deeper into Elvira's death. The thing is— we did pretty well for amateurs. There was a lot that we got right."

Sunny grinned. "We got the wrong Olive Oyl."

"For sure." Verity smiled.

"Did you ever find out the identity of the woman the doctor visited?" Chaundra asked.

"She's Elvira's estranged sister," Verity said. "Apparently, the two women hadn't spoken in years. She didn't come to the funeral because she was on a business trip to California. John knew about her but had never met her. He tracked her down and informed her about Elvira's death but she was already on the West Coast. He drove out of town to visit her after she returned; she had asked him to tell her what he knew about her sister's final hours."

"Verity wasn't as convinced they were lovers as I was,"

Sunny admitted sheepishly. "She said the kiss was a tell. Too tame for them to be romantically involved."

"Maybe we should vote. You know, whether or not to keep the EPIs in action," Mary Beth suggested. "We could be a citizens' support group for the sheriff's office."

Just as Verity was taking a sip of her mint tea, two uninvited guests appeared behind Denise and Chaundra. Verity inhaled sharply, choking on the mouthful of tea.

"You alright, sweetie?" Sunny asked while Verity gasped for air.

Mary Beth thumped her on the back.

"They can't see us," Anna Louise giggled. "We just had to be here. We felt so left out."

"We did rescue you, after all," Percy said, hand resting on the hilt of his sword as he struck a proud military pose.

"You did indeed," Verity croaked.

"I did what?" Sunny scowled, looking confused.

"Just, ah, talking to myself." Verity cleared her throat. "Yes, voting is a good idea. But we need to also decide what we can actually do for the sheriff without riling the man. He may not want us involved at all."

"She right," Fumiko's black eyes sparked with excitement. "If no can do murders, we find lost kitty cats. Catch bad children who skip school. Nab the peeping Thomases."

"Peeping Toms," they corrected her.

"Let's just vote," Denise said, "we'll figure out what we can or can't do later. Those who want to be part of a real private investigation service, raise your hand."

Kate and Mary Beth, in spite of their former resignations, looked at each other and then grinned and raised their hands. So did Percy and Anna Louise. As did everyone else.

And so, with seven live votes and two deceased votes in favor, the motion passed.

———

"You do realize you can't be official members," Verity informed her housemates later the same night.

"That sounds spectrally biased," Percy complained.

Verity rolled her eyes. "I don't even think that's a thing."

"You shouldn't hold our being dead against us."

"I don't. It's just the way it is. You're dead, so you can't own land, vote in an election, have children, eat, drink...or, apparently, enjoy unlimited travel. I'm sorry, but since you can't be seen by my friends or anywhere in public, you can't be official investigators."

"We can choose to be seen at important moments," Anna Louise suggested, "like when we came for you at the quarry. Or when the sheriff makes an arrest."

Verity picked up a kitchen towel to dry the dinner plate she'd just finished washing. They were like children, begging for a second dessert. "No," she said firmly.

"Never?" Anna Louise whimpered, looking at her with puppy-dog eyes.

"That may work on Percy but it sure won't work on me. Listen, if you two came out for my friends, it would be only a matter of days, maybe hours before the entire town knew about you. And that would change everything."

"Why?" Percy asked.

"You think the crowds of leaf peepers who arrive every fall are annoying? Wait until you see how many tourists show up to see real ghosts!"

"Oh," her two housemates said.

"Believe me, you don't want that headache." Did ghosts get headaches? "Besides, you don't know if you'll even be here a year from now, or next month, or tomorrow. Whatever glitch in the heavenly system has kept you in the land of the living might suddenly get fixed. And off you'd go." Strangely, she felt a lump in her throat at the thought.

"I know." Percy stared dismally at the tips of his immaculately polished boots. "It *is* what we wanted. To move on, into eternity." He turned to his wife and she twitched her nose at him.

Verity still couldn't read their private sign language. Was that cute nose tweak a silent communication of affection? Verity narrowed her eyes at the pretty Southern belle. Or was Anna Louise telegraphing: *Ignore the mortal, she doesn't know what she's talking about.*

Verity turned away to place the towel and plate beside the sink. When she turned back, Anna Louise was smiling innocently at her.

"Listen, you two. As far as I'm concerned, the important thing is that you were there for me when I needed you. So, thank you. And, I should add, you've been surprisingly good company. Most of the time."

"We can stay?" squealed Anna Louise. "We can live in our... your house?"

It actually hadn't occurred to Verity that she had a choice. Could she have simply told them to leave? "I guess so. You are part of my family, by marriage. As you're Mark's ancestors, I think he would have wanted you to stay. We can agree to share the house." However, one reservation came to mind. "But stay off my telephones."

"Of course, Miss Verity," Anna Louise cooed, clasping Percy's hand. "We wouldn't have it any other way."

ABOUT THE AUTHOR

Kathryn Johnson (aka Mary Hart Perry/Nicole Davidson) has authored over 40 thrilling mystery, suspense, and historical novels for adults and young readers. Her books have been nominated for the prestigious Agatha Award and won the Heart of Excellence and Bookseller's Best Awards presented by the American Library Association.

Kathryn loves teaching the craft of fiction writing at The Writer's Center (https://writer.org), in the Washington, DC area, as well as throughout the world via live workshops on Zoom. She has developed seminars for and spoken at the Smithsonian Institute, Library of Congress, Mystery Writers of America, International Thriller Writers and many regional writers' conferences.

As the founder of a writer's coaching and editorial service, https://KathrynJohnsonLLC.com, Kathryn is bursting with pride for her amazing author clients as they pursue their own publishing careers. Her nonfiction book, The Extreme Novelist is based on her popular 8-week course for fiction writers.

Kathryn is thrilled to be joining the Oliver-Heber Books family and introducing the Haunted Farmhouse cozy mystery series, featuring the intrepid Verity Cade, two ghosts who have lost their way to the Afterlife, and a cat named Lady Macbeth.

A small press bound by the belief that every voice matters.

Sign up for our newsletter to learn about new releases and more.
https://oliver-heberbooks.com/subscribe/

Follow us on social media:

facebook.com/oliverheberbooks

instagram.com/oliverheberbooks

amazon.com/oliverheberbooks

youtube.com/@OliverHeberBooksPublisher